CENTURION
Dark Genesis

Christofer Nigro

Cover Art: <u>rizkynugraha</u>

https://www.fiverr.com/rizkynugraha

**Special thanks to Gordon Long and Matt
Hickman for their adept editing chores and
advice; and to David MacDowell Blue and Elden
Ardiente (https://ldnrdnt.com/) and
(rdnt.arts@yahoo.com.au) for helping me put
the finishing touches to the cover.**

CENTURION: DARK GENESIS

Christofer Nigro

DEDICATIONS

This novel is dedicated to my grandmother, Gertrude "Trudie" Nigro, for loving me as much as anyone possibly could despite our various disagreements over the years; to the memory of my grandfather, Thomas J. Nigro, for being a father figure throughout my life and the remainder of his after I came into this world despite all of our differences; and mother Patricia Nigro and my uncle, Thomas F. Nigro, for putting up with me my entire life and helping me whenever they could; and to the memory of my aunt, Concetta "Connie" Denisco, for always supporting me and believing in me; and to the memory of my Uncle Pete and Aunt Marie for likewise always supporting me and seeing the good in me.

... To the memory of my friend Dennis MacMillan Jr., for teaching me what it's like to be courageous in the face of the greatest adversity of them all; to my many other friends who honored me by seeing positive qualities in me; and my many colleagues in the creative arts for helping me fulfill my lifelong dream of putting my ideas to paper (particularly Jean-Marc Lofficier for giving me my first big break).

... And to the many creative minds, past and present, who helped forge the super-hero genre from its dramatic beginnings to its gradual ascension from the fringe of cultural acceptability to the mainstream over the past 80 years... with special thanks to Jerry Siegal, Joe Schuster, Bill Finger, Bob Kane, William Moulton Marston, Otto Binder, Gardner Fox, Jack Kirby, Joe Simon, Stan Lee, Steve Ditko, Alan Moore, Mark Gruenwald, Frank Miller, Mark Millar, Paul Levitz, John Ostrander, Geoff Johns, and many others too numerous to mention for their bold vision and the lifelong inspiration they provided to me and so many others for several generations.

Christofer Nigro

Table of Contents

CENTURION: DARK GENESIS

Part 1: Power, at Last

Chapter 1: Everybody Hates Benny

Benny Lonero was nervously walking down the corridor on the second floor of Buffalo Historical High School. His plainly average looks were further marred by a slight case of acne and a moping expression as he strode down one of the brightly decorated corridors of this small but respected institution of secondary education.

He carried a small duffel bag filled with a few required texts, various writing utensils, and two 32-bit flash drives that stored several of his completed assignments in digital format. During that hallway strut to his first class of the day, several strong emotions pervaded his psyche with the intensity of super-heated plasma. These ranged from a deep envy of the popularity and attractiveness of the athletes amongst the male student body, to the unrequited love and/or lust he felt for several of his female peers.

Having recently started his sophomore year in high school, he dreaded having to awaken so early every morning on weekdays. He knew doing so would entail spending eight hours per day in a setting where he was disliked by the vast majority of its small student population. His low status on the social totem pole caused him to be marked as the target of sadistic emotional and physical abuse by his fellow students.

This effect on his psyche wasn't helped by his constant stress over the fact that he had to struggle just to maintain a level of passable grades. He found it absolutely humiliating that his academic performance was so much lower than that of several fellow students whom he simultaneously admired and envied. This was the case despite his writing skills, and an intelligent mind that simply wasn't suited to the specific learning methodology imposed on students by the schooling system.

Like many individuals in his specific predicament, Benny's thoughts continuously wavered between a desire to take cruel vengeance on those 'higher-up's' who routinely reminded him of his lowly status, and an equally strong desire to share *their* exalted position on the social hierarchy. Of course, both conflicting desires were but fanciful daydreams to him. He often prayed to the 'powers that be' in the universe to grant him a radical change, some opportunity for elevation above the station that fate seemed to have cruelly thrust him within.

These daydreams and mental pleas would abruptly end when a teacher reminded him that he wasn't paying attention to their lecture, or a fellow student launched a spitball at him, etc. *Gotta love sweet reality*, he would silently remind himself as the real world demanded his acknowledgement once more.

As Benny began his daily routine in this dreaded institution by tinkering with his combination lock, his attention was drawn to a conversation that was taking place two lockers away. The participants were a tall athletic boy named Jeff Wolfe from Buffalo's North Side, and a girl he wasn't too familiar with, a brunette of average height but exquisite looks named Leah Stanton. Benny turned his head in the direction of his two peers as they talked and laughed about Leah's planned birthday party, which she was hoping Jeff would attend. A few seconds later, Leah turned around and found herself making eye contact with Benny.

Just as Benny noted to himself how attractive Leah was, the shapely girl uttered the first words she ever spoke to him, which came in an eruption of extreme anger and hatred that startled even a seasoned target of such antipathy like Benny.

"What the hell are *you* looking at, faggot?" she said with no small amount of fury in her voice.

"Geez, why do you have to be so hostile? I wasn't doing any harm…" Benny replied, only to be abruptly cut off by Leah's next verbal onslaught.

"You were looking at me, and that's *a lot* of harm, you little douche bag!" she spat in his face.

"So, you're acting like this just because I *looked* at you?" Benny asked with a confused expression.

"I think he wants you, Leah!" Jeff yammered sarcastically. "He was admiring your merchandise; I saw him doing it. You're so damn hot, you just converted the fag! Ohh yeah!"

Leah began yelling a series of choice expletives at Benny. Then, after being spurred on by Jeff, she rushed towards the thinnish boy and shoved him hard, making a point to painfully dig her long fingernails into his chest as she did so.

"Don't you ever let me catch you near me again!" she screamed at Benny as he backed away in both shame and further confusion. "I'll kick your ass all over the hallway!"

"If you wanna do that, Leah, then you'll have to get in line," Jeff noted with a grin. "Go get him before the daily line forms! You'll probably make horse manure out of him! But if he takes a swing back at you, I'll step in and put his head through that locker. Because where I come from, a guy doesn't hit a lady."

Unfortunately for Benny, another unfriendly participant was about to enter the fray. Mickey Judge, a talented hockey player and friend to Jeff and Leah, overheard the conflagration from his locker across the corridor. Within seconds, he was at the pretty young woman's side.

"Is Lonero causing you trouble, Leah?" Mickey asked with a sneer on his face.

"Yea, he is!" she responded, still enraged. "That faggot was looking at me like he wanted to jump me! I'm gonna kick his ass if he ever gets near me again!"

Mickey walked over to Benny, grabbed the shorter boy by the lapel of his shirt, and slammed him against one of the locker doors. That caused a loud clanging sound which reverberated down the corridor.

"You stay away from her, you got that, asswipe?" he ordered the greatly humiliated young man as his long right index finger stabbed into the bridge of Benny's nose.

"Dude, I don't even know her," Benny pleaded in his defense. "I didn't say anything to her! She was talking to Jeff near my locker, and I just turned and looked. I didn't do or say anything…"

Benny's plea was suddenly cut short as he practically had the wind knocked out of him when the much bigger and stronger Mickey slammed him hard against the locker again.

"I don't give a shit, you faggot!" Mickey screamed in Benny's face. "She hates you, something I can totally relate to! Every time I see your little punk ass I hope you give me one good excuse to…"

Mickey's attention was then distracted by the sound of Jeff's voice exclaiming, "What are *you* looking at?"

Another person had clearly entered the vicinity, and not someone whom Jeff and Mickey were friendly with. Both Benny and Mickey turned their heads to see Jeff approaching a very tall, corpulent boy with glasses. This turned out to be Craig Minkel, another frequent target of popular ire, who was practically Benny's only friend at the school. He was, predictably, a fellow social outcast whom virtually no one other than Benny was willing to befriend. And vice versa, of course.

"Did you come to help your partner-in-buggery?" Jeff asked Craig with a combination of sarcasm and hostility.

Following that half-hearted question, Jeff pushed the tall rotund boy into one of the lockers. The impact nearly knocked his glasses off.

"I have no idea what's going on here," Craig stated matter-of-factly. "I just came to my locker and saw you and your clique buddies assaulting my friend again. And probably for no reason at all, as usual."

"Someone like him *exists*; do we need any other reason?" Jeff replied with further hostility.

"Yeah, I think you do," Craig said bluntly. "Because if that's all it takes for you to hate someone, you should disband the hockey team and start a Neo-Nazi club in its place."

"Ohhhhh, the king of stomach rolls just pwned you, dude!" Mickey sardonically mocked Jeff, attempting to spur on the impending beating he was hoping to see Craig receive. "You should open up a can of 'whup ass' on Stinkel Minkel for that!"

"Thank you for the cute nickname," Craig said with a forced fake grin.

"Why don't you shut up, you're so *stupid*!" Leah verbally pelted the tall social outcast.

"No more stupid than that stuffed bra of yours," Craig retorted with a snigger.

Without hesitation, Jeff punched Craig hard in the stomach, causing him to exhale in agony as he slumped halfway to the floor. Shouting another series of expletives, Leah rushed towards Craig and began pummeling him furiously. Jeff stood in front of the melee to intimidate their target into making no attempt to defend himself.

"Kill him, Leah!" he shouted. "Tear his fat ass up! Woohoo, you go, girl!"

Yelling an obscenity at his tormenters, Benny attempted to break free of Mickey's grip to run and seek the aid of a teacher. He struggled briefly with the larger boy, who soon overpowered him and slammed him against two locker doors. Benny wailed in pain as a metal handle bit into his left kidney area. Mickey then kneed his target in the groin, sending Benny down to the floor.

While on his knees with his hands covering his throbbing testes, Benny looked Mickey directly in the eyes and told him, "You just went too far."

Upon hearing that, Mickey lifted the shorter boy off the floor by his shirt and slammed him against the lockers yet again. "So, what are you going to do about it? Go all Columbine on us?"

His face filled with pain and humiliation, Benny fought past the agony to affect a rare moment of direct eye contact with the taller boy. Then he said, "Keep this up and maybe I will."

"Oohhh really, rainbow-boy?" Mickey retorted with a grin that sent a sensation of icy fear throughout Benny's battered body. "Let's just see you get a gun or some other weapon in through the metal detectors and the security check at the front door in the morning. In fact, now that I heard you say that, you can bet I'm gonna talk to Ned and have his security boys strip search you every morning. I hear they're *really* thorough in their searches. I bet you'll actually enjoy that, huh?"

"I bet you'd enjoy watching, otherwise you wouldn't ask your security crew buddies to do it," Benny snapped back. "How much will you pay them for the cam footage of my search? They'll probably charge you extra for the several extreme close-up shots you'll be demanding."

Mickey responded by kicking Benny in the side of his upper torso, causing him to grunt in pain. The tall, well-regarded champion of bantam league hockey then raised his fist in preparation for pounding the side of his target's face.

Just then, however, the familiar voice of mathematics teacher Dean Zach was heard inquiring,

"What's going on over here?"

As the popular students ceased their respective barrages and turned to face an angry-looking Mr. Zach, Leah spoke up first.

"Lonero was bothering me, and these guys were just defending me," she explained with barely contained fury. "And then his friend stepped in and started with us."

"You know that's a bunch of bull," Craig lamented as he forced himself back to his feet, still not fully recovered from Leah's relentless assault on him.

"It's enough bull crap to fill the Augean Stables beyond even Hercules' capacity to clean it," Benny metaphorically remarked while continuing to wince in pain. "I wasn't doing anything to her, I was just standing at my locker to get my stuff, and she came over to Jeff and started talking to him right near me…"

Leah then cunningly interjected, "Lonero was ogling my body, and that other perv friend of his made a comment about my bra. That's when Jeff slugged him. He doesn't like seeing a girl getting harassed like that."

"But he loves encouraging you 'girls' to dish out harassment of your own kind to the low-ranking beta students every day, right?" Benny said. "And let's not start about your fondness for homophobic zingers…"

"You just shut up and don't *ever* talk to me!" Leah yelled in response. Jeff then put his arm around her in a protective manner, and she rested her head on his shoulder.

"Okay, I'll take care of this," Mr. Zach said. "You guys go to your next classes, and Mr. Minkel, you head down to the office. I'll deal with you down there later."

The balding, usually avuncular teacher then turned to Benny, who was now inching back to his feet. "Mr. Lonero, please come with me. You and I are going to have a little chat."

"Oh c'mon, I can't believe this!" Benny exclaimed. He shot a distinctly malicious glare at his tormenters while Craig huffed off to the office to face the not-so-tender mercies of Principal Wilson.

Mr. Zach pulled Benny aside and put a meaty hand on his left shoulder, a look of concern and disappointment marking his ever-distinguished countenance.

"First of all, are you okay?" the tall bespectacled math teacher asked the boy.

"No, I'm not okay," Benny decreed. "Those creeps pick on us every day. I'm gonna kill them!"

"Stop that, Benny, now! You're better than that, and you know it. I've heard from Mrs. Metcalfe that you have potential with your writing, so don't blow it."

"I'm sick of this, Mr. Zach. Sick of seeing those idiots do whatever they please, with nothing remotely resembling consequences. I never hear a single teacher suggest that *they* need to visit the guidance counselor's office for one of those embarrassing 'evaluations,' like they do with me. As if the way *they* act is considered 'normal' or 'acceptable.'

"But *noooo,* the school *love*s sending the less popular students like yours truly for these 'evaluations.' I guess a lack of popularity counts as a sickness in their eyes, while savage behavior and intolerance is just 'kids being kids'."

Mr. Zach's grip on Benny's shoulder tightened, grave concern filling the hazel eyes behind his thick bifocals.

"Benny, I've known those kids you were having that altercation with since they were in middle school. You may not believe this, but they aren't bad people at all. They just get stupid sometimes, as young people tend to. Not only that, but they have a lot of stress on them, what with the hockey team and the cheerleading squad taking up so many of their spare hours, and all the expectations placed on them…"

"So, you're saying I would be showing some good school spirit by overlooking what they do to me and Craig every day? That our agreeing to be the equivalent of a cat's scratching post while they get to be the cats is a fair way for the unpopular to 'bend' for the popular?"

"Benny, stop getting wise with me, you know I didn't mean it like that."

"I think I heard what you meant loud and clear, Mr. Zach. Do you think what they do to me every day doesn't stress *me* out? Do you think maintaining my website to showcase my writing in the hope of attracting a publisher after I graduate doesn't put as much stress on me as their precious high school sports does for them?

"*Ohhhhh* wait, I forgot! Those popular guys who have all the girls fawning all over them and treated like the royalty of the school because of their great ability to throw a ball across a field or knock a puck around a floor of ice are *soooo* valuable to this school! Certainly much more than someone whose talents lie in the power of the pen rather than the far greater power of the hockey stick, or the kicking foot. My bad!

"So how do I deal with *my* need to let off steam, huh, Mr. Zach? Maybe go outside and kick the neighbor's little brother around a while? I mean, that little boy agreeing to serve as my personal punching bag is the *least* he could do for an upstanding, stressed-out writer like me, right?"

"Look, Benny, you're feeling sorry for yourself right now, and self-pity is never a productive emotion under any circumstances. But more than that, you're starting to smart off to me, so lose the attitude, go to your first class before it starts in a few minutes, and think things over. Or I'm going to be the *next* one to lose his temper on you."

"Fine, I'm out of here," Benny said softly as he shuffled down the now empty corridor towards his first period class.

I'm going to hurt them just like they always hurt me and Craig, he thought to himself as the twin inferno of rage and bitterness began consuming his soul like a gasoline-soaked rag put to a flame.

13

Chapter 2: Escalation

Benny trod down the mean streets of Buffalo's Upper East Side after vacating the less-than-hallowed halls of Buffalo Historical School. He cringed at the sight of the decrepit houses dotting the landscape like oozing sores on septic flesh. To him, this rampant urban decay embodied a concrete manifestation of the corrupt social values engendered by the system that only encouraged the worst in humanity. He planned to one day put his revulsion towards the world order he lived under to paper (or its modern digital equivalent), hoping to do his small part to incite reform--or, better yet, a full revolution.

His loathing of the system that allowed such decay in its architecture—which he felt naturally extended into the attitudes of the people who populate such an environment—was likely matched by his detestation of himself and what he believed to be his lot in life.

Needing a sounding board to vent his usual frustrations, he pulled out his cell phone and typed a text message to Craig, asking why their situation should contrast so heavily to that of the 'royalty' of the student hierarchy.

"Dunno," Craig sent back in a text filled with all his usual misspellings and grammatical errors. "I not filosipher. Plz stop with big words ur killin me with them."

"You're no help at all, dude, you know that?" Benny quickly typed and sent back.

"i only cann tri," was Craig's snide response.

Benny closed his cell phone with a huff of annoyance and continued the several block trek to the home he shared with his grandparents and uncle, just as he did each school day upon disembarking from the subway station. During his walk home, his thoughts were a morass of existential contemplation.

Okay, I'm aware that nobody's life is actually perfect. But compared to my life, it certainly seems that way. Why are the lives of people like Craig and I so low on the metaphorical rung of our peers' social ladder? I hate self-pity, and I hate envying nearly every other person in that freaking school. But if almost everyone you spend five days a week with for nine months out of the year abhors the very ground you walk on, how can you not come to hate yourself just as much? How can I have confidence in myself when everyone else around me considers me a total waste of oxygen consumption?

Why can't the Powers That Be in the cosmos either strike me down, or offer me a major change in my personal status quo? What did I do in this life, or a past one or whatever, to merit this suckish existence? If there isn't a force for Justice in this universe, can't there at least be a force for Mercy?

Benny finally had enough of feeling sorry for himself. *Oh, geez, would you stop with the chronic internal whining, Lonero? You're actually starting to annoy* yourself *here!*

Of course, whatever respite his home life may have given him from school was frequently diminished by the actions of his two well-intentioned surrogate parents. His relationship with them was heavily strained. After all, how can you support someone that you do not understand, even if you genuinely love them?

Hence, Benny knew he had little to look forward to in the walls of the domicile he called home besides a warm bed and good dinner. In fact, he constantly worried over what may trigger another violent confrontation with his formidable grandfather.

His psyche then became filled with fantasy scenarios illustrating the many ways he wished he could make those who raised him--but refused to understand him--suffer retribution alongside those who willfully misunderstood him during his life at school. Needless to say, Benny wasn't exactly proud of many of the thoughts that comprised his daily internal monologues.

***

As Benny entered the front door of his grandparents' modest but comfortable home on Buffalo's West Side, his grandfather, Dominic D. Lonero, stood in front of the youth with his patented expression of anger; it was a look that the distraught adolescent had grown to dread. Dominic wasn't tall in stature, and in fact barely matched Benny's 5 foot 6-inch height.

However, his musculature was impressive for a man well into middle age, the product of over two decades of hard labor and beneficial eating habits. He had endured the tough streets of Buffalo's less savory areas as he grew up, and it most certainly showed in every aspect of his being. The wisps of slowly graying black hair on his head which were all that remained of a long-departed coif only seemed to enhance the tough features and aura of menace that he exuded if you dared get on his bad side.

"I heard the way you talked to your grandmother this morning," Dominic said with a volatile tone. "You need to understand whose house this is, and how easy we could have you put away if you continue to act like this."

"Oh, yes, I forgot," Benny replied with his usual acerbity. "If you provide for a child materially, he owes you the same deference that a serf owes the king for allowing him a few little tracts of land on his property. After all, it's not like you actually *chose* to take care of me when I didn't go with my mother, as if it was actually a *responsibility* of some kind. Nope, it's all due to your good, altruistic nature, and nothing more. Oh wait, I forgot—you don't have a naturally altruistic nature! My bad!"

Benny moved to walk past Dominic, who stepped in front of him, barring his path into the living room.

"Don't be a wise ass with me, kid," the burly man said. "You don't appreciate anything we do for you. Remember, you need us, we *don't* need you. So, you better watch it."

"I'm not economically dependent on you by choice," the boy spat back. "If you and my grandmother gave me the emotional support I needed and didn't think providing me with material necessities was all it took to be a good parent or grandparent, maybe you would have earned my respect!"

"We don't owe you any respect! This is *our* house, not yours!"

Benny struggled to hold back both his temper and his tears. "Look, please leave me alone. I had a bad day at school today, and I don't want to fight with you again."

"Of course, you had a bad day at school. I know that nobody there likes you, except for that Craig screwball you bring around here. I don't blame those kids for treating you that way, because I know how you are."

"Okay, that's enough! Leave me alone, *now!*"

Dominic grabbed his less muscular grandson by the left arm, squeezing it hard. "What did I tell you about giving orders in his house? I'm the boss, not you! This is my home, and you're just a guest!"

"Get your hands off me!" With that firm request made, Benny swatted his grandfather's arm. Dominic then grabbed his defiant grandson and pushed him against the front door. This caused the adolescent to suffer a flashback of what occurred earlier in school with Mickey Judge and Jeff Wolfe.

Finally losing his temper as a result, Benny grasped Dominic by his bulky shoulders and began fighting back, despite not being able to match the older man's strength.

"You better get your hands off me!"

"Why? You couldn't lick a stamp and you know it, you no good little bastard!"

"Maybe you'd be happy if I just blew my brains out!"

"Go ahead, you animal! Everyone in this house would cry for two days, and then we'd forget all about it! Do you hear me? You're no goddamn good!"

As the fight began to escalate, Benny's grandmother and Dominic' wife, Grace Lonero, came rushing into the front room, nearly tripping on the flowing gown she often wore during her leisure hours.

"Alright, stop it now!" she yelled as she pulled the two apart. She then turned to her now nearly berserk grandson, careful to stand in front of Dominic to keep her equally fiery husband from striking down Benny where he stood. "Benjamin, are you causing trouble again? Like you did this morning?"

"Yeah, you and my grandfather have such stellar personalities, anyone who gets into it with either of you has to be a 'troublemaker,'" Benny answered with biting irony. "Only an ungrateful punk like me could possibly live in this house and avoid developing a severe case of scoliosis for not constantly bowing down before your gracious majesty."

Dominic then redoubled his efforts to get his hands on his grandson, prompting his wife to increase her restraining grip on him. "He's no good, Grace! He's an animal! Why don't we just put him away?"

Benny angrily turned and punched the front door, leaving a visible indentation in the wood. The degree of emotional pain that assailed his mind overwhelmed his recognition of the physical pain now afflicting his throbbing knuckles.

"I'm out of here!" he said as he opened the door and stormed out.

"But I'm making dinner right now!" Grace protested.

"Give my portion to the birds outside!" Benny shouted as he huffed out of the front hallway.

"You little son of a bitch!" Grace bellowed.

"Maybe he'll jump in front of a car while he's out there!" her husband said.

"Shut up, Dominic!" his wife yelled in the robust man's face. "You can be a creative troublemaker around here too, you know!"

***

Back at Buffalo Historical School, the lights remained illuminated in the gymnasium as Mickey Judge and Jeff Wolfe practiced after school for their hockey team with a few fellow members of the Icemen. Leah Stanton and her friend Marissa Robbins were also present, leaning against the bleachers as they offered supportive caterwauls to the players. The team had been doing quite well for the duration of the semester, and much of it was thanks to these two boys and their dedicated, skillful performances on the rink.

The attractive smiles and admiration of girls like Leah and Marissa was another major incentive to good performance, of course. It was certainly one of the 'major perks' of athletic success and the accompanying social popularity, as Jeff often put it. Though the girls were themselves star athletes for the champion volleyball team that routinely made the school proud, the support they gave the boys was well reciprocated.

"Shake that booty of yours down the ice and whack that puck like you mean it, Mickey!" Leah shouted with euphoric glee. "You're lookin' *goooood*, dude!"

"Give those Hut Tek players hell on ice, Jeff!" was Marissa's loud contribution to the supportive verbiage. "You're so totally hot I'm surprised the ice doesn't melt beneath 'yo feet during a game! Haha!"

Life seemed good for all concerned in this gym, and despite having the everyday problems that typically afflicted adolescents, their regular routine was one they greatly looked forward to. None of them knew what the future had in store for them, but they all felt that there was no reason why it wouldn't be a bright one.

As they ran across the shiny floor to practice their skills and stay in shape for the upcoming game against North Park, doing their best to simulate being on actual ice, Mr. Zach entered the gymnasium. He had to stay late for a staff meeting, and he wanted to take advantage of the extra time by having a talk with some of the school's premiere students.

Whistling with his fingers to get the small crowd's attention, Mr. Zach motioned with his hand for Mickey and Jeff to approach him. The man then looked at Leah, who was still observing from the same spot at the bleachers, and he indicated for her to likewise come forth.

"Hey, Mr. Zach!" Jeff greeted the popular teacher with high enthusiasm. "The Icemen are gonna kick some major North Park ass come the 4th of next month!"

"Actually, Mr. Wolfe, it's on the subject of ass-kicking that I want to talk to the three of you," the bespectacled, earnest-looking man said.

"Please don't tell me you're going to lecture us about Lonero and Minkel," Mickey said with a roll of his eyes.

Leah shook her head and uttered a very audible sigh.

"Listen, all of you," the math teacher stated firmly. "Is Lonero really so bad that you kids have to dislike him that much? I know he's far from perfect, and that he can be irritating at times, but have you ever considered that some of his more annoying behavior can stem from his acting out as a result of the treatment you all deliver to him every day? Don't you think he has feelings too?"

"Mr. Zach, all Lonero ever does is act like a nerd everywhere he goes," Leah said. "He totally brings that treatment on himself. And I don't care for the way he looks at me, either."

"I see lots of the boys looking at you 'that way,' Leah," Mr. Zach noted. "And this includes your friends on the team there. Yet I don't see you crying harassment when they do it."

"That's different!" she exclaimed. "They know how to earn a girl's respect. Lonero and that friend of his are just… okay, I won't say what they are, but you know what I mean."

"I can vouch for that," Jeff added.

"Seriously, Mr. Zach, don't you think it would be more productive to give Lonero a lecture for the way he acts than the way we and others treat him *because* of how he acts?" Mickey queried with barely concealed contempt for the subject of the unwanted conversation.

"I have spoken to him, Mr. Judge," Zach assured the young athlete. "In fact, I've spoken to him more than once, including earlier today. I want you all to be honest with me here. Was he really to blame for what took place this morning? Or should all of you have gone to the office along with Mr. Minkel?"

"Hell no!" Leah spat. "*I* sure wasn't the one who ogled *him* up and down like some kind of perv!"

"I was only trying to defend her," Jeff said. "Does she have to put up with that, Mr. Zach? And do we have to put up with *him* and the Minkel Monster every day?"

Mr. Zach frowned. "Miss Stanton, would you have gotten half as angry if you were 'ogled' by a boy you didn't know but whom you happened to find attractive? And Jeff, do you honestly believe that Miss Stanton here really needed you to play knight in shining armor, or was that just an excuse to pummel someone you dislike? And someone who also just happens to be an easy target, as well?"

"I can't believe you're taking that little poindexter's side, Mr. Zach!" Leah complained.

"I'm not taking the side of anyone in particular," Zach stated curtly. "Rather, I'm trying to take the side of honesty. No doubt Mr. Lonero brings the proverbial ax down on himself enough times in his wrong-headed attempts to get the type of attention he doesn't receive legitimately, but you kids are often thought of as leaders of the student body. Is this how people who are supposed to provide positive examples for others supposed to behave?"

"I can't believe we're hearing this," Mickey said almost under his breath.

"And I can't believe I *need* to tell you this, Mr. Judge," was the last thing the well-respected teacher retorted. "Try to show a bit of empathy for those you view as beneath your status in life.

I just hope this doesn't get completely out of hand, because you don't need a math teacher to explain the statistical probability of things like this going very bad if you take it too far."

With that said, Zach turned and departed, hoping that the faith which the entirety of the staff had in this trio of well-liked students was merited.

"Hmmm, I think I need to have a 'talk' with Benny-boy myself tomorrow," Mickey noted aloud, with a heavy degree of ire evident in his voice.

"No doubt," Jeff remarked with a smile. "Need any help?"

"None at all, but it's still more than welcome," Mickey replied. "It wouldn't be fair that I was the only respectable member of the sophomore class who got a piece of him."

"So where is this 'talk' going to take place?" Leah asked with anticipation.

"In the boys' locker room tomorrow, right after the last class is over," Mickey answered.

"We'll need your help, and the help of Marissa, to get that punk in here at the right time."

"Believe me," Leah said, "Marissa hates him even more than I do, if that's possible,

especially after she found out that he has the hots for her. Do you have any idea how disgusted she was? She'll be more than happy to get involved in this."

"Cool," Mickey replied through clenched teeth, with the thought of inflicting harm upon Lonero filling him with a heated sensation.

***

Benny Lonero aimlessly ran about the deteriorating urban environment that he has always called home for over a half hour until it occurred to him to send a text to his one actual friend. He let Craig know that he needed to talk, and fast, since the thoughts he was now contemplating were potentially life-threatening. Despite the fact that the Pine Harbor apartment complexes were in a decrepit low income area of Buffalo's West Side, the presence of his close friend there made him perceive them as a second home despite their squalor.

Benny hoped and prayed to no deity in particular that his cell phone would emit its characteristic jingle to let him know that his text was answered as he strode about the congested side streets of the inner city environment. He knew that worse cities existed across the U.S., and certainly in Third World regions elsewhere on the globe, but this didn't do much to improve his thoughts of living in a blighted urban cesspool of a 'lesser' severity.

Finally, after roughly ten minutes, the jingling tune of "Dream Weaver" by Craig Wright notified the melancholic young man of an incoming phone call. A quick, instinctual perusing of the caller I.D. informed him that it was the much-desired response from Craig Minkel.

"What's wrong, bro?" uttered Craig's concerned voice as soon as Benny hit the touch screen's 'answer' button.

"The usual," Benny replied through an irritated sob. "I had a fight with my grandfather again."

"So what else is new, dude?"

"I know, but this was one of those bad ones that really get out of hand and leads to fisticuffs, and… well, I had to get the hell out of there before it went any further. Do you mind some company right now?"

"Sure, use any excuse you can to mooch a meal off me, huh?"

Ben snickered. "Thanks. I could really use a talk in addition to that meal that I'll be mooching from you. I hope I don't deplete your supply of macaroni salad again."

"I would worry more about depleting your overall welcome, dude. But far be it from me to disrupt our usual routine for exchanging shoulders whenever one of us needs to be convinced that life is worth living, right?"

"Yes, I know. Woe is we, huh?"

"Just get your silly ass on over here, and we'll talk over some chips and dip. And maybe even some macaroni salad if I'm still in a generous mood by the time you get here, dude."

***

Another 30 minutes later, Benny sat across from Craig on the ancient but reasonably intact couch in the small living room of his mother's apartment. Like all flats in the glorified project area known as Pine Harbor, it was a modest, poorly heated residence that Craig's divorced mother, Jewel Minkel, at least nevertheless kept provided with all modern accoutrements, such as digital cable and an Xbox 360.

The fact that Craig himself was highly adept with putting together most types of gadgetry insured that every device they had worked much better, and far longer, than their respective manufacturers ever intended.

"Damn, you sure are putting away those chips," Craig told his friend as he watched him voraciously consume the snack. "One would think you hadn't eaten in a week."

"Or at least not since lunch in the school cafeteria earlier today," Benny replied with his mouth stuffed full of nachos. "Don't forget, you decided not to let me have the macaroni salad when I got here, and I also took a rain check on dinner at home, so my grandfather and I didn't kill each other."

"Dude, you really need to get out of that house before the old man finally does you in."

"And I really need to get out of that school, too. And I often feel I really need to get out of this *life*. How can I run away from absolutely everything I know? I'm sick of being hated at both school and at home."

"I'm not sure what to tell you when I don't even know what to tell myself, considering I have the exact same life as you do. Well, minus the total nerd thing you have going on, of course."

"Right. The respect you receive compared to me is so evident. I'm sure Leah really wants to jump your bones. Your rather *big* bones, that is."

"Funny. The way you scarf down those chips, you may end up fat by the time you reach the big two-one, dude."

"You know, it really sucks that those jock asshats get all the attention from girls like Leah. And Marissa doesn't even look at me except to call me things like 'faggot' and 'loser.' And that's when she's in a good mood."

"I'm not sure how else you expect those girls to react to us. What would we have to offer them, exactly?"

"Look, we may not be attractive like the jocks, and we may not be able to run down a field with a funny-shaped rubber ball in our hands as fast, or hurl a round version of that ball through a hoop extended ten feet in the air as well, or swat a flattened vulcanized rubber object down an ice rink with a crooked stick as skillfully as they can. But it's not like we're totally without talent. I can write a story without having to be assigned to do it by the English teacher, and you're capable of actually building a CD player out of spare parts taken out of a garbage can. Why aren't these things considered impressive or attractive?"

"You forget that it's not exactly exciting to watch a bunch of nerdy guys sit in a room and compete with each other to see who can be the first to write a coherent story; or a bunch of fat boys in greasy blue work outfits scramble to assemble a Blu-ray player faster than another team like that. But like Mr. Walters once told us, watching a group of attractive guys with rippling muscles and six-packs running down a field, or skating down a rink showing off how fast they can move and how strong they are compared to another team of guys …"

"…well, it's a really *visceral* experience that makes the chicks excited to the very depths of their hormones, man," Benny concluded for him. "Yeah, yeah, I know, I was there too when those words zinged out of his mouth. C'mon, it was my complaints about the 'sitch that prompted those pithy words of his in the first place, remember?"

"Of course, and maybe that's your major problem. You complain all the time, but whenever I suggest you try to do something to improve things, you tell me that there's nothing you can do about it. Remember what Mrs. McCall said about succumbing to fatalism and cynicism?"

"More sage advice from someone who doesn't have a life anything like ours, and probably never did."

"So, she isn't worth listening to for that reason?"

"Look, I don't exactly see you being proactive and rising above your less-than-exalted status in the social hierarchy either. And I don't see your home life as being one you're eager to brag about any more than mine, bro."

"Okay, so what do you suggest we do? Buy a gun from Ratfink on the corner of Niagara and wipe out everyone at the school who ever treated us like cow dung, as a psycho would? Or point it at ourselves and pull the trigger instead, like a coward?"

"It's getting to the point that I no longer care about going down either path. I just can't take this anymore. I want it to stop."

"We're better than that, man."

"Maybe you should speak for yourself, Craig."

"Look, I don't like choosing between being a psycho or a coward, instead of looking hard for a third alternative. If I didn't think you were better than all of that, I wouldn't be your friend and let you mooch my nachos like I do; not to mention my treasured supply of macaroni salad."

Unable or unwilling to think of an appropriate response to that, Benny put his face in his hands and sighed, allowing despair to claim him as its own.

***

The following day was a Friday, and Benny reminded himself when he was rudely awakened by his grandmother to get up for school. He tried to console himself by noting that after today he would have a short but much needed reprieve from the peer bullying he routinely received. And he could sleep in to avoid much of the conflict at home for two consecutive days.

He was thankful that his grandfather had already left for his city job by the time his grandmother woke him up at approximately 7:00 AM every usual weekday morning during the school year. The risk of getting into a major fight with one of them was a bad enough way to start the day, but he considered his grandmother the lesser of the two 'evils' since she was less inclined to try and thrash him—not that she didn't often want to just as much as her husband did.

Benny left the house without more than minor bickering with his grandmother, and he thanked the Fates for one of the rare small favors they granted him while he approached the school with the usual degree of anxiety. Little did he know how justified those usual feelings of trepidation would turn out to be, considering what a few of his least favorite peers had in store for him at the end of the school day.

Much to his pleasant surprise, he saw little of Mickey and Jeff that day, and he was only subject to taunting by many of the other students, who usually did so to a lesser extent if they weren't spurred on by one of the ringleaders of his extensive personal hate brigade. But a much bigger pleasant surprise—or so it seemed—appeared to him as he prepared for his last period class.

He quietly stood at his locker, this time determined not to play the clown at any point during the day, thus decreasing his chance of garnering any potentially negative attention. As he retrieved his required text book and flash drive for his seventh period class in computer programming, he suddenly turned to see the lovely face of Marissa Robbins looking up at him with what actually appeared to be a friendly smile.

He was initially taken aback by the lovely sight before him, as this frequent subject of his dreams had only entered his presence on previous days to inform him of how much she despised the very atmosphere he breathed. She had also never before approached him sans the company of her fellow tormenters-in-crime.

After the surprise had worn off and he realized this wasn't just another of his usual fantasies involving her, he found himself utterly captivated by Marissa's soft features, freckled skin, bright emerald-hued eyes, flowing shoulder-length brown hair, and firm petite figure. As always, the sight of her put him in a state of awe, only this time it wasn't from a distance, nor at the opposite end of her savage vitriol. As a result, he found himself atypically bereft of any words, sarcastic or otherwise.

"Hi, Benny," she said in her characteristic soft voice that never failed to mesmerize him when he heard it, despite the fact that he usually heard it projected at him in harsh tones.

"Um… hi yourself, Marissa," he replied with a notable degree of caution.

"Are you surprised to see me say 'hi?'"

"In a word… *yes*. Considering that, in my recollection, 'faggot' was the nicest thing you ever said to me before. When you said anything at all to me, that is."

Her pouty lips smiled in response. "Well, I know I gave you a hard time in the past, but I've been doing some thinking." She then suddenly glanced a bit closer at his body. "Wow, have you been working out lately?"

"Actually, I do work out a few days a week at home. You noticed?"

"Yea, I certainly did. It's been showing. Your biceps and your abs have been getting… bigger." She smoothly moved her small, soft hand over his right arm, and then over his stomach region, to feel the contours of his muscles. His entire body enjoyed a pleasant tingling sensation that caused him to jerk involuntarily at her touches.

"Oh, did I make you nervous? I'm sorry."

"No, no, it's okay. I'm just… just curious as to what you want, Marissa, considering you've never shown… yanno, any interest of this sort in me before, to put it mildly."

"You mean, because I've been starting to notice you in a different way now?"

"Yeah, pretty much. I'm sorry that I feel the need to ask this, but is this some sort of game?"

She giggled in a fashion that he found highly cute and appealing. "I understand why you feel that way. I certainly haven't treated you very well before. I guess I deserve the skepticism. But maybe we can talk about it in private later? I think I certainly owe you that much, considering how I've treated you in the past without thinking."

The expression on his face made it clear that he had now become completely dumbfounded. He still couldn't resist feeling utterly love struck by the short brunette girl standing before him, a girl whom he considered akin to a goddess on Earth despite her ill treatment and contempt of him in the past. At the same time, though, he couldn't just forget her ill treatment of him in the past, and how it always made him feel afterwards. Thus, the young man found himself torn between two powerful but opposing inclinations.

"Um, look, Marissa, I like you despite everything, but…"

She looked down for few seconds. "I can understand why a part of you might hate me just a little."

"No, I don't hate you, I just… I dunno, I guess I just don't know whether or not to believe you."

"I told you, I understand your wariness. Look, I won't ever bother you again, okay? I guess I owe you that much, to leave you alone if you hate me and don't want me near you."

She turned to walk away, and Benny found his inner conflict leaving him in a psychic tug of war between two courses of action that competed strongly over his next decision. He had but seconds to allow one to win out over the other. In the end, he couldn't be sure if the decision he ultimately chose constituted weakness on his part or the taking of a courageous chance.

"Wait, Marissa! You don't have to go. I didn't mean to act that way. I just have a few trust issues, as I'm sure your figure… I mean, as I'm sure you can *figure!* Look, I'm willing to meet with you after school so we can talk."

She turned around and gave him a satisfied, wondrously beautiful smile that pleasurably bore into the center of his soul, making him tingle all over again. When she verbally responded, it sounded to him like a verse from a heavenly hymn.

"Awesome. How about downstairs in the gym room? Mr. Robin and Mr. Frost are out at this time, and I know for a fact that no practice by any team will be going on today. So, we'll have the place to ourselves to… you know, talk."

"Are you sure that no afterschool practice will be going on?"

"It's the third Friday of the month. I'm very down with the schedule of the teams, remember?"

"Of course, you are. I mean, yes, I know. Okay. Okay, I'll meet you there and we'll… talk."

"I look forward to seeing you."

"Ditto to the max."

"Bye for now, Benny."

With that said, she smiled and gently rubbed her thin, long-nailed fingers over his left hand. He flinched in excitement, doing his best to conceal it so as not to embarrass himself by looking as smitten as he actually was. *Get a grip, Ben. She's only a girl. And one who happens to hate you. Well,* used *to hate you, I guess.*

Marissa then beamed that captivating smile of hers again and quietly walked off to her final class of the day. He couldn't help staring at her figure and buttocks as she strode away and noting how her clothing was form-fitting enough to her show off her shape to anyone with the gift of vision. He considered her nothing less than a living work of art, and he wanted more than anything else in the world to be justifiably flattered by her apparent overtures of interest, no matter how she may have acted in the past.

Should I trust her? he pondered interrogatively. *Isn't it totally conceivable that she could have changed her mind like she said? I mean, I have been working out. I know she likes athletes, so I may have become more attractive since 'hitting the iron.' If I give in to fear and mistrust, I may be losing the chance for something that I've always wanted but never imagined could possibly come true. The Fates may finally be compensating me. I have to believe this could be true, and not let fear stop me from giving this a chance. I need to allow for positive thinking, just like Mrs. McCall always advised.*

With that decided, Benny Lonero made the decision to descend into the arms of the Devil, while willing to believe that an angel awaited him instead. It was a decision that would lead to severe repercussions for everyone involved, and arguably a turning point for the entire world.

For the planned set-up wasn't the only thing that Benny would be inadvertently wandering into in the near future; the Warp Event was but a few hours from manifesting in Buffalo.

***

Benny walked out of his seventh period class filled with an unbridled enthusiasm and sense of excitement that he couldn't stifle despite trying to look as nonchalant as possible. Thankfully, his worst 'haters' were nowhere in sight.

Maybe their opinion of me will go up a notch or two if Marissa and I… well, yanno, actually became an item or something, he thought to himself. He had already told Craig that he wouldn't be riding the bus home with him this afternoon, and exactly why he wouldn't. His only close friend wished him all the luck in the world, despite the notable uncertainty in his tone that conflicted with his desire not to rain on his friend's proverbial parade.

Quickly storing away everything he didn't need for the weekend in his locker, Benny looked around to make sure the hallways were clear of any possible hostiles. Since they seemed to be, he quietly wandered the building for another several minutes until most of the student body and teaching/administrative staff had left. He was aware that the doors would be open for another two hours since the custodial staff had to stay on site to complete their jobs. Just two security guards would remain on the grounds during that time. Knowing their habits, Benny easily evaded them and headed down to the bottom floor where the gymnasium was located.

He entered the correct hallway at the pre-designated time, wondering if Marissa would truly be there and fully expecting her not to be. This is when he received his next pleasant surprise—or so he thought--when he found her standing outside the entrance to the gym with a wide beam on her attractive face. He noticed that she had since dispensed with the long-sleeved shirt she wore during the school day and was now clad in a more casual but very enticing tank top that fit her petite body quite snuggly, while baring two inches of her midriff in the process.

Unable to suppress a smile, Benny couldn't help being both ecstatic and incredulous. *Wow, is this really happening? To me, of all people? Should I maybe pinch myself, to make sure this isn't another of my daytime fantasies where she is my passionate co-star?*

"Hi, Benny," she said in the soft, slightly squeaky voice that he found so appealing. "I'm glad you made it. I was getting a bit worried that you stood me up."

"I would never do that," he insisted. "I'm glad you waited for me."

"Of course, I did. Believe me, I wouldn't miss this."

She then quietly walked into the entrance of the gym, and he eagerly followed her. He now allowed himself further hope that the Fates and other cosmic powers of the universe had decided to give him the karmic equivalent of an income tax return.

As he entered the room, he saw her standing there and smiling at him in all her lovely glory. Her gleaming expression seemed designed to ease him into putting any remaining fears of fully entering the gymnasium completely behind. It worked, and he did just that.

No sooner had he walked in and approached her than he was startled when Mickey Judge suddenly rushed out of the side door leading into Mr. Robin's office, grabbed him, and dragged him inside the boys' locker room with a single strong pull of his athletically-honed musculature. Inside the locker room stood Jeff Wolfe, who wore a vicious sneer as he stepped in front of the door to block a possible exit attempt by their target.

A second later, Jeff opened the door to allow Marissa to enter the usually off-limits-to-girls room, as she was eager to see what was about to take place. This was agreed upon in exchange for her essential part in the scheme.

"Hi, Benny-boy," was Jeff's mock salutation to Benny, rendered in an obviously poisonous tone.

"What the hell?" Benny shouted in a combination of shock and horror as reality cruelly crashed down upon him with the force of a wrecking ball. He then turned to the still smiling Marissa. "You set me up, didn't you?"

"Duh!" she said in response. "Someone give the faggot a gold star!"

"How could you do that?" he asked her in a stammering fashion that reflected his horrific disillusionment.

Her pretty features took on a menacing expression. "Um, maybe 'cause I hate you? Could that be it? Use what little brains you have, freak!"

"You bitch!" he hollered back.

Mickey responded by grabbing the less athletically built Benny and slamming him hard against the concrete wall. "Don't you *ever* talk to her like that! You hear me?"

Benny turned towards the girl whom he now felt incredibly foolish for trusting. "I'll kill you!"

Marissa extended her middle finger to him and calmly replied, "Fuck. You."

Mickey then expanded upon that reply by kicking Benny in his gut, causing him to gasp and fall to the floor. "I told you not to talk to her like that! You're the one that's gonna be dead, you little punk!"

Benny found that he could take no more, and he screamed in rage as he rushed towards Mickey and punched him clear in the nose. The athlete's head snapped back upon the impact, but he stood his ground. He then felt a trickle of blood flow out of his left nostril.

"Damn, he made you bleed, Mickey!" Jeff observed aloud.

With a look of pure evil taking over his usually Adonis-like visage, Mickey retaliated with a punch to Benny's face that sent the shorter boy back up against the wall, followed by a blow to his stomach that brought him down to the floor. Benny spit a stream of blood from his mouth and looked up to see Mickey standing over him with the same expression of abhorring antipathy.

He extended his index finger towards Benny's face and told him, "*I hate you.*"

Forcing himself to his feet again while still consumed by his rage, Benny lunged towards Mickey, swinging at him with a stream of vicious punches. His bigger and stronger tormenter was quick to retaliate with an equal degree of aplomb, and a vicious fight began.

"Smash him, Mickey!" Marissa screamed.

After several moments of furious mutual pummeling, Benny was clearly receiving the worst of it, having his lip split wide open and the right side of his face swollen. He was soon knocked back into the wall by a particularly strong blow. Mickey then kicked the object of his wrath hard in the chest. His smaller opponent quickly fell to the floor again.

"Jeff, grab his arms!" Mickey hollered to his friend and accomplice. "Hold him! I'm gonna give him a nutcracker!"

"Yeah, crush the family jewels!" Jeff shouted back as he leapt upon Benny and held his arms in as tight a grip as he could muster.

Benny began struggling and kicking wildly, doing all he could to prevent the very painful assault that Mickey was determined to inflict upon his anatomy. He continued to let his fury flow through him like lava erupting from the maw of a volcano, and he managed to hold Mickey at bay for several seconds.

"I told you to hold him!" Mickey yelled.

"I am, man, but he's struggling like a mad dog!" Jeff replied. "Hurry and give his lower bits the treatment!"

"Do it!" Marissa shouted as she ran forward and stomped her foot down on Benny's stomach as hard as she could. This painful move caused him to gasp intensely as the wind was forced out of his lungs.

But as Mickey then ran forward to deliver the planned punishment, Benny suddenly summoned the will to kick forward with his right leg, striking his aggressor exactly where the athlete intended to hit him. The tall sportsperson winced in pain, involuntarily clasped his hands over his throbbing extremities, and fell back against the opposite wall.

The still raging young boy then bit as deeply into Jeff's right hand as he could, causing the larger youth to bellow in pain and release his grip. The young athlete looked at the bite indentations in his skin and turned back to Benny.

"You are *so* dead, you little punk!" Jeff shouted.

Realizing that his rage, no matter how great, could not bring him a victory in this situation, Benny ran towards the door with Jeff in pursuit.

"Get 'im!" Marissa yelled to Jeff as she tended to Mickey.

"I'm okay, I'm gonna kill him!" the recovering Mickey spat as he likewise took off after their fleeing target.

Benny knew he wasn't likely to outrun his faster pursuers, but somehow the realization of what he would receive if the two champion hockey players caught him filled the boy with sufficient adrenalin to enable him to swiftly clear the corridor. Benny shouted like a banshee in agony to attract any possible attention to his plight by the remaining school security guards and custodians as he fled in desperation. Upon turning another corridor, he nearly ran into Daniel Woody, a security guard and good friend of Mickey and Jeff, standing there.

Woody grabbed the angst-ridden boy by the arm before he could rush past him. "Hey! What's going on here? Why are you still in the building? Dismissal for the day was a while ago."

Seconds afterwards, Jeff rushed around the corner, followed within moments by Mickey. "We were just chasing him out of here, Dan... Mr. Woody. We have hockey practice, and he came back there to bug Marissa."

Benny gritted his teeth, the fury still coursing through him like a vat of highly corrosive acid. "You are so full of...!"

"Enough!" Woody yelled at Benny while shaking him harshly. "Get out of the building, and don't let me catch you causing trouble here after closing time again! Got that?"

Mickey looked Benny straight in the eyes, the glare of pure unadulterated mental bile pouring from his expression like a wave of streaming solar particles from the Sun. The tall athlete then clearly lip-synched the word "Monday" to Benny, the meaning being immediately evident.

Benny promptly pulled away from Woody's firm grip once it relaxed a bit and rushed out of the building as ordered.

His mind was filled with thoughts of revenge and hatred, with as many of those ill feelings directed at his own person as against his three tormenters. He silently cursed the Fates for their cruelest act against him yet. *And in a lifelong series of cruel events, that's* saying *something,* he mused to himself sadly as he rushed down the streets of Buffalo's East Side, with no heed for what direction he was heading.

Chapter 3: Cosmic Intervention and Warped Perceptions

Benny was unable to recall how many hours had passed since he fled the school. His mind was in a state of complete turmoil, his perceptions blinded by a burning rage. All he knew is that he didn't want to return home in this state of mind. That carried the risk of having his grandfather tell him yet again that he completely deserved the treatment routinely meted out to him by his peers. The fact that he believed there was actually some validity to this opinion only increased his searing sense of torment.

Considering the season of the year, the hours of daylight were waning by the time Benny realized he had wandered into the Marina, several miles from his home. He hadn't bothered to send a text to Craig, as he had no inclination to talk to anyone. No other soul was out and about, and the boats tethered to the docks sat quietly on the calm surface of Lake Erie, the moonlight casting a shimmering gleam over the water. The entire area appeared strangely silent as he dropped to his knees and leaned his shoulder against an abandoned SUV which was parked on the grass a few hundred yards from the docks.

The rusty decay of the vehicle's metal husk appeared to match the mood now pervading Benny's battered mind. It truly seemed like appropriate company for the troubled young man as the internal rage and tumult continued to boil within his psyche like a bowl of water in a microwave oven. He pounded on the chafed door of the SUV several times with both fists to vent his anger but succeeded in doing nothing more than to inflict stinging pain on his knuckles. The vehicle may have been well past its prime, but the metal plating was still quite strong, and it would not yield to the pitiful blows of any mere human.

Seeing the futility of venting in this manner, the young man fell to his knees and continued to pound ineffectually on the old vehicle's door; eventually, his hands began to swell as if stung by a swarm of bees.

It was after several interminable minutes of this that it happened. This would be the moment he would forever remember as having changed everything. Not only his own life, but the destiny of the entire world.

The end of all that Benny knew before began when the eerie silence, initially broken only by his pain-wracked sobbing, was suddenly interrupted by something else.

It first made its presence known to him as a bright whitish-blue flash of light that he caught in the corner of his tear-soaked eye. It was intense enough that it caused him to remove his face from where it was buried in his hands and look up into the star-flecked heavens. He then noticed that the entire surface of the night sky was ablaze with that light. It appeared to flare with a level of candela that outshined the Sun on the brightest day, yet it didn't cause any retinal discomfort. Instead, it seemed to evoke a powerful tingling sensation that appeared to permeate his entire body on a cellular and even sub-atomic level.

The English language—or any other lingual tongue known to humanity—lacked the capacity to readily express what Benny had begun to experience. All he could say was that the light grew increasingly bright with each passing second, and the sensation of being somehow 'altered' in a fundamental manner increased exponentially along with it. His mindscape was filled with a kaleidoscope of imagery that he would likewise find exceedingly difficult to describe. The closest he could come to that would be to say that he saw myriad worlds, levels of reality, and beings that even his creative mind could scarcely imagine.

These images appeared to coalesce into what his perceptions roughly translated as a huge triangular construct decorated with flashing star-like lights, all emanating from what appeared to be a series of glass-covered portholes. It had a metallic sheen to its surface that possessed far greater luster than the dull rusted casing of the SUV he leaned against. The construct appeared to hover miles into the sky yet was large enough to take up the bulk of his visual range. A deep whining sound appeared to be emitted by the construct, and it seemed to be attempting to penetrate into his mind as if it was guided by some nigh-incomprehensible intelligence.

Finally, the construct began to vibrate oddly and was soon joined by two other equally large triangular constructs, which intersected each other at distinct angles to form a triad. The three interconnected constructs then seemed to shatter, only to be replaced by what seemed to be the imposing countenance of a man with a flowing mane of cloud gray hair and a long beard of the same color; the face lacked one of its eyes, the empty socket covered by a patch. The face evoked a sense of vastly powerful authority and majesty.

The visage appeared to project information and imagery directly into every aspect of his mind at once, as if he was subjected to a forced download of what he could only describe as 'cosmic gigabytes.' The face appeared to say words in a thunderous voice: "Know this. The time has come. All must change. All must grow. All must evolve! You and everything! Harbingers of the new way are needed!"

The young man could swear that for a brief moment the mien of a beautiful, flaxen-haired young woman appeared in place of the terrifying older man's face, offering a reassuring smile that greatly contrasted with the male face which preceded hers. He couldn't be certain, however, as the male visage seemed to reappear so quickly.

He couldn't make sense of the reverberating message, but it bore so deeply into his mind alongside a salvo of unidentifiable symbols that he held his hands to his head and screamed. It was too much for a mere mortal of limited mental acuity to handle. Benny Lonero's poor little mind was overwhelmed, and the sound of his agonized scream seemed obfuscated by the whining begun by the first construct, which seemed to interpenetrate every part of the universe.

Then… it was over.

***

How long the entire experience lasted, Benny was unable to discern. He was well aware that it wasn't his imagination, because as he recovered, he could see the last vestiges of the amazing bluish-white light fading into the normal blackness of the sky. It was akin to the sight of the glare from a light bulb quickly fading as its coils shorted out. Further, the tingling sensation which felt as if it encompassed every atom of his body remained, though not as intense as before.

He could barely recall any of the imagery he saw, as if it was too much for his conscious mind to process. But both the intersecting triangular constructs and the imposing male visage remained superimposed in his thoughts like a dream too intense to forget upon waking, or an afterimage burned onto a computer or television monitor.

The normal sounds of the evening had commenced again, as if some mysterious cosmic 'pause' button which caused the previous unnatural silence was now turned off, and 'play' had been re-started. He felt a constant surge of energy in his body that was extremely euphoric, as if he were being electrocuted in a way that empowered him rather than causing any pain or discomfort.

Variations of one overriding question were foremost in his mind. *What the hell happened? What did that… light… do to me? I feel… well,* incredible. *Invincible.*

Benny found himself able to cast aside his fiery rage, if only momentarily, to stand up and take full measure of the changes he could sense having undergone on a fundamental level. He glanced at his clenched fist, which he felt charged with pulsating energy. Turning around, he resolved to both test his newfound mettle and vent his anger by summoning the courage to punch the strong metal side of the SUV with all his might.

As it turned out, his new level of might proved to be immense. That single punch caused the side of the car to completely cave in, as if struck by the type of battering ram used by law enforcement officers to smash open a heavily bolted door. In fact, the metal of the vehicle had crumpled inwards like a wad of crushed tinfoil. Further, the boy's knuckles barely felt any pain at the impact.

Incredible, he thought to himself. *I mean, totally incredible! I can't believe this has happened. I'm not sure if my strength is on the level of that Prometheus dude, let alone Ultimus, but it's way up there! More than the strength of any human being who isn't, well… metahuman.*

He then reached his hands under the SUV, gripped its metal rim tightly, and casually lifted it over. It took but a minute amount of effort to accomplish this. And though he was no expert on vehicles, he knew that SUV weighed well over two tons.

"Un-freakin'-believable," he whispered aloud to himself. "Benny, you just hit the greatest jackpot in the world. Nobody is going to mess with you again." The fact that he wasn't quite the only metahuman in the world then occurred to him, as such beings seemed to be appearing across the expanse of the planet in notable numbers over the past few years. "Well, most people won't, anyway, and no one without the risk of getting back whatever they dish out."

I just… so can't believe this. I have to know this isn't just part of some weird dream caused by that flash of light. I mean, I know I could have just gone nuts because I finally went through too much at school today. But, the thing is, I read about other strange events over the past few years happening right after some weird flash of light. So, this might be real. It just has to be! Please, God, don't make me 'wake up' and find out it's not real!

He then took stock of the energy he felt coruscating through his cellular matrix.

I also get the distinct feeling that this isn't all I can do. I'm not sure exactly how I know it, but I do. And I need to put it to the test. Right now.

Determined to further test the reality of his 'unbelievable' new status, Benny decided that the SUV husk would again serve as his proverbial guinea pig. Walking fifteen feet away from it, he clenched his right fist again. He then concentrated on the energy coruscating through his body, attempting to consciously focus it towards congealing into his hand. He felt the energy pour into it with great intensity, and a moment later it physically manifested in a form resembling crackling bluish arcs of electricity, yet somehow not truly electricity.

"Whoa!" he shouted as the flowing energy built to a crescendo, and the flicking arcs sizzled like the sound of several steaks cooking atop a blazing grill.

He pooled his resolve into focusing the energy outward, pointing his fist directly at the SUV. Less than a moment later, a glowing beam of searing bluish energy was projected forth, appearing to sizzle the very air molecules directly around it. The beam struck the thrashed side of the vehicle, causing it to shatter as if a hundred pounds of TNT had detonated within. An ear-splitting boom accompanied the spectacular explosion, and scraps of burning metal accompanied by shards of melting plastic and splintered glass fell to the ground, setting a series of mini-fires on the grassy ground.

"Holy...!" Benny exclaimed with a feeling of pure euphoria.

He then looked at the arcs of sapphire energy still coruscating around his fist, unclenched it, and willed the energy manifestation to die down below visible levels. Within a second, it did just that. The surge of energy he released was considerably more powerful and destructive than he hoped for, as he didn't want such a loud blast to result. Now he knew that he had to flee the vicinity before police and fire trucks arrived.

I need to be careful with that, he reminded himself. *I need to practice, get that more under control. But I'm not going to need these energy discharges to deal with those bastards at school anyway. Monday is going to be payback time.*

Before leaving he took one final glance at the glorious display of his newfound power before him and smiled. The feeling of sheer exhilaration coursing through him was beyond measure. He believed that the Powers That Be in the universe had given him the means to show the world that it's no longer permitted to mess with Benny Lonero.

Interlude: The Valis Institute

Former special ops agent turned paranormal investigator Donovan Jakes leaned back in his office chair. The office itself was secretly constructed beneath a gymnasium which recently opened on Niagara Street. Located just a few blocks from Benny's home, it was one of the many global sites of the Valis Institute, an organization established in 2006 to study the unusually intense set of astronomical phenomena that began occurring soon after the 21st cemtiru had begun. These events were referred to by the press as *Warp Events*.

This particular location was constructed in Buffalo based on an intense prediction made almost a year earlier by Claire Boone, one of the Valis Institute's best psychics. Boone's natural born ESP abilities became greatly enhanced following a Warp Event that manifested over the San Francisco Bay area. As for Jakes himself, he was a former military man who encountered much over the past 25 years that left him eminently qualified to head the metahuman research division of the organization, including the equivalent of what its members half-jokingly referred to as its 'police' wing.

This covert institute was funded by several individuals and organizations of considerable means, all of whom preferred to keep their involvement 'off the record.' Mounting evidence suggested that the cosmic events of unknown origin being studied by the Institute may have actually altered the very physical laws governing space and time in the localized region of the galaxy that includes Earth's solar system.

Other strange phenomena connected to these Warp Events included the alleged widespread opening of dimensional portals and the emergence of strange creatures from these quantum rifts; new and often exotic technology that wouldn't work under established physical laws before suddenly becoming operable; and espers & "indigo children" across the world experiencing a dramatic surge in their psychic abilities accompanied by disturbing nightmares that included apocalyptic scenarios.

Different divisions of the company were dedicated to studying and assessing these other singularities. Jakes had strong connections with each of them, as the diverse phenomena connected to the Warp Events would sometimes overlap, thus necessitating periodic cooperation between the institutes' different departments.

The Institute was completely off the books, and the powerful individuals funding its amazing but clandestine activities seemed to have more than enough influence to circumvent government oversight or control. It was entirely non-profit, and Jakes often wondered where the funds to continue its elaborate and rather extensive operations kept coming from; not to mention the highly advanced cutting edge technology the institute had exclusive access to. He wanted to ask more questions but had thus far convinced himself to ask as few as possible. At this point he simply didn't want to risk being investigated or ousted, as he not only found his job here valuable, but he also wanted to keep the organization under his purview.

As long as Donovan held his current position at the Institute, he could use the organization's unique resources to personally monitor emerging metahumans. And he could then act to help them… or to stop them, whatever any individual case may require.

True to Boone's considerable prescience, the major Warp Event she predicted would hit the Western New York area had come to pass. She further predicted that a greatly powerful metahuman would emerge in the wake of this particular Warp Event; a metahuman who would end up playing a pivotal role in world affairs.

According to Boone, whether this metahuman's major effect on the world would be for good or ill depended on many constantly fluctuating factors that hinged on certain specific decisions, which in turn led to myriad possible outcomes. The gifted, Warp Event-enhanced esper often explained to Jakes and others at the Institute that the future isn't set in stone. Rather, it more resembles a cascade of many possible results stemming from a certain likely catalyst incident.

Because of this, Jakes decided to relocate to Buffalo so he could personally operate this specific branch of the Institute. If the stakes were that high with this soon to emerge metahuman, he wanted to be there himself. He would do his best to insure a positive outcome to the impending event, even though he knew he was risking much, including his own life. But if he could avert a catastrophe for the entire planet stemming from the strange new physical laws that allowed previously 'impossible' events to occur with alarming regularity, it would be a risk well worth taking.

As he sat and studied the reams of information that streamed across his monitor, he began scratching his close-cropped brown and gray beard. This was something he did whenever he was both focused and concerned at the same time. In fact, some of the reports he read more than warranted that concern: A teenage boy with the power to control electricity was reported to have been involved in several incidents over the past few days in Kentucky. A girl who evidently had the power to morph into a cat-like creature had apparently made headlines in Ontario, Canada.

"Jesus, how far is this going to go?" Jakes quietly asked himself aloud.

Just then, he heard the chiming sound which indicated Boone was attempting to contact him over his private communications system. He immediately voice activated the intercom that would allow him to speak directly to her in wireless fashion.

"Donovan here. What's up, Boone?"

"Donovan, it's happened!"

"Can you be a bit more specific?"

"His power just emerged. The metahuman I told you about. The degree of Odic energy he unleashed was so strong that sensing it gave me the queen of all migraines. I threw up twice before I was able to make this call. Donovan, we need to go to yellow alert. Now."

"Will do, Boone, and thank you for what you go through for us, not to mention the world. In the meantime, take some meds and relax. I've got this."

Chapter 4: No Train, No Gain

For the first time in Benny Lonero's memory, the weekend couldn't pass fast enough for him. He pooled as much of his will as he could muster to avoid speaking to his grandparents and his uncle, as well as his mother, with whom he was estranged. As difficult as it was for him to get along with his grandparents and their son, his relationship with his mother was worse, and he previously decided it was supremely wise not to live with her. But that was something he would deal with in due time. The problems with his family could wait until he figured out how his new status would impact upon that particular situation.

In fact, he spent most of the weekend away from the house. In the early morning he boarded a bus to an area on the outskirts of Buffalo's West Side where O'Reilly's Salvage, a large sprawling junkyard, was situated.

Upon first arriving there on Saturday afternoon, he peered through the bolted gate barring ingress to the yard. It was littered with numerous examples of vehicular debris that would be perfect for him to test his newfound powers on. All of this served as preparation for Monday morning. Not only was utilizing these incredible powers even more exhilarating to him than he imagined sex would be (though he hoped to use his new status to help him succeed in that area, too); but it also provided him with continued elated proof that what the Warp Event had done to him was not just an extended dream or hallucination.

Early that morning, he had discovered that the 'Warp Event' was what both the media and astronomers were calling the bizarre flash of light that astounded the residents of the Western New York area Friday evening. And which clearly resulted in his incredible transformation. Reading that report on *The Buffalo News* website before leaving in the morning provided further validation for the reality of Benny's experience.

He further read that the press and scientific community struggled to come up with an explanation for this stellar anomaly, which was actually one of several such 'events' of varied intensity that had been manifesting over disparate areas across the globe during the past few years. The number of these events precluded the rare singular occurrence of a super nova in nearby space, or a huge comet combusting in the upper atmosphere.

Since Benny was curious about the true nature of the Warp Event that transformed him into something akin to a demi-god, that was something he would have to investigate later. More immediate matters of concern held his attention this day, however.

Benny peered through the gate which led to the spacious junkyard, and he saw no other living creature. As concern for being caught trespassing built up in his mind, a strange tingling sensation suddenly coursed through the contours of his skull and converged in the center of his forehead. It felt as if the unknown energy now saturating his entire cellular matrix was centering there much as it did when he focused it into his fist to project an energy discharge.

For a quick moment, it appeared as if his mind was expanding outwards and 'probing' the immediate vicinity. He was aware that several small rodents and a plethora of insects were present in the junkyard, but no life forms larger or more sophisticated than that.

Whoa whoa whoa! he thought to himself. *What the hell was that? It's like I… I dunno, like I 'scanned' the junkyard to see who or what else was there, and then the answer was somehow… just given to me.* He couldn't describe it any better than that for the nonce, but it gave him an elated 'rush' much as he imagined one may get after partaking of a strong pharmaceutical stimulant. *I need to learn the full parameters of these powers, but like I said, only the metahuman strength I have is needed for dealing with the 'crew' on Monday. Though this 'probing sense' or whatever I might call it will sure as hell come in handy for avoiding the security guards and other staff when required.*

Now that he 'knew' beyond a shadow of a doubt that the coast was clear, he decided to test his strength by seeing if he could rip open the gate's deadbolt. He grabbed the strong solid steel lock and squeezed it with all his might. The square-shaped piece of metal crumpled like a tin can. He then pulled it as hard as he could, and the steel chain snapped off the fence as if it were a thread of silk.

"Whoa," he said quietly to himself with a grin. "This totally kicks ass. And it's soon going to help me do that in a totally literal sense. Heh."

Benny pushed the gates open and entered the junkyard. He spent the rest of the morning testing his newfound superhuman strength on any item he could get his hands upon. He bent discarded mufflers and tail pipes like they were composed of cardboard. He punched through plate glass windows with ease and incurred no damage to the skin and bone of his hand. He tore the trunks off the discarded vehicles as if they were little more than plastic covers attached to a cup of margarine.

After a half hour of this, it took a strong effort of will not to raise his arms to the sky and scream in pure, unbridled elation.

***

After returning home late Saturday afternoon, he ordered a pizza, so he could fully avoid contact with his grandparents at the dinner table. He didn't want to risk an altercation, since he wasn't yet prepared to use his newfound strength against his grandfather, despite how much he hoped to show the intimidating patriarch of the house that he was now a greater force to be reckoned with. He succeeded in evading his erstwhile father figure throughout the evening.

On Sunday morning, he was back outside the junkyard, where he quickly learned that his break-in the previous day was discovered. Consequently, a new padlock had been placed over the gate. *I think it's safe to assume the owner may have increased the yard's security measures. And this gives me a chance to concentrate and try that mind thing, that total mental awareness, or whatever you might call it, that I did yesterday without actually trying. Here goes…*

Benny concentrated and focused, and he again felt the sensation of the incredible energies which now permeated his atomic structure stream to a central point in his forehead. That was followed by the impression of his mind flowing out from his skull and interpenetrating the physical environment, absorbing information from the entire surrounding area. Within a moment, he 'knew' there was now a hidden security camcorder sequestered in a telephone pole located near the center of the junkyard.

"Damn, it worked," Benny said to himself. *There's a security cam located there,* he silently noted in regard to the telephone pole. *And I certainly can't let documented evidence of me using my powers be recorded here.*

Grinning slyly with a hint of malicious glee, Benny saw this as the perfect opportunity to test his energy discharges. He knew that he had to get that power under better control if he hoped to use it against threatening targets in the future. And he had the distinct premonition that he would soon be required to do exactly that.

He moved back several feet to make sure he was out of the cam's recording range. He then pointed his fist in the direction of the large metal circuit box attached to the pole, as it was there that he knew the cam was concealed. Focusing his cosmic energies to congeal into his fist, he then concentrated into projecting it outward as a sizzling bluish-hued beam. In just over a second, the beam projected as he demanded, only this time he attempted to willfully rein in its intensity. The air crackled and smoked directly around the discharge beam as it projected forward and struck the pole about a foot and a half below the intended spot.

41

The heavy wooden pole was split in half by the power of the beam, and though he missed the box containing the hidden cam, the recording device was nevertheless smashed to pieces when the several hundred pounds of wood came crashing to the ground. This was accompanied by a thunderous echo that reverberated throughout the space of the junkyard.

"Damn it!" he yelled. *I only intended to hit and shatter the box, not smash the pole. No doubt that's going to attract some attention. I really need to gain better control over this power, but right now I have to get the hell out of here…*

It was then that Benny's thought was cut off as he heard someone shout, "Hey!"

He turned around and saw that the owner of the junkyard had just shown up, and he had a vicious and snarling Rottweiler on a leash. Evidently, the man had decided to patrol the area for additional security. He was standing far enough away that he could barely make out Benny's features.

"Aw, shit…" was all Benny had to say in response to this.

"You bastard, you!" the owner shouted back to him. "What the hell did you just do? You're the prick who broke in here yesterday, aren't you?"

It was then that Benny realized his power of cosmic awareness was less than perfect, but he would have to wait until another time to find out why its reliability factor fluctuated. He turned to run but would find that his attempt to flee the premises was about to face some opposition.

"Sic 'im, Gronk!" he heard the man holler as he released the harness on the leash holding back the dog.

Snarling and salivating with rancorous fury, Gronk rushed at Benny with impressive speed. But as the animal reached the startled young man and leapt for his throat, Benny reflexively swung at the attacking canine. The backhanded blow struck with sufficient force to send the dog's heavy body flying through the air until it slammed into another telephone pole. The animal then hit the ground hard, where he lay whimpering and twitching in agony.

"Gronk!" the owner bellowed. "Jesus!"

As the man ran to check on his injured pet and would-be junkyard guardian, Benny ran towards the fence on the western section of the yard at a level of speed surpassing that of the dog. He then leapt over the ten-foot high fence with little discernible effort. Landing on the sidewalk outside the junkyard, he subsequently took off down the street as fast as his enhanced leg muscles would carry him. He was never a fast runner and was quite inefficient at most competitive sports as a result. But since he had evolved to his metahuman form, the pace he now displayed would make any Olympic athlete seethe with envy.

His once poor stamina had likewise given way to a degree of endurance which made it appear as if his altered physiology produced no fatigue poisons. He ended up running the many miles it took to reach home in under a half hour, and without becoming the least bit winded. All of this was done as more or less a reflex action borne of his haste to escape being identified by the owner of the junkyard; and to avoid having to hurt him as he did the dog.

I can't believe I just K.O.'d a Rottweiler. And I reacted so swiftly, it was never able to reach me in the first place. I always had fast reflexes, but this… this is uncanny. And also totally bad-ass.

A malicious grin of satisfaction now shone across the young man's face as he pondered what he would do upon arriving at school the following morning.

Chapter 5: No One Messes with Benny

Benny wore a strangely calm expression as he exited the West Utica Street subway station on Monday morning. Buffalo Historical School was a mere two block strut from that location. He ignored the quintet of giggling female classmates of his who stepped out of the subway exit at the same time he did. They ignored him in turn, as was usually the case.

Just you wait, he said to them silently. *You don't know it yet, but as of today, I'm now the ultimate 'big man on campus.' Let's see whose attention you'll be clamoring for soon.*

Benny clenched his right fist as hard as he could to vent and control his festering anger. The now familiar tingling sensation of the amazing energies that coursed through his cellular matrix gave him a quick boost of confidence. For the first time in his tortured life, he didn't feel helpless and vulnerable. He didn't feel as if he had to avoid or fear anyone. Just to grant himself further reassurance that he didn't wake up from an incredible dream this morning, he ducked behind the subway station and punched the side of its marble wall. His fist sunk halfway into the hard ivory-hued mineral, with the resulting hole surrounded by a web of zig-zagging cracks.

Benny grinned with great satisfaction as he looked at the impossible damage he did to the side of the station, once more reminded that the fantastic was no longer limited to his imagination or daydreams. This was followed by an approving glance at his still clenched fist. The skin was barely even skinned by the full impact blow he had just delivered to hard marble. He then resumed his walk towards the school, barely able to keep a malignant beam of anticipation from appearing on his face.

***

As Benny entered the front door of the school, Craig Minkel saw his friend step in and ran to catch up with him.

"Hey, dude, I never saw you clamber into the building like you owned the place like this before," Craig noted with a sarcastic gleam. "And where the hell were you all weekend? You weren't answering your texts, so I figured your date with Marissa didn't go very well. If it did, you would have called and told me. Unless she invited you over her house on Friday night and you ended up staying all through Sunday, in which case…"

"I don't want to talk about it right now," Benny replied firmly.

He still had no idea if it was a good idea to tell Craig everything that happened to him over the weekend. He certainly didn't believe that the time, if it ever came, was the present. But he did know that he needed Craig out of his way for the duration of the school day. He couldn't risk his one good friend getting involved in the events Benny was planning to initiate.

"So, who pissed in your corn flakes this morning? Did you get into another fight with your grandparents or something?"

"No, I just have a lot on my mind right now. I'll call you later if I need to talk. As of today, I have things to take care of, so expect me to be scarce, alright?"

"Fine. I just wanted to know how things went, but I think you just gave me the answer. I'm sorry, I know how much you liked her. I figured it wouldn't turn out good, but I didn't want to piss all over your party. See you later, man."

With more than a tinge of attitude in his tone of voice, Craig huffed off to let his friend deal with whatever he was dealing with on his own.

With that taken care of, Benny strolled to the corridor where he knew he was likely to find Marissa Robbins at her locker. The girl's schedule was well known to him, since he had admired her standing in front of that locker often enough to have it committed to memory.

Right on schedule, Benny thought to himself upon noticing she was indeed there, as per usual for this time. As he walked over to the attractive young woman, he realized that now the sight of her no longer filled him with awe and desire. Those feelings were now replaced by a loathing that easily matched her own. His previous daydreams of affectionate intimacy with her were replaced by images of using his newfound power to incinerate her face.

Upon approaching Marissa, the changed young man moved ever so slightly into her personal space and leaned against the locker next to hers. He knew she would quickly notice him that way despite being busy rummaging through the contents of her locker. It took the petite brunette less than three seconds to notice Benny's always unwelcome presence. She was clearly startled to see him boldly standing so close to her, especially after the events of three days prior.

45

"What do you want?" she said, with a bit of nervous tension evident in her tone. "Did you tell? If you did…"

"No, of course I didn't," Benny replied with a sardonic smirk. "I just wanted to thank you for our 'date' on Friday."

"What the hell? Have you lost it totally, you little fag?"

"Actually, I've never thought more clearly. I wanted to thank you because it made me realize what scum those boys you drool over so much actually are. Now I'm glad that I'm *not* like them, rather than wishing I was."

"They're better than what you are any day!"

Benny shrugged that one off, never losing his discomfiting grin. "It also showed me what type of girls you and your friend Leah are for finding boys who do things like that to be cool and attractive. And you especially, for going along with their plans to hurt me like that. The fact that you could actually do what you did to someone who you knew liked you so much, no matter how unattractive you find him…"

"I strongly suggest you get away from me right now, Benjamin Lonero, or I'll give you another beating right here."

Marissa angrily threw one of her textbooks down on the floor as hard as she could to emphasize that she was more than livid enough to make good on that threat. She was completely unaware, however, that she and her cohorts were no longer capable of carrying it out. For now.

"I'll be glad to go, right after I give you a message to deliver to your boyfriends. Tell them the rumors I heard of their mothers having intimate relations with four-legged animals of various species must be true, considering how they turned out. Oh, and please tell Leah I heard that she has a very unhealthy degree of fondness for her own dad, even when he isn't on one of his drunken binges and two-timing her mom with his own daughter. Think you can see to it that they get those messages?"

Benny grinned in satisfaction as he saw the startled look on Marissa's attractive visage. The girl was unable to fully believe that she had just heard what her ear drums had collected. Her own anger simmered to a boiling point, which was evident with the way she clenched both of her fists and gritted her teeth.

"You little douchebag! When I tell all of them what you said, they're going to make Friday seem like a pleasant dream."

"So, I *can* count on you to get that message to them, then? Cool! The basketball team always did mention how reliable you are about giving so many things, if you get my meaning."

Benny ended the hostile conversation with a sarcastic pursing of his lips, pretending to throw her an imaginary kiss from a distance. After he saw the look of fury and disgust on her face, he smiled and walked away. He knew he could count on her to give his message to her "crew." He also knew they would be more than pissed off enough to attempt to catch him alone later that same day. The bitter young man planned to make the opportunity come easily for them.

Right after gym class. Benny's heart was pounding with anticipation. *Last class of the day. How differently today is going to end compared to last Friday. Yup…*

***

A swirl of conflicting emotions ran through Benny's pain-riddled psyche throughout his first six classes. He went out of his way to act as if nothing was unusual, but some of his teachers seemed to realize he was atypically quiet. No sarcastic responses were uttered from his infamous mouth that day, to be followed by a combination of laughs and jeers from his fellow students.

But his seeming ennui didn't appear serious enough to merit asking him if he needed to talk, either to them or to the guidance counselor. His instructors well knew it was usual for Benny to be depressed; it just wasn't usual for him to be so quiet, considering how he most often acted like the annoying clown to vent his frustrations.

As the soccer game that took up his physical education class near the end of the school day was wrapping up, Benny began preparing for the confrontation that was to come. He knew Jeff Wolfe and Mick Judge were going to wait until he was alone, and he had plans to see to it they would "accidentally" find him that way. As he expected, the two popular athletes pretended not to have received his message from Marissa, even though he knew she would have made a point to tell them as soon as she could after he had his "conversation" with her that morning.

In short, Benny had much unfortunate experience with how they operated. They would likely believe he was off-guard due to their failure to say anything to him earlier in the day. But he knew better.

They must think I'm really stupid. Just as I figured they would. How nice to see their overconfidence work to my advantage.

Benny didn't participate in the soccer game, so he wouldn't inadvertently display any of his newfound power. The gym instructor, Mr. Frost, didn't pay much heed to it, as he knew how useless Benny was to any team he was on, and how badly ridiculed he would be by his peers for each poor performance if he insisted on the boy's participation. So, the teacher felt that he was giving a break to both his star pupils and Benny by looking the other way.

As the last few boys cleared out of the locker room to head back to their home rooms for dismissal, Benny feigned his time in there to simulate being off his guard. While he was looking in a mirror and combing his thick brown hair, waiting for the inevitable arrival of his adversaries, he was suddenly surprised to find his

47

conscience gnawing at him. He initially believed that after Friday, he had lost all vestiges of it. He now realized that wasn't the case, however.

The tormented young man couldn't help the pensive musings that began flowing through his mind like rapidly moving water in a creek. *Should I really be doing this? I mean, doesn't this make me as much a bully as they are? I know that a lot of the teen heroes I read about in the comics--like The Fly and Invincible--wouldn't do something like this.*

But hey, I'm not them. I'm not going to pretend to be a wimp! These asshats deserve what they're going to get! Did they care about bullying me? Did they even acknowledge me as a fellow human being, with feelings? I'm not going to wuss out...

"Yo, rainbow-boy!" The sound of Mick's distinctive voice cut off Benny's troubled thoughts.

The young man turned to see both Mick and Jeff enter the locker room. He then saw Mick use what were obviously a set of Mr. Frost's keys they were given in trust to lock the door behind them. The advantages of being prized athletes gave them privileged access to much more than the hearts and bodies of their female peers, he noted.

"We got your message, fag," Mick told him with an extremely incensed tone. "You won't get out of here this time. Now, how about you give us that message to our faces?" The tall and lanky but well-toned athlete then looked back at his accomplice. "Hell, you stay out of this, Jeff. I want him to say it to *my* face. I don't need your help to lay him out."

Benny knew he had no reason to be afraid... except, perhaps, for what he now wanted to do so badly to the boys now confronting him; what he now *could* do to them. He was aware of his own complicity in this latest confrontation due to his morning exchange with Marissa. He put himself—and them—in this position. His inner sense of scruples screamed to him that it wasn't right. He didn't want to care. But a strong part of him did nevertheless.

"Look, Mick," he said, raising his hands in a conciliatory gesture. "I'm sorry I said that stuff, okay? I was just very upset after last Friday. What you guys did was 'eff'ed up, and you know it, so how did you expect me to feel? But..."

Mick refused to hear the words. He simply continued to walk slowly towards Benny, his face red with burning ferocity. It was an expression Benny had viewed only too often, but this time it was worse than he'd ever seen it before.

"I hate you," Mick told him with a stiffly pointed index finger just a few inches from his target's face.

Benny put his hands up again. "Mick, listen, please. Something... happened over this weekend. I'm not like I was. I can hurt you badly. I *wanted* to hurt you badly, for what you did. But... but I don't want to now, alright? So, can you please accept my apology, and let this go? For once? I won't ever say anything to you or about you again, I promise."

"*I. Hate. You,*" Mick said once more, this time with more phonetic emphasis on each word, as he continued to move forward.

"Just kick his ass, Mick!" Jeff yelled in encouragement. "Do it! Or I will!"

Mick continued advancing slowly towards Benny, as if salivating with anticipation over what he was about to do.

The sight of this caused the beleaguered young target to suddenly find himself beset by a kaleidoscope of memories. These were comprised of all the things said and done to him by Mick and his cronies in the past. Now Mick and Jeff wanted to do something like that to him again. And he was still in terrible pain over what Marissa did at their behest on top of everything else. Upon being besieged by these memories, he knew he couldn't take it anymore.

"You won't hurt me again!" Benny shouted in extreme defiance.

The enraged youth rushed towards Mick and struck him directly in the sternum. Much to the athlete's shock, the unbelievable force of the blow felt as if it caved his entire rib cage in as it sent him flying back over two dozen feet to impact against the wall on the far side of the locker room. Mick gasped for air and put his hand over his shattered chest as a thick trickle of blood dribbled from his mouth.

"Oh Jesus…" Jeff stammered. "Mick… how the hell…?"

Now driven completely over the edge, Benny roared in fury and ran towards Jeff. Too startled to move, and too slow to evade Benny's incredible burst of speed at any rate, the athlete found his left arm crushed in the smaller boy's vise-like grip. Benny twisted Jeff's arm, watching him scream in agony as the bones made a cracking sound not unlike an eggshell being stepped on.

"I warned you!" Benny bellowed as he continued to twist and fracture the strong athlete's arm as if the bones were strands of uncooked spaghetti. "But you had to do it anyway, didn't you? I can't take this anymore! And now I don't have to! Do you hear me?"

Benny then lifted the injured Jeff off the ground as if he weighed less than an ounce and hurled him towards the opposite side of the room. A loud crunching sound was heard as the tall young man's airborne body struck the surface of the wall ten feet to their left.

Several feet away, Mick slid down to the floor while coughing out streams of blood, unable to utter a word, and helpless to aid his friend as his ribs poked into his lungs with every slight move he made.

Still maniacally out of control, Benny rushed over to Jeff, who lay twitching on the ground. The young man again lifted the much taller student into the air as if he were nothing more than a roll of newspaper. He found himself unable to temper his rage as the memories of all he had endured at their hands--and the hands of others--through the years continued to flutter through his mind like the rapidly changing scenes of a filmed training montage.

Yelling in anger and turmoil, Benny slammed Jeff into the wall again. He heard a sick squishing sound upon the impact, accompanied by the clear sensation of more of the boy's bones cracking.

"I've had it with you! Do you hear me?"

But the sight of Jeff's limp form quivering in his hands as blood trickled out of his nostrils suddenly gave Benny pause. The former's eyes were wide open, as if glaring accusingly at Benny, even though no words left his gaping mouth.

"Oh man…" was all Benny could choke out as he released the grip he had on his adversary's shirt. The athlete's limp body fell to the ground with a dull thud.

Jeff continued to move in spasms, and his lips shook as if he was trying to say something with great desperation. However, he was unable to muster the energy to release a single sound louder than a series of airy gasps. He was obviously going into shock, and the blood that suddenly spurted from his mouth in fountain-like fashion made the extent of his injuries quite clear.

"God, what did I do?" Benny yelled as he covered his face.

The boy turned towards Mick, who lay in a sitting position with both hands covering his broken chest, his mouth and eyes wide open. He also looked as if he was trying to say "look what you did" to Benny, but all that could be heard were a few sickly gurgles that accompanied the blood continuing to stream out of his face's main orifice.

"You made me do this!" Benny screeched at him with an extended index finger. "Why did you make me do this?"

Screaming in rage at himself and the rest of the world, Benny punched the side of the wall above the sprawled and damaged form of Jeff Wolfe. His fist smashed clear into it, leaving a cavernous hole in the plaster. He then ran towards the locked door, easily pushing it open by breaking the lock with a single forceful shove.

Benny ran through the now mostly empty school with such speed that he deftly evaded the security guards and custodial personnel who remained in the building. He rushed through the front doors, once again not knowing nor particularly caring where he was headed. His mind was filled with a barrage of painful thoughts, and he wanted the entire world to pay for what he was now on the road to becoming.

Chapter 6: Turmoil is the Worst Kind of 'Moil

At the Valis Institute sequestered underneath a "dummy" fitness club located on Buffalo's Lower West Side, special agent Donovan Jakes suddenly found his mid-afternoon coffee break rudely interrupted. The disturbance was the result of a nearly panic-stricken Claire Boone—the gifted head of the metahuman research organization's psychic Esper Division—who managed to take the man unawares despite his decades of experience in clandestine military operations. He really hated when she did that.

"Donovan!" the curly-haired woman exclaimed as she burst into his quarters. "It's happened!"

"Jesus, Claire!" the heavily trained but fully human special agent shouted as he leapt to his feet in a combat-ready position. "Did you forget how to knock? I've actually killed people who snuck up on me like that in the past."

"Never mind your macho posturing right now, Donovan! It's happened! I just sensed a spike in both his power and his emotional state! Each was strong enough to indicate some serious poop is now hitting the fan."

"Who? Do you mean the Lonero kid? I'm guessing it's him, considering you instigated our sponsors to establish this Buffalo branch of the Institute exclusively for the purpose of monitoring him."

"Yes! The Lonero kid! After 'feeling' the spike—it really hurt like hell, I thought it was going to give me a cerebral hemorrhage or something—I checked the police band radio. Sure enough, no more than fifteen minutes from the time I felt the psychic surge, a call was placed to the BPD from Buffalo Historical School, where Lonero is a student. Something involving him went down there, Donovan! A metahuman incident! I'm telling you, we should have been keeping a closer look…"

"Claire, calm down and clear your mind of the empathic detritus you picked up from the kid and the others involved in whatever happened there. Did you get any 'picture' of what he did?"

"No clear images, just a blurry but potent sense of chaos and turmoil. And that energy surge. It wasn't anywhere near an omega-level spike in power, but it was clearly enough to indicate a dramatic display of metahuman force. Not only that, but I sensed great emotional agony emanating from three individuals... and extreme physical pain from two of them."

"Jesus H. Christ. Okay, I need to get a task force over there right now. I have to locate Lonero and deal with this before something worse happens. Including but not limited to his getting into a firefight with the cops."

"Please be careful, Donovan. He seems to have snapped or something. You'll be in my prayers."

"Pray for Lonero instead. I suspect he's in need of them more than me right now."

***

The late afternoon sky had taken on an aptly overcast appearance as Benny Lonero sat curled up in a small tool shed located in the back of a residential home on Buffalo's East Side. He had no idea who lived in that house, nor did he care in the least. He felt the need to hide from the world, and this place would serve that purpose for the moment. Despite the incredible power he now possessed, his entire body was trembling from spasms caused by sheer emotional anguish and confusion.

What did I do? Benny asked himself this question repeatedly as slow-motion visions of the bloody and broken bodies of Mick and Jeff cascaded through his mind, refusing to cease, offering him as little mercy as he gave them. Moreover, the usual torrent of mental imagery consisting of the abuse he frequently received from his fellow students was now intermixed with these equally disturbing images of his infliction of the same upon two of his worst tormenters.

"But they deserved it!" he screamed to himself, breaking the collage of emotional repetition.

Benny then lashed out physically by smashing his diamond hard fist through a thick oak wood cabinet inside the shack as if it were built out of cardboard. He no longer cared if his verbal venting attracted the attention of the owners of the home whose backyard he had taken uninvited refuge in. After all, he was now pretty much a demi-god, and accordingly, he no longer needed to fear anyone. The exhilaration of the new immunity from fear that this power afforded him conflicted with an equally strong terror over the havoc he knew that he could now wreak upon others at will.

And why shouldn't he? His entire short lifetime was filled with many who amused themselves and vented their own frustrations by hurting him, both physically and emotionally. Wouldn't it simply be just retribution on his part? Weren't they facing a creation of their own cruel and thoughtless actions? Shouldn't they pay for all the hatred and abuse they hurled at him on a regular basis?

In addition to pondering such questions, Benny also felt that reparations from the universe were his rightful compensation. All the acclaim and respect his tormenters enjoyed would now be his for the taking. *Anything* he wanted could be his for the taking, in fact.

But the unfettered thrill of these thoughts was continuously replaced with feelings of horror. The fear of what would happen to him each day was now intermittently superseded by a fear of what *he* could and might do to others.

Benny Lonero screamed another curse as he again used his now herculean strength to kick the well-built oaken door of the shack clear off its hinges.

"They're all gonna pay," he said to himself as he wiped his eyes to clear a stream of tears. "Marissa, you're next."

When the name of this girl came to mind, he began planning to exact brutal comeuppance upon the young woman who had shattered his heart and eagerly led him into the waiting arms of those who wanted to hurt him. *Then I'm gonna get all the rest of those a-holes who went along with them. And then I'm gonna move onto everyone who made my life a veritable hell in middle school.*

Benny sobbed as he began to walk out of the unfamiliar yard. Before he could leave, however, he was intercepted by the owner of the house who unexpectedly exited the back door of his home, clearly concerned about the commotion he was hearing outside. The homeowner was Willie Morris, a middle-aged sewer worker of strong constitution who grew up afraid of no one he had ever met. But that would change in just a moment.

The man was startled to see a crying, clearly emotionally distressed teenaged boy standing before him. His first instinct was to ask the boy what was wrong, until he noticed the severe amount of damage wreaked upon the tool shed which he had worked so hard to build with his own two hands the previous summer. His concern was now replaced with anger at the sight of what he believed to be a youthful vandal in his midst.

"Hey, what the hell did you just do to my tool shed?" Willie demanded to know, not caring what the answer would be. "You little bastard, I'm gonna drag your ass right to the police station myself!"

But Benny no longer feared any threat wearing human skin. Not even from a man whose burliness rivaled that of his grandfather, and who was clearly just as fearless. His tortured gaze caught that of Willie's, and the man suddenly knew fear when he saw the young boy's eyes take on a bluish luminescence. Sparks of sapphire-hued energy were arcing around the fingers of the youth's right hand, accompanied by what appeared to be the ozone-like stench of burning air.

"You think that tool shack is damaged now?" Benny hollered. "Then watch *this*, you ignorant geezer!"

Benny pointed his hand at the shed and focused the torrents of energy gliding through every cell in his body into his fingers. A sizzling projection of radiant bluish energy was projected from the young man's hand into the sturdy wood of the shack, causing the entire structure to explode upon impact. Shards of wood and metal fragments from what was left of Willie's precious tools were strewn about in every direction, and the older man covered his face as smaller pieces of the debris landed throughout the backyard.

"Dear... God..." was all Willie could say as terror overwhelmed him.

The homeowner slumped to his knees as Benny angrily approached him and stuck his index finger near the older man's face, the arcs of azure energy still flickering about the extended digit. Willie forced himself not to pee his pants or beg for his life, reminding himself of the dignity he valued more than anything else.

"Do you want to try to bully me now, old man?" Benny yelled. "Do you now? Just try it!"

The horrifying situation was then interrupted as Willie's wife Elaine walked out of the house.

"Willie, what's going on out there?" she managed to ask before gasping in shock at the sight of the strange glowing-eyed boy threatening her normally plucky spouse.

"Elaine, get back in the house..." Willie choked out after hearing his wife's voice.

As the trembling homeowner spoke, Benny's entire body shook with the force of the conflicting emotions that now tore through his psyche with a force of a geyser.

"Please don't hurt my husband..." Elaine pleaded as Benny turned and looked at her.

The anguish-ridden young man appeared to think the impassioned request over for a moment. Benny then turned and retreated from the yard, sparing Willie Morris mortal harm, and his wife the trauma of having to witness it.

The woman ran and embraced her husband of 24 years, falling to her knees beside him and crying with a combination of fear and relief.

"Oh, thank the mercy of the Lord," Elaine said as she and her husband held each other tightly.

"Willie, who was that boy? Why were his eyes glowing like that? Why was he here?"

"I dunno why he was here," her husband replied. "But I don't think he was human. I think he was probly one 'a them metahuman people. He blew up the shed just by pointin' at it, and there was some kinda blue electricity or sumthin' comin' outta his body." Willie took a deep breath before uttering the final part of his description to his terrified wife. "And there was sumthin' seriously wrong with him in the head."

***

Benny ran down the darkening Buffalo streets as fast as his now superhuman leg muscles would allow him as his mental breakdown continued unimpeded. The destruction he had just perpetrated upon innocent Willie Morris's world filled him with pangs of remorse that were partially flooded out by another stream of consciousness montage which poured through his battered mindscape like torrents of water through a shattered dam.

As he passed an alleyway on a side street, Benny suddenly sensed a tremendous surge of energy that was quite unlike the Odic forces he had recently begun commanding. It seemed to emanate from the alley he just passed, and he instinctually turned to peer into the passageway between tenement buildings.

He saw what appeared to be a taller man with a white beard wearing a pair of bifocals and clad in a black shirt with a Pink Floyd logo on it. But it was clearly a different man than the one he saw in the visions he received during the Warp Event, despite the similarity of the age and the gray beard. For instance, this man had two eyes, not just one.

"I can't believe what a bloody mess you are at this point," the man said in a British accent.

"Worse than that counterpart of yours who morphs into the wolf. He'll be blinkered out of his mind if I should tell him about this. Wish I could help, mate, but it's out of my hands. Try not to cause too much trouble in the meantime, okay, kid?"

Before Benny could react, the figure was suddenly gone, and the strange energies he sensed seemed to fade along with the image.

Considering the psychic melt down he was now undergoing, the adolescent metahuman shrugged off the sighting of the strange British man and his inexplicable statements as a bizarre hallucination. If this had been anything more than a hallucinatory apparition, it wouldn't be until sometime in the future that Benny would find out who that man was and what, exactly, he was talking about.

For now, though, the continued flow of disjointed feelings was all that passed for thoughts in his highly distraught psyche as he resumed his mind-addled trek across the neighborhoods of Buffalo's East Side.

***

Within the hour, Donovan Jakes walked into Buffalo Historical School in a suit and tie with a convincingly forged detective's I.D. He watched as EMTs carried two teenage boys out on gurneys towards a waiting duo of ambulances. Though not in possession of a medical degree, Donovan had seen more than enough injuries on the battlefield, and he could readily discern with a cursory glance that these boys' injuries were quite severe.

Not wanting to interfere with the important work of the EMTs, Donovan approached what he recognized as a woman in uniform who possessed a standard officer level rank. He pulled out his false badge, confident that his contacts who forged it had done so to perfection and introduced himself to the officer.

"What happened here?" he asked the lawwoman.

"We have two male students who were severely beaten," she responded. "Only a custodian and two security guards were still in the building when it happened, but I highly doubt any of them were responsible. We're still questioning these three employees now, though."

"Did they say if they saw who did this?"

"They say they didn't. As for the victims, they are known to have been popular athletes, so they're wondering if the perps may have been members of a rival hockey team. This school's team, the Icemen, are known to have a bitter rivalry with the teams from both Hut Tek and Rivertown High. During the second semester of the last school year they had a brawl with visiting students from Rivertown who tried tearing down one of their team's victory banners."

"Do you agree this may have been over a petty high school sports team rivalry?"

"These athletes tend to take their sports very seriously, since it's a major factor behind the popularity they enjoy. This has been known to cause them to engage in acts of thuggish and even gang-like behavior towards rival teams whom they mutually view as a threat to each other's social status among peers."

"Hmm. I would like to see the crime scene."

"Follow me, Detective."

Donovan did indeed follow the officer, hoping to distract any attention from the fact that Benny Lonero was behind this. He needed to handle this situation himself and minimize the chance of a direct police confrontation with the young metahuman. He knew that Benny—and the world—would be far better off if the boy ended up in the hands of the Valis Institute rather than any government agency.

As the incognito Donovan was led to the door of the boys' locker room in the gym, he immediately noticed how the lock was broken from the inside.

"It's quite strange that the door's lock appears to have been smashed by someone breaking out, as opposed to someone breaking in," the forensics officer on the scene noted to the faux detective. "Equally strange is the fact that these two boys were athletic types, yet despite the struggle they must have put up, only their blood seems to be present on the scene."

"So, there is no discernible sign that the perps were injured during the assault?" Donovan asked.

"Well, we won't know for certain until we analyze the samples I just collected. However, based on the dispersion path of the blood around both victims, it doesn't seem like the perps suffered any harm. The injuries that the victims received, though quite severe, were not bullet or knife wounds; in fact, no puncture wounds of any type were in evidence following a cursory examination by the EMTs. Of course, we won't know for certain until they get to the hospital and the doctors are able to give them a more thorough examination. They may have been struck with blunt instruments of some sort, including pipes or baseball bats, but again, we can't know for certain until they can be fully examined at the hospital."

"I see."

Jesus, it looks like this kid used his bare hands to do this. Just how strong is he? Hard to tell when you consider these boys were mere humans, however athletically inclined. Still, I had better assume Lonero is quite the powerhouse before I confront him.

"And there's another odd bit of evidence," the forensic officer pointed out to 'Detective' Jakes. "The wall here is damaged, and it appears that it was made by… well, a human fist."

"A fist?"

"Yes, the knuckle indentations in the material are clearly evident. But considering how thick that plaster is, the amount of strength it would take to punch a hole like that into it is, well, rather incredible. Especially considering there's no sign of blood or fragments of flesh surrounding the damaged area. I'm still going to scrape for possible skin samples, of course. If I find any, then we have a good chance for a DNA match with any eventual suspects."

That statement didn't sit well with Donovan. *Hmmm, I had better make sure our contacts at the police department check for any samples that may be found in the forensics lab. If they are, we can't let them be traced back to Lonero. If the police should attempt to arrest him… and if the government ever got their hands on him before we did… well, that could be bad.*

57

"Okay, I'll let you get back to your work now. I'm going to ask the three employees who were in the building when this incident occurred a few questions."

"Alright."

But Donovan already knew those three claimed to have seen nothing. The two guards were extremely worried they might lose their jobs for something like this happening on their watch, but Donovan wasn't the least bit concerned about that. The former special ops soldier knew that it might be only a matter of time before the guilty party was suspected of being a student at the school rather than a group of outsiders. Or the act of a single individual, as he knew to be the case.

Moreover, Donovan's perusal of Benny Lonero's file at the Valis Institute database indicated he might eventually become a suspect, though likely not right away. It was probable a group comprised of a few fellow athletes from a rival school, or of members from the emerging street gangs in the city, would be considered more logical culprits. At least initially, that is.

Donovan then realized he had to leave the scene, because time was now very much of the essence. Benny was out there somewhere, obviously in a state of extreme emotional distress. Claire didn't yet know how great his power level was, but she said it appeared to her psychic senses to be "off the scale." If so, that would potentially make Benny an omega level metahuman. He knew Claire's penchant for dramatics did not include a similar proclivity for exaggeration. Benny had to be found before something truly tragic happened.

As Donovan left the school grounds, he activated a secure line on his watch communicator. "Len, we have a situation here. I need a team of about four men, with a suit of plex body armor and U-3 model plasma rifles prepared for each of us. That's five, if you had trouble counting.

We're damn lucky those plasma rifles started working as intended following the Warp Event in Austin last year. And I need all this *yesterday*.

"You also need to get Agent Boone on the horn and tell her that she needs to find our quarry's location *fast*, even if that means she has to use those cerebral enhancement drugs. She has my full authorization for that, and I'll take full responsibility for any possible consequences. Agent Jakes out."

Donovan let out an exasperated sigh as he closed communications. *Dammit, kid, you better be salvageable. If not, a lot of people are going to be in a world of festering horse dung. I know you're in a lot of pain, so please don't make me have to end you. And please be so kind as to refrain from ending me, or any of my team.*

Chapter 7: The Point of No Return

Obviously, Marissa Robbins had never given Benny her home address. However, he was aware that several of her friends and partners-in-hate against him did indeed have that information. At the very least, her number was in the address book of their respective cell phones. To acquire it, though, he would have to force it out of one of her friends.

Considering his current state of mind, and the way most of her friends had always treated him, Benny was more than willing to go this route. He also knew exactly where he could reliably locate at least one of these friends.

Several of his classmates frequently congregated for socialization at the Crimson Room, a club located close to their school. It was geared entirely towards serving teens eighteen and under and was known to be rather rough despite billing itself as an "alcohol free zone" for obvious legal reasons.

Because many of his chief tormenters were among the usual patrons of that club, Benny avoided it like the meeker residents of a South American jungle would avoid the territory of a cannibal tribe. He always resented being ostracized from such a popular social atmosphere, and he couldn't help evincing a pang of dark satisfaction at finally being able to enter the location without fear for his safety.

Revenge would be sweet, and thoughts of it were effectively beating back the conscience that was desperately struggling within Benny Lonero to quell the path he was now treading towards.

A large but nondescript SUV was driving around the West Utica Street area of Buffalo's East Side with an extremely important purpose. Within its spacious interior was Donovan Jakes, accompanied by four other armed agents of the Valis Institute, one of whom was driving. Sitting next to Donovan in the back seats of the van was the now anxiety-ridden super psychic Claire Boone.

"Do you sense his presence anywhere around here, Claire?" Donovan asked his partner with clearly mounting impatience.

"I'm trying to pick up details, but you're making me really freaking nervous, Donovan!" she replied in irate fashion. "Do you know how dangerous it is to confront a metahuman with this level of power?"

"Do you know how dangerous it is to others, not to mention Benny himself, if we *don't* confront him, Claire? This is a steep responsibility, and you agreed to the requirements of this job along with the rest of us when you joined the Institute. So, you need to pull yourself out of this funk."

"Donovan, I signed on as a member of the Esper Division for detecting potential metahuman manifestations, I'm not a goddamned soldier! All of us are likely to get killed! Why couldn't I stay back at the base and report on what I sensed of his whereabouts via communicator?"

"Because your abilities are less efficient and accurate from a distance, damn it! Claire, I need you to get hold of yourself. You may not be a soldier, but you're really needed here in the field. The crew here needs you... and so does Benny. We have to find him and stop him from doing whatever he's planning to do before something horrifically tragic for everyone involved happens."

"How are you and a mere four soldiers going to stop him?"

"Because despite his level of power, these abilities are very new to him, and he's likely unable to make full use of his capabilities at this time. He also has no training yet, whereas the five of us are veterans at combat situations. We've also received a few years of additional training geared towards dealing with dangerous metahumans, and we're armed with special weaponry designed to handle extra-conventional threats, most of which didn't even work before the Warp Events allowed such tech to become functional. There is still no guarantee we'll come out of this intact, but..."

"Which means its highly *experimental* weaponry, Donovan! How often has that equipment or your training really been put to the test?"

"Dammit, Claire, you listen to me!"

Donovan's voice trailed off for a moment before he sighed and continued.

"Claire, we all need to put ourselves on the line here because as far as we know, Benny may be worth it. The police aren't trained or well equipped to deal with the likes of this, at least not in a way that will minimize casualties. This is our job, and however unprepared you may think we are, we're certainly much more prepared than the conventional authorities. I know you're scared, and you have good reason to be, but you must get hold of yourself because we need you. Okay?"

Donovan placed a reassuring hand on the trembling Claire's shoulder. She sucked in a lungful of air and nodded weakly.

"Okay. I can do this. Just let me concentrate, alright?"

"Certainly. And thank you, Claire. Thank you so much. You don't have to be a soldier to be brave.

***

Given his current level of energy and speed, it didn't take very long for Benny to make his way on foot to the door of the Crimson Room.

Forcing himself to look as nonchalant as possible despite his state of emotional anguish, the newly evolved young metahuman entered the establishment for the first time. The two always alert security guards on watch looked at him oddly, as he was an unfamiliar face; however, it wasn't all that unusual for new teen patrons to enter the club.

At first, the alert guards glared in the newbie's direction as if sensing something "off" about the newbie, and Benny found himself hoping he wouldn't have to deal with them as he did with two of his tormenters earlier that day. After all, he understood they were just employees doing their job to keep the patrons and property of the club safe.

Fortunately for the bouncers, they shrugged off their "sixth sense" feelings of unease since Benny was a relatively short and fairly skinny kid that didn't look like any kind of threat. Moreover, the metal detectors at the entrance registered no firearm or bladed weapons on him. Little did they know, however, that the strange boy in their midst was a veritable living weapon, packing unimaginable firepower within his altered cellular structure.

Having casually gained ingress to the club, Benny walked around scoping the premises for certain familiar—but unfriendly--faces. He saw many stunningly attractive girls on the dance floor with their arms wrapped around boys, and occasionally each other. Some of them were engaging in what was popularly called "twerking" with their fellow dancers, and all of them were dressed to impress.

Benny began seething with a combination of yearning and envy upon observing this pleasurable and fun interaction between boys who were many popularity levels above him, and attractive girls who would almost certainly shun him with all due prejudice if he attempted such public intimacy with them.

That's all going to change soon. Because, to paraphrase a certain comic book character: you just hit the jackpot, tiger! And Lord help anyone who tries to deny you access to this aspect of life anymore.

As Benny admired the beautiful bodies of the girls who were variously gyrating on the dance floor and chatting with friends at the juice bar, his gaze finally came upon a male peer whom he recognized. He gritted his teeth in anger as his eyes locked on the haughtily smiling mien of Les Gurgleworth. Despite this boy's blatant lack of good looks, he was accepted by the "in" crowd for reasons Benny didn't readily understand, but likely had to do with the fact that his way of thinking and acting was in no way "outside the box" (one thing Benny had learned was that cruelty and intolerance were acceptably "inside" the proverbial box). This fact was made clear by the several girls who gave Les affectionate hugs and clamored to take turns sitting on his lap.

Knowing this adversary of his was part of the popular social circle that included Marissa, Benny walked just close enough to be noticed by Les. The latter glowered at the very unexpected interloper with a look of incredulity, as if he couldn't believe that this social pariah dared to enter the Crimson Room. Benny responded with a sarcastic grin and a stiff projection of his middle finger in Les's direction. He then turned and headed towards the boys' washroom.

"Omg, do you know that assmunch, Les?" the girl presently sitting on his lap queried. "I've never seen that dork in here before. Why did he flip you the bird like that?"

"That's Benny Lonero," Les responded with grating anger in his voice. "I can't believe he walked in here. He gave me the finger? He *seriously* gave me the finger? In *here*? Could he really be that incredibly retarded?"

"Go kick his ass, Les!" another girl zealously insisted. "Security won't see it go down in the pisser."

"Just wait here," he said as he headed towards the men's room. "I'll be right back."

Les entered the bathroom to find it occupied only by Benny, who was standing in front of one of the filthy porcelain urinals. He wasn't relieving himself, however; he was just standing there with his back to the entrance, as if patiently waiting for someone to enter. That someone had just done so.

Les wasted no time engaging Benny. "Lonero, what the hell are you doing in this club? And who the hell do you think you are for giving me the finger? Do you want to die or something?"

Benny simply stood there quietly, as if he didn't consider Les important enough to acknowledge.

Les became even more incensed at this apparent dismissal of the threat he tried to present. "Did you hear me? I'm talking to you, faggot!"

He stormed over to Benny and shoved him from behind. "Huh? Do you hear me?"

After pushing him a second time, Les was thoroughly startled when Benny turned around and seized him by the throat in a blur of motion. Before the popular young man could even consider an appropriate reaction, he found himself effortlessly slammed against the wall with sufficient force to crack the plaster. The degree of strength displayed by Benny was immense and extremely unexpected. Les had the wind knocked out of him, and the cheek under his right eye immediately began to swell into a purple mass. His throat felt as if a steel vise was tightly enclosed around it.

"Give me Marissa's address, Gurgleworth," Benny demanded with a coldly vicious tone.

"Oh man," Les gasped, struggling to come to his senses. "Who – who – what? Do you mean Marissa Robbins?"

"What other Marissa do we both know, you snotwad!" Benny hollered as he bent Les' left arm behind his back with enough force to inflict hairline fractures on the bone.

Les bellowed in agony, and Benny responded by painfully pulling his head back by the hair. It took a good effort of will for him to resist doing this hard enough to rip out a handful of follicles by their roots.

"Tell me or I'll hurt you bad, Gurgleworth. Just like you and your friends always used to hurt me! And if I find out you lied, or you told anyone about this, I'll come back for you. And nobody will stop me from getting my hands on your worthless, intolerant hide again. *Nobody*. Do you understand?"

"All right, all right, I'll give it! Just don't – don't bend my arm anymore! Please, man."

"Give up the address and I'll stop. That's more mercy than you ever showed me, you dick."

The girls at the juice bar looked in the direction of the boys' washroom with expressions of utter bafflement and dread since it was Benny, and not Les, who exited first. Even worse, Benny looked unscathed, and Les didn't follow him out. They wisely declined to approach the young man as he quietly but fervently headed towards the front door of the club and left the establishment.

He walked as if he had a purpose, and unfortunately for Marissa Robbins and her family, that purpose was a trip to their place of residence.

***

About fifteen minutes following Benny's departure from the Crimson Room, a certain specially designed but inconspicuous-looking SUV pulled up outside the teen club.

"Are you sure he was here, Claire?" Donovan asked his psychic colleague.

"Yes!" she replied fretfully. "He was! If he's not in there now, he was in there very recently. I'm sure of it. His psychic energy signature is like nothing I've ever experienced before. Oh my god, Donovan, please *please* be careful. His energies are so strong that he could still be in there!"

Donovan gently but firmly grabbed Claire by the shoulders before full-fledged panic could set in and overwhelm her. "Claire… chill, okay? Just focus on the task at hand, and let's do our job. We need to get in there now, but you can stay in the van, okay?"

She nodded while taking deep breathes to staunch an oncoming panic attack. Just in case, though, she began reaching for a bottle of mild prescription sedatives she kept handy in her coat pocket.

"Alright, people, let's head out," Donovan addressed his four-man-and-woman team of discreet, specially-trained-and armed soldiers. "And like Claire said, be careful; we're facing a very powerful and very emotionally distraught young metahuman."

The crew simultaneously nodded an acknowledgement.

"We're prepared, Col. Jakes," Agent Brett Silver assured him.

"Let's do this," Agent Gail Parker said.

The five of them exited the SUV through sliding side doors, with Donovan in the lead. Just as they approached the door of the Crimson Room, the Valis task force suddenly heard the doors slide open behind them again. Claire cautiously stepped out of the vehicle, taking a series of deep gasps as she did so.

"I'm – I'm coming with you," the potent esper said. "I need to – to be there for you."

"Are you sure?" Donovan asked with respectful concern.

Claire nodded frantically, fighting to keep the courage ascendant over her fear. "Yes. Yes, I'm sure. I'm sure."

Donovan and his four comrades-in-arms walked through the front door, their body armor hidden under long dark trench coats (though not a soldier, Claire wore a version of the body armor for safety's sake, since she was in the field). Each of them was partially incognito by wearing simple but effectively distracting dark shades. The two security guards saw these strange adults enter the teen club and moved to intercept them.

"Hey, you can't come in here!" one of them said as he grabbed Donovan by the shoulder.

"Yes, we can," the battle-hardened soldier countered as he shoved an official-looking but bogus badge in the guard's face. "We're FBI, and we're here to investigate one of your young patrons."

The guards looked at the badge carefully, but neither was well-versed enough in official government credentials to determine its authenticity. And both knew the club didn't need any trouble with the law, particularly from agents of the federal government.

"Who are you looking for, exactly?" the second guard asked.

Before Donovan could think of a convincing response, his attention was drawn to an injured Les Gurgleworth stumbling out of the boys' bathroom. His left eye was almost swollen shut, with both eyes streaming tears. He was grasping one of his arms and was obviously injured, though not severely.

"Donovan, I sense *his* aura all over that boy, and I'm getting sensations of extreme pain from him…" Claire whispered to the leader of the Institute's away team.

"We're looking for *him*," Donovan said to the guards while pointing at Les. He then turned to the four fellow soldiers that comprised his team. "See that the bouncers behave while I go talk to the boy. Agent Boone, you're with me."

As Les walked about awkwardly, not knowing what he should do next, he suddenly found himself accosted by a tall and handsome but mean-looking bearded man and a chestnut brunette woman with plain features but intense eyes.

"Young man, you need to come with us over there," Donovan insisted, while gesturing towards an area of the club where no other patron was congregating. "Now."

Not in any shape to even begin to resist or question such a steadfastly direct order by the likes of Donovan, the still shaken Les did as instructed.

As they reached the semi-secluded area of the club, the task force team leader grabbed Les by his non-injured arm and looked him straight in his tear-soaked eyes.

"Did you just have an encounter with Benny Lonero?" the soldier asked him.

Les nodded with a blank expression. "Yeah, yeah, and there was something messed up about him. He never came in here before, and he was never strong like that…"

Donovan shook the boy a bit, causing him to wince in pain. "Why didn't he beat you down completely? What did he want from you?"

"He - he told me to give him my friend Marissa Robbins's address. And – and he told me – told me not to say anything to anyone. But – but you seem to already know this, so I'm not – not – giving this up to you. Jesus, I didn't want to give it to him, but he was hurting me, I thought he was gonna kill me. God, this is so messed up…"

Jesus H. Christ, Donovan thought to himself just before he turned to his comrade. "Agent Boone, what are you getting from this?"

Her visage went almost chalk white. "I'm getting… a combination of horror and complete sincerity from him. Oh, dear God, he's going after that girl, Colonel."

"We have no time to lose," Donovan said as he turned to Les and again grabbed him rather firmly by his non-injured arm. "You need to give us that address now, young man. This is not a request. And then you need to get some medical attention and not say a word about what really happened here. You tell the doctors that you got jumped by a group of kids in the bathroom, and you had no idea who they were. Give false descriptions if you have to. But don't mention Lonero's name."

"And prepare to see us again. These are direct orders and you had best follow them *to the letter*, do you understand me, young man? Otherwise I won't be such a good a mood when you see us again."

Les slumped back against the wall while he nodded desperately, wanting this ordeal to be over.

Donovan then shifted his gaze to his psychic comrade. "Claire, come on, we need to get the team to that girl's place of residence immediately! I pray to God we're not too late."

***

About thirty minutes after Benny departed the Crimson Room, all appeared momentarily calm outside of the Upper East Side apartment complex where Marissa Robbins and her family lived. This family consisted of herself, her mother, and her younger brother, Danny, who was eight years of age.

Her mother was away at her place of employment, while Marissa worked with her brother to fix dinner for the two of them. Also present was her older male cousin Ted, eighteen years of age, who often lent Marissa a hand in looking after the household and her younger brother when her mom was working.

"Are you really sure you know how to make tacos, 'Rissa?" the tall and burly young Ted Robbins asked his cousin.

"Man, she barely knows how to make a peanut butter and jelly sandwich," Danny snidely remarked.

"Shut up, you little poozer," Marissa snapped at her younger sibling. "Like you can cook at all, right? That's why Ted and I have to do this for you."

"Hey, I know how to cook!" Danny insisted. "You just never let me, so we're always stuck with *your* cooking."

Marissa held up a plastic spatula in a mock threatening gesture. "Give me one good reason why I shouldn't crack you over the skull with this, you little pimple with legs?"

"All right, you two, can't we all just get along?" Ted queried with an exaggerated sigh and rolling of the eyes. "We'll all make dinner together tonight, so if it turns out bad then all three of us share the blame equally, okay?"

Marissa sniggered. "Sure, sure, fine."

But the girl's jovial interaction with her two cherished family members was very rudely interrupted when the locked door leading into the front room of the small apartment was suddenly kicked open. The padlock securing the entrance was broken with ease.

All three members of the Robbins family turned their heads, startled at the unexpected and violent intrusion. Marissa was by far the most startled of the three when she saw it was none other than Benny Lonero standing in her home. A look of pure hatred and fury was manifestly evident on his face.

"Marissa…" he hissed upon seeing her. "It's so nice to welcome myself into your humble home."

He then shut the door behind him and began approaching the astonished girl.

"Lonero!" she shouted. "What the hell are you doing at my house? How did you get my address? How did…?"

"You know this guy, 'Rissa?" Ted asked her. "Who the hell is he and how the hell did he kick the door open like that? I know I locked it!"

Recovering from his momentary shock, Ted stepped in front of his cousins, determined to protect them from whatever type of threat Benny may have posed. Unfortunately, he had barely begun to suspect just how great a threat that actually was.

"Dude, I have no quarrel with you," Benny told the muscular young man barring his way. "I don't know what you are to Marissa, but know she set me up to get attacked by two of her friends at school. She planned the whole thing out with them and pretended to like me so she could lure me into the place where her friends would jump me. She's always hurt me in other ways too! She and her friends went too far, and they're not going to get away with it this time! Not when I can finally do something about it!"

Ted turned to Marissa. "Whoa *whoa*, what the hell is this guy talking about? What did you do to him, Marissa?"

The girl's lower lip began quivering as she forced herself to push past the shock for a reply. "I just…"

A moment later the shock was replaced by a wave of anger. "Just get the hell out of my house, you little faggot scum!" she shouted at the intruder.

"Not even an apology, huh, Marissa?" Benny yelled back. "Not that it would be for any reason other than to save your stupid, lying little hide anyway!" He then took a few steps closer to the startled Robbins trio. "Why did you always hate me, Marissa? What harm did I ever do to you? Did you think I'm just going to let all that go now that I can do something about it? You made me think you really had feelings for me, and you lied! Wasn't everything else you were doing enough to satisfy your sadistic need to hurt someone you dislike for whatever petty reasons that you dislike me?

"Did you think I had no feelings? Or did you just fail to consider them worth your concern?

"And you set me up for Jeff and Mick to hurt me really bad! Well, guess what? I hurt them bad instead! And now I'm going to hurt you!"

"Oh my God…" she stammered. "What did you do to Jeff and Mick?"

"Exactly what they intended to do to me, you stupid bitch!" was Benny's reverberating reply.

"Oh no, not Jeff and Mick," Marissa whimpered as tears began streaming from her reddened eyes. "Please, don't hurt my family."

Benny stepped forward with his right fist raised, while his eyes began emanating a shiny azure radiance. Similarly-colored waves of energy soon started arcing around his clenched hand. He pointed towards Ted and Danny with his other hand.

"Tell these two to step aside or get the hell out of here and I won't hurt them," Benny said.

"Okay, enough of this!" Ted hollered as he moved closer to the advancing Benny. "Look, man, I'm not saying what my cousin did was right, but I'm not going to let you hurt her, okay? You need to get out of this house right now! *Now*, or I'll throw you the hell out!"

"Really?" Benny sneered. "Just a few days ago, you probably could have done that easily. But now the Fates have reversed the advantage. Get out of the way, man, or I'll *knock* you out of the way. And it won't be pleasant."

"I'll kick his ass!" Danny yelled just before he attempted to rush towards Benny to defend his family until Marissa grabbed him and sabotaged the move.

Deciding to act rather than talk any further, Ted hurled his strong athletic form towards Benny and swung at him with all his not inconsiderable might. Benny's enhanced reflexes responded incredibly, and he easily side-stepped the incoming blow even though it likely wouldn't have done much damage had it succeeded in striking him. He then grabbed the young athlete by his shirt and effortlessly flung him several feet across the apartment.

The airborne youth smashed into the living room wall, leaving a huge indentation in the stucco. Ted Robbins bounced off the wall and landed on the floor. He wasn't seriously injured but quickly realized that he had incurred a cracked collar bone that debilitated him with searing pain.

"I warned you!" Benny shouted at the young man as he laid on the floor grasping his pain-wracked shoulder.

Throwing her brother safely aside Marissa grabbed a cast iron cooking pan by its handle and attacked her long-time object of ire. Once again displaying enhanced reaction time, Benny dodged the blow and snatched the pan from the girl's hand in a blur of motion.

Then in a display of his newfound power designed to terrify the former object of his heart, he grasped the strong metal cooking implement between his two hands and concentrated on summoning forth the Odic energies seething through his cellular matrix. The bluish energy crackled about the metallic substance of the pan, causing it to rapidly tarnish and smoke before quickly melting from his hands into a boiling mass of ferrous liquid that dribbled down onto the kitchenette's floor.

"Oh... hell..." Marissa gasped.

"Speaking of Hell, that's what you've made my life for the past year," Benny said through gritted teeth. "Now I'm going to send *you* there."

He again raised a still energy-encompassed hand at Marissa, while his glowing blue eyes appeared to reflect the intensity of his anger and inner turmoil.

"Benny, no..."

The girl who formerly served as the focus of many of the tortured young boy's dreams covered her face while she prepared for the coming blow, hoping that Benny would show her just enough mercy to end things as quickly as possible.

Just then, however, Danny ran over to the dangerous home invader and began pummeling on his back, albeit to no effect.

"Leave my sister alone!" he bellowed at the top of his lungs. "I'm not going to let you hurt her, no matter what she did to you! She's my sister!"

Benny halted his action and shifted his gaze to the boy. "Your sister is a no-good piece of..."

"She's my sister!" Danny yelled through tear-soaked eyes as he continued punching and kicking Benny to no avail. "Don't kill her, don't kill her, don't..."

Benny found himself hesitating as something deep within him was moved by the boy's heartfelt pleas. He had no reason to fear anyone in that house, and he didn't; yet a feeling much like fear began rushing through his psyche nevertheless. Consequently, he stayed his hand long enough for another set of trespassers to enter the scene and intercede.

"Benny, stop what you're doing!" declared an adult male voice reeking with authority.

The young metahuman turned his now luminescent blue eyes around to see Donovan Jakes standing in the front room and pointing an object that resembled an odd-looking firearm at him. Just behind the bearded soldier were five other individuals, three men and two women. Four of them held similarly designed firearms and were clearly fellow soldiers.

The fifth individual, a woman, stood behind all the others, holding no weapon and looking at Benny with an expression quite unlike that of the four stalwart soldiers. Benny seemed to feel a strange sort of rapport, something he couldn't think of sufficient words to describe, with this woman. Claire Boone radiated a sensation of extreme fear that she was struggling to hold at bay, and the boy could somehow pick up on this.

"Who are you?" Benny asked as he turned his raised fist in the direction of Donovan and his team. "Are you the police or something?"

"No, we're not the police," Donovan said with calm conviction. "We're people who are actually capable of stopping you if it comes to that. But please listen to me, Benny, because I don't want it to come to that. And I don't think you really want to hurt anyone. So please listen to what I have to say before you do anything..."

But Benny was too aggrieved by his pain to fully listen. It was immediately obvious to everyone concerned that diplomacy would not prevail.

Christofer Nigro

Chapter 8: It All Hits the Fan

"If you're not the police, then who the hell are you?" Benny demanded of the Institute agents now confronting him. "And why are you pointing those funky-looking guns at me?"

Donovan couldn't help noticing that the crackles of coruscating energy which surrounded the boy's hands were building in their intensity. They soon began appearing to encompass his entire body, as his eyes flared an even brighter level of incandescence.

"Oh my God, Donovan," Claire whispered as loudly as she could. "He's about to…"

The veteran soldier wasted no time in diving to the side to evade the oncoming energy bolt that Benny projected from his extended right hand. Agents Gail Parker and Brett Silver did the same, but Agent Eddie Marks wasn't as quick on his feet. When he was in mid-dodge the searing beam of bluish energy struck him in the side, sending his body clear out the door and into the hallway. He impacted with the far wall outside the apartment and laid still on the floor, while a thick thread of smoke was seen billowing out from where the beam had impacted his hip region.

"Eddie!" Claire screamed as Agent Sasheen Kahn ran to his injured comrade's side.

After quickly checking his vitals, Sasheen looked up and said, "He's alive! But he's really hurt."

"Damn you, kid," Donovan uttered as he quickly jumped back to his feet. "You just had to do this the hard way."

The soldier then promptly pointed his plasma-projecting taze rifle at Benny and depressed the trigger. He found it remarkable that the untrained boy managed an incredible leap across the kitchen to avoid being struck by the spherical discharges of incapacitating energy. Landing on the other side of the apartment, however, Benny lost his footing due to the poor condition of the rug. It was then that

71

Donovan's firearm found its target, knocking Benny off his feet with three direct hits by the fast-traveling mini-spheres of plasma.

Taking advantage of the time he just bought himself, Donovan turned to his team.

"Sasheen, get Eddie back to the van! Gail and Brett, get the civilians out of here and clear out the building! Claire, stay with Eddie and give him emergency medical aid! One of you stay for crowd control, but the rest of you get back here ASAP!"

The three remaining agents moved to follow their leader's orders as fast as any human possibly could. Sasheen carried out his fallen comrade, while Eddie rushed to the injured Ted Robbins and helped him out of the apartment.

Gail rushed over to the terror-stricken Marissa and Danny Robbins, motioning for them to follow her out the door. "Let's get out of here now, people! Move!"

Before Marissa could exit, though, Donovan grabbed her by the arm and spoke to her with a strong tone. "You and I are going to have words over your part in this whole affair later, young lady. In case you were wondering, you aren't getting off scot free."

After the girl fearfully nodded her head to show she understood, Donovan released his grip on her arm and she promptly followed Gail and her little brother out the door. The soldier approached Benny and once more pointed his exotic piece at the young metahuman, who was still lying insensate with scorch marks marring the three spots on his clothing where the taze rifle's plasma projectiles had struck.

"Benny, if you can hear me, please stay down…"

As if on dramatic cue, Benny suddenly opened his still glowing eyes. With a flash of movement that was scarcely a blur, the superpowered adolescent grasped Donovan by his wrist and easily bent it away from him. The teen's grip was irresistibly strong, and the soldier found himself taken down to his knees. The teen metahuman was clearly fully recovered from the three direct hits by the taze rifle.

Damn it, I should have accounted for such a level of resilience, Donovan silently admonished himself.

"I heard what you said to Marissa before she got away," a fuming Benny told the now pain-wracked Donovan. "You know what she did and you're still sticking up for her!"

"Benny, listen…" Donovan said while his strategic mind was analyzing a way out of this unfortunate predicament.

"How do you know who I am?"

"As you get to know me better, you'll find out how far my resources go." Donovan gritted his teeth and focused on speaking coherently despite the pain now assailing his entire arm. "Now, listen to me. I know what that girl and her friends did to you. You have every right to be angry. I understand why you want to get back at them. But this is still wrong. This is not the way to go about it."

Benny gritted his teeth in anger, and his eyes seemed to glow with a greater luminosity. "You're just like the rest of them! You care more about what I'm doing to them now than what they've been doing to me for the longest!"

Donovan could feel Benny's crushing grip tightening around the fragile human bones of his wrist. The grizzled warrior could also see the energy arcs surrounding the youth's body begin to spark with more intensity in concert with the radiance of his eyes. He realized that he but had a few seconds at most to act before crippling injury (or worse) ensued.

Reacting with decades of experience and intensive training, Donovan quickly slammed his booted foot directly below Benny's knee, where he knew a sensitive nerve was located. As the boy lost his balance, the soldier jumped upwards and slammed his forearm into the teen's sternum as hard as he could. This effectively took the powerful young metahuman to the floor. The surprise of this maneuver caused Benny to loosen his grip, and Donovan was able to completely wrench free of it.

The veteran of combat then rolled over on the floor, recovered his taze rifle, and again aimed the exotic piece at his target.

However, the soldier once more underestimated Benny's recovery time. The youthful superhuman had sufficiently shrugged off the effects of Donovan's move to project a powerful beam of energy in the latter's direction while still on the floor. Luckily his aim was poor from that position, so Donovan was able to leap out of the way, albeit barely. The beam continued past him and struck the wall next to the door, blasting a huge hole clear through it.

I hope my team managed to evacuate this building, the soldier thought to himself, *'cause it may not be intact for much longer.*

"Benny, stop this nonsense! Now!" Donovan pleaded as he leapt to his feet and fired two more medium-intensity plasma projectiles at the boy.

The still off-balance metahuman managed to dodge one of them, but the second flaring projectile hit him directly in the chest. Benny shouted in both pain and rage while stepping back a few feet. This time, though, he didn't fall.

Oh, man... Donovan griped to himself. "Benny, don't make me fire at you again! I only want to talk to you, okay? That's all. I'm not taking the side of those kids who hurt you, but you need to understand that what you're doing here is no different than what they did. I know that deep down you're not like them, so you have to stop this."

"I don't have to do *anything* I don't want to anymore!"

With that declaration, Benny screamed in an incoherent rage and projected another sizzling bolt of energy from his hand at Donovan. Again, the soldier's battle-honed reflexes enabled him to dodge; this time, however, part of his left arm was skimmed by the beam. It seared through the sleeve of his body armor and scorched the outer dermis of his skin.

"Arrgh! Damn you, Benny! You're beginning to seriously piss me off now!"

Forcing himself to remain on his feet, Donovan pointed his rifle and returned fire. Benny evaded the marble-sized sphere of plasma with superhuman reflexive precision, and again retaliated with a beam of sizzling azure energy. Donovan somersaulted out of the way, with the beam consequently shearing clear through the living room couch and blowing out the wall separating the front room from Mrs. Robbins's sleeping quarters. Her clothing dresser was shattered, and her entire queen-sized bed was knocked over and strewn across the room by the force of impact.

Further, the explosive destruction inflicted by the stray bolt of energy caused the entire ten-floor apartment complex to begin shaking on its foundation. Donovan continued with his desperate attempts to talk the anguished teen down, certain it would be possible to reach him.

"Benny, I know you went through a lot, and I'm trying to be patient with you, but this has to stop!"

"Nobody tells me what to do anymore! Are you going to try?"

"Damn straight I am, kid!"

Summoning as much of his speed and audacity as he could muster, Donovan rushed towards the boy before suddenly dropping down into a semi-crouched position. As he hoped, the feint was successful, and Benny's next energy beam sizzled over his head, striking and smashing the open door into hundreds of wooden smithereens.

The charging soldier moved under the sizzling blue energy and slammed into Benny's diaphragm. The impact knocked the boy back against the wall next to a large window with such force that the glass on the pane was cracked. Donovan's body armor just barely shielded him from the sting of the energy arcs which crackled in the form of azure sparks all over Benny's body.

The veteran soldier knew he had to act quickly now. He made use of the startled metahuman's off-kilter state by slamming his elbow hard on the teen's jaw. Donovan immediately followed that move with an even stronger blow to the side of the boy's face with the weighted handle of his piece. He finalized the assault by delivering the hardest punch he could muster to Benny's solar plexus region. The combo of moves finally seemed to stagger the powerful teen.

"Benny, listen to me, goddamn it! I'm here to help you!"

Despite being moderately stunned, the young man was now far too strong and resilient to be taken down with just a few blows from a normal human being, no matter how expertly placed. Shouting once more in unmitigated fury, the younger combatant grabbed Donovan by the lapels of his trench coat and effortlessly slammed him into the section of the wall next to them. The soldier gasped in pain as the wind was cruelly knocked out of his lungs.

Benny then had more words of his own to hurl at Donovan as he was stunned up against the wall.

"No, you're not here to help me! You're here to help *them*! Just like all my teachers at school! Just like my own grandfather treats me the same! I'm tired of being hated! Now I'm going to hate back! Let's see how *they* like being constantly terrorized by someone stronger than them!"

Upon saying that, Benny pulled Donovan forward and slammed him into the wall again, this time sending him halfway through the stucco. The soldier struggled to regain his senses and regain the offensive before he was torn apart. That would constitute a fate he knew may next befall the remainder of his task force, to be followed by any number of civilians before the police or military managed to take him down.

Having been overcome with his own emotional anguish, the youthful metahuman raised his diamond-hard fist, clearly intending to send it sailing into Donovan's fragile human face. However, thinking about what he was about to do appeared to cause Benny to hesitate for just a moment.

That was all the time it took for a powerful beam of whitish-blue energy to come crashing through the window and slam into the teen's left shoulder. Struck by a force that was obviously far more powerful than even the highest intensity setting of the taze rifle could produce, Benny was knocked clear off his feet. He landed on the floor outside the kitchen, momentarily stunned.

This bought Donovan the seconds he needed to himself to recover. The soldier pulled himself out of the wall's stucco and quickly glanced out the shattered window pane to view the source of the beam that saved him. He saw a clear silhouette of what appeared to be an adult male figure hovering in mid-air, with a hint of a glimmering silvery attire being discernable.

Whoa, that must be Ultimus! Donovan mused to himself, recalling the reports collected by the Institute regarding North America's most powerful--and thankfully heroic--metahuman to emerge since the first Warp Event of the 21st century. No sooner did he make this seeming realization than the hovering figure suddenly turned around and soared out of the area at tremendous speed.

"Hey, wait, I can still use some help in here!" Donovan barked out the window at the fleeing figure. "I'm not sure if that was enough to take the kid down for the count!" *And how the hell did he know I needed him here, anyway? Talk about a real-life* deus ex-machina*!*

However, the apparent intervention of Ultimus was to prove but a temporary reprieve, and not quite the *deus ex-machina* that Donovan had hoped for. Within a second and a half of the flying hero's departure, Benny recovered and abruptly sat up. Wisps of smoke could be seen billowing from the material of his shirt where the beam had struck him.

"What the hell was that?" the no longer dazed boy demanded aloud.

Oh, shit, I knew it, Donovan lamented to himself. *It never fails.*

The soldier swiftly pointed his rifle at Benny, letting off another shot at the teen metahuman before he could get back to his feet. This time, however, the youth's preternatural reflexes proved fast enough to counter with a lower-intensity beam from his fingertips. The sizzling sapphire beam successfully hit and dispersed the oncoming plasma projectile a few feet short of its target.

Damn, that kid is quickly getting the hang of those powers, and he can really think under pressure. I need to end this fast.

By that point, Benny was back on his feet and angrier than ever. "Who did that to me?"

The still dazed teen looked around and saw no one other than Donovan, nor did his enhanced senses pick up the hidden presence of another party. He then shrugged off the mysterious attack and returned to his spiel.

"It doesn't matter who did that anyway, because you see that you can't take me down! You're not going to stop me from getting to those people! Did anyone stop *them* from hurting *me?*"

Benny raised his arm again, and once more the energy arcs dancing around his form like the sparks emitted from a pinwheel began increasing in number. This by now signaled to Donovan that the projection of another energy beam was imminent. Before the combat veteran could attempt an evasive move, Agents Gail Parker and Sasheen Kahn entered the now smashed doorway behind him, their taze rifles raised and ready.

"Donovan, get down!" Gail hollered.

The leader of the team wasted no time heeding this warning while his two teammates unleashed a salvo of plasma projectiles from their taze rifles. Struck by the multiple bolts, Benny was knocked back several feet towards the window. He still didn't go down, though his wobbly state clearly indicated the salvo of plasma had caused him severe pain and numbness.

Gail was determined to take no chances after the way Eddie was injured. "Hit him again, Sasheen!"

The two soldiers released another fusillade of plasma bullet, and Benny was in no shape to dodge them. This time the impact from the multiple spheres of stinging energy knocked the boy clear through the window, where he landed hard on a fire escape situated about a dozen feet below. The already cracked glass was shattered as Benny was sent through it, and the shards showered down past his dazed form as it lay on the metal grating.

Donovan was by then back on his feet, and he was determined to press this advantage and end the conflict on his own terms. And he needed to do so with haste, as he knew the building would soon be surrounded by both pedestrian onlookers and police cars.

"Well done!" he barked to his team members. "But I'll take it from here!"

"What do you mean, Donovan?" Gail asked with more than a hint of concern.

Donovan wasted no time answering, however. Instead, he ran towards the broken window and jumped down to the fire escape below. As intended, he landed directly upon Benny's sternum while the teen metahuman was still not fully recovered from the combo of the plasma salvo and the fall. The young metahuman gasped in pain when Donovan's full weight came crashing down on him from twelve feet up.

The veteran combatant was determined to continue pressing the advantage, likewise taking no chances considering how powerful Benny had already proven to be. He quickly unleashed a series of punches to the boy's face, never taking the risk of pulling a single blow.

"Dammit, kid, stay down!" the soldier roared as he delivered the severe pummeling. "I know you're not really a killer! I can tell you've been holding back your full power whenever you attacked someone!"

He delivered another punch before grabbing Benny by the lapel of his shirt and shaking him before continuing his impassioned lecture. "You have to let your conscience fight past the pain and come to your senses before you do kill someone, or we're forced to put you down! Whichever may come first!"

Donovan then struck Benny in the face as hard he could once more. "Do you hear me, kid? I've had about enough of this from you today! So, stand down and stop this tantrum of yours or you'll force me to keep hitting you until you do!"

Despite Donovan's best efforts he noticed that Benny's meta-resilient skin was just barely showing any sign of bruising under his severe pummeling. Before the boy could be rendered unconscious, his rage kicked in again and he pushed against the soldier's chest with his palms.

Though he couldn't bring his full strength to bear, Benny's superhumanly enhanced musculature was still sufficient to hurl Donovan into the metal steps of the fire escape a few feet behind them. He then managed to get back to his feet again, and the bruises on his face and the rest of his body were already beginning to vanish completely.

Donovan managed to get back on his feet in record time, only to find that he and Benny were facing off again. The boy raised both of his fists, and the rage boiling within him caused the sapphire-hued energy popping about them to resemble sparks flitting about a live wire. His eyes were now glowing with a fearsome intensity comparable to lighthouse beacons.

Before Benny could make a move, though, he found himself under assault by another salvo of plasma projectiles, these fired out of the window above them by Gail and Sasheen. The impact of the glowing red spheres struck their target and knocked him back against the side bars of the fire escape. The teen grabbed onto the metal with great force and just barely managed to prevent himself from falling over.

With surprising speed Benny gave as good as he got by firing a bolt of energy back at the window. Gail had seen him telegraph the move, however, and shouted the warning to her comrade. Though they both managed to jump out of the way, Sasheen did so with only partial success, and was grazed by the edge of the beam's corona as he leapt back. He yelled in pain and fell down to his knees. The right side of the window pane was blasted away by the force of the beam, sending a spray of splintered glass and other debris into the already devastated apartment.

Gail quickly ran to her fellow soldier and helped him to his feet. She promptly checked the wound on his right shoulder and was relieved to see that it was only superficial; thankfully, his body armor spared him the worst of it.

"Stand down, all of you!" Donovan shouted up at his team. "I've got this!"

In the meantime, the grizzled soldier took his biggest risk yet by turning to face Benny and raising his hands to show that he didn't have a firearm or any other weapon. "You see I'm unarmed, right, Benny? I'm sorry I had to give you that beating, but it's not like you couldn't take it. And you know you didn't exactly give me any other choice. Now, will you please listen to me? Don't you at least owe me that much?"

Benny stood with his hands still raised in preparation for an attack. Both his hands and his eyes continued to blaze with an intense blue radiance. His teeth were still gritted tightly and his lower lip trembling in a state of fury. But he seemed to be momentarily listening as per Donovan's request. Hence, the soldier continued his talk, trying to make his words as gentle as he could despite maintaining a firm tone.

"Thank you. Now, listen, Benny. I know you're hurting. Please trust me when I tell you that I don't want to hurt you further. I know you've been through hell for many years now. I know how those kids treated you, and I can imagine what your home situation is like.

"But this is wrong. I'm saying this to protect you as much as them. These powers you were given by the Warp Event are a tremendous gift. You can do much good with them. Please don't give into the pain and become a worse bully than the people that hurt you ever were. I know you're better than that despite all the pain controlling you right now."

"I'm not letting them get away with this!" Benny shouted back. "They need to pay for making me become... what I've become!"

"And they will pay," Donovan replied. "But not like this, Benny. Hate and revenge are wrong. They're self-destructive, and right now you're standing on a very dark precipice. I know you're not a bad person, so please don't let your pain turn you into one. Don't force me to take extreme measures to stop you. Please stop yourself first."

Benny didn't move back, and the energy arcs continued to blaze about his upraised fists like plumes of blue electricity. His eyes continued to glow with a piercing incandescence, but suddenly they appeared to be flickering rather than blazing with a piercing intensity. It seemed as if something from within his being was fighting to temper his fury. But it was seemingly losing that fight quite rapidly.

"I don't want to do this! But I have to! I'm going to make them stop! And I'm going to show them what it's like!"

Donovan then decided to take a further risk and take a few cautious steps closer to the enraged boy. His hands were raised in a gesture of extending the olive branch.

"Benny, not like this. You know it's wrong, and I know you don't want to become like them, only worse. Right now, you must make a decision. One that will have huge consequences upon not only the direction of your life from this moment on, but likely the entire world. For God's sake, please make the right one."

Agents Gail Parker and Sasheen Kahn continued to peer out the window, but sans their firearms raised. Nevertheless, they still had them in hand, prepared to go into action at a moment's notice. They also found themselves really wishing they hadn't left Agent Brett Silver to remain outside of the apartment to maintain crowd control. It appeared they would soon need every able-bodied member of the team to have a fighting chance of containing this situation, and they were ready to call for reinforcements.

"Donovan, I hope you know what you're doing…" Gail whispered within ear shot of Sasheen. "You better survive this, so I can slap you in the face later."

Benny had clearly listened to Donovan's impassioned words, but the rage continued to show evidence of seething out of control. Both the metahuman youth and the hardened soldier began wondering if the emotional damage was too great for any inkling of conscience or empathy to rise forth and stem the tide. Was the young man now past the point of no return?

Benny began advancing upon the grizzled warrior before him, his fists still raised, his expression remaining indicative of a person needing to cut loose. Donovan steadfastly maintained his "at ease" stance and braced himself for what now appeared to be coming. He was nevertheless determined to play out his big gamble to the end.

"Donovan…" Gail whispered aloud as she quietly went against his orders and raised her taze rifle.

Sasheen pushed her hand down. "No, Gail. Let Donovan carry this out his way."

After approaching within a few inches of Donovan, Benny found himself looking at the unarmed soldier eye-to-eye. The boy's teeth were still gnashed in an expression of rage and his eyes glowing with furious intensity, but the older man didn't flinch. Instead, he kept eye contact with Benny while sustaining a fearless but calm expression.

After this stare down continued for what seemed like an eternity, Benny then made his move. The boy stepped forward and wrapped his arms around Donovan. But the teen didn't exert any superhuman force as he did so. When Benny sunk his face into the soldier's coat and began crying uncontrollably, it became evident that the tight but not constricting grip was simply an embrace.

"I don't want to become this!" Benny shouted through the tears. "I'm out of control, and I need help. Please just make it stop!"

Donovan returned the embrace as he breathed a huge sigh of relief and silently thanked the God whose existence he was very agnostic about until this very moment.

"At ease, kid. It's going to be okay. You made the right choice. It was the hardest thing you ever had to do, but you did it. From this point on, it will never be that hard again."

A few seconds later Donovan heard the distant sound of approaching police sirens blaring a few blocks away to interrupt the moment. He then realized that he and his team needed to quickly vacate the area now that the matter was resolved. And they needed to do so with Benny in their custody. *Luckily, it took long enough for the boys in blue to get here. Gotta love the inner cities!*

"It's going to be all right now, Benny," the soldier again assured the boy. "The worst part is over, and we can start healing and training you. But you have to come with us, because the police are on the way and we can't let them find you here like this. And we can't just let you go free. I'm not going to lie to you. There will be consequences for what you did. We're going to have to take you into custody and put you under lockdown before we can start helping you, because right now you're a danger to both yourself and the public. Do you understand this, Benny?"

An emotionally drained and repentant Benny Lonero silently nodded a tear-moistened face as he voluntarily allowed Donovan to lead him down the fire escape towards the waiting SUV. He was en route to the Valis Institute, and a major new chapter of his life awaited him there.

END PART 1

Part 2: The Long, Hard Road Begins

Chapter 9: Consequences Are a Bitch

Claire Boone couldn't help but glare at the melancholic figure of young Benny Lonero through the thick, rectangular ultra-thick glass window—"almost like transparent steel," as Donovan described it--adorning the containment cell's reinforced steel door.

The thinnish but well-toned boy sat silently on the cell's bunk, his hands clasped over his face whilst his mind was contemplating things she could scarcely guess. He displayed no other type of motion, nor any verbal utterance since surrendering himself to Donovan's task force just fifty minutes previous. Further, he had refused food and water when it was offered to him, and this prompted Claire to begin pondering a series of unsettling questions.

Did he even truly need to eat or drink any longer? How much of his humanity did he retain since the metamorphosis? What in the name of Lady Freya had he become? And how many others like him were out there now in the wake of the most recent Warp Event? Did their rapid appearance over the past several years signal the beginning of a grand new world? Or was it a precursor to the Apocalypse, Ragnarok; the veritable twilight of humanity?

Claire forced herself not to try and formulate answers to these questions flowing through her mind as she continued monitoring the seriously troubled young man. *Or is that young* demi-god *now? Stop thinking these things, Claire Ann. You need to get a grip with yourself as it is. Don't let Donovan and the rest of the Institute know exactly how much this whole affair is freaking you the hell out.*

Yet the powerful esper couldn't help picking up on the waves of tortured emotions flowing from Benny's mind as he sat there unmoving like a statue of one of the Greek gods she had seen in an art museum years ago. The woman was simultaneously terrified and fascinated by the young man; so much of the former, in fact, that she had secretly put on an adult diaper before monitoring him in case her bladder suddenly gave up its contents. She managed to prevent such a sudden loss of bodily waste thanks in part to the fact that she sensed nothing from the boy that so much as hinted at the intention to go on another destructive rampage.

But how long would this last? How unpredictable might this strange and troubled new metahuman be? Could he actually break out of a cell specially designed to hold dangerous metahumans? Claire didn't want to find out the answers to these disconcerting questions, and she firmly hoped the answers wouldn't come during the span of her watch.

Because of her state of mind, the potent esper involuntarily jumped and almost fulfilled the purpose of her diaper when the door leading to the lower chambers suddenly hissed open. Turning around, she was relieved to see it was only Donovan, accompanied by an armed Agent Gail Parker.

"At ease, Claire, it's only us," the goateed soldier said reassuringly. "And well done on your part, I must say. You held your station just fine."

"Thank you, thank you..." the overwrought psychic nervously gibbered in reply. "But what took you so long?"

"I had to confer with the staff and touch base with Ms. Concord herself to figure out a plan to clean up the mess that Mr. Lonero made for us and himself. We need to talk to him now. You aren't required to stay, because you've already done your share. But if you don't mind, I'd like your continued presence here regardless."

Claire hoped that the soldier didn't notice her shudder at his request. "Okay."

Donovan punched a code into the small panel to the left of the cell door, which resulted in a clanging sound that indicated the heavily reinforced lock was now disabled. The ingress to the cell could now be opened by a casual shove of the hand. Claire couldn't help but shudder again at the realization of her unshielded exposure to Benny.

As for Donovan, the grizzled veteran soldier couldn't help being impressed by all the advanced technology which the various private sponsors of the Valis Institute had collectively provided for this cause. He was still determined to look more into these sources in the future; he was a squaddie for the military-industrial complex long enough to know that nothing was truly provided for purely altruistic purposes -- at least not in the prevailing global system that put the acquisition of money and power over all else. But that was an "elephant in the room" that he had to look away from for the moment.

Benny removed his face from the cover of his hands and looked up as he heard the clanging sound of the lock release. His expression was one of disquieting unease, but his rage thankfully appeared to remain fully spent. For now, anyway.

"Hello, Benny," Donovan said with an uncharacteristic composure as he pulled a chair from the desk inside the cell and took a seat. "Thank you for your patience, and for remaining calm. We can now proceed from here."

"What's going to happen to me now?" Benny queried with an understandable hint of anxiety. "Has this Institute found an effective way to execute metas like me?" The sarcasm in his tone was biting.

"Stop it, Benny. I said we were going to help you, not exploit you or hurt you anymore than you already have been. That will remain the case for as long as you work with us rather than against us, and do not lash out at the world like you did earlier today. And I do not break my word."

The manner of Donovan's enumeration was refreshingly convincing. This was reflected in Benny's continued tranquil demeanor despite the nature of his next question.

"Okay, let me get the main thing out of the way first: I'm going to have to be punished, right?"

"What do you think, Benny?"

The young boy looked down and closed his eyes. "Yes. I know, and I understand. I messed up really bad. Simply saying I'm sorry, no matter how sincere, won't be enough. But is it too much to hope that you won't see this as a one-sided issue?"

"That's not too much to hope for, Benny. Quite the contrary, in fact. I'm going to have words with those peers of yours who drove you to this. And I'm going to see to it that they own up to their part in what happened. But, as for you…"

Benny closed his eyes tighter at Donovan's slight pause. *Here it comes, dude…*

"To start things off, you need to be closely monitored by the Institute for a while."

"How long is 'a while?'"

"It's a unit of time that basically translates as, 'until I say otherwise.'"

"Yeah, I figured that was your working definition."

"Mmm-hmm. During that time, you're going to be trained in the responsible use of your power. We have some really good facilities for that here, and you'll also have access to all the equipment and instruction you will need for getting a handle on those powers.

"You're also going to receive counseling with specially trained psychologists, to deal with the anger, bitterness, and depression eating away at your soul. Two outcomes may be the end result of all this:

"One, you will learn to deal with these emotional scars and become a force for good in the world.

"Or two, you will remain a vengeance-driven metahuman thug that needs to be put down; one who *will* be put down, under those circumstances.

"Lashing out at others because of what society has done to you is not a valid way of dealing with the pain. I'd say I'm sorry it has to be that way, but I'd be lying to you if I did; and I'm going to give you all the honesty you can handle. I'm not sorry about doing what it takes to keep people safe from metahumans threats, and I mean it. So, *don't* become one of those threats. Do you understand that, Benny?"

"I do, Donovan. But I also want to make something clear, lest you think I'm going to be a passive little kid who only does what some dude in a uniform tells him to do. I understand all that you just said, and I agree. I understand that I need help, and I do want to use my power for the greater good.

"But I *do not* consider the 'greater good' to be whatever the United States government tells me to do. Nor will I agree to be used as a living WMD to subjugate other nations on behalf of building the American Empire for the wealthy few. If this is what you're getting at, then I ask you to execute me right here and now and be done with it."

Benny's non-threatening but firm tone made it clear to the soldier that he wasn't the only person in this room who indisputably meant whatever he said. Donovan couldn't help finding such an attitude and set of ethical principles to be admirable, as it reminded him very much of himself in a way. It actually served to bolster his conviction that there was indeed hope for this young metahuman.

But the long-time legionnaire well knew that enough rage and hurt remained in the boy's soul to make this an up-hill battle against an extremely strong force of metaphorical gravity. He wasn't prone to kidding himself any more than he jested others.

"I assure you that will not be the case, Benny. Even though I served as a soldier for a long time under the auspices of the U.S. military, I saw more than enough during that time to fully understand the folly of using metahumans as defenders of any particular national world power. The Valis Institute is not a branch of the U.S. government, and in fact it's mostly funded by private scientists and artists of considerable means who are interested in positive change for the world. We believe that metahumans are citizens of the entire world no matter what national boundaries they were born within."

"This doesn't make me feel much better, Donovan. I smell the rotting stench of covert corporate interests here. Maybe international in scope."

"Benny, the Illuminati does exist, but for the most part it's not actually secret. And as smart as you seem to be, I think you know that."

"The Illuminati sometimes does put on masks when operating in public, Donovan. Or pull a sheepskin over its coating of wolf hide, like the Man of the Dollar Sign pretending to be a Man of God. And I think you know that too."

Donovan scowled, both annoyed and a bit further impressed with the young man before him. Then again, he understood this explained a lot; intelligent and creative individuals tended to be prone to either being crazy or being driven crazy by a world that refused to understand them. It's much easier to demonize and reject what you don't understand than to find it of potential interest or benefit. And one of the main things Donovan learned about people through his many years in the armed forces was their tendency to take the expedient route.

"Look, Benny, you're going to have to trust me, okay? The alternative, which is just letting you run wild right now, is not an option that would benefit anyone, least of all yourself. I know trust doesn't come easy to you, but you're going to have to trust someone sooner or later. Because if you don't, your bitterness and anger will never be fully healed or under control. As we used to say it as I was growing up: Do you dig it?"

The soldier's last question had an extra sting of firmness to it. That was intentional on his part, of course.

"Yeah, I do 'dig it,' Donovan. And again, I understand that's the way it has to be for now. I don't pretend to trust myself any more than you do at the moment. And I know respect is something that I have to earn. And that I need to give it myself if I hope to receive it, blah blah blah, yadda yadda yadda.

"But you have to earn it from my end too. I've met more than my share of adults who expect to receive it without earning it, simply because they've been on this planet more years than me. They've made too much of a mess of this world to claim they have some special sort of esoteric wisdom unique to 'grown-ups' alone."

Gail chortled, and then mumbled, "As if you kids could run the world any better."

Benny immediately snapped back, "As if we could possibly run things any *worse* than you esteemed fountains of wisdom and stellar judgment. And FYI, I'm not suggesting we should be fully in charge, just given a voice and seats at the table…"

"Alright, enough of this," Donovan interjected with his left hand rising in a heavily emphasizing "halt" position. "Gail, this is not the time for that, and you know it. Same with you, young man. We have more important things to discuss here, and political debates about fringe issues is not on the itinerary."

"Fine," both Gail and Benny said simultaneously with a concurrent sigh of exasperation.

Clearly, though, Gail was quite perturbed with the young metahuman over the injury he caused to her friend and colleague Eddie Marks. She needed and wanted every excuse she could find to lash out in his direction. Donovan realized he would have to take this important and potentially troublesome matter into account, which would include keeping Gail as far away from anything that involved Benny as possible for the foreseeable future.

"At any rate, your request won't be a problem, Benny," Donovan continued. "I'm not averse to earning respect instead of always just demanding it. And I know what it's like dealing with authority figures who demand unswerving obedience. I see where that too often leads, especially if they are not people of good judgment or scruples.

"But for the time being, because of what you did—not simply because you're a 'mere' teen—I *will* call the shots on many things. Either that, or I turn you over to the police, and you deal with the type of authority *they* represent. I'm sure you completely relish the thoughts on how that would turn out."

Benny sighed again. "Yeah, no doubt."

"Also, consider this: I'm going against the law and calling in many favors by not throwing you to them, and having the Institute deal with you and your little fiasco instead. This is no small thing, and you *will* give me due consideration because of it. Can you dig that too, young man?"

Benny gave an acquiescent nod to those conditions. He then immediately began voicing the next set of his own.

"Please understand this too, Donovan. And I can call you 'Donovan,' rather than 'Sir' or 'Sensei' or 'Master' or 'Your Excellency,' or anything like that, right?"

"By all means, smartass. I'm not your master or commander, but I am your keeper and caretaker for a while. Just to make that clear from the get-go. Now what else do you think I need to understand? Please let me know, and then I'll let *you* know whether or not I agree that it needs to be understood by me."

"I'm not going to do the Peter Parker/Clark Kent thing from the comic books and pretend to be a meek, pathetic little nerd so that no one suspects what I really am. That just invites exactly the type of treatment that I experienced which... you know, led to all of this. I realize what I did was wrong, but that doesn't mean I'm going to continue taking it from them too. We need to find another way to keep the 'secret identity' thing going, okay?"

"I already have a plan for that. So, here's the deal, in every conceivable nutshell:

"As I said before, I'm going to have some words with the worst of your tormenters. My sympathy for them is not exactly high, trust me. I'm not going to ignore the problem they present and tell you to just suck it up and take it all up the business end, if you get my meaning. You can bet that I wouldn't. But here's the thing...

"You can't just go apeshit and do the meta-on-the-rampage thing every time someone pisses you off. You need to act civilized if you expect civility in return, let alone build a better and more civilized world. I'm sure you already know what using military-style shock and awe measures to solve every single problem gets you in this world. I sure as hell do, especially after having been in the thick of that quagmire for so long."

"Yeah, I know, but..."

"Don't interrupt me, Benny, because I was just about to answer your main question. We're going to have to do some type of 'make-over' for you. It will be tricky, and you have to follow my instructions to the letter in order to pull it off accurately. You need to write '*to the letter*' on the blackboard a few hundred times, as often as it takes for that to sink in. Do you hear me?"

Another of Benny's patented sighs permeated the atmosphere. "Yeah, I get you. I dig it. Whatever way you want me to put it. I'll even write it in some funky italics-looking font to make the emphasis clear."

Donovan grinned in semi-satisfaction. "Good. Now, here is how we're going to deal with the matters of school and your living arrangements. Listen carefully, because life as you knew it is over for good.

Also, in order for you to return to that school, we're going to have to use some contacts to see to it that a few Institute members become employees of Buffalo Historical."

"Seriously?"

"Very seriously. Not only do you have to be watched while you're there, but we must make sure that the school suddenly becomes more concerned about preventing bullying in general. Admittedly, this is more for the sake of the bullies than you or the other bullied kids right now, but it will be beneficial for all students there in the end. So, expect to see three new staff members at the school when you return to school."

"When do I have to go back there?"

"You will go back there after the municipal government decides to re-open the school following that little incident you pulled. I'll let you know when that is but count on it being about a week and a half."

"Swell."

"Next up, I'm sure you understand that there is no way in hell we can let you go home to your grandparents. At least, not until you've had a good share of counseling in self-control and anger management, as well as further training in mastering your powers. In fact, based on the research I've done, I'm not sure it's a good environment for your mental health at all. So, here's what we have to do…"

Chapter 10: Basic Training is Also a Bitch

Benny's mouth gaped in astonishment at Donovan's pronouncement regarding his living conditions.

"Dude, you can't be serious!" he proclaimed. "How can you convince my family to let me stay here?"

"Leave it to us, Benny," Donovan replied with his characteristic sense of confidence. "You know you can't return to that house until you get some serious counseling, not to mention sufficient training in the use of more fully controlling your power. I'm not going to put your family at risk, or you in a situation where you're likely to get provoked. Our intel has made it clear that you have your share of trouble at home too, right?"

Benny sighed audibly. "Yeah, I do. My family doesn't really understand me, and my grandfather can be a very harsh man if you get on his bad side…"

"Something I'm sure you do with regularity, considering you're who you are, and he's who he is. Correct?"

Benny sighed again. "Another gold star for you."

"We already did more than enough research on your parents, also. Your dad has never been a part of your life, and your mother and stepfather…"

"Yeah. It would be even worse to have me go and stay with them. I'm with my grandparents for good reason. Even if that didn't exactly turn out to be copacetic either. But it was most def the lesser of two evils."

"Well, I was never a fan of 'lesser evilism.' So, you need to stay away from that family of yours for a while, at least until we can work on things."

"Fine. I have no great desire to go back there anyway, especially not after this. But what about the police investigation?"

Now it was Donovan's turn to sigh. "That is going to… take some effort. And it's not going to be taken care of easily. One of the things I need to do is talk to those two boys you put in the hospital, before they talk to the police."

The soldier turned to Claire, the look on his face evoking an obvious question.

The powerful esper was quick to respond. "Based on their emotional state and a quick scan of likely possible futures over the next few days, I'm going to venture a very educated prediction that it will be around three days that they will each be able to speak coherently again. But it won't be until Monday afternoon that the doctors deem them well enough to give detailed testimonials to the police. Prior to that, they will be too doped up with pain killers to even give their own names accurately."

"Good," Donovan said. "That gives us a bit of planning time, though not nearly as much as I'd like." He then turned a firm gaze back at Benny. "You're going to owe me big after this, young man."

The youth looked down slightly. "I know. And I'm sure you'll never let me hear the end of that."

"Of course, I won't. Which leads me to my next question. Are you serious about wanting to learn to use your power for the greater good?"

Benny's countenance suddenly beamed an expression that, for the first time in many hours, was even remotely indicative of a positive emotion. His response barely concealed his level of anticipation. Was this opportunity really happening, considering what happened earlier?

"I can't think of a better way to live my life and to make up for what I did, Donovan. I'll follow your lead, because even though we just met barely two hours ago, I already owe you a lot. As long as we understand that the type of hero I'm going to *try* to become will be at least partly on my terms."

"Don't get too big for your silly little britches already, guy. And don't get overly pretentious. You have potential, but it's going to be a long road and a lot of hard work before you have any right to call yourself a 'hero' by any proper definition of the term. I know because I've met more than my share of true heroes, and a far larger share of pathetic souls who only *thought* they were.

"And no, in case you're wondering, I *do not* consider myself among the honored ranks of the true heroes. I'm simply a battle-weary soldier who tries to aspire to certain codes and principles rather than just obeying the orders of authority figures in uniform. You will be working *with* me, and not *for* me, the government, or any corporation. However, the Institute will be on you like mold on weeks-old cottage cheese for the entire ride. Count on that."

Benny looked up at the stern but invariably fair-minded figure before him. "I… don't consider that to be a bad thing, Donovan."

The soldier now allowed himself to smile, once again filled with a feeling of hope for this young metahuman's prospects. But it was a very cautious and tentative form of hope.

***

The following day, Benny found himself with little opportunity to recover from the emotional tumult he had experienced a mere thirty hours earlier. As it turned out, Donovan had other things in mind bright and early that morning. These plans entailed having the young metahuman awakened and reporting to the Buffalo Valis Institute's cavernous training chamber. This was located much lower in the hidden underground facility than the main laboratories, control center, and living quarters.

"You could've warned me about that alarm buzzer you had in the cell that is now my bedroom, Donovan," Benny griped to his new mentor.

"Of course, I could have," the soldier retorted. "But I obviously chose not to. I've always noticed that people are more on their toes when their training begins at an unexpected time. Especially when that time is several hours north of noon."

"I'm used to sleeping in on Saturdays."

"Then you need to get used to *not* sleeping in on Saturdays. Which brings up an important question: Have you even noticed yourself getting tired anymore since those cosmic energies altered your physiology?"

Benny thought about that query for a second. "Actually, now that you mention it… no. Because of my depression, I used to sleep all the time, and I never seemed to get enough sleep. But since the change, I don't really feel myself getting tired anymore, and I seem to sleep just to put my mind at ease and dream. Though my dreams were really messed up last night."

"And they will likely continue to be for a while, but we'll work on that. Which brings us to this training chamber, one that I like to call The Stadium. The reason why will is about to become obvious now that your training partner has just hit the entry request bell on the door."

Donovan hit the "enter" button on the smart panel connected to his wrist watch, which caused the automatic sliding door on the far end of the chamber to hiss open. Through it emerged a rugged looking and husky young man with brown hair slightly lighter than Benny's own. His complexion was olive, and his musculature looked quite impressive, as if he worked out intensively.

"Benny, meet Mac Campton. Or, as his ego prefers we call him, Brick."

"Real cute, Donovan," Mac rejoindered as he cracked his knuckles in a posturing manner.

The soldier grimaced in response. "Mac, meet Benny Lonero, who hasn't chosen a code name yet."

91

Benny reached out to shake Mac's hand, but he refused to accept the gracious gesture. Instead, the burly youth simply looked the smaller boy over for a moment while bearing a countenance of disdain.

Mac was then predictably quick to utter a complaint. "Wait a minute, Donovan. Are you serious? This is the guy you expect me to--you know--spar with now?"

Benny suddenly developed a look of incredulity upon his boyish face. "Donovan?"

The grizzled veteran grinned to himself again. "Yes, to your direct question, Mac; and the same to your implied one, Benny (based on your expression). See, not only do both of you start your training today, but you both also need to let off some steam in the worst way. And it's much better you do that with a fellow metahuman than your non-powered and non-trained peers."

"You mean this guy is a metahuman, too?" Mac queried with his index finger rigidly pointed at Benny. "He don't look like anything at all. Does he know how strong I am?"

"Not yet, but Benny is quite strong too," Donovan noted. "And we have yet to try testing his upper limit. So, as strong as you obviously are, as far as we currently know, he may be even stronger."

"Oh, bullshit, man!" Mac exclaimed with waving hands. "This kid is as scrawny as a set of pipe cleaners! And just look at me compared to that."

Mac flexed and flaunted his prominent biceps to emphasize the point.

Benny rejoined simply with an angry glare. The young man called Brick reminded him of a few choice athletes that he knew from school.

"Who the hell do you think you're eyeballing, man?" Mac asked with a clearly hostile tone and a thick index finger poking his smaller sparring partner in the forehead.

Benny's reply to that was a gritting of his teeth almost immediately accompanied by a sudden conversion of his dark brown eyes to a luminescent blue. This was followed in turn by a crackling corona of bluish energy that appeared around each of his tightly clenched fists.

"What the hell is all that?" Mac said, as he stepped back involuntarily.

"Benny, calm down," Donovan stated firmly but soothingly, while risking a painful injury by putting his hand on the boy's shoulder.

After a moment of strong effort, Benny did as requested. The glowing coruscations of energy quickly buzzed out of existence while his eyes lost their luminosity in unison with his hands.

"Mac, I'll have you know that learning not to underestimate someone you're facing in combat, even during a simple sparring match, is one of the most important lessons I can possibly teach you," the soldier lamented upon turning his attention back to his other young charge. "Let me inform you that Benny here may not look nearly as tough as you, but he's proven capable of doing an incredible amount of damage. Show him the respect he's earned."

Mac shook his head. "Whatever, man. When are we going to get this thing started? My *Wizard of Warcraft* crew across the world awaits my return to the computer."

Donovan wasted no time with his response. "No need to delay any further. I'm going to start your joint training by teaching some basic moves from American boxing. I'll give you two your own pair of specially constructed padded gloves. What I want to see first is not only a comparison of your respective strength levels by facing you off against each other, but also to see what type of natural fighting skills each of you may possess."

"Pshht!" Mac sputtered with a roll of his eyes. "I just got these powers a few months ago, and before that I kicked more ass than a cowboy's saddle has ever seen."

Benny sniggered at that comment.

"You find that funny, man?" the tightly muscled youth heckled his smaller opponent.

"Since you asked, I find you *highly* amusing, Mac," was Benny's comeback. "And what's the source of your power, by the way? Do you draw strength from your own cockiness? Sort of like Anteaus does from the Earth?"

"What the hell is an 'Anteaus?'" Mac enquired. "You're really stupid, man."

"No doubt," Benny quietly retorted. "I'm really stupid for thinking you might be educated enough to have actually read Greco-Roman mythology."

With that said, Mac jumped into a defensive stance. "Why don't you make a move, you little dickweed?"

Benny quickly duplicated both the stance and the attitude, as Mac's gesture triggered a deluge of highly unpleasant memories. "I'll make *several* moves, you jock piece of trash!"

Elsewhere in The Stadium's spacious chamber stood Agents Sasheen Kahn and Helda Bauer, both of whom now suddenly took on expressions of alarm. In accordance with their security duties, each of them began drawing their high-powered taze rifles. Having immediately noticed this action, Donovan signaled them to stand down; that he had this situation in hand.

The tough-as-nails soldier stepped between the two angry young metas and simultaneously gave both of them a hard shove to the chest with each hand.

"Enough, guys!" Donovan commanded. "As I said, you'll both get your chance to let off steam this way, but only under my direction and control! And within the confines of mutual respect."

He then turned to the larger of the two combatants. "Mac, no more provocation of your fellow meta trainees, understand? You can't afford to be running around in common society acting like that, or you'll just put me and others in the position of taking you down. I'm here to train you and see to it that you use your power responsibly, with enough training so that you can. There is no place for the street punk mentality among the ranks of heroes, you dig that?"

Mac lowered his arms in a huff. "Fine. I'm cool, okay?"

Benny followed suit and stepped a few feet back. "I'm cool too, Donovan. But I didn't start this…"

Donovan raised his right hand to stifle any further verbosity from his trainee. "Let it go, Benny. I already saw who started it, and I stopped it so you didn't have to. *Don't* get it started again. Okay?"

"Yeah," the dark-haired boy replied with only a slight hint of vexation in his voice.

With matters now apparently under greater control, the two contestants were directed to the middle of the chamber, where there stood a large cage-like structure. It had a lock just above the lever on the door that resembled a souped-up deadbolt.

Mac pointed at the construct. "Seriously?"

Benny looked at the metallic mesh structure with equal surprise. "What he said."

"Hey, if this worked for the MMA tournaments, we figured it would work for our purposes too," was all Donovan had to say in response. "And I think we were right. Now get inside, please. Oh, and in case you're wondering, the mesh of The Cage—yes, we call it *The Cage*, because that simple name fits it just fine—is a titanium alloy."

The two boys grudgingly entered, slipped on the special hand gloves that were given to them, and stood several feet apart in opposite corners as Donovan entered alongside them.

"Are you sure it's wise for you to be in there like that when the two of them start going at it, chief?" Helda hollered from across the room.

"Absolutely not, ma'am," Donovan replied with grudging honesty. "But I think it would be even less wise for me *not* to be in here."

"Do you at least want one of us to go in with you?" Sasheen asked, also via raising his voice from across the room.

"No," Donovan confidently answered. "I'll signal if I need you. Until then, I got this."

He then directed Benny and Mac to stand at ease before each other. After he insisted that the two bow to each other to display mutual respect before starting the slug-fest, Donovan braced himself a moment before uttering the word everyone in the chamber was anxiously anticipating.

"Fight!"

Mac immediately proved himself the more aggressive of the two by charging forward like a maddened rhino and swinging a right hook at his much smaller opponent. He was startled by Benny's reflexes when the latter easily evaded the blow, and then avoided its immediate follow-up with similar ease.

Having now become a bit more confident with the full realization of the edge his enhanced reflexes afforded him, Benny threw a punch capable of smashing clear through a cinderblock wall at his larger foe. To his consternation, Mac caught the fist in his meaty left hand, barely evincing any pain at doing so.

The bigger youth then tugged Benny forward slightly and laid a crushing haymaker clear across his chin. The brown-haired meta of Italian heritage was sent airborne by the force of this blow, his flight halted only when he crashed into the metallic mesh a about twenty feet behind him.

Ooooh, Donovan said to himself.

Benny landed hard on the mat and stumbled back to his feet. The fact that he could receive serious pain from another powerful metahuman was now made unnervingly clear to him.

He instinctively moved his tongue around the interior of his mouth to check for broken teeth. Finding none, Benny forced himself back to his feet and resumed his fighting stance.

Mac danced around in the center of the cage and struck his fists together a few times in another posturing motion. "You done? Because if not, I'm going to hurt you worse."

For a moment, the same fears of being beaten upon by stronger individuals that Benny had lived with every day of his life prior to the metamorphosis infested his mind. And it did so like a horde of filthy rodents that find a way into the sanctity of one's home through the toilet.

However, the boy would be damned if he was going to allow this situation to follow him into the new circle he had just entered.

With this determined resolution, Benny's fear was quickly replaced by an utter refusal to end up on the lower pecking order of the dawning metahuman population. He would not allow himself to be forced into a position amongst the emerging gods that was comparable to the one he experienced amongst the mortal peasantry.

Benny felt a powerful inner imperative to evolve in more ways than one. For a brief moment, the young metahuman saw a replay image of the bearded one-eyed man with a thunderous voice and uber-authoritative disposition that he experienced as a vision on the night of the Warp Event. He still had no idea what that terrifying and powerful image meant, but the deluge of emotions it triggered was quite evident.

Prompted by these strong feelings, Benny raised his right fist and lunged at Mac. The larger youth reacted as expected and ran to meet the attack blow-by-blow.

But as Benny approached within inches of his opponent, he didn't throw the predicted punch. Instead, he utilized his enhanced leg muscles to leap clear over his challenger. Mac threw a cuff of his own, but it ended up connecting with nothing save thin air.

Landing behind his bulkier opponent, Benny took full advantage of the mighty lad's momentary confusion by running towards him and slamming his entire upper body into Mac's stone-hard back.

Pain inundated the brawny metahuman's shoulders and arms like numerous bee stings upon the collision. At the same time, the force of its impact caused him to be briefly smashed up against the mesh of The Cage.

As Mac bounced off the flexible mesh immediately following impact, Benny charged forward and struck him hard in the side of his jaw. Mac was staggered by the unexpected power of the blow, as he never experienced pain like this since his metamorphosis to meta-humanity.

Benny then moved in and struck again, this time directly to his opponent's sternum. This time Mac found himself sent clear off his feet and onto his back.

For a second, Benny moved back into a fighting stance, his self-assurance further boosted. But that was to be short-lived. The following moment, a very irate Brick sat up again, his olive-hued face almost turning bright red with anger. This being the first time he had ever been hurt since his transformation, he wasn't going to leave this affront unpunished.

Uh oh, Donovan thought to himself as he moved a bit closer. *The shit is about to knock the fan clear off the table.*

Now having returned to his feet, Mac clumsily charged his smaller opponent like the Wild Bull of Thessaly did Hercules. His several swings proved incapable of overcoming Benny's greater speed and reflexes, and the latter managed to land a reciprocal blow direct to Mac's lower abdomen. The bigger contestant bowled over in agony but was still not taken out of the fight.

The robust youth with the rock-hard musculature retaliated by back-handing his challenger in the stomach. This brutal blow caught Benny off-guard and proved that his enhanced reflexes weren't perfect.

Benny was again sent flying back into the mesh of The Cage. The Italian metahuman was stunned by the force, and he barely managed to regain his senses by the time Mac rushed at him again. Before the young man code-named Brick could make contact, though, Benny managed to shrug off this inflicted stupor just in time to lay a haymaker to the right side of his opponent's jaw.

Mac was knocked back several feet by the impact of this punch. After he recovered his senses a moment later, he noticed a stinging sensation on his lower lip. Rubbing his hand over his mouth, he was astounded to see a streak of blood rub off on his fingers.

Mac was truly flabbergasted by the sight of his own blood. He didn't think he was capable of bleeding any longer, as his skin had withstood being stabbed by knives and struck by baseball bats without having drawn blood, or even so much as a bruise being formed. This, coupled with the fact that the blood which flowed from his mouth was more a purplish hue than red in color, was highly disconcerting to him.

The large metahuman's apprehension was quickly replaced with anger over this gross violation of a dermis he had previously taken for granted as being indestructible. Overwhelmed by these extreme emotions, Mac ran towards Benny with an enraged scream that a banshee would envy. Benny unleashed his own pent up wrath by responding in kind.

The two frenzied meta-youths met in the center of The Cage and grasped each other in twin grips of steel. Each had their respective hands on the others' throat in an apparent contest to see who could strangle the other first. Both boys were exerting their superhuman levels of strength to the fullest, with each of them utterly refusing to give ground to the other.

Donovan couldn't deny being fascinated by what he witnessed, as well as observing that the two metahumans seemed roughly equal in regard to sheer strength. Seeing these angry young titans clash, even under such controlled circumstances, was truly a sight to behold.

Nevertheless, an unfortunate development which he felt, in retrospect, that he should have anticipated sooner, proved quick to ensue.

Despite what appeared to be matching degrees of indignation and strength, Benny's furious struggle to overcome his foe soon acted as the catalyst for something else. It began with the familiar, trouble-indicating glow of sapphire in his eyes. It predictably continued when it was swiftly followed by sparks of similarly azure-hued energy coruscating across his arms and hands.

As his fury grew over the next several seconds, so did the intensity of these arcs of energy until they expanded to a luminescence that fully encapsulated his body.

This all-encompassing glow delivered a continuing series of extremely painful shocks to Mac. His mighty superhuman body underwent what resembled intense spasms, is if he were subjected to an epileptic seizure of titanic proportions.

This grotesque tableau continued to escalate as the radiant blue Odic energy seared through Mac's every cell. The degree of agony it produced caused him to scream with such reverberation that all present were worried that his larynx might burst.

As the force emanating from Benny's grip continued to increase over the next several seconds, so did the tenor of his opponent's pain-riddled bellows. By that point, Mac's eyes were rolling back into his head, giving his irises a ghastly white sheen, while his wide-gaping mouth began to extrude copious amounts of foamy sputum.

Though Donovan wanted to intervene, the intense glow of the energy all but blinded him. Further, the sizzling of the air around Benny's immediate vicinity stung his skin like hundreds of needle pokes.

This forced the all too human soldier to step back rather than proceed any closer. He knew Mac was extremely tough, but could he handle a cellular assault by such powerful energies? And would Benny regain sufficient self-control to stop before it was too late? Donovan silently cursed himself for thinking he had this under control.

Just then, however, he noticed that Mac suddenly released his rugged grip on Benny after a hugely stubborn effort of will to maintain his superhuman hold at all costs. Shouting with a fiery ire reminiscent of a djinn being released after centuries trapped in a bottle, the still-glowing Benny hurled his now limp opponent through the air with a single mighty heave.

Mac's midair form smashed into the eastern end of The Cage's metal shielding, after which it landed on the mat with a loud thud. He was still moving, but he appeared in no hurry to rise to his feet again. Instead, he just lay there writhing and groaning in distress, his stone-hard flesh being riddled with small burns and exuding wafts of steam.

Benny released another scream while the bluish glow of Odic energies continued to spark in all directions from his body, making him resemble a human-shaped neon flare. After all that energy and emotion was released from his system, though, he seemed to clasp his fists tightly and force himself to desist. *Get a grip, Lonero...*

The penetrating glow then began rapidly fading in its intensity. Within about a minute the few remaining arcs of visible energy burned themselves out of existence. In tandem, the azure candela of his eyes was replaced with their more familiar dark brown irises and surrounding white. The young man seemed to take a few deep breathes as he looked at Mac's pain-wracked form wriggling pathetically on the mat.

As Benny's composure returned, he couldn't help but notice the concerned look on Donovan's visage. He further noted the startled expressions on the faces of Helda and Sasheen, both of whom now stood a few feet from The Cage with their taze rifles drawn. The victor of this metahuman contest wanted to kill the tension by saying something. When he opened his mouth to do so, only one question came out.

"This counts as a win, right?"

Chapter 11: If the Costume Fits...

"How long do you expect to stay at Craig's house?" Grace Lonero shouted through her grandson's cell phone, her tone saturated with the usual attitude.

"I don't know," Benny replied with grudging honesty to his grandmother. "Things were bad at home, and I had to get away..."

"Did you hear what happened at your school on Friday?" Grace interrupted nervously. "Some gang members or something beat two hockey players badly enough to put them in the hospital. Did you happen to know Mikey something or other, and that Woof kid?"

"Yeah, I knew them, but I wasn't at the school when that happened. I was at Craig's house discussing my staying there..."

"Your grandfather and I thought something happened to you when you didn't come home on the same night those gang members broke into the school! Were those boys' friends of yours?"

"He doesn't have any friends at that school, Grace," Benny heard Dominic Lonero mutter in the background. "Except for that screwball Craig, and that's only because no one likes him either."

"Shut up, Dominic!" Grace yelled. "You don't need to be instigating this right now."

"*You* shut up!" Dominic yelled back at her. "This is my house, and I'll 'instigate' all I want! Let him stay there with that goofball! I was about ready to put him away anyways."

"See what I mean?" Benny said, beginning to respond in kind to his grandfather's resentful anger. "I need to get away from that house for a time, or... I don't know what I might do. I can't take it anymore. Craig's mother is making lunch for us now, so I'll call you back later."

The embittered young man quickly hit the "end call" tab on his cell phone before he got angry enough to crush the device in his hand. He found himself thankful that Donovan insisted he stay at the Valis Institute. All he needed to do now was to call Craig and convince him to go along with the ruse.

Due to the nature of the last words he spoke to his best and practically only friend, the young metahuman wasn't surprised that Craig didn't call or text him all weekend. Benny sent him an apology text, along with a typically abbreviated request to call him immediately.

"I didn't like your attitude when I last saw you, man," were Craig's first words to his fellow social outcast when he complied with the call request. "You're lucky I didn't punch you in the face right there…"

"I apologized, and I wasn't exactly in a good mood that day," Benny responded before his friend pushed the antagonism any further. "I'm sorry."

"Look, don't worry about it. I know I can be an ass sometimes too. Anyway, did you hear what happened to Judge and Wolfe? Could it possibly have happened to two nicer people?"

"Yeah. I did. And no. It couldn't."

"Rumor has it that the same thugs who did that broke into your 'girlfriend' Marissa Robbins's house and attacked the bitch and her family. Some metahuman fracas went down around her 'hood that night, so it may have been a coincidence. Who knows?"

"Yeah, I heard about all of that. But look, I have something else I need to talk to you about now. I was having problems at home, so… I'm staying at my Aunt Mary's house right now. But I don't want my grandparents to know about it, so I told them I was staying with you. Can you please go along with that for now in case they call you?"

"Aw, man, do you have to put me in the middle of your family problems?"

"Look, I already talked to them, and things have gotten bad enough there that I told them I would only be dragged back over my dead body. Or maybe *theirs*, to be a bit more realistic."

"Ha! Benny the Badass. I'm sure your grandfather trembles at the thought of getting on your bad side."

"Dude, stifle the sarcasm! Something else happened; something I need to discuss with you, but… not now, and not over the phone. We'll talk about this when we get back to school. After we leave for the day, that is."

"Okay, well, you know it's closed until Thursday. Of course, they're only going to close it long enough to get the blood stains off the wall in the locker room and fix the lock on the door, and not so much as a minute longer than that. Then again, if the hiatus went on any longer, they would only end up taking our Easter vacation away."

"Craig, enough about that, okay?"

"What's your problem? Why are you still in such a pissy mood?"

"Like I said, something happened, okay? But I don't want to talk about it right now. Maybe I'll come by your place on Tuesday if I can, and…"

"Benny, did you have something to do with what happened to Judge and Wolfe?"

The young metahuman suddenly felt as if he would choke. "What would make you think that?"

"I'm not stupid, man. You were acting weird before that shit went down on Friday, and you're sure as hell acting weird now. And then you suddenly picked that night to run away to your aunt's house/ On top of that, the mere mention of the incident at the school bothers you so much when you really shouldn't give a royal screw about what happened to Judge and Wolfe. Especially considering, you know, how they always treated us like something you find buried in the cat's litter box."

"I told you, Craig. We'll talk later, not now."

"Shit, Benny. What in the hell is going on?"

"I'll text you later, alright? I have to go now, so please don't say anything to anyone about any of this. And remember what to say in the unlikely event my grandmother should call you, okay?"

Benny quickly ended the call before Craig could protest or ask anything further. He then backed up against the hard concrete wall of his assigned quarters before sliding to the floor, tossing his cell phone on his bed, and covering his face with both hands.

Oh, man, Craig suspects everything. So, do I tell him the whole story? Or do I just keep lying to him? Lying to practically the only friend I have is not the same as lying to everyone else. I know what Donovan would tell me if asked him for advice on this, but it's not like I'm going to just mindlessly do every single thing he ever tells me to do. I have to learn to think for myself even when I'm following the lead of another.

Damn it. If only there was someone I could talk to about this who would be more concerned with me doing the right thing than the expedient thing…

***

Early Monday morning, Benny was back in the training chamber, with Donovan and a duo of armed security guards present as per usual. This time, though, he noticed that Gail Parker wasn't among the two. The "vibe" he had gotten from her over the past weekend since the altercation at the Robbins apartment made him wonder if there was good reason for her reassignment. But that was yet another concern he had to put aside for the nonce.

The young metahuman found himself standing "at attention" in front of a huge, 300-pound cinderblock clasped tightly between a pair of solid steel clamps.

It was just over fifteen feet from where he stood, which was described by Donovan as the ideal distance for the test that was about to supervene.

"Alright, Benny-boy, we're now going to teach you to control the intensity of those nasty energy beams of yours," the soldier-turned-drill-instructor informed him.

"So, you don't want me to just try to smash that big ass cinderblock to millions of tiny shards?" Benny asked.

"No, no, I don't. I suspect you're fully capable of generating more than enough power to do that. What I want you to do here is see if you can willfully temper the power output so that the damage you inflict upon the block is minimal. It's essential that you learn to control the power output of those energy beams. So that you can simply stun normal human beings, as well as fellow metahumans, without blasting them to pieces; or causing a hell of a lot more property damage than any given circumstance may warrant."

"'I shall try, master, I shall try,'" the young man responded in satirical imitation of the young genie from one of his favorite vintage fantasy films, *The 7th Voyage of Sinbad*.

Having managed to catch the pop cultural reference, Donovan rolled his eyes while muttering, "Smartass."

"Hey, being a smartass is much better than being a dumbass, right?" Benny retorted as he extended his arm and clasped fist in "firing position."

As he began to concentrate, Benny felt the familiar tingle and rush of the incredible degree of Odic energies inundating his entire cellular matrix. Within a fraction of a second, he could feel these energies being "pushed" down the extremity of his arm and focused through his extended arm.

The bluish, crackling energy bolt was projected from his hand as initiated, its sheer intensity literally burning the air immediately surrounding its contours. The cinderblock was struck dead on, and it blew to pieces with a massive blast of force.

Donovan and the two security guards covered their ears in rapt discomfort.

"Geez," one of the guards could be heard whispering.

"Whoa," was all Benny had to say.

Donovan walked over to the smoking remains of the cinderblock and inspected it glumly.

"Impressive, huh, boss?" the youth said proudly.

"Impressive maybe, but way off the mark, kid," the soldier replied. "I'm not sure how much concentration you put into reining in your power flow, but you still destroyed most of the cinderblock. That means if the beam had struck a human being full on, it would have been lethal. The person would likely have been cut in half or had a quarter of his body shredded into little bloody pieces."

"I tried, Donovan."

"Then it looks like you need to try harder. And keep trying until you learn to control the power flow. Because you're not going out there into the field, so to speak, until you do."

The leader of the proceedings clicked a small button on his arm band to activate the intercom system. "Len, have another 300-pound cinderblock brought in."

"Fun, fun," Benny murmured to himself in anticipation of what he knew was going to be a grueling day of training.

***

Several miles away, in the business-heavy section of Buffalo's Sheridan Drive area, stood a recently established research outfit called Osmos Exploration. The fledgling company's already well-known mission statement was the following:

"Using state-of-the-art technology to investigate the emerging scientific anomalies of the present era, Osmos is dedicated to using such knowledge to facilitate advances in the growing energy needs of human civilization. The establishment of affordable alternative sources of energy production that eliminates the need for reliance on fossil fuels without undermining the profitability of the many corporations that make America the world leader of industry is our goal and our privilege."

Of course, the average working person paid no heed to the presence of this research facility in favor of tending to the all-important concerns of earning a living and raising their families. Those few who did pay attention, however, knew exactly what "anomalies" and opportunities Osmos was referring to.

Many corporations were eager to invest in metahuman research, and the government was just as keen to provide generous finance subsidies and contracts for the same. The executive board of Osmos was confident that before long the facility would be "too big to fail." The rarely seen head of this company, Martin Teasil, was an enigma, but apparently well-respected by the money-movers on Wall Street.

Amongst the many separate laboratories within the sprawling complex was the one that was headed by Prof. Rutger Kaiser. A research physicist, the fairly tall man had a mop of unkempt graying hair stop his head, and his exquisitely unattractive face was marred by the scars of what was clearly the result of having suffered a very severe case of acne during his adolescence. His grating voice was tinged with a slight German accent that drew shivers from every lab assistant and colleague who had to hear it. He wore a pair of thick, strap-on goggles of his own design that doubled as protection from the light effects generated by his various experiments, and as a corrective remedy for his far-sightedness.

This particular afternoon Kaiser's pale eyes, which looked twice as big as they normally were due to the concave lenses of his goggles, were focused upon his latest handiwork: a full-body, thin suit of shiny blue material covered with circuitry-like attachments, the main part of which appeared to be a bronze-colored metallic circular device connected to the sternum region.

The suit was displayed within a plexi-glass chamber where it was soon to be subjected to a final few operational tests. The scientist smiled smugly at the glittering garment before him, an action much disliked by his colleagues, since it exposed a mouthful of crooked yellowing teeth.

"Beautiful, isn't it?" Kaiser asked no one in particular.

"Yes, yes, it's quite an accomplishment, Professor" answered his lab assistant Renee Mack with a nervous stammer. "Glad I could be involved in this."

"If only your job didn't depend on you never saying otherwise, huh, Ms. Mack?" the scientist snapped back, just to make it clear that he wasn't a fool who couldn't recognize insincerity when he heard it.

"Um…"

"So, are you happy with the results, Prof. Kaiser?" his other lab assistant, Myron Wexler, quickly interjected to rescue Renee from what would likely be an awkward response.

"I expected no other outcome, Mr. Wexler," was the scientist's curt rejoinder. "I am hardly an ineffectual loser incapable of producing results. That is why I am where I am and… well, others are lab assistants, no?"

Myron exhaled slightly to signal being put off. "Well, Prof. Kaiser, it is late and well past quitting time. So, if you are no longer needing our services…"

"Do feel free to vacate the premises, Mr. Wexler," Kaiser said. "I no longer need any gopher work done this evening."

Without saying another word, both Myron and Renee stormed out of the lab, making sure to keep their opinions of Kaiser to themselves until they were well beyond the corridor leading away from his lab.

The scientist made no attempt to be courteous to others, as he long ago abandoned any belief that his fellow human beings were worthy of such niceties. The abuse and rejection he had endured in his youth and young adulthood due to his less than appealing appearance and unorthodox interests had resulted in his writing off the human race as a point of consideration. He owed his success to the support of no one else. In fact, his employment by Osmos was merely a means to a personal end as far as he was concerned.

The dumpy-looking scientist walked towards the plexi-glass case where the suit he constructed was confined and put his hand to the surface of the glass, directly opposite to where the suit was strung up. A crackling field of energy jumped between the circular apparatus of the outré garment's sternum region and the surface of the glass where Kaiser's hand was pressed. It much resembled the effect observed when one puts their hand to the glass of a plasma ball one can buy at a novelty shop, but considerably more intense.

"Yessss…" Kaiser slurred to himself while he remained transfixed upon the energy generating suit. "You are going to be my road to the power I've always lacked. This entire city, and the world beyond it, will pay for what the depraved human species has done to me. We will see how the residents of this backwards city enjoy receiving a dose of the hell that people have always subjected me to."

His smile then took on a vicious countenance of contempt, his yellow teeth gritted tightly together like the maw of a predatory creature savoring the thought of a soon to commence kill. With this change in mood came a noticeable increase in the intensity of the energy pouring between the suit and the palm of Kaiser's hand that was still tightly pressed to the surface of the glass.

***

Tuesday morning was quick to come, and with it the ever-reliable wake-up buzzer that forced Benny out of his slumber. He was at least thankful that he didn't seem to get tired anymore, or to wake up feeling like he had just finished running a fifty-mile marathon stretch (which had previously made him extremely crabby in the mornings).

Nevertheless, he came to find that he needed the sleep, if only to enter a form of meditative trance which he appeared to naturally drift upon entering the REM state. Many strange images passed within his mind while in this mode of consciousness, which he knew served roughly the same purpose as the symbolism of dreams. They differed from standard dreams, however, in that they tended to be much more vivid and full of information.

These nightly meditative forays were accompanied by the overwhelmingly peaceful sensation of making a powerful psychic connection with the ultimate intelligence of the universe itself. To his perception, this eternally vast universal intelligence seemed to be "downloading" such symbol-laden information into his organic neural hard drive (read: his brain). Discerning their meaning was a challenge, but one he was determined to undertake.

Once again, however, Benny had to put such concerns aside and report to the training chamber. This time, though, he was to receive quite an interesting surprise.

"If you're going to play the role of a hero who deals with the type of menace that the Warp Events have proven capable of producing," Donovan told him, "then you need to dress the part."

"Please don't tell me that you got me a tuxedo," Benny replied with his usual acerbity.

"No, silly-ass," Donovan said. "I'm talking about a fully functional outfit and disguise that I think you're familiar with from reading those dreadful comic books; not to mention watching those CGI-saturated movies based on them that have recently become such popular money-makers for God knows what reason. Those funny books and the movies based on them just encourage metahumans to do stupid shit."

Benny exhaled a sigh of indignation. "Are you talking about a costume?"

"That is precisely what I'm talking about. Take a look at this."

Donovan walked over to a plastic suitcase on a nearby metal stool and opened it. Out of it he produced a monochrome black and white full body suit that included a cowl which covered the head and the top part of his face. In its center was a white insignia that resembled an inverted triangle surrounded by a disc. The uniform came equipped with sturdy-but-comfortable-looking gloves and boots, along with what appeared to be a sort of white utility belt around the waist area.

Donovan smiled upon presenting the costume. "So, what do you think, guy?"

"It... looks okay. Is that a utility belt?"

"Yes, as you will need to carry certain types of equipment at times."

"And what does that emblem in the chest area mean?"

"It's a Tetrad of Pythagoras, lined with Nordic runes. The circle around it represents a mystical field of protection for medieval wizards who summoned all sorts of weird entities into the triangle, where they would be trapped. Classic occult symbols that Claire suggested, which she felt was just somehow 'right' for you. Hey, it's not like we just put a big 'S' symbol there, huh? But it gets better.

"The uniform is made of a special type of polymer that a certain research facility was able to create just a few years ago. Not coincidentally, nothing like this was able to be produced prior to the global onset of the Warp Events, which seem to have changed what is and isn't possible to invent, let alone actually make work. This material has been referred to as *bio-mimetic polymer*, and it duplicates the properties of the wearer's skin to an approximate extent."

"Ah, sort of like those 'unstable molecules' invented by Reed Richards in the *Fantastic Four* comic book."

"Not having read any of that junk, I'll take your word for it."

Benny scowled. "Comic books are very influential on all aspects of culture and science, dude. In fact, you're now seeing what was once considered to be exaggerated pseudo-science in their pages becoming a reality following those Warp Events. So maybe you should show those books and what they represent and have always foreshadowed with a bit more respect, huh?"

"Look who's suddenly giving *me* advice on showing respect. Anyway, this bio-mimetic polymer will effectively become as tough as your own skin when you wear it, even though you shouldn't expect it to be indestructible. Hence, you should be able to project your energy discharges at full force without shredding the material. And their highly adaptive structure has one more very cool feature that I think you're really going to like."

"I already like what I see here. Please do tell me about whatever property this suit has that's even better than *this*."

"The polymer is 'energy-responsive.' Since it will instantly adapt to the energy frequencies produced by your cellular structure whenever it's in contact with your skin, a short-wave omni-directional discharge of your energy, if properly focused into the clothing itself, will cause the suit to expand and take on its regular appearance."

"Meaning…?"

"Meaning, that your entire regular wardrobe--just about any type of clothing imaginable--can be altered by a procedure we have access to that will convert its sub-atomic structure to bio-mimetic polymer. It will then become adaptive enough that the pattern and shape of this suit can be invisibly grafted into its matrix by a process we call *sub-atomic overlaying*. So…"

"So… when I produce that omni-directional burst of energy, my clothing that is overlaid with the pattern of this suit will quickly change color and expand to instantly cover me in this costume! Sort of like what Ms. Marvel could do in the comics! That is so far *beyond* cool that a special adjective needs to be created for it!"

"You can invent that adjective yourself, being an aspiring writer. In the meantime, you need to try on this outfit, and you need to spend the rest of the day practicing how to precisely use such an omni-directional energy discharge to initiate the morphological alteration effect on your clothing. That also means, of course, that we have to give your entire wardrobe the sub-atomic alteration and overlay treatments."

"Let's get to it, then. And I can't wait to see how this sub-atomic alteration process works. This place is more awesome than I ever imagined! Do I ever have to go home?"

Chapter 12: Picking Up the Pieces

Head Nurse Beverly Tanner found herself utterly charmed by the tall, early-middle-aged man with a prominent athletic build and a thick, salt-and-pepper mustache that, unbeknownst to her, was dyed black. He resembled nothing less than a classic movie star hero with the way he proudly stood over her front desk on the 4th floor of Kenmore Clemency Hospital.

The nurse was curious as to what color his eyes were, but they were concealed by dark shades which made him look like a figure right out of 1980s action cinema. Of course, Beverly hadn't the slightest idea that the gently speaking man was actually Valis Institute agent Donovan Jakes utilizing a false identity.

"Well, I think it's very sweet of you to stop by and bring flowers to your nephew, Mr. Wolfe," Beverly said with a sly wink of her eye. "He just recently regained enough health to speak after that horrid beating he took at the school. Your whole family must have found this quite difficult to deal with. My heart goes out to you."

"Thank you for the condolences, Nurse Tanner," said the incognito Donovan. "And yup, 'difficulties' is certainly something that Jeff's situation has brought to everyone concerned. And you say he's sharing a room with Mickey Judge, the other boy who was hurt along with him?"

"Please call me Beverly," the faux blonde nurse stated with another clearly flirtatious tone. "And yes, Jeff is sharing a room with Mickey, as both their parents felt it would be better for their spirits if…"

"Much obliged for telling me where the room is… Beverly," the disguised Donovan said with a friendly though not flirtatious smile. "Here, please take this as a token of my appreciation."

He reached into the package containing the chrysanthemums he was carrying and handed one of the flowers to Beverly.

"Oh my," she said, graciously accepting the purple floret with a swoon.

Before she could say another word, or even come close to working up the nerve to inquire about whether the handsome gentleman was single, the undercover agent of the Valis Institute had already begun storming down the hallway towards the room housing the recovering Mickey Judge and Jeff Wolfe. His expression was no longer one of a good-natured uncle, but an angry soldier on a mission.

The still badly injured but now conscious Jeff and Mickey found their mutual semi-slumber rudely interrupted when the clandestine Donovan suddenly barged into their room and discreetly shut the door behind him. His dark shades, dyed hair, long overcoat, and large cowboy hat did an effective job of detracting from his naturel distinctive features. The overall demeanor he exuded before pronouncing a single word froze the two young patients to the core of their currently wretched being. He was clearly a man used to inspiring such feelings and commanding immense respect with his mere presence alone.

"Mr. Judge, Mr. Wolfe," Donovan greeted the two still heavily bandaged young athletes. "I'm Corporal Bob Taylor, and I'm here at the behest of the Federal Bureau of Investigation."

He then brandished a realistic and official looking identification badge to show them. In fact, the insignia truly was crafted by the U.S. government for him to facilitate an actual undercover mission years ago.

"Are you… here to take our statements 'bout about who did this to us?" Mickey croaked out, making it clear that speaking was still difficult for him.

The youth's enquiry, however, confirmed Claire's prediction that they were not yet questioned by the police. The former soldier never doubted her, but still felt a pang of relief at this verification.

"Not actually, boy," Donovan said. "I already know of Mr. Lonero's involvement in your sorry situation right now. Moreover, I'm aware of what you little miscreants and your lady collaborators did to drive that kid to do what *he* did to you two. I know it was self-defense on his part."

"Not… entirely true," Mickey insisted. "He called us names… he provoked us…"

"Something you and your sycophantic followers never did to him many times before, right?" Donovan interjected rhetorically. "I know all about the dementedly cruel little scheme you two concocted in league with Miss Robbins to lead Mr. Lonero into your planned dressing room encounter. That was really low, and for what I understand about you guys, that's sure as hell saying something."

The two boys looked at Donovan's icy glare with expressions of mounting fear.

"Let this be known to the two of you," the disguised Valis agent said with the firmness of a bamboo stick. "Mr. Lonero has always secretly been working for us. He was trained by us. You don't need to know the details behind that, as it's information highly classified by the Homeland Security Department.

"Your constant provocation of the kid caused him to snap and display his true prowess. He's being dealt with by us, but what the two of you and your cohorts did to Mr. Lonero over a prolonged period to make him lose his cool and force him to defend himself and reveal his true capabilities means that you're all in some majorly huge trouble with the government. I'm talking about the type of trouble that makes even the bravest Navy Seal stain his pants if he so much as *imagines* being in it.

"You are now privy to highly classified government secrets, and I have the authority—at my discretion—to have both of you detained and 'disappeared' over to Guantanamo or some other 'black' prison of my choice, if you get my meaning there."

"Shit, man…" Jeff groaned.

"'Shit's' the word all right, kid," Donovan concurred.

"Look, are you… saying you're just gonna let him get… get away with this?" Mickey queried, summoning a hint of discernible anger through his fear.

"No, kid, I'm not," Donovan replied. "As I said, he's being roundly censured for what he did. But considering he was bullied and provoked by you fine gentlemen and your lady cohorts for so long, and considering he needs to be where he is as per classified government plans, he will be back at the school when you return there."

"Do you mean…?" Jeff began saying.

"Yes," Donovan confirmed. "Out of consideration for your injuries, I won't haul your sorry asses into federal confinement. But there are two big stipulations involved with that very generous decision of mine.

"One, you will both cease provoking Mr. Lonero when you return to the school yourselves. You will cease encouraging others to do the same. You will leave him the hell alone. Because I can't be held responsible if you make him snap again. And if you do, you will be in so much trouble with the federal authorities that you had better pray to whichever big names in world mythology you happen to pray to that Mr. Lonero kills you next time.

"Because if he doesn't, where you end up afterwards will be far worse than any conception of Hell you might have. Within a few months you'll be suffering from Stockholm Syndrome so badly you'll consider Mr. Lonero and every agent of the government to be the greatest thing since free condoms."

Both boys were silent for a moment.

"Okay…" Jeff said weakly.

"But after what he did to us…" Mickey chimed in.

"Mickey, man… let this go," Jeff interceded. "Just… look at us. And this is… the government. And you gotta… admit, what we did…"

"Fine," Mickey squeaked. "Okay."

"I'm going to hold you to that, Mr. Judge," Donovan informed him with all due seriousness. "Now for the other condition required to stay out of Guantanamo.

"When the local police come to question you soon, you *will not* tell them of Mr. Lonero's involvement in this whole affair. You will both agree it was hooligans from the New York Boys, that dangerous East Side street gang currently active in the Fruit Belt area, who wandered into the school and did this to you. Both of you think you saw four of them, but they took you gentlemen by surprise and hit you too fast to properly defend yourselves. You have no idea why they entered the school, but you suspect they may have been scoping for drug customers. Got it?"

The two young athletes gave a weak but noticeable nod of the head in agreement.

"Good. Keep in mind that I represent a government authority far higher than the local police who will be investigating this case. We will remove the jobs from any officers whom you may tell of Mr. Lonero's involvement. We will indefinitely detain any members of your family or friends whom you tell, or we have reason to believe you plan to tell, to keep this secret if necessary. Then you two will be similarly detained, even if only one of you spills the beans. Miss Robbins is now being interrogated by another agent and she will be under similar restrictions when next you see her.

"*Don't mess with the FBI*, gentlemen. We are bad ass mo' fo's the likes of which wannabe bad ass mo' fo's like yourselves can scarcely imagine. And I don't think you two want to run afoul of the real deal in bad-assery twice in one week, especially after the first time didn't work out so well for you."

Both nodded again, this time more nervously.

"And one more thing before I leave. You now know that Mr. Lonero is much more than he seems, and always has been. Consider that he could easily have killed you both with the training he was given. But he didn't. He stopped before dealing you fatal blows. He showed you mercy when some would argue that you deserved none.

"He made it clear that he has a good shred of decency in his heart despite having snapped. What he did was wrong, and he is in big trouble for it; but what you and your peers did to provoke him was 'wronger' than wrong. So, suck this whole thing up to a very painful learning experience, heal up, go back to your petty but popular little lives for as long as the high school party lasts, and change your ways or else you may someday end up in a worse place than even Guantanamo."

Donovan then left the flowers on a small table next to Mickey's catheter bag.

"Oh, before I forget… these are for you guys. Just to show there are no hard feelings from the Bureau. I would have brought candy, but neither of you looks like you're able to eat solid food right now."

Donovan made the sign of a cocked gun with his fingers and grinned just before departing the room, as if leaving Jeff and Mickey with one final warning to keep to their deal.

For their part, the two boys sat for a long time in silence, neither attempting to engage the other in any talk about the matter. If anyone could be completely convincing in a subterfuge like this, it was Donovan Jakes. And the evidence that Benny was more than he appeared seemed to speak for itself.

***

After exiting the hospital, Donovan brandished his communicator, which was cleverly disguised as a cheap smart phone. He entered a special short code on its digital keypad that connected him to fellow agent Helda Bauer.

"Helda, my part of the job is done. I take it you were equally successful with Miss Robbins, her cousin, and her sibling?" He received an answer in the affirmative. "Good. Of course, we'll have to keep watch over all involved. And this will be clear to Benny once he meets the new staff members upon his return to Buffalo Historical. Wish I could be there to see the look on his face when he finds out who's joining him at the school."

Chapter 13: First Night Out

"And they seriously believed that smelly load of dung you threw at them, Donovan?" the soldier was asked by an incredulous Benny following the former's return to the Institute.

"Most certainly," Donovan replied.

"They may be jocks, but they were also good students in terms of academic merit. I hope you don't believe the stereotype that jocks are typically dumb. They simply put greater value on their athletic prowess than they do their grades, since they get rewarded a lot more for the former than the latter. You know, just like the culture they're so proudly a part of does. But that doesn't mean they underestimate the importance of keeping the grades up, though. They know they have to do that, so they can keep playing their sports, keeping enjoying the popularity, be liked by the teachers, and qualify for a sports scholarship to college."

"Keep the bitterness and lack of faith in the disposal bin, Benny-boy. I'm an expert at interrogation. I know how to play the secret agent, because I actually *was* a secret agent for a long time. And trust me, the man may leave the agency, but the agency never leaves the man, to paraphrase the hicks."

"But, Donovan…"

"Don't 'but' me, kid. They were in a highly confused state of mind due to recently receiving those very humbling injuries from a certain asshole whom they never imagined could do something like that to them. Then, when they're still injured and vulnerable, a guy like me walks into their hospital room, flips them an authentic-looking government badge, and gives them the third degree about being thrown in Guantanamo.

"Those boys were already emotionally shaken, with their perception of the comforting reality they always knew torn to shreds as surely as their innards were. They were in no mental shape to consider questioning things. Nor was Miss Robbins and her two unfortunate relatives after the epic scare you put into them."

"So, I'm really going back to the school in two days?"

"Yes, you're really going back to the school in two days. That's when the extended weekend your psychotic episode generously gave to your fellow students ends. Hence, that's when you'll be going back. We don't need an absence on your part to be cause for suspicion or further rumors."

"Thank you for the helpful words, Donovan."

"You'll always get my support as long as you play the straight and narrow, but never will you get any coddling. That's not my way, and I don't think that's of any benefit to certain emotionally disturbed people who need to be responsible and get healed instead of expecting special entitlement to lash out at others. *Capisce, mon frere?*"

"You just mixed two different languages."

"Yeah, I did. Deal with it if you didn't like it. Anyway, you're not leaving this facility until we let you out for school on Thursday morning. Doctor's orders, with me being the de facto Surgeon General around here."

"Yeah, yeah, I just wanted to visit Craig, okay? I can use the support of my best friend right now."

"We at the Institute are your current best friends for the time being. You can see Craig when you get back to school. And since it's only a day later than you asked, and it's not a life or death type of situation, I don't think you have much to complain about. The only way out of here without you blasting your way out is with the special code. I just changed the code, so only the head of security and myself has it for tonight.

"And if you're fool enough to manage to blast your way out, we'll know faster than you can take your next breath. You do still breathe, right?"

"I seem to, yeah. And fine, I get the gist."

"Good. Then take the gist to bed with you now. It's almost time for lights out."

"Hey, no problem. I have some serious meditating to do tonight anyway."

***

A few short hours later -- at 1:23 AM, to be exact -- Benny opened his eyes. He had just come out of his latest meditative trance, with this one directed towards a very specific purpose.

The practice of probing the universal ether for answers to questions has been given various names through the ages, many of which he learned over his weekend computer research: "cosmic consciousness," "cosmic awareness" (his personal favorite), "reading the Akashic record," "probing the collective universal consciousness," among others. This is precisely what he had attempted to do, all to acquire a very simple answer to a very important query.

I'm very confident those sequential numbers and letters I received in the trance are the no-longer secret security code to this place. I can't freakin' wait to see what else I can do with the psychic aspect of these powers.

Benny now had several hours of practice behind him using a low-level discharge of omni-directional energies at a very specific frequency to morph his bio-mimetic attire into the outward appearance of his costume. He was further confident that he had the process down pat. But he didn't want to take the chance of initiating the sartorial morphing procedure while still in the facility, since he somehow just "knew" special sensors would detect the unavoidable energy surge and alert the security staff. Especially considering the presence of any espers who happened to be present overnight in the facility.

Nonetheless, his newfound power of cosmic awareness that he usually accessed only while in a sleep-like trance was already serving him well.

Benny was determined to get out into the mean streets of Buffalo's West Side after dark to test his mettle as a super-hero. He wasn't going to do everything on Donovan's time table. He realized that he was due many of the restrictions he now had imposed on him by the Institute, but he was determined to never let anyone control him completely.

For the past weekend the metahuman youth studied the facility layout and patrol sequence of the overnight security to know how to make his way to the heavily reinforced exit door on the sneak. He strongly suspected his ability to subliminally but effectively access his cosmic awareness would help in this stealth-oriented task as well.

Benny's faith in his new abilities and early training proved spot on as he quietly reached the dense metal door that led to the stairway, which in turn led to the seemingly ordinary weight-training facility acting as a cover for the Valis Institute. The young man was just about to punch in what he believed to be the exit code on the control pad when a thought suddenly occurred to him.

Wait, shouldn't I come up with a swanky code name before going out for the first time? Yeah, I think I should.

Cosmic Boy, maybe? Nah, that's taken by a character from DC Comics. Cosmic Kid? No, too similar. Hmmm, how about... Centurion? *Yes! I can't exactly go wrong naming myself after a Roman military soldier, right? So, from this night onwards, let the people of this city know that* Centurion *has entered their midst! Woo hoo, w00t w00t, and every other example of positive exclamatory slang I can't think of right now!*

The newly christened hero-in-training carefully punched in the code and found to his delight that he had indeed successfully "pulled" the correct sequence out of the cosmic ether. This was confirmed by the small red light at the top of the keypad turning blue, and the appearance of the *"You May Now Exit"* notation across the digital screen directly to its right.

"Yes!" he shouted in a whispery tone. Then he quickly admonished himself—silently this time—for letting his enthusiasm break his quiet.

Benny slid the heavy door open with no difficulty, albeit as slowly as possible to minimize any accompanying sound. The youthful metahuman then closed it from the other side just as carefully. He found no trouble sneaking out the hidden side door of the surface gymnasium which Donovan had showed him the first night he was taken to the Institute.

The fledgling hero then quickly made his way a few buildings down the street and stepped into a small alley between a tenement building and a small Hispanic smart phone shop to "morph" into his costume. He wanted to put a few buildings between himself and the Institute's sensors, just in case.

Benny stood in the middle of the alley and concentrated. The by now familiar tingle of energy could be felt coursing through his cellular structure, and he released it from every cell of his body in all directions simultaneously.

The low-wave frequency didn't affect the atmosphere, or any surrounding object save for his clothing, which within the span of 1.5 seconds took on the appearance and texture of his costume. Upon its overlay pattern being thus "activated," the now molecularly altered attire fully expanded so the cowl surrounded his head and the gloves covered his hands, with his sneakers and socks appearing to transfigure into the costume's white boots. A quick flash of blue-ish light accompanied the energy emission that triggered the sartorial morphing, as did a short buzzing sound made by the crackling discharge.

Centurion had now successfully donned his costume for the first time in the field. However, the quick moment of illumination that came with the transformation process thoroughly startled a hobo whom he failed to notice was laying curled up in the side of the alley just a few feet from where he stood.

"Huh, wha?" the homeless man uttered as he jumped up into an almost sitting position.

Oh, great, Centurion thought to himself. *I hope he didn't get a good look at me before I morphed into my costume. I doubt it, though, given the darkness of the alley and his obvious state of inebriation. I really* do need to better develop my cosmic awareness, so it warns me of things like this.

"At ease, Mister," the hero-in-training said to the trembling tramp. "It's only the city's newest super-hero. There aren't any phone booths available anymore, so I had to use your alley to change into my working threads. I'm Centurion, by the way. Take care, and, um… get sober, I guess."

With that said, the youthful metahuman shook the hobo's hand and darted out of the alley at great speed. He swiftly proceeded down the lengthy darkened boulevard of Niagara Street. It was a locale where bad things were known to happen all too often, particularly during the night.

"Holy beans," the vagrant said to himself as he checked his bottle to see how much of the cheap whiskey was left. "Did I jest imagine thet? Hope not, 'cause this city rilly needs some he-roes."

He then belched, downed a gulp of hooch, and attempted to go back to sleep in the alley that served as his bedroom.

***

Benny was aware of what an exceptionally dangerous area of Niagara Street the Shoreline Apartments neighborhood happened to be. This was from years of visiting his close friend Craig, who lived just behind the mammoth apartment complex in the section containing the Pine Harbor apartments.

The number of thugs who regularly wandered this area at night to prey upon and intimidate the unwary was something he had personally experienced on more than one occasion during his frequent visits. This included a large number of fellow teens much like those who tormented him at school, but sans any veneer of civilized respectability. He was accustomed to being greatly cautious when meandering about this area, but tonight he finally had the power to reverse the roles by giving a taste of terror to the malefactors who believed they ruled the night here.

The rumor that members of the recently flourishing West Side street gang who called themselves the State Boys had reportedly begun staking out territory here only further disposed the young metahuman to reclaim the streets for the common person. He fully believed that battling the symptoms of crime was no replacement for dealing with the source, which he attributed to the system itself; but he knew that he had to work his way up to that. And sometimes immediate symptoms had to be dealt with, as anyone who ever came down with a case of the flu could readily attest.

Don't be nervous, Benny, he reminded himself as wandered about the strangely Aztec-like architecture of the low-cost Shoreline tenements. *This time,* you *have the power, not the punks who generally terrorize the area.*

Centurion concentrated to summon forth the Odic energies now roiling within his atomic structure. The intense tingle their frequency harmonics sent throughout every cell in his body became clearly discernible to him, which gave further comfort and reassurance that his silent proclamation wasn't just bravado.

He also began focusing his mental faculties to see if his "cosmic awareness" could somehow lead him towards a congregation of "punks" who needed being put paid to. Upon doing so, he did experience a sensation that resembled a notable urge to walk in a specific direction along the south end of the tenement complex.

It was an impression akin to a psychic with a dowsing rod seeking out hidden supplies of water.

This equivalent of a directional tingling sensation, as if he was extracting information directly from the etheric firmament of some vast universal database, proved on target when he reached the designated area of the complex.

There the rookie hero saw a quartet of young men, each of whom appeared between the ages of fifteen and eighteen, pushing a smaller boy in their age group against a side of the tenement's wall. Centurion well understood how painful the ridged stone and mortar of those tenements felt to a mere mortal who was shoved against it.

The sight of that enraged him to the core of his metahuman being, and the powerful Odic energies which now saturated his cellular enclaves began involuntarily surging. His eyes took on their fearsome azure glow as these energies leaked out of his ocular sockets. This luminescence only intensified as memories of the abuse he himself had taken all too often from such individuals began cascading through his mind, much like a series of crude cel animation pages being rapidly flipped through.

Control yourself, Benny, he reminded himself firmly. Accordingly, he struggled to keep his disturbed emotional state and inner rage at bay. Still, sparks of cerulean-hued energy began sizzling around his tightly clenched fists like a swarm of electromagnetic mayflies cavorting over a bluish-hued lamp.

"Let him go," the young hero-in-training commanded. "Or deal with someone who can actually fight back, not to mention annihilate all four of you." *Geeze, that sounded corny. I need to work on my threats.*

"Who in the hell is this?" the tallest gangmember wondered aloud.

"Dunno, he ain't wearing any colors I recognize," said his shorter but bulkier partner-in-terror. "Or any kinda outfit I recognize either. But he makes demands of us in our territory. No one does that."

Attempting his best Michael Keaton imitation, the monochrome-clad metahuman gladly answered the question of the first gang member as to his identity: "*I'm Centurion.*"

The stares of incredulity he garnered in response prompted him to follow that statement up with, "And let me give you fair warning that I can—and will—hurt you badly if you don't release the boy, pack your bags, and move out of this city faster than it took any of your fathers to conceive you. Which I imagine was probably less than a minute."

The tallest of the four hooligans whom Centurion now fully recognized sniggered loudly. "We're the State Boys, bro. This territory is ours. This little freak was trespassing, just like you are. But he wasn't stupid enough to insult our fathers."

So, we're gonna make a bigger example out of you. You're gonna bleed like it's comin' out of a hose, man."

The thug pulled out a retractable switchblade and extended the shiny, razor sharp knife hidden within. He rushed towards Centurion like a cat lunging at an unwary grounded bird, his mouth practically frothing in anticipation of the blood he planned to spill.

Though his training had only recently begun, the young metahuman's reflexes were superhumanly keen, and he easily evaded the slashing blade directed at his throat.

Centurion then instinctively swung his fist in backhanded fashion, moving with such swiftness his arm appeared almost a blur to the human eye. The back of his fist struck the youthful gangbanger in the side of the face, cracking his facial bones from the cheek to the jaw and sending him flying backwards over two dozen feet.

"Holy shit, man!" exclaimed a heavy-set member of the now truncated quartet. "He must be one of those metahumans! Like that Ultimus dude! You're still dead, bitch!"

Centurion found himself genuinely taken aback when the young gang member quickly brandished a concealed firearm. This was an eventuality he failed to consider.

"Waste 'im!" the burly gangbanger shouted.

At this command a shot was fired. Centurion now instantly realized the vast emotional difference between watching a gun pointed at someone on TV and actually having this happen in real life.

Thus, the rookie hero failed to dodge the bullet that was fired at him, and the lead projectile struck him directly in the gut from a few feet away. The impact of the small metallic object carried a force akin to what he always imagined a mule kick to the lower abdomen would feel like.

"Gods, I've... been shot," Centurion choked to himself as he grabbed his stomach area with both hands and fell to his knees.

"Aaahh Jesus!" the gang's young victim screamed. "You shot him! You shot him!"

The gun-wielding gangbanger then turned the weapon to the direction of the screaming young man who was still at their mercy. "Shut 'yo smooth little ass before I put the next one right in 'yo family jewels."

This brief distraction was all it took for Centurion to realize that while he felt the painful wallop of the bullet, it didn't penetrate his skin. No hole was evident in his bio-mimetic costume either, which added further validation to this. No blood could be seen despite his expectation that his hands and the ground directly beneath him would be stained a wet crimson.

Within a moment, his state of shock was replaced by a build-up of anger even greater than that which he felt during his recent encounter with Jeff Wolfe and Mickey Judge.

"You shot meeeeeee!" he bellowed while reflexively extending his arm in the direction of the gunman and summoning the powerful energies his atomic structure was now saturated with.

A searing bolt of sapphire-tinted energy was projected from his cupped hand at the man holding the firearm. The now terror-stricken gang member managed to barely dodge via his street-honed reflexes. That move didn't enable him to escape the effects of the beam unscathed, however.

The bolt of energy hit the brownish surface of the Shoreline tenement just to the side of the remaining trio of gangbangers and their hapless victim. The mortar that was struck exploded outward, spraying the general vicinity with numerous chunks of rocky shrapnel.

The stone debris projected from the damaged infrastructure ripped the skin of both the gun-wielding gang member and the gang's victim in several places. Neither were fatally injured, but both screamed as they hit the ground due to the sizable degree of skin they each had torn from their bodies.

A third member of this party of State Boys, who stood to the left of both, was similarly flogged by debris. This one, however, was more seriously injured when a particularly large shard of mortar smashed into his face, pulverizing his nose into a mass of dripping gore. No scream was emitted from him upon being struck; just a deep sound reminiscent of someone attempting to forcibly vomit before his body met the ground.

In the meantime, the gun-wielding thug laid on his stomach screaming and writhing his extremities like a deranged break dancer. Numerous small shards of mortar were embedded into the tough leather jacket of his back and the denim covering his buttocks, penetrating the clothing and flesh underneath. After coming to a semblance of his senses, he began reaching for his dropped firearm, which now laid a few feet from him.

The still infuriated Centurion was not about to let him retrieve the weapon for another shot, though. That is when something quite unusual happened.

Resulting from a combination of rage and instinct, a pair of twin yellowish beams were unexpectedly projected from Centurion's eyes. These beams focused on the firearm, causing it to burn white hot within seconds of contact.

When the gangbanger grabbed the now shimmering white firearm, he hollered in extreme pain as the skin on his fingers literally cooked upon touching the super-heated metallic surface of the gun. Numerous pus-filled boils became visible on his now deeply red appendages.

Centurion's continuing pain and rage prevented him from fully acknowledging the previously un-manifested use of his power he had just displayed, however. Instead, the livid metahuman rushed towards the final standing gang member, grabbed him by the scruff of his jacket, and hoisted him off the ground with ridiculous ease.

"Easy, man! I can get y'all a good deal on some really good stuff…!"

But Centurion wasn't listening. Instead, he simply flung the gang member up against the still intact portion of the stone-ridged tenement. He could hear the youth's ribs and possibly some of his vertebrae crack upon the impact. A trickle of blood dribbled down the side of his mouth as he slumped to the grass unmoving.

"Oh, my gods, what did I just do?" the hero-in-training said to himself while literally shaking with recriminations. "I lost it again. The guy I was trying to help was injured. No no no, this is not how the first outing of a super-hero is supposed to go. It never happens like this in the comic books."

Centurion rushed towards the fallen bodies before him to see to their condition. He first tended to the boy whom he tried to save from the gang. The young victim was shuddering in pain and shock, the only words leaving his mouth forming a repetitious series of statements alluding to how much pain he was in.

"I'm so sorry…" Centurion said with an overwhelming level of remorse.

The youthful superhuman suddenly became determined to attempt using the Odic energies for healing. He placed his palm on the injured boy's chest and concentrated on building an entirely different frequency of energy. It pulsated with gentler but still intense rhythms, and he let it pour in flowing streams directly from his hand and into the victim's cellular structure.

This type of energy manifested as a slightly lighter hue of blue luminescence, akin to the sky on a sunny cloudless day. Though it caused no further damage, it didn't seem to have any beneficial effect either. At least, none that were readily discernible. The injured boy merely seemed to gasp a bit louder as his chest took on an eerie blueish incandescence for a few moments.

Centurion finally gave up, after which he pulled out the special cell phone the Institute had given him. It was a device that sent out texts and calls along a private and heavily encrypted satellite receiver, and he used it to summon an ambulance.

Knowing that the rescue vehicle would be along soon, he fled the area and headed back towards the neighborhood where the Institute was located. The adolescent hero lacked any inclination to speak to the police, whom he knew would doubtless also be arriving; and he felt he had already sufficiently apprised the EMT dispatcher of the situation despite the haste he felt was necessary.

Centurion quickly headed back towards the Institute, intending to sneak back in with no one the wiser. However, as he moved within one block of the hidden

Christofer Nigro

location, the young man caught sight of something that made him wonder if having confronted the police would have been easier to face.

It was none other than a very irate-looking Donovan Jakes, with two fully geared up Institute security guards flanking him.

"Benjamin," the lead agent said with a scathing deep voice. "Come with us. *Now.*"

"Oh crap…" were the only words that the would-be hero's larynx could form.

123

Chapter 14: Year of the Cat

Tabatha 'Tabbie' Morales was used to running away. She had been doing so since she was a wee lass of eleven, and at this point in her young life—the age of fourteen—she was no stranger to living on the streets. They were as much home to her by now as the interior of any particular house, no matter who its owners may have been.

Never, however, did she expect her life on the streets to take the turn it would once she was exposed to the local Warp Event when its otherworldly energies blanketed the Buffalo area in a moment of intense fiery blue candela. Her rapidly fading human thoughts recalled how she was squatting in a Lower West Side back alley to relieve herself when the strange flash suddenly seemed to envelop the entire world for a brief two seconds.

Her personal world was to be immediately altered in a most nightmarish manner.

At first, Tabbie bid this eerie light little attention due to its extreme brevity. She likewise attributed the strange images that filled her mind during the light show to be the result of hunger-induced hallucinations, or something like that.

But within several seconds of exposure to this mysterious light, she first noticed the intense itching sensation over every inch of her skin. She scratched until she made herself bleed in several places even more intensely than the deliberate cutting she used to inflict upon her mocha-colored skin as a means of venting her feelings of anger and lack of control over her life.

Within an hour she began seeing the beginning of the strange hairs emerging from her outer dermis. They appeared first in the sections of skin on her arms that she cut open with her incessant scratching. This process grew more pronounced over the following two hours as her nails grew longer and sharper, and the light ochre-colored but smooth hair began covering more and more of her body.

By the middle of the evening, she was so uncomfortable in her clothing that she tore much of it off, shredding it with her now talon-like nails as if it were paper.

Tabbie then realized her body had become almost entirely hirsute, with a covering of hair that much more resembled the smooth coat of fur which belonged to a cat than anything human. The light ochre coat had many darker stripes running through it.

Upon seeing this, Tabbie attempted to scream, "Oh my God!" in Spanish, but the words instead came out resembling a scratchy, barely intelligible string of sounds.

The freakishly transformed young girl then felt the urge to seek cover. To that end, she began darting about with a degree of speed the best athletes in her former school's cross country team couldn't match. Accompanying her lithe movements was a display of agility greatly surpassing any feat she or her co-players on her old middle school gymnastics team had ever accomplished. The color imagery which her visual acuity was accustomed began being rapidly replaced with dull but vibrant patterns of heat.

The girl's initial terror and revulsion at what she had become, along with the startling confusion over the myriad scents that began assailing her olfactory senses, were quickly replaced with far more simple thoughts and feelings. These included a sense of oneness with the urban streets and back alleys that she now considered not merely a home, but her territory.

These feelings of possessiveness towards the back alleys in her claimed vicinity led to extreme anger directed towards anyone or anything that dared to enter what she felt to be her rightful domain. This feeling was primal, and nothing her formerly human mind could ever conceive of or relate to.

A few days later, mailman Ernesto Gutierrez was to be the first unfortunate individual to inadvertently cross into Tabbie's newly claimed territory. This occurred in the earliest hour of his usual route, as he walked past an alley on Budd Street.

As he did so, Ernesto heard an intense and rather disturbing sound that resembled an animal ravenously eating a moist fruit. His curiosity being piqued, the mail deliverer stepped slowly into the garbage-encrusted contours of the narrow passage between two abandoned houses from which the sound appeared to have originated. The courier then adjusted his vision to see what he at first took to be a large ochre-colored dog tearing away at the flesh of a smaller dog that to his eyes was most likely a terrier.

It was when this creature looked up that Ernesto suddenly observed, to his unremitting horror, that it was no large breed of dog he was looking at but something human-shaped. Its slim bodily contours suggested a female, which appeared even more terrifyingly clear to him when he saw that the upper abdomen of this creature appeared to have two rows of four small breasts.

The face of this creature vaguely made him think "human" ... but *only* vaguely. Her protruding ears were pointed upwards; the nose was small, hairless, and tan; her eyes, greenish with a horizontal slit denoting the iris; and her razor-sharp teeth were gluttonously devouring the innards of her slaughtered prey. The latter of which turned out to be, on this closer inspection, not a small breed of canine but a large rat.

Upon having her meal interrupted by this interloper, the female creature gracefully but frighteningly jumped to two feet in a crouched position, and then pulled back a set of thick red lips to bare her blood-covered incisors. She emitted a dry hissing growl of clear and present hostility that chilled the reliable mail-deliverer right down to the marrow of his bones. He screamed in terror and fled the alley.

But the roughly humanoid animal that was once Tabbie Morales would forgive no such intrusion on her domain by one of those fragile hair-deficient creatures that infested the urban landscape she called home. The newly transformed Tabbie couldn't kill them all, or even most of them, but she would gladly make exceptions for those who directly invaded whatever alley or other space served as her personal sanctuary at any given time.

Ernesto ran impressively fast for a mere human, but he couldn't outrun the thing that Tabbie had become. She dashed with an odd but effective ever-changing combo of bipedal and quadrupedal locomotion that overcame the man's panicked sprint within seconds.

The girl-beast leaped upon his back and tore clear through the material of his uniform, ripping deep into the muscle of his flesh. Ernesto screamed in agony and even more terror as he realized that he was now paralyzed since his bestial pursuer dug into his spinal cord and severed numerous key nerves along the way. Before he could regain any semblance of his senses, the she-predator had torn several chunks of his buttocks and legs from his body.

Though members of the species she used to belong to weren't Tabbie's usual prey of choice, she found the meat taken from them to be pleasant enough to her palate. And despite the abundance of rodents and a fair supply of stray dogs to serve as her primary food source, the former Morales girl would never refuse any good meat from another source that opportunistically came to her attention.

***

When the EMT's pulled Ernesto Gutierrez into the ambulance, he was barely alive and most definitely not intact. Tabbie didn't leave much flesh and skin on his lower extremities. Worse, the man had lost even more blood than flesh. As he was hauled into the rescue vehicle to be rushed to the hospital, the victim of the she-creature's ghastly predation drifted into and out of consciousness; during the brief and tortured moments when he was awake, only two words left his mouth.

The EMT that rode in the back of the ambulance with him briefly lifted the oxygen mask to hear what he was trying to say. "*Niña Gata*," was all that was uttered.

Being of Latino lineage himself, the EMT realized these Spanish words translated into English as "cat-girl." They would be the last words ever spoken by Ernesto before he mercifully drifted into a coma.

***

"Look, I never said I was going to let you control me completely, Donovan!" Benny protested from within the confines of his detention-cell-cum-quarters. "I tried to do the right thing! It's not like I targeted former classmates who bullied me this time. These were gang members who were assaulting an innocent victim."

The deep red pallor on Donovan's face didn't fade in the slightest at the metahuman youth's statement of defense.

"First of all, Benny-boy, this is not about taking fascist control over you. Like it or not, you are still my prisoner for *your actions* upon acquiring your powers, not because I'm some black ops general looking to conscript metahumans in the service of war! You need to be put under some measure of lock and key until you can be properly trained and healed of the emotional scars that caused you to become a public menace!"

"I know, but…"

"I wasn't finished! Don't interrupt my disciplinary spiel again, kid. Especially not when I'm on a roll."

Benny lifted his hands in an "okay, fine" gesture and remained silent.

"Secondly, because you're under detention right now, you can't just slip out of here! And considering how Claire let me know that you were likely telling the truth about how you obtained the special pass code, because of you this entire facility will be on complete lock-down over night. No code will be capable of opening that door until then; it can only be opened by a special electronic key that has no code with symbols that you can pull out of the ether, or wherever-the-hell you snatched them out of! And only two people on this planet have such an electronic key, one of whom isn't anywhere in New York State.

"As for your attempt to play hero without proper training, you not only severely injured those gang members, but you also injured the kid you were trying to save just as badly! And that's not to speak of the property damage you caused that's going to come out of the city's already strained budget."

Benny looked down and clamped his eyes shut. "Okay, okay, I done messed up. I know that. But I was just a bit eager to make up for what I did…"

"You will pay off your debt to society on *my* frigging time table, not yours! Do you realize the trouble you caused? The media already reported a new 'hero' in their midst, and Commissioner Frakes is having a pissing fit over it."

"Didn't you mean 'hissy fit?'"

"Shut up! I'll use whatever terminology I please to make my points, kid! You're now under more severe detainment! A less comfortable room, as well as all cell phone, Internet, computer, TV, and video game privileges removed! And no writing outside of your school assignments until I say different."

"Donovan, I understand you're quite peeved right now, and that I brought it on myself again. But I'm hoping to make a living off my writing…"

"You don't have to worry about making a goddamned living while you're a prisoner of the Institute! We pay the bills for your upkeep right now! Do you dig it?"

"Okay, okay. I dig it. And I'm sorry, alright?"

"Not nearly as sorry as you'll be if you even consider committing another infraction of any sort! If I find out that you so much as left the toilet seat up, you'll be going into third level detainment!"

"Donovan, what difference does it make if I leave the toilet seat up when the only toilet I can use right now is in the detention cell with me? And besides, I don't even seem to really need to use the bathroom anymore…"

"Shut up! It's bad enough I have to let you return to the school tomorrow to avert suspicion from your involvement in this. But you will be returning there with a few hidden escorts."

"You seriously mean…?"

"I was never *more* serious! You messed up, so you're getting babysat until I'm confident that you will trust me enough to play things my way."

"Look… I know I messed up. I'll follow your lead from now on in terms of timetable. I really want to use my power for the right reasons. But my principles and autonomy will always come first, as soon as I've served my 'sentence' or whatever words you would use to describe it."

"I think 'sentence' fits your situation just fine. But I have to grant you the equivalent of 'school release' during the morning and early afternoon hours. Then you come directly back here, and here you stay until I say different. And that will be your routine until after you've completed a lot more training to control those powers and received a good deal more counseling to control those damaged emotions. Understand?"

Benny stood at a mock "at ease" position. "Sir, yes, sir!"

Donovan glowered. "You're in no position to be a wise ass right now, kid."

***

The training chamber was momentarily filled with a bright blue incandescence as Benny utilized one of his energy beams to punch a small hole in a huge cinderblock. It was projected from the tip of his extended right index finger.

He then immediately turned and released another bolt of azure energy from his outstretched hand, this one much greater in width but packing less of a punch. That second beam knocked a duo of weighted human-shaped mannequins off a platform where they were situated.

"Excellent work, kid," the supervising Donovan Jakes said with genuine approval. "You successfully focused your first beam to do only very precise, localized damage to the cinderblock. That means you're capable of busting a lock on a door without blowing it off its hinges and taking the surrounding wall with it.

"As for the second target, you knocked those specially weighted mannequins down without smashing them to pieces or punching holes through them. That means, based on the empirical lack of damage and the degree of force measured by the computer, you're fully capable of hitting a pair of humans with just enough force to knock them silly without causing serious harm or death."

"Go me!" the teen self-cheered with a raised fist.

"Don't get too cocky, Benny-boy. You still have a long way to go before you can even begin to feel secure in the control of those powers. For instance, you still haven't figured out how to project different forms of electromagnetic energy despite managing to let loose those ocular heat beams while under extreme emotional duress during your unauthorized night out.

"And then there's the full extent of those strange ESP-like abilities you refer to as 'cosmic awareness' to contend with. This power appears similar in some ways to those of our own espers, but also dissimilar in other ways; not to mention covering a far wider range of potential uses. It somewhat resembles a form of psychic surveillance referred to as 'remote viewing.'"

"I spent the past six days in constant training for eight hours at a time, starting immediately after returning from school. That was followed by twelve hours throughout the day on weekends with no personal time allotted to me. I'm trying to put forth a real effort to make amends and finish serving my 'time.'"

"Did that statement include a veiled insinuation that you would like to know when you're going to be released from your 'grounding?'"

"That's a fair assumption to make, Donovan."

"And I answered that question more than once already: When I feel you have both acquired sufficient training to control those powers effectively and healed enough that your mind is no longer filled with thoughts of hatred and revenge. Then there's the matter of your much-deserved punishment being fulfilled to my satisfaction."

"You're just loving this power trip, aren't you, dude?"

Donovan literally raised his left eyebrow and anxiously scratched his goatee. "I beg your pardon, kid? As in… *excuse me?*"

"I just want you to be upfront with me about whether or not I'll ever be free to operate as a hero according to my own volition. I told you, I'll graciously accept the punishment and training, but I won't accept being lied to, or controlled indefinitely."

"And I told you that I won't lie to you, kid. You're just going to have to trust me on this."

"Donovan, for cripe's sakes! You're not accountable to anyone, including any laws that may guarantee me a finite amount of time in confinement if I fulfill the obligations and pay my debt to society. 'When Donovan Jakes feels like letting you off' doesn't sound like any form of due process to me."

"But you're going to have to accept it as the way things are. Because that *is* the way things are, Benny. Your debt will be paid in accordance with my discretion and judgement."

"I think it's at least time you told me where all the funding for this very elaborate Valis operation is coming from. And how we can both be sure that it's not actually about conscripting and controlling metahumans as involuntary soldiers or corporate-controlled mercenaries for the U.S. war machine."

"I've seen no sign of suspicious activity or foul play in this set-up so far, Benny. I give you my word on that."

"But you have suspicions that this whole operation may not live up to what it purports to be, right? I can sense those doubts in your mind, Donovan. Don't give me any bullshit."

"You're claiming to be empathic now?"

"Yes. I was straight with you about this, so *don't* lie to me about the Valis Institute."

Donovan paused and took a loud exhalation of frustrated acquiescence. "Okay, look, kid. What I just told you was the truth. You have my word on that. I too have some questions about where the funds are coming from, though I assure you that I'll look into the matter every spare moment I have. Alright?"

"Slight amendment to that: *We'll* look into the matter during *our* spare time. Do not expect me to be passive about the whole thing while you play Sherlock Holmes on your own. I plan to earn your trust, but you and Valis need to do the same in return."

Donovan paused while gritting his teeth. "Fine, kid, but we pursue this thing my way. Investigations also require finesse and training. So, if you even *think* of going into this half-cocked…"

Suddenly, the familiar screech of the facility-wide intercom beeper reverberated through the training chamber. Donovan looked on his watch-shaped wrist communicator, which identified the call as coming from Claire. He knew she wouldn't interrupt these training sessions unless the matter was urgent.

The soldier tapped the button on his communicator, which was disguised as the crown of the stop-watch. "What's going on, Claire?"

"Donovan, there's been an incident in the city that I believe involves a rogue metahuman. And it's nasty enough to require your immediate attention."

Donovan shook his head. *Like I need another one of those right now,* he thought. "All right, I'll meet you in the tactics chamber. Donovan out."

"Let me come and help," Benny practically pleaded. "If you're serious about letting me become a bona fide super-hero, and happy with the progress of my training, then at least let me attend the briefing. Let's hear what Claire has to report, and you can determine if I might be of some help."

"Benny…"

"Donovan, please don't '*Benny…*' me. I need to know you were serious. And I need to know you believe I can be of help. I both want and need to make those amends we talked about."

The young metahuman's tone was both calm and impassioned, with no hint of rudeness or demand. And its high level of sincerity washed over Donovan like a spilled bucket of warm water.

"Come with me, kid."

The veteran soldier walked out of the training chamber with a smiling Benny Lonero tagging close behind. The teen's first mission against a metahuman threat was soon to commence.

***

"This is a pic of the victim acquired from the crime scene," Claire Boone said in a somber tone. "He slipped into a coma while en route to the hospital. His injuries appeared to have been inflicted by some wild animal with claw and tooth marks somewhat resembling a cougar, or some other big cat. In fact, according to the EMT who rode in the back of the ambulance with him, the last thing he was heard to say before going comatose was 'Niña Gata,' which is Spanish for 'cat-girl.'"

Benny looked over the grotesque digital photos of Ernesto Gutierrez's injuries displayed on the screen in front of them with a combination of intrigue and revulsion. The young hero-in-the-making was both nervous and excited about the prospect of pitting his newfound powers against the might of whatever could wreak such horrific damage upon a human being. And he prayed his own power and training would be up to the task, lest he end up the same way as the unfortunate Mr. Gutierrez.

"Are you saying this is the work of an out of place animal that's currently loose in the city?" Donovan queried. "There have been reports of strange teleportations of that nature in areas struck by the Warp Events, and…"

"No, I'm pretty sure that's not the case here, Donovan," Claire politely interjected. "The impressions I received upon concentrating was that of, well, a big feline of some sort that was once… well, human."

"You mean like a were-cat?" Benny asked.

"I mean, like a metahuman whose metamorphosis following exposure to the Odic energies of the Warp Event took an extreme bestial form," Claire replied. "There are also reports of a runaway teen girl last seen in that area just before the Warp Event, and I get the strong impression this 'Niña Gata' creature may be… well, her."

"Have there been any unusual cryptid sightings fitting your given description in the designated area over the past few weeks?" Donovan asked.

"I looked through all the databases that collect such reports," Claire responded, "and the answer to that is 'yes.' But the reports are very furtive, as the creature in those sightings appears to be as stealth-capable as the typical cryptid. But I doubt this formerly human creature is an etheric entity that engages in temporary quasi-corporeal manifestations, as many cryptids actually are. I think she is fully biological and permanently corporeal in nature."

"You're correct on that, Claire," Benny said with full confidence.

Both Donovan and Claire turned their heads from the data appearing on the large flat screen monitor mounted to the wall before them.

"What makes you think that, Benny?" Donovan inquired.

"I just focused my own degree of concentration into this situation," the young fledgling hero said. "It's not as effective as when I go into a full meditative trance, but I did receive the, I dunno, the impression that this is a biological creature resulting from a human being mutated—or whatever you want to call it—by the Warp Event energies."

"Oh God…" Claire muttered. "Donovan, we need to bring this girl in and help her. I know what she did was horrible, but I don't think it was out of malice or mental instability. The thought impressions I get from her are so primal, as if she is operating on the level of a particularly cunning animal. But taking her in without killing or severely injuring her will be exceedingly difficult, not to mention incredibly dangerous for any agents you may send out."

"Not all my agents, Claire," Donovan said as he turned to the boy sitting beside him. "Benny, do you think 'Centurion' is ready for a serious field mission?"

"Just point me in the right direction," Benny replied with forced self-assurance. "I totally got this."

Chapter 15: Centurion vs. Niña Gata

It was a damp Friday evening as the first sign of the bitter Buffalo winter to come had chilled the air. It was this same evening that Donovan Jakes had decided Benny would be up for his first metahuman confrontation, albeit one carefully monitored by the Institute.

The sight of the young metahuman in his costume, along with the mission commander and fellow soldier Sasheen Kahn attired in his discrete combat raiment, had caught the eye of Gail Parker as she passed them in the corridor.

"Um, out for a stroll this evening, are we?" she remarked with a bitter tone. "I see the kid's detention turned out to be short after all."

"At ease, Parker," Donovan said. "This isn't a night on the town for him. He's going to make himself useful by dealing with our problem down in the Virginia Street area."

Gail huffed loudly. "Seriously, Donovan? After what this little prick did to Eddie? What he did to those other kids? And after the way he recently broke out of custody and wounded a civilian while haphazardly trying to play 'hero?' You're letting him out and trusting him to do *this?*"

"Whoa, Gail," Sasheen reacted with instinctive concern. "That was a bit harsh, don't you think? He's trying to make amends…"

"Bullshit!" Gail exclaimed. "Eddie has a hole the size of a fist in the side of his abdomen thanks to this little bastard!"

Centurion wisely kept his mouth shut, but his countenance still took on an angry expression. Small arcs of energy began forming around his now tightly clenched fists. This did not escape Gail's notice. She immediately brandished her taze rifle and pointed it at the young man.

"Go ahead and raise a hand to me, you son of a bitch!" she hollered. "Do it!"

Donovan quickly stepped between the two and shoved Gail's hand down. "Parker, let's step into the office over there. Now!"

The tough brunette agent forced herself to withhold uttering any further statements in the corridor and took an angry stride into the nearest office her commanding officer pointed to. Donovan followed her in and shut the door behind them, but not before he turned to the two young men standing outside.

"Sasheen, keep an eye on him while I deal with this," he commanded. "And Benny, you keep your cool. That's an order."

"Yes, sir," Sasheen said in compliance just before putting a reassuring hand on Centurion's shoulder.

"Please stay at ease, Benny," the tough albeit good-hearted soldier said. "You need to understand that Gail didn't mean that. She was just good friends with Eddie, and…"

"Sasheen, I've had enough people hate me to realize that she *totally* meant it," Benny replied. "I know what I did was wrong, and I'm trying to make up for it. I plan to earn my respect here. But she is never going to let this go, never going to abandon this reason to hate me; and sooner or later she is going to make a serious move against me. When that happens, I'm not going to have any choice but to…"

"Now it's my turn to tell *you* 'whoa there!'" the thin but strong soldier of Middle Eastern descent interjected. "Donovan is going to handle this. I'm a friend of Gail too. Neither of us are going to let it come to that. You and Gail are on the same team, and in time, she will realize that.

"And by the way, Eddie is going to be all right. You didn't seriously injure him thanks to his body armor and you holding back like you did. He's just under medical observation right now."

"I appreciate your telling me this, Sasheen. And I have no doubt that you and Donovan will do all you can to keep Gail from going postal over this. But it's not going to matter, I can tell you that right now. No one who has ever hated me has ever 'gotten over it.'"

"Stifle the cynicism due to the past, my friend," Sasheen advised. "Your life is completely different now. I believe in you, and Donovan believes in you. You have a lot to look forward to in the future."

"But not all of it good, I'm guessing."

Centurion's voice had a solemn and ominous pretension when he said that.

***

Behind the closed door of the conveniently chosen office, Donovan was making his displeasure with the scene Gail had just caused in the outside corridor quite clear.

"What in the hell was that all about, girl? You should have known better than to provoke Benny like that, after all the time I've spent trying to rehabilitate him!"

"Oh, come on now, Donovan!" Gail rejoined. "That little punk is a menace, and you know it! He should never be trusted on a mission, let alone one as important as this! He's already proven what a dangerous and unstable psycho he is, and he already made an unauthorized departure from this facility! Even putting Eddie aside, does it make no difference to you what he did to those fellow students he attacked?"

"Of course, it does, Gail. Which is why he's under my confinement and rehabilitation! What he did was very wrong, but those kids and others like them pushed him relentlessly, over and over again, until he snapped; and his home life wasn't so great either. He had virtually no support from anywhere. And the thing is, he never attacked an innocent. It's obvious he actually held back while attacking those idiotic bullies."

Gail's voice increased in fevered volume as her eyes began producing tears. "No innocents? What about Eddie! *Eddie!* Who was injured while trying to stop that little maniac! Did you forget Eddie?"

"Eddie was a soldier who attacked Benny first, even if it was the right thing to do. The kid was in a terrible state of mind, and he simply defended himself. Yes, Eddie was in the right, and he's a good soldier and a true hero. And because of that, he knew the risks of the job. But he was *not* an innocent! He was a combatant who fully realized his target would likely return fire."

"And it doesn't matter what Lonero did to Eddie while he was under your command? He hurt Eddie and could have killed him!"

"What happened to Eddie affected me strongly, Gail. But as I said, he's a soldier who knew the risks, and on top of that, Benny held back while attacking him too. He could have blown Eddie in half, but he didn't. And Eddie received no injury he won't fully heal from in time. You need to deal with this and stop letting your personal feelings for Eddie cause you to provoke Benny every time you see him!"

"Dammit, Donovan, you're acting more like a social worker with that kid than a jail warden! As far as you seem concerned, he's not getting punished, but he's become your newest recruit and prize student! You even let him go back to school as if nothing happened! And after what he did there!"

"He's being monitored at the school at all times. A few Institute agents have been assigned there posing as staff. Nothing will happen that they cannot nip in the bud, or that I won't know about."

"And are these agents sufficient to take Lonero down if he does go crazy again? How many innocents might he take with him to get at the next kid who says a few harsh words to him?"

Donovan had finally had enough, and he was determined to make this clear.

"Alright, I'm *ordering* you to stop this, Gail. Now! You're beginning to head down the same road that you're condemning Benny for going; and for the same reason he did. Yes, he is my newest recruit, because he's not a bad kid! He's deeply emotionally scarred, and he did an awful thing as a result. But he didn't go so far that he can't be redeemed. I've seen worse than him turn out okay when the proper degrees of training, respect, purpose, and responsibility were given to them."

"You know that's a load of bull, Donovan! You just feel sorry for him because he's a stupid kid…!"

"No, it's not a load of bull, Gail! I'm a prime example of the point I'm trying to make here! I was once more messed up inside than him, even if not for the same reasons. My life would have turned into a serious tragedy if I hadn't met Sgt. Miller at exactly the time that I did. He believed in me and saw the spark of good I had buried within; something that I, and practically no one else in my life, knew was there. So, don't you go telling me that I don't know what the hell I'm talking about!"

Gail tried very hard to remember the respect that her commanding officer had legitimately earned, not to mention that which was due to him based on chain of command protocol. She thus struggled to control her growing ire.

"That kid is *nothing* like you, Donovan. Nothing whatsoever!"

"You only think that because you didn't know me back then, Gail. I'm thankful you didn't, otherwise you would probably have had a similar hissy fit with Sgt. Miller."

"You're making a big mistake here, Donovan. I'm not going to just ignore what he did to Eddie and all the rest because of this misguided soft spot of yours for punks like Lonero."

"Okay, let me end this waste of time argument by saying this.

"You are under strict orders to leave Benny alone. That means *you stay the hell away from him*, in case you need that spelled out for you. You will not approach him under any circumstances without my authorization. You will not speak to him under any circumstances without my prior authorization. You will not be assigned to any detail that is connected to him in any way, save possibly for certain extenuating circumstances that I, and only I, may authorize.

"If you have any problem with this then I order you to come clean with me about it right now, and I will reassign you to a facility in another warp-affected city that is outside of New York State. Or maybe it would be best to remove you from 'defense' and place you in an administrative position instead, if you can't emotionally handle the rigors of this station. Speak now or forever hold your peace on this subject!"

The tough as nails young woman gritted her teeth with such force that she thought their enamel might crack. But after a few seconds of silence, she reined in her fearsome temper, and the reddish pallor that stained her lovely facial features promptly dissipated.

"No… *sir*. I have no problem with these orders."

"Good. Because that is the end of this." Donovan went silent for a moment, then spoke again in a gentler tone.

"Listen, Gail… I respect you and trust you a lot, because you've earned it. There are few soldiers I'd rather have at my side than you. So, *do not* make me and everyone else concerned regret my not re-assigning you to another facility right here and now. You're dismissed, Agent Parker."

Donovan then turned and walked out the door, leaving it partially open. Gail remained inside with a heated expression marring her attractive visage. She was determined not to leave the room until Centurion was completely out of her line of sight.

This isn't over, you little bastard, the formidable femme ruminated to herself as she struggled to maintain her silence.

***

Virginia Street was known to be one of the most dangerous and crime-ridden boulevards of Buffalo's Lower West Side, but this evening Centurion traipsed across its dark thoroughfare with no fear of any human opposition. He was quite anxious, however, about the imminent prospect of knocking heads with some serious *metahuman* opposition that was outside the controlled circumstances of The Stadium. This was serious stuff, the veritable real deal, and he pushed himself to show courage in the face of it.

Centurion had actually come to respect Donovan Jakes, and wanted to prove that the soldier's faith in him was justified and not a miscalculation on his part. The hero-in-training couldn't stomach the thought of embarrassing both himself and Donovan by proving Gail Parker and other detractors correct.

Centurion scanned the decrepit houses and darkened driveways with eyesight superior to that of a normal human. The sorry condition of the surrounding infrastructure and rows of cheap cars in poor condition gave the area a grimy look that made him cringe. His own neighborhood was nothing to be impressed about, but it didn't compare to this degree of decrepitude.

Donovan is insane if he ever expects me to be loyal to a system that forces people in today's day and age to live like this. But as he would tell me if I commented aloud about it right now, "Keep your damned idealistic politics to yourself and focus on the task at hand, kid!"

Centurion called upon his recent training and endeavored to keep to the shadows as much as possible while he commenced his search for whatever awaited him here. At the same time, he attempted to focus his "cosmic awareness" to alert him to anything dangerous that may be lurking beside him in the grungy darkness.

"Are you okay out there, Centurion?" Donovan asked over the mini-communicator embedded within the youth's right ear.

The fledgling teen hero put his finger to his outer canal and voiced a response. "Yes, Mother, I'm fine. I even made sure to look both ways when I crossed the street."

"Don't be your usual wise ass self, kid. Agent Kahn and I are in the van two blocks down, but right now, you're on your own. This is your first time in the field against…"

"… a metahuman threat," Centurion finished for his mentor and commanding officer. "Yes, I understood that by the fifth time you explained it to me. But so far, all is quiet, and… wait."

A strange, intense sensation began permeating the interior of his skull, as if some sort of warning beacon was triggered. A nightmare-inducing image suddenly filled his mind.

"What is it, Agent Centurion? Do you see something?"

"No, not exactly. But I seem to be sensing…"

The young champion's sentence was abruptly cut off as a powerful hirsute form leapt out from under a concealing pile of refuse and slammed into him with sufficient force to knock him clear off his feet.

He landed in front of a nearby driveway to find himself under the savage assault of a bestial creature the likes of which he never imagined existing outside of the horror films he frequently streamed online. The adolescent hero could feel this entity's extended claws raking gashes through the super-durable skin on his facial area. The suddenness of the brutal attack and the pain he felt as a result caused him to panic.

"Ahhhhh shit!" he shouted, while he struggled to shove the fiendish attacker off him.

Niña Gata's only reply was a wicked and savage hissing growl that mirrored the maniacal fury of her attack.

"Centurion, what is it?" Donovan queried frantically over the communicator. "Do you need assistance? You better not have just stepped in dog shit!"

But Centurion was in no position to tap the mini-device with his index finger and reply. Rather, he was in the desperate position of trying to prevent his eyes from being clawed out of their sockets.

Clearly not expecting the levels of strength, speed, and sheer ferocity wielded by the cat-girl, the inexperienced young hero was becoming overwhelmed with sheer terror and physical pain as the she-beast continued ripping into his facial skin. Within several seconds, though, that feeling was replaced with anger and a determined resolve to get that creature the hell off him.

By forcing himself to act Centurion finally managed to grab the creature's wrists and pull them away from him with a towering strength that surpassed her own. He then buckled his legs underneath the female manimal until the soles of his boots were pressed against her lower abdomen.

"Get… off!" he hollered as he pushed his legs forward with all his superhuman might.

The resulting double kick flung Niña Gata through the air for over a hundred feet, until she made a painful crash into several large plastic garbage containers that were issued to all residents of the city. Her agility proved astounding, however, and she quickly leaped into a quadrupedal stance.

Though taken aback by the atypical power of this seemingly human transgressor of her territory, the bestial femme fatale's animalistic rage allowed her to ignore the sharp pain cutting through her rib cage like several hot needles.

"Graahh!" Centurion bellowed in fury as he jumped back to his feet and released a beam of incandescent bluish energy in his adversary's general direction.

The cat-girl managed to leap out of the way at just the right second, causing the searing ray to instead strike the downed garbage dispensers. The thick blue plastic sizzled away as the refuse contained within was blown across the driveway by the force of the blast.

"Agent Centurion, you had best tell us what the hell is going on, or we're coming out there now!" Donovan demanded.

"I have contact with the enemy, for crying out loud!" the teen responded as quickly as he could. "She's a nasty little number, but I'm going to *bust her ass*!"

"Her?"

"She… it… whatever! It sort of looked like a girl, okay? I have to sign off, I'm on this!"

So, Claire was right then, Donovan thought to himself. "Hold it! What type of damage did you do with that energy beam we just heard you discharge?"

But Centurion didn't respond. He took on radio silence to focus his full attention on rushing into the driveway and looking in every direction for his quarry, determined to strike her before she struck him again. Though he wasn't yet fully aware of this, the vicious cuts permeating his face were rapidly healing.

As he ran into the section of the expansive yard that led towards a garage capable of holding the cars of four residents, the buzzing sensation in the front section of his skull suddenly "went off" at full intensity again. This time the youthful hero reacted to it just quickly enough to turn as Niña Gata leapt at him from atop the roof of a nearby tool shack.

The ferocious cat-creature again struck Centurion with enough force to send him back against the wall of the home covering the eastern section of the driveway. And once again, she attacked her monochrome-clad opponent with an incredible degree of inhuman fury, hissing and howling with sounds akin to an enraged bobcat combined with a woman's shriek.

The beast girl tore at her opponent's face a few times before his superhumanly keen reflexes and recent training combined to enable him to block her furious fusillade of blows. Nevertheless, her powerful talons cut through the sleeves of his costume and ripped into the uber-tough flesh below the bio-mimetic material. The material immediately began resealing along with his skin, but the amount of damage his adversary was inflicting began taxing his Odic-charged healing ability.

This time, though, Centurion's feeling of desperation and fear quickly escalated into a primordial wrath of his own. His inner resolve now refused to allow him to tremble helplessly while he was brutalized by another, no matter how vicious or strong they may be.

Shouting once more in defiance, the young hero grabbed one of the cat-girl's flaying arms along with her throat in his steely grip. Niña Gata struggled with relentless fury to get loose, but Centurion's grip prevailed for the moment.

Despite being rapidly choked into submission with one arm held fast and the other unable to find a position to strike, the cat-girl's cunning would quickly prove as formidable as her strength and ferocity.

She lifted both of her legs, extended the claws that were once human toenails, and used them to slice Centurion's stomach area. Both his bio-memetic uniform and skin beneath received two sets of five deep tears. Blood flowed out of the hero's gut in concert with a sharp pain exploding across his abdomen.

"Aaarrggh!" Centurion screamed. "Oh, you bitch!"

Even though the sudden painful injury caused him to release Niña Gata, he was angry enough to push past the pain and get into a practiced fighting stance. The cat-girl rushed her adversary, hissing and growling with an unbridled ferociousness. She slashed maniacally with her hand claws, forcing Centurion to the defensive and he instinctively placed his forearms in front of his face and eyes to protect them.

More tears in his uniform and skin were received even as the cruel wounds on his abdomen began sealing, with the bleeding already having almost completely ceased.

The she-beast then jumped forward and closed her jaws on her opponent's left arm, sinking her small but razor-sharp teeth deep into his skin. Centurion yelped in pain and found himself driven back against the tenement wall behind him. Niña Gata then leapt on the costumed teen and her needle-like teeth went for his face.

However, Centurion's reflexes proved even faster than her feline-like speed. Before her teeth could bite into his forehead region the hero grasped her throat in both of his hands, holding her in a choking grip and spoiling the move. She struggled furiously but was again held fast.

"You are really starting to piss me off!" Centurion decreed.

He then immediately pulled her felinoid head towards him as he delivered a nasty headbutt to her nasal region. Niña Gata's cat-like nose was smashed, and the severe pain caused the were-feline to back away. Severely stunned, she covered her face with both hands. Blood could be seen spewing out the gaps between her hirsute fingers.

"Time to end this!"

Centurion took advantage of his foe's debilitated state by rushing forward and delivering a powerful reverse punch to her jaw that sent the ochre-coated cat-girl flying across the alley. The shaggy she-beast slammed into the wall on the opposite tenement building that framed the lane, with three ribs cracking upon impact.

After the cat-girl fell to the filthy ground of the alley, Centurion rushed her again. He lifted Niña Gata as if she were a hairy rag doll and slammed her up against the wall, making sure to brace his right arm against her throat, both to exert a choking pressure on her trachea and to keep her from biting at his face again. The felinoid hissed and struggled furiously but was still too stunned to make good use of her free claws.

Centurion was not about to give her time to recover and inflict another injurious attack on him, though. As he held her against the wall with strength that exceeded her own, he began concentrating on summoning the extraordinary Odic energies flowing through his cellular composition. His eyes began taking on a bright glow, with his entire body quickly becoming surrounded by a radiant nimbus of a whitish hue.

The end result of this energy build-up was an omni-directional pulse of extraordinarily brilliant white light that flared from every cell in Centurion's body, displaying a sufficient candela to illuminate the entire section of the neighborhood for a split second.

Niña Gata's sensitive pupils reacted to the incredible pulse of pure light as if a phosphorous flare was blown up directly in front of her face. She howled in both surprise and agony, feeling as if her retinas were scorched by miniature flashes of fire. This caused her to suspend her struggle against her opponent's grip.

Centurion had once again unwittingly utilized an entirely new manifestation of his power: pure blinding light.

Having temporarily blinded his bestial foe, Centurion pummeled the light-dazzled Niña Gata in the side of her somewhat elongated face. The force of his superhuman blow cracked the felinoid's jaw and sent her sliding across the alley.

Despite her injuries and temporary blindness, the once-human beast was a noble creature who refused to go down. The creature once known as Tabbie Morales fluttered her eyelids repeatedly in an instinctual attempt to shake off the effects of the light burst and restore her full visual acuity. While doing so, she began violently lashing out with the talons of all four limbs in the general direction her keen hearing sensed the movements of her adversary.

Centurion charged the she-beast again but was forced to block one of her frenzied slashes, which tore three deep gashes in the flesh of his stomach.

"Graah!" he shouted in defiance once more. "You are so going *down!*"

At this point Centurion again began summoning forth the powerful energies flowing within his cellular matrix. His eyes released their distinctive azure luminescence as sparks of energy began visibly coruscating from his clenched fists. He didn't want to risk projecting a beam of his deadly energies at such close range of his opponent, so this concern prompted him to resort to an entirely different type of attack.

Centurion noted that his foe's vision appeared to be rapidly returning, so he realized that he needed to press whatever advantage he still possessed. After he noticed that the sparks of his flowing energies seemed to be greatly unnerving the cat-girl, who began swinging her claws around much more erratically in response, he rushed towards her a third time.

"Don't like the light, huh?" he said aloud. "That is really useful to know."

Centurion's charge broke through the cat-girl's defenses and smashed her up against the wall with staggering force, the impact of which stunned her for a moment.

Then, upon firmly gripping her shoulders he released paralyzing jolts of his cellular energies directly from his hands into her body. This he appeared to do more instinctually than with full intention, as if he was allowing his anger to unlock more aspects of his potential.

In response, Niña Gata's greenish-colored eyes rolled back in her head as her nimble form was aglow from the painfully searing energies that sent her into spasms. Her dislocated jaw was partially forced open as dribbles of foamy saliva streamed out of one side of her maw; every strand of her thin coat of ochre-colored fur seemed to stand on end for a moment as a result of this horrendous energy assault.

Using his own judgment, Centurion forced himself to quell his rage from going any further, and he succeeded in "powering down" his energy flow in concert with his will. The youthful champion then moved back from his foe, and watched her limp form slide down to the garbage-encrusted ground in a state of unconsciousness.

Wisps of smoke could be seen billowing off Niña Gata's furry body and out of her partially open gullet, due to the sizzling effect of the energy he poured into her. However, the steam soon dissipated and the cat-thing appeared otherwise fully intact despite a broken jaw and a trio of cracked ribs.

Just a split second later, Donovan and Sasheen rushed into the driveway, where they stood beside the triumphant young hero with taze rifles at the ready.

"Too late, leader-man," Centurion said with nervous gumption. "You didn't get here in time to help me do what I was able to do on my own."

"Ha!" Sasheen grimaced, as he patted the teen on the shoulder.

Donovan gave the unconscious Niña Gata a quick once-over before turning back to his youthful charge. "You did good, kid. Minimal damage to your foe, and minimal damage to property. And those gashes on your face and gut are already closing up; you barely lost any blood. Your bio-mimetic suit should self-meld as your wounds heal."

"Thank the gods for small favors," Centurion said, actually sounding exhausted. "Though I think my guts almost fell out of my stomach when this thing slashed me there. I'm just lucky she didn't go just half an inch deeper. Come to think of it, this is the second time I almost lost my guts in as many field missions."

"Colonel, we need to get whatever the hell this creature is into the van and get out of here," Sasheen reminded the grizzled veteran of war. "Thankfully the people who heard all this were smart enough to stay in their houses, but at least one of them is bound to have called the police."

"I'm no rookie, Agent Kahn," Donovan snapped back. "That's why you're calling *me* 'colonel' instead of the reverse. Let's pick this beast girl up and get her back to the Institute before the boys in blue show up."

While moving quickly but cautiously, the three men had the cat-girl secured in the back part of the van designed for holding metahumans. They then headed away from the grubby neighborhood several minutes before the police arrived on the scene.

I actually did it, Centurion told himself as he helped shackle his defeated adversary. *I mean, I really actually did it! But don't make an ass out of yourself by shouting "woo hoo!" or something like that. Otherwise, you will totally deserve the lecture you'd receive from Donovan about not getting too cocky. I have to show him I can keep proper perspective without his iron hand around my neck 24/7.*

When the police did finally arrive, the citizens who witnessed the events outside of their windows recognized the description of the new hero from the recent article that appeared in *The Buffalo News.*

The next day, Centurion's code name would again appear in the headlines, where witnesses gave him due credit for ridding the area of a dangerous creature apparently spawned by the Warp Event. His reputation as a hero had begun. But where would it lead? This was a question both he and Donovan were secretly asking themselves with just a smidge of trepidation.

Okay, perhaps *more* than just a smidge.

Chapter 16: Back to School

As noted, Benny's return to school had to be carefully planned by The Institute, and what ensued when he did is recorded in this chapter. Consider it a flashback if you prefer! By the way, this is the Omniscient Author speaking *waves to the readers*.

A look of unease permeated Benny Lonero's plain features as he entered the halls of Buffalo Historical School for the first time since what he had been referring to as "The Incident." He thought long and hard about the lessons imparted to him by Donovan and the rest of the Valis Institute staff. These lessons were, of course, in regard to the importance of controlling his baser inclinations now that he was a metahuman of such formidable power.

He knew that Mick Judge and Jeff Wolfe would not be returning to school for at least another month; and he also knew that Marissa Robbins was being treated for "shock" at the local hospital and would not be back for at least a week.

Nevertheless, the familiar corridors looked strangely narrow and bleak to him considering the history they had accumulated in his mind. It was quite unpleasant for him to go back to the school. But he understood the necessity of acquiring a diploma, and he had to attend school in order to help allay any suspicions being directed towards his complicity with The Incident.

Benny's new resolve was about to be put to the test immediately, however. No sooner did he stride towards his locker than he happened to simply look up and catch the gaze of Leah Stanton, who was passing him on the way to her own locker.

"Ewwww, it's Lonero," she said to Rick Kelley, a friend and frequent co-conspirator walking alongside her. She made a point to say it loud enough for Benny to hear, and the look of disgust on her face was palpable.

Benny walked past her without uttering a word, but he gave into the temptation to respond by lifting his middle finger in her direction.

"Yo, douchebag! Did you just give Leah the bird?" Rick said loudly.

Benny continued to walk, and this time he forced himself to pay his tormentors no heed. It didn't work, however, as both Leah and Rick ran over to him. The two clearly had a lot of anxiety to work out of their system due to the emotional tumult of what happened to their friends, even though they would never suspect that Benny could have been responsible. Rick caught up to their target and shoved him from behind.

"Hey, I'm talking to you!" Rick shouted. "Don't you ever give the finger to Leah again, you hear me?"

"I don't need your help kicking his ass, Rick!" Leah stated boldly.

Now irritated beyond measure, Benny turned and angrily confronted his duo of aggressors.

"I'll give the finger to anyone who deserves it," he said.

"Oh, really, you little dickhead?" Rick rebuffed as he took an angry step towards the schoolmate whom he despised.

But before Benny could react, a large beefy hand clasped Rick's shoulder from behind.

"Do you have a problem, young man?" said the deep voice of a tall and muscular African-American man with movie star good looks and dressed in a school security shirt.

"Huh?" Rick reacted with clear intimidation.

"Allow me to introduce myself," the tall man said, never releasing his painfully tight grip on the boy's shoulder blade. "I'm Al Garrison, and I had the pleasure of starting my job as a security guard here today. And no sooner did the first minutes of my first day on the job start than two troublemakers made a point to identify themselves to me."

"What do you mean?" Leah asked with faux incredulity. "Lonero gave me the finger! Rick was only sticking up for me…"

"No, you made a comment to him first, which provoked him," Al said, making his witnessing of the event quite clear. "There's been enough trouble at this school lately, and I've been hired to help prevent more of the same from going down. So, you can bet that I'm not going to tolerate any bullying. Whatever was going on here before stops on my watch. And my watch extends to the same five days and eight hours that you attend class here. Both of you report to the office and stay there until I show up."

"Seriously?" Leah replied, throwing her hands in the air.

"Yes, *seriously*," Al said with strong emphasis. "This business ends now. You had best never let me see either of you do something like this again, or you will be looking for a new school to attend classes. Now get to the office, and don't make me have to tell you again."

"Man!" was the last thing Leah said in protest as she and Rick began heading towards the dreaded domain of the principal.

One of the other security guards who was friends with these students looked on from the end of the hallway with an expression of surprise. But he knew that Rick and Leah started the whole thing, as usual. Hence, he wasn't about to come to their defense at that moment, or his favoritism to them might become obvious to the new security man on the team.

"Thank you, Mr. Garrison," Benny said with a sincere smile. "I'm glad you were hired."

"Don't thank me, Mr. Lonero," Al replied with a hint of anger. "The 'they' who hired me to *get hired* by the school was the Valis Institute."

"Say what?" Benny said, obviously taken aback.

"And I saw what you were clearly considering doing to those two," Al continued.

"I hate to reiterate what Leah said, but... 'seriously?'" Benny queried, while throwing up his arms in mock imitation of the girl.

"And I'll reiterate what Al said in response to that irksome young lady: 'yes, *seriously*'," came a gravely female voice from behind the boy.

Benny turned towards the source of the voice, only to find a statuesque, lanky woman just a few years short of middle age with curly blonde hair standing before him. She was dressed in professional business attire with her hands clamped on her hips.

"I'm Tatti Lawson," the woman said, in answer to the obvious question on Benny's mind. "But that's *Mrs.* Lawson to you, young man. I'm the new guidance counselor here, and you are wanted in my office several minutes ago. Don't worry if you forgot where it is, as I'll be pleased to escort you there."

Aw, crap... Benny thought to himself as he followed the Institute agent to the office where she would now be working. *Donovan, I am sooooooo gonna kill you!*

***

Benny didn't like the gaze that Tatti Lawson focused on him from across her desk. He saw that her counter was adorned with a bare minimum of personal items, as if she had no actual life, just the role she was playing here. This seemed to put light years of cold distance between the two. Something about the woman greatly unnerved him, however, and he knew she was no average agent of the Institute.

"Donovan seriously placed agents here in the school?" Benny asked through slightly gritted teeth. "To babysit me?"

"Damn straight he did, little boy," Tatti said. "Agent Garrison was hired as a security guard. He's a veteran of as many wars as Donovan, and he will do his considerable part to see that the bullying that drove you over the edge will be kept to a minimum. I'm here to keep an eye on you, and everyone around you. And you can rest assured that nothing escapes my eye. That is the reason I was so valued as a spy for a government ops unit I won't mention. Nothing gets past my notice, which is why I was so often called 'The Noticer' by those who worked with me and secretly feared me."

"Oh, come on now…" Benny stated with one hand over his face.

"I'm just glad you've been getting your anger out of your system by pummeling the walls of the recreation room in the Institute's third floor instead of people you dislike."

"What? How did you know that? Were you spying on me there too?"

"No, I didn't start spying on you until today, and only in and around the grounds of this school. I do have a life and career apart from you. I know you've been doing a number on those walls because I just noticed those creases on your knuckles. They so happen to resemble the distinct shape of the ridges which I previously noticed as the texture of the cinderblocks from the wall on the third floor recreation room at the Institute.

"I further noticed that the same cinderblocks have mysterious cracks in them indicative of the pattern that punches would make on such a surface. I knew right away that it was either you or Brick that was doing the mystery angst-relieving pummeling, because only you two are strong enough to get away with that sans any serious hand injuries. But those ridges sure as hell imbed themselves in the skin!"

"I don't believe this…"

"Says the kid who projects funky blue beams of energy from his hands and snatches numbers out of the ether. I just want to make it clear to you that The Noticer is watching you. So, don't do anything stupid. Because if you do, then it *will* get noticed. Are you capable of behaving like a meta-gentleman, Benny?"

"In other words, I no longer have any privacy here. Great."

"Benny, you're still under lock and key for what you did. You have to continue attending school if you don't want suspicion for that to enter the minds of the police, students, and staff of this school. That would ultimately take your punishment out of the hands of the Institute and into the hands of the state apparatus. So, don't forget for a second that you're under Institute custody. Worry not, though, since I'll be here to constantly remind you of that."

"How did the Institute manage to do this?"

"Oh, we have our ways."

"I'd like to know exactly what those ways are, and how the Institute comes by its very impressive resources."

"I'm sure you'd like to know what half the girls in this school look like naked too, but that also ain't gonna happen, kid. Anyway, I'm going to write you a pass now and you'll go attend the remainder of your first class and keep out of trouble. Agent Garrison and I will do our best to see to it that you do. And our best is pretty damn good."

Benny snatched the hall pass out of Tatti's hand and walked towards the door.

"Oh, and Benny? You might want to wear matching socks next time."

"Huh? How did you notice…?"

The woman's only reply was an obnoxious snicker planted on her face.

"Oh. Right. 'The Noticer.' Geez, you're annoying…"

With that response made, Benny was glad to exit the guidance office and head towards whatever awaited him for the rest of the school day. Almost anything was better than being in the presence of The Noticer.

***

Rutger Kaiser found himself willfully strolling up the northern end of Prospect Avenue. A fiendish beam adorned his pock-marked face, which exposed his crooked, yellowing teeth to anyone who may have had the happenstance to pass him on the street. But none did so this early in the morning, as he made a point to be out just before the sun had fully risen.

It was time to put the Odic-energy channeling suit he had created to a small test outside of laboratory conditions. And what better test, he mused, than using it to silence the annoying old dog that ran to the edge of his owners' fence and barked at the scientist every time he walked past each day. It seemed like that damn dog was always outside, as if the owners wanted the animal to send an unfriendly message to any passerby who had the temerity to walk past the metal gate surrounding their yard.

Let us see how that beast enjoys being on the receiving end of another's hostility, Kaiser thought to himself. *Oh yes, let us see!* The embittered scientist couldn't help giggling aloud like a child anticipating a desired birthday gift at the thought of what he was about to do.

Kaiser's stride was slow but methodical as he approached the corner to the street where the house in question was situated. He was dressed in a long, dingy brown trench coat that he didn't wear often, and a large fishing hat that mostly concealed his unruly mop of graying brown hair. He wore a pair of bifocals that were much more conventional than the specialized goggles he designed and usually had over his eyes. He hoped that he wouldn't be so easily recognized in this irregular garb, in the unlikely case a neighborhood busybody happened to be up unusually early this morning to witness the imminent test.

Kaiser finally turned the corner onto Prospect where the offending house with its rusty metal fence surrounding the yard was located. As per usual, the old white dog darted to within an inch of the fence's enclosure and began barking at Kaiser as if he was some type of common undesirable (as opposed to the very *atypical* undesirable that he was). The canine pushed his two front paws against the fence repeatedly as he yelped, as if to emphasize how much he desired to get past the enclosure to the man on the other side.

"I have a surprise for you today, you filthy animal," Kaiser said with a churlish grin.

As dog yipped away in protest to the fact that the man stood in front of the fence rather than just walking by, the scientist removed his glove and rolled up the right sleeve of his trench coat. Upon doing so, he exposed the shimmering blue gauntlet of the suit he created. As he practiced numerous times over the past week, Kaiser focused his thoughts into summoning forth the powerful energies stored within its specialized circuitry, a technical innovation he could only have perfected following the change in physical laws initiated by the Warp Event.

Since Odic energies were so receptive to human thought and imagination, spirals of crackling energy began arcing about from the fingers of the glove, seeming to change from multi-colors to a bright solid orange every few seconds. The sight and "feel" of those energies terrified the dog, who added impassioned whining to his yelps.

Kaiser uttered that horrific giggle of his again as he forced himself to cease being mesmerized by the energies visibly coruscating from the gauntlet and to instead point his arm towards the now cowering and whimpering canine. The scientist then focused his thoughts to something akin to what a person thinks when they aim to strike at an irksome fly buzzing about their head.

Immediately after the thought passed through his mind, a bolt of pure cascading energy burst from the extended fingers of the gauntlet. This beam melted clear through the metallic loops of the gate as if they weren't even there and struck the still yelping canine in the side of his body.

The animal let out that familiar whine of pain that one often hears from an injured dog as a full third of his body and the internal organs within were burned away. The agonized whine was a short one, as the canine was dead within a second of being struck. The power discharge was relatively low-level, but it was more than enough to leave the animal a mutilated husk with portions of a charred rib cage and the darkened remainder of his viscera laid visible to the world. The fence sported a still smoking hole three feet in diameter to mark the passage of the destructive beam through its looped metallic mesh.

The satisfied and elated scientist focused his thoughts into those of rapt satisfaction. As he did so, the twirling arcs of energy around the gauntlet faded from visibility.

Kaiser then rolled his sleeve down, put his glove back on, and swiftly but casually turned and walked away from the ruined fence and the smoldering carcass that was once a living, barking dog. A vile smirk contorted his acne-scarred features as he departed the scene of the carnage. One thought flowed through his mind as he did so: *Initial field test successful. And with it, came the expiation of an ugly animal that did nothing but take its misery out on others.*

The mousy scientist left the vicinity without realizing the unmitigated irony of his last musing.

***

"So, can you explain to me what a hypotenuse is, Mr. Lonero?" queried Benny's math teacher Dean Zach, determined to make sure that the young man was paying attention (and he usually wasn't in math class).

"Yes, I can," Benny replied with an enthusiastic smile. "It's the longest side of a triangle."

The expression on Mr. Zach's face was one of only partial satisfaction. "But what kind of triangle? Not all triangles have sides of equal length, remember? That's the only hint I'm going to give you."

The first word that came to mind for Benny was "equilateral," which he believed he remembered to be a triangle with three equal sides... though something felt wrong about that response. Deciding to conduct a silent experiment, he focused inward, attempting to probe the depths of the universe for a response. His mind was suddenly flooded with a variety of shapes that appeared to be, for want of a better explanation, a wave of Euclidean concepts manifesting in metaphorical imagery that were comprehensible to him on some subliminal level.

"I'm waiting, Mr. Lonero," Zach lamented impatiently. "Preferably while you're still young, and I'm not yet old enough to die."

"He's an idiot," Leah Stanton whispered to her friend Darcy Majors, who nodded in agreement.

"A right-angled triangle," Benny suddenly answered. *Whoa, I really seemed to fish the answer out of the universal "database" or whatever you call it.*

"Right you are," Mr. Zach stated with an approving smile. "There's hope for you in this class yet, Mr. Lonero."

"I guess I get a cookie then, right?" Benny remarked flippantly.

"He's such a retard," Leah said, albeit slightly louder this time.

"Miss Stanton, can you be so kind as to remove yourself from the room?" demanded Mr. Zach.

As Leah opened her mouth to protest, the bifocal-wearing teacher cut her off by saying, "And yes, *seriously.*"

The young woman simply huffed audibly and stormed out of the room. Darcy gave Benny a menacing look in response, which he met with a pungent stare of his own.

Shortly afterwards, the class was adjourned, and Benny walked into the hallway to find himself face-to-face with an obviously irate Leah. He turned and walked in the opposite direction, but the angry girl kept her gaze focused on him.

"Don't even think about it, Miss Stanton," came a female voice from behind.

Leah turned to find the new guidance counselor, Tatti Lawson, leaning against the lockers directly behind her. The girl was unaware that she was facing none other than The Noticer.

"What? I wasn't doing anything."

"You were about to. I noticed that you walked out of the room a short while before class ended, and didn't return to it; instead, you just proceeded to hover around your locker. That indicated you weren't going to the john or running an errand for Mr. Zach but were told to leave.

"When the class was released, I then noticed you giving Benny Lonero a look resembling that which a cat gives to a mouse just before it's ready to pounce on the rodent and tear it to bits. The reason you were thrown out of the class then became obvious to me. Based on what I noticed about your expression accompanied by that slight shift in your body language, it's clear you were contemplating a move towards Benny."

"I didn't do anything! And besides, if Lonero didn't act like such a retard all the time, people wouldn't hate him so much. You don't have to deal with him like we do."

"As if his having to deal with you as a peer doesn't constitute an ordeal on *his* part, right? Listen, Miss Stanton, and listen carefully. I know Benny's way of going about things makes him an acquired taste. He has a lot to learn about social graces. But if you don't like his personality, then I'll thank you to just stay away from him and not say anything to him. Trying to hurt someone just because you dislike them is no longer acceptable in this school. If he bothers you first, then you come to me, and I promise I'll deal with it. But you don't say anything to him as long as he extends you the same courtesy. Got that?"

"What seems to be the problem here, Mrs. Lawson?" inquired Mr. Zach as he walked out of his room.

"I was just telling Miss Stanton here about some of the changes in the school following the unfortunate incident last week," Tatti replied.

"To the office, Leah," Mr. Zach said. "Now."

"Fine," the girl responded with more than a hint of attitude.

"I'm glad you noticed that trouble brewing," Zach said.

"I notice *everything*, Mr. Zach," Tatti rejoined with her characteristic smirk.

***

Two classes later, Benny finally came across Craig Minkel in the hallways. The two friends simply looked at each other for a moment, and then Craig turned to move on.

"C'mon, man, I'm sorry about how I've been acting lately," Benny pleaded sincerely.

"Mmm-hmmm," Craig said as he turned back. "That's why you used me to cover for your running away, and in return gave me the attitude and the run-around."

"Look, dude, a lot has gone on since last week."

"No kidding! And I think you know a lot more about it than you told me so far. Don't lie to me, man."

"I'm not going to lie to you anymore, okay? You've been practically the only friend I've had since I got to this school, and you have a right to know. But I need to tell you that in the privacy of the A.V. Room during study hall. Okay?"

"Why not after school?"

"Because I have to go straight to… where I've been staying afterwards, and nowhere else."

"Which isn't really your aunt's house? Which means that's another thing you've been lying about, huh?"

"I promise the lying stops here. You'll understand why I did that after I tell you what's been going on, and what type of… changes I've been through. Okay?"

The towering, geeky young man sighed at his much smaller friend. "All right, the A.V. Room during study hall. Mrs. Metcalfe will be out half the time, as usual, so you can tell me whatever it is that you have to tell me then. It better be good."

"You can't imagine *how* 'good,' dude."

With that decided, the two young men parted for their respective classes. As they did so, however, they were observed by Leah, Darcy, and Rick, who were congregated at the opposite end of the hallway. And the two outcasts were very much the subject of the trio's conversation.

"That new security guard has been on my ass big time about messing with Lonero and Minkel," said Rick.

"Yea, and so has that new guidance counselor," Leah responded. "They expect us to just ignore them when they act like retards."

"Well, you two have no idea what I heard," Darcy said.

"Don't keep us in suspense," Leah insisted.

"Hell no I won't," the girl with the braided blonde hair replied. "Word is, Lonero and Minkel are responsible for what happened to Mick and Jeff."

"You're serious?" Rick said. "How could those two losers have done something like that to them?"

"They couldn't," Darcy answered, "but they could have hired someone to do it for them."

"Seriously?" Rick asked.

"Wait, think about it a minute," Leah said. "Melissa told me that Benny said things to her about Mick and Jeff's mothers, or something like that, as if hoping she would get back to them with it. He knew they would come after him if he did that. They knew he had gym class with them last period. Whoever he and Minkel hired must have snuck in the school and took our guys by surprise."

"But who could they have hired?" Rick queried.

"Word is, it must have been the State Boys," Darcy said. "That gang has been all over the news! Lonero lives on the West Side, and I hear his neighborhood is close to their territory. He and Minkel probably sold drugs or something to save up enough money or whatever, and then hired members of the gang to… you know, do what they did to Jeff and Mick."

"Yea, you're right," Leah agreed. "And since those nerds know the routines of the security guards, they could have shown those gangbangers how to sneak past and hid them in the boys' locker room until Mick and Jeff went down there. There was probably like at least six of those guys, with baseball bats and pipes and stuff. Mick and Jeff never had a fair chance!"

"Those assholes!" Rick practically shouted.

"Tell me about it!" Darcy said. "Mick and Jeff are our friends! They were two of the best athletes our school ever had, and they were student council leaders. They did a lot for us and the school. Now they may never be able to play sports again because of what those dickheads did to them!"

"Which leads to an important question," Leah said, while her eyes squinted in a devilish fashion. "Do we just let them get away with it?"

Chapter 17: Light Stings... All Over the World!

(With major apologies to the 5th Dimension!)

"I need a drink," Craig Minkel said, as he leaned against the A.V. Room table, apparently to prevent himself from keeling over. "I totally cannot be seeing... what I think I'm seeing."

He was speaking about the sizzling blue arcs of Odic energy that were manifesting around his best friend Benny Lonero's tightly clasped fists.

"No, you're not imagining this, bro," Benny assured his best mate. "I'm Centurion. The Warp Event that hit Buffalo a few weeks ago did the most incredible number on me."

Craig pushed himself back into a full standing position, his considerable height made evident in the process. "So... so, you did... you did what was done... to Mick and Jeff?"

"Lower your voice," Benny reminded his friend quietly but sternly. "Then again, if anyone was within hearing range, I'm sure my 'cosmic awareness' would let me know. At least I think it would, anyway; I'm still trying to figure out exactly how it works, and what its limits are. So, in the meantime, we need to be careful about what we say, and where we say it."

Craig was still attempting to catch his breath and didn't bother to re-assure his anxious friend that the A.V. room was usually clear at this time of morning and left in his care by Mrs. Metcalfe.

"Dear Jesus, Benny. And you're... not in jail or wherever they put criminal metahumans these days because of this... 'Institute?'"

"The Valis Institute, yes. But you can't mention a word about them either, okay? I'm in their custody, but I have to continue attending school here to keep suspicion off of myself. And I have to report to them after school, and all weekends, for a while yet. They've been training me, and helping me to become…"

Benny ceased speaking when he noticed the pale complexion on Craig's visage appear to grow even more alabaster in tone.

"Are you okay, dude? I know this was a lot to take in, and…"

"A lot to take in? Benny, that's *the understatement of the century*. This is, like, neutron star heavy. You not only gained these awesome powers, becoming who knows what in the process, but you… did what you did."

"Craig, you know what *they* did to *us* every day. I lost control when they tried to hurt me again. Okay, I know I provoked them that day, but it would have come to what it did sooner or later anyway. I'm not just making excuses; you know that's probably true!

"And at the time, I didn't know about Valis, where I could have gotten help before losing it like I did. But I'm making up for what I did with my efforts as Centurion. I've thinned out the activities of the State Boys, and I took out my first metahuman menace recently: that cat-chick who was slashing people up over on Virginia Street. I'm trying to make amends, and I like to think I'm off to a good— if sometimes, um, rocky--start."

"Benny, considering what's happened, and what you did… I just need time to take this in."

The young metahuman began staring at the floor for a few seconds, with an expression that seemed to suggest shame. "I know this is scary. I know this is a lot to deal with. And I know what I did was… out of line. But I promised I wouldn't lie to you anymore, and I need the support of my best friend. I know I can do good for this world, but I need help. I've got too many emotional scars and psychological issues, so I can't go it alone."

Craig exhaled loudly and ceased leaning against a table that held a wide array of TV equipment. He stood up in a full stance, seeming to ponder a wide variety of considerations and all their possible consequences. The tall, flabby teen then extended his hand to his only close friend of three years.

"Thanks, man," Benny said as he reached to take Craig's hand and shake it. "This means a lot. I won't let you down."

The young man seemed to tremble and grow pale again upon shaking hands with Benny, though.

"What's eating you now, Craig?"

"I dunno, I was frankly a bit concerned that you would accidentally fry my hand down to the bone, or something."

"Nah, that wouldn't happen. Unless you gave me good reason, of course."

"Dude, that wasn't funny."

Benny frowned. "I know. Sorry."

***

"Kaiser took the suit out for a field test, and neither of you had the good sense to report this to me?" shouted a very red-faced Grant Denning, the Western New York branch manager of Osmos Exploration.

The suit-wearing executive's high octave scolding was directed at Myron Wexler and Renee Mack. These two being the hapless lab assistants of Prof. Rutger Kaiser, the inventor—but not the owner—of the miraculous Odic-energy absorbing suit that seemed borne out of the Warp Events as surely as the metahumans who had recently begun appearing all over the world in alarming numbers.

"Sir, we didn't know he took it out," Renee pleaded with the frantic manner of someone who realized their much-needed job was in jeopardy of ending any second. "We were under his authority, and…" She choked.

Myron did his best to calmly finish what he felt was a very important point his colleague was about to make. "Mr. Denning, what she means is that, honestly, it wasn't our job to keep tabs on his activities. As lab supervisor, it was his job to do that with his assistants, which was—I mean, *is*--us, and, and…"

"Don't give me those excuses, you idiots!" Denning interjected with the ferocity of an angered big cat. "You are both well aware of the lab protocols, and what he did was a severe breach of one of our most important rules! Both of you are responsible for a failure of Herculean magnitude to this company!"

Myron and Renee gulped in tandem, both terrified over how they expected this lecture-cum-interrogation to culminate.

"Sir, we didn't know the suit was taken out until we got here this morning," Renee said, again desperately attempting to placate her infuriated boss. "We had no reason to suspect that he…"

"Shut up!" Denning howled.

He then forced himself to desist, and his face turned beat red with veins bulging like greenish-blue water tubes from every possible spot in his neck and temples. The livid executive reminded himself of his hypertension and the need to maintain at least a modicum of decorum in a professional setting, even when confronted with the peons in his midst.

"Look," Denning continued, trying with visible effort to lower his voice and get his temper under control. "Do you happen to know when that son of a bitch checked the suit out of its containment chamber?"

Hoping to keep her boss at an even keel at all costs, Renee rushed to the empty plexi-glass containment unit and checked the log data on its sophisticated digital lock.

"5:37 AM, sir," she stammered. "He checked it out at 5:37 AM this morning. Two hours before Myron and I punched into the lab."

"Jesus freaking Christ," Denning uttered through an exasperated sigh. "He's outside the walls of this facility? With the suit? We need to call our private security force immediately and get his sorry ass back here!"

The three then turned around as the beeping sound that signaled the opening of the lab door announced Rutger Kaiser's arrival. He was still wearing his old trench coat and trousers, a sight that made him look like nothing more than a decrepit hobo to his co-workers.

"Greetings, Mr. Denning," the scientist said, his disposition still far too ebullient to bring him down at the generally unwelcome sight of the branch manager in his lab. "What can I do for you this fine morning?"

Kaiser's exuberant, giddy mood was even more unsettling than his usual aloof, narcissistic demeanor to Renee and Myron. They instinctively took a step back behind Denning.

"You took the suit out on a field test, you bastard?" the irate manager asked.

The wide, ugly beam on Kaiser's face dwindled in size just a bit before he responded. "Yes, Mr. Denning, I did. And I am pleased to announce that it operates beautifully, more than even I could have hoped for! It absorbs the Odic radiations that have super-saturated the planet's atmosphere and very quantum signature following the multiple Warp Events of the past several years.

"It can then project that energy outwards in a variety of ways, all in accordance with the wearer's will. It's marvelous! It was if the physical laws of the universe itself were altered to allow me to successfully invent this suit! In fact, when I first activated it, I saw strange worlds, and worlds beyond worlds! If only you would have been fortunate enough to have experienced it for yourself! It was wondrous, Mr. Denning, truly wondrous!"

Renee and Myron each took another step backwards. They weren't in the least concerned if either Kaiser or Denning saw how much they were visibly trembling. *Please, please don't let this cause my I.B.S. to act up,* Renee silently begged the universe as the first unpleasant squeezing sensations in her lower intestine became evident.

"You son of a bitch!" Denning bellowed at the still beaming Kaiser, while jutting his extended index finger in the scientist's dumpy facial features. "Do you realize how many company policies and official protocols you breached by initiating such an unauthorized field test? Do you realize what your thoughtless actions may have cost us if anyone saw you do whatever it was you did with that suit?"

Kaiser's wide beam faded. It was an action that cloaked his unseemly yellowing teeth but somehow extenuated his severely pocked facial skin in their place. His eyeballs looked bulbous as ever due to the modified bifocals he wore.

"Yes, I realize as much, Mr. Denning," the squat scientist replied with just a hint of growing anger in his tone. "But I am beyond caring any longer. The power I summoned... the things I felt... when I first used the suit made me realize I no longer have to take what this world has thrown in my face for the entire span of my life. It made it clear that I can now hurl back far more than others can throw at me.

"And with that realization in mind, Mr. Denning, would you be so kind as to remove your finger from my face? As in... *immediately*."

Denning did indeed remove his finger, but only so he could move his hand down to his hip and coil it into a fist. His face again turned beat red, and he began trembling with rage. He then reached down and pressed the large red button on a small signal device that was clasped onto his belt.

Myron and Renee each shared a look of extreme horror; it was as if they both just knew that after the next few moments, *nothing* in their world—or the *entire* world, for that matter—would ever be the same again. The last thing they could possibly want was to be at the epicenter of such an occurrence.

"Did you just summon security, Mr. Denning?" Kaiser asked with a vile grin and a passive aggressive tone.

"Yes, I did, Kaiser!" the manager replied. "You're in some serious trouble now! *Serious* trouble!"

"Oh, really now, you pompous ass?" Kaiser retorted with another wide beam that exposed his yellowing, plaque-encrusted teeth. "Are you certain I'm the one who is facing such a serious debacle?"

Within seconds, the loud emergency override beep was heard at the sealed lab door, and two armed security guards entered the room.

"What's the problem, Mr. Denning?" the lead guard asked.

The manager pointed at the still grinning Kaiser. "I would like both of you to demand that Prof. Kaiser tell us where he has the suit he was working on in this lab! Then I want you both to take this son of a bitch into custody while *neglecting* to be gentle about it."

Both guards put a strong hand on each of Kaiser's shoulders. He never lost his grin, or even seemed to acknowledge the tight grips.

"Please tell us what Mr. Denning just asked, Prof. Kaiser," the lead guard insisted firmly. "And please do not make us have to ask again."

"Not a problem, sirs," Kaiser said. "You see, I never removed the suit from my person after its test run this morning. It's very compact despite the circuitry and hardware it contains. Hence, I'm still wearing it under my trench coat and trousers."

Kaiser's sadistic grin then seemed to intensify as he raised both of his arms and gritted his teeth as if concentrating heavily upon something. What that concentration was focused upon became obvious a mere second later as his body suddenly appeared to be enveloped in a fantastic pink luminescence. The flare swiftly intensified until nothing in the room was visible save for that trans-spectral light.

This dramatic surge of energy was accompanied by a deep heat effect that was felt by Denning and the two lab assistants who all stood several feet away. These effects, in turn, were accompanied by a loud sizzling noise and the ear-splitting screams of the two security guards.

When the dazzling light had spent itself, all that was visible was the still grinning but now glowing form of Kaiser, along with the burned remains of the two security officers laying at his feet. Their light body armor and firearms had melted like wax exposed to a flame, and their blackened bones and steaming internal organs were visibly hanging from their gutted forms.

Kaiser pulled the tight mask of the now incandescent blue suit over his face; its own lens openings fitted neatly over his special bifocals, as specifically designed. The external circuitry crisscrossing all over the outer frame of the suit glowed a glittering mauve-pink against the bluish radiance of the rest of the cosmic garment. Clearly, he was absorbing and emitting several different "frequencies" of the fabled Odic radiations at once.

"Impressive," Kaiser said aloud as he examined the human remains at his feet. "The degree of bodily damage done to these guards from a close-range omni-pulse did considerably more damage than the single projected beam I inflicted upon the dog from several feet away. Just as I anticipated. Heh."

Myron and Renee had both fallen to their knees, and the woman was by now beyond caring whether the stench of her ejected bodily wastes was noticed by the three other people in the lab. Far greater concerns now obviously occupied her mind.

The usually fearless Denning fell back against the nearest table. He struggled to maintain a degree of his famed composure, something he had practiced every day of his life. Because of the highly privileged upbringing he enjoyed, Grant Denning grew up fearing almost no one, including his flighty parents, so what he now experienced was horribly unfamiliar to his senses.

"Dear God," the foul-tempered executive said. "Kaiser, please... please be reasonable. We can work out a deal regarding an ownership share in the suit."

"Like most of your ilk, you only show respect to someone whom you happen to fear," Kaiser said with disdain, as the gauntlet of his raised fist crackled with an orange-hued aura of cascading energies. "Which isn't many when it comes to silver spoon sucking slugs like yourself.

"Normally, that odd person you fear would only be this company's 'esteemed' CEO, Martin Teasil. But now it's me. And I'll remind you why you should fear me far more than that paper-pushing chair warmer. I'll show you why no one will ever disparage me again! I'll make this entire pathetic world pay for what it's done to me for the entirety of my life!"

The incomprehensible energies channeled by the suit began flaring in concert with Kaiser's temper as he reached towards the now quivering form of Denning. The still-luminous scientist grasped the executive's wrist and clasped it tightly.

"For God's sake, Kaiser, don't do this!" was all Denning had time to scream before a coruscating wave of energy ran from the scientist's illumined gauntlet and traveled up his former branch manager's left arm, much like sparks dancing up a live wire conduit.

With but a moment of concentration, Kaiser caused the tracks of energy to flare until the glow fully encompassed Dennings's limb. The smartly dressed man screamed in unimaginable agony just before falling to the ground. The cessation of the flare's candela revealed that Dennings's left arm was burned to ashes. Shredded tatters of his immaculate suit's sleeve that previously covered his now non-existent limb fell slowly to the tiled lab floor like wispy lint snowflakes.

Myron and Renee screamed in concert as Denning mercifully passed out following a few seconds of his own screaming. Rising his now luminescent arms above his head in a self-worshiping manner, Kaiser released a shout that was a combination of defiance to a world that had long scorned him, and the intense elation that came with the feeling of having ascended to a higher form of life.

Determined to further display the newly acquired power granted to him by his miraculous suit, Kaiser projected a beam of orange-colored energy from his right gauntlet that completely obliterated an entire large metal table and all of its myriad contents. It ultimately smashed a five-foot hole clear through the reinforced cinderblock wall directly behind the table.

The cosmic-powered scientist then turned to his two former lab assistants. The two cowered on the floor before the superior being facing them, wrapped in each other's arms like lovers who embraced just prior to one leaving for a long trip apart from the other.

"Do you two fools have anything to say to me, albeit in front of my face this time?" the scientist asked them with a still exuberant tone in his voice.

"Please, Prof. Kaiser. We... we didn't do anything..." was all Myron managed to splutter forth.

"No, I'm not the much hated, much disrespected 'Prof. Rutger Kaiser' any longer," the now fully deranged scientist stated bluntly. "I have transcended that wretched figure. I am now like unto a god, a veritable lord of light. Yes! I am now... Light-Lord!"

The last things Myron and Renee heard before all went black was the clanging of the emergency fire alarm as it reverberated alongside the scientist's incessant and maniacal laughter.

Chapter 18: Something Tragic This Way Comes

Benny strolled down the usual byways of the Buffalo Historical School corridors with his mind stuck firmly upon the ginormous revelation he made to Craig scant minutes earlier.

I know telling Craig was the right thing to do. I just couldn't lie to him anymore; he's been my friend when practically no one else in this school wanted to be. For three years now! I can't rely entirely on Donovan, great as he is, or the rest of the Valis staff, for support on something so big. And it's not like I can go to my grandparents or my uncle about this. And my mother and stepfather… pfft!

It was after traipsing to the middle of the corridor where his own locker was located that Benny beheld the lovely figure of Carolyn Marsden, a fellow sophomore who was quite unlike every other girl he knew at the school. She was a fairly petite, slimly built mix of African-American and Hispanic; her flawless, mocha-colored skin and raven black shoulder-length hair highlighted this blend quite perfectly.

Benny always found her unique facial features to be exotically appealing, like his personal idea of what a girl of Egyptian royalty would be like. Beyond that, her behavior and general disposition further singled her out amongst Buffalo Historical's female high school populace. She seemed quite "bookish" and intellectual, and not as fixated on sports—let alone the boys who played sports-- nor the latest trendy fashions, or just about anything else which the "in crowd" seemed to invest a priority of their interests.

Benny didn't know Carolyn too extensively, as she began her tenure at Buffalo Historical during the second semester of her freshman year after moving to the Queen City from Boston. Nevertheless, he had spoken to her several times during the previous semester, even if relatively briefly, whenever he worked up the nerve to approach her. And during those fleeting conversations, never did she speak to him disparagingly, or call him anything remotely like the usual expletives and pejoratives that the rest of the student body were so fond of verbally pelting him with. Moreover, she never visibly cringed when he spoke to her, the girl seemed enamored of his social company.

Further, Carolyn seemed perfectly content to limit most of her in-school socializing with her same-aged niece Jane, along with a small clique that also appeared to have no major interest in pursuing entry into the popular crowd. This kindly little social circle hardly stood out, and the main student body harbored no dislike for them. They simply weren't part of the upper social tier. The students at the top of the school food chain merely exchanged polite salutations with Carolyn's group during the occasions they would interact in the hallways, or if paired together for class projects.

In other words, Benny respected Carolyn as much as he was attracted to her. The "respect" part of the equation certainly wasn't the case with Marissa Robbins and her circle, who seemingly loathed the very oxygen molecules which sustained; and who made a point to remind the unpopular teen of this disheartening fact at every opportunity that presented itself.

Upon seeing Carolyn this particular morning, Benny suddenly found himself wondering why he never made an effort to get to know her better--besides the fact that both his self-esteem and social popularity were lower than the planet's subterranean molten core, that is. He simply dared not approach her in that way before.

But since gaining the power and identity of Centurion, he felt pleasantly emboldened.

It's time to make a move, Lonero. Don't be such a wuss. Carolyn would deserve much better, and you know that. Besides, since you got caught in the Warp Event, there are few other people in the world who can give her the security that you can now. You're practically a freaking god. And no one—mortal or otherwise--would appreciate her more than you do. Sorry Apollo and Zeus, but this one is going to be mine.

With that decided, Benny nonchalantly walked up to Carolyn as she dug through her locker for her next class' textbooks and required supply of flash drives. As he did so, the meta-teen immediately became aware that Al Garrison stood watch at the far end of the corridor. The burly guard's arms were folded in an "at ease but ready for anything" stance, and he made a point to establish eye contact with the young metahuman.

Benny felt simultaneously relieved that Al would keep the usual suspects from interrupting a conversation with Carolyn, and uneasy that his every move was being scrutinized. Nevertheless, he was put more at ease when Al gave him a genuinely kind smile, as if wishing him a sincere bit of luck with the girl whom the young man had now set his eyes upon.

Of course, Benny was also aware that should he ever start dating Carolyn (or any other girl, for that matter) he would be under more intensive scrutiny than ever. He knew he would have to do something about that if the time ever came, but right now he needed to focus on the task at hand.

Geez, I wonder if Apollo ever got such a swarm of gastro-intestinal butterflies when he approached the most amazing forest nymph he ever met. Then again, there's no way I can be the only demi-god, or whatever the hell I've now become, who ever got nervous in this situation, right? Still, it's not like I have Zeus's ability to shape-shift into a form resembling Adonis, or Brad Pitt. I still look like, well... me.

Benny began feeling quite irritated with his reticence to take the plunge. *Just get over the damn fear and do this, Benny. You're Centurion, dammit! This can't be as bad as facing down Niña Gata!*

"Hey," Benny said in a casual but friendly manner to Carolyn.

"Hey yourself," the girl replied in her characteristically spunky fashion.

"So, what're you up to?"

"Oh, just dealing with split ends, new shoes that don't fit properly, a new cell phone that only receives texts when it feels like it. In other words, the usual. How have you been? Has the usual crew been giving you grief again lately?"

Benny pretended to react well to the girl's good-intentioned query with a forced smile. In actuality, though, he was determined to downplay how much he disliked being reminded of the fact that he was so often defined as the hated and besieged social outcast, especially by a girl whose respect and approval he wanted so much.

"Things have been totally copacetic lately. Especially now that we have better security."

"Oh, yea, because of what happened a few weeks ago to Mick and Jeff, right? That really scared me. I hope they catch the lunatics who would do something like that."

Benny forced himself not to frown in shame over Carolyn's comment. He also thought better of giving into the temptation to make critical comments about Mick and Jeff, let alone providing his educated opinion that "The Incident" wasn't a one-sided altercation.

Don't you dare, Lonero! She doesn't share your opinion of them, because they never did to her what they did to you and Craig, and she's very upset about the whole thing. She also doesn't know you well enough yet. This isn't the time to confide in her like that.

"Yeah, no doubt. But don't worry, I'll protect you if danger ever rears its ugly head while I'm around. I promise." He topped that comment off with a pleasant and sincere smile.

Carolyn's returning smile was one of the most beautiful things Benny had ever laid his dark brown eyes upon. "Awwww. My hero. Anyway, I'm off to class now. I'll see you in sixth period?"

C'mon, Lonero, don't chicken out! You're not that little wuss any longer. Act like what you've since become, not what you used to be.

"Cool! But before you go, I was sort of wondering… well, since we do have lunch during the same period, and Craig will be off to the Skills Center for the second half of the day, and I have no one to sit with that I actually care to sit with… um, would you like to have lunch with me? I enjoy your company a lot, and it just so happens I accidentally packed an extra can of Dr. Fizz. Like those annoying TV adverts say, it's made from real fruit, and it tastes awesome!"

Carolyn gave another genuine smile. "Aww, that's really sweet of you, Benny. I like talking to you also. But since I always sit with Jane and our friends, why don't you come and sit with us? They're as fun to talk to as I am, and I think they would really appreciate that sense of humor you're so 'infamous' for." This was followed by another sincere smile from the plucky and good-humored girl.

Benny tried hard not to visibly frown. "Well, yeah, I'd like that, but you know, I was hoping you might like to sit with just me, so we can talk about stuff we may rather… you know, talk about privately."

The full-faced girl patted his arm soothingly. "Benny, don't be so shy. You can say anything in front of them that you might ordinarily say to me when we're talking alone. They're a cool group of peeps! My crowd likes the intelligent type of person, one who actually knows that 'two' is not just a number, but is also represented as, well, two different grammatical variants. As in, T-O and T-O-O. They like talking about funky but brainy stuff like that. So please don't hesitate to join us. I'll see you there, but I have to get to third period now, 'kay?"

Benny managed to cover the fact that he was gritting his teeth. "Yeah, no problem. I'll see you later, Carolyn. It was nice to talk to you."

Carolyn shined her very pretty beam at the young man, which made his heart flutter several times, and scampered off towards her next class. Benny clasped his right fist tightly as a strong feeling of dismay began rapidly morphing into rage. It took every iota of willpower not to utter the words that blazed through his mind aloud.

Damn it all! Would she be so quick to reject me if she knew what I really was? What I can do is far superior to what any of those stupid jocks who're so popular can do. I can actually save the entire world! I can protect her from anything! Can they do that?

It was then that Benny felt the dramatic tingling surge of powerful Odic energies building up in his cellular matrix like water boiling in a heated pot. In response, he clenched his fist harder and fought to keep the building energy flow from surging into a visible manifestation. He was doing this successfully when he was startled by a sudden hand on his shoulder.

"Benny, are you okay?" came the too-familiar voice of Tatti Lawson. "You seem a little... tense. And this was after you talked to Carolyn, whom I noticed seems to be quite nice to you."

"Huh?" Benny jumped with a start. *Damn it, why didn't my cosmic awareness let me know I was being observed by The Noticer? I need to figure out exactly how this power of mine works.* "Um, Mrs. Lawson, what are you doing here?"

"My job," she firmly stated. "What are you doing in the middle of the hallway watching Carolyn going to class instead of walking her there yourself? Especially since your own class is located on the same corridor."

"Well, I hated to see her go, but I loved to watch her leave, yanno what I mean?"

"Funny, Mr. Lonero. Real funny. Now get to class, you have an education to pretend you're serious about getting."

"Right. Wouldn't want to neglect such a life-affirming pretense."

As Benny strode towards his class, Tatti turned and headed to the opposite side of the hallway where Al still stood a watchful guard.

"Al, we have another possible problem, and a big one at that," she told the muscular guard and fellow covert agent of the Valis Institute. "Did you notice what I just did?"

"Um, if you're referring to our boy, then yes, I noticed that Benny was talking to that girl," the bogus security officer said. "He seemed cool about it, and she's always seemed cool with him. Why? Was there more to it than that? Something that may be of concern?"

"Her name is Carolyn Marsden, and she's a very nice and level-headed girl, not part of the 'in crowd' at all. I don't think she would ever hurt Benny. At least not on purpose, that is. The point of concern was what happened at the end of their conversation. I noticed the expression Benny had on his face, as well as the way he clenched his fist, as she walked away. I think he likes her as more than a friend. She seems happy to welcome him into her life and crowd, but *only* as a friend."

"So, our boy done got himself stuck in the friend zone. And you don't think Benny is going to take that well?"

"No. I don't. Not after all he's been through, with his present state of mind. Keep a tighter eye on him during the coming days, especially when you see him interacting with Carolyn, her niece Jane—that's the much taller girl she always hangs with—and anyone else you identify as part of Carolyn's circle. If she ever gives him her phone number, do not authorize his calling or texting her, save for under extenuating circumstances that are first cleared with me or Donovan. Is this understood?"

"Perfectly, Tatti. But, he's been coming along so well, and I would hate to ruin the possibility of his making another friend. And if he never learns to deal with the normal types of disappointment that all people have to face at one time or another…"

"Yes, I get that, Al. But Benny is *not* a normal kid anymore. He's got the power of a demi-god. And his emotional wounds are very deep. He has a good soul and a sincere desire to be a hero, but that goodness is currently buried under the emotional equivalent of scar tissue. Let's not forget what he's capable of if he loses it; and let's also not forget that he is under our custody for doing exactly that once already."

Al fidgeted with his baseball cap for a moment before resuming eye contact with Tatti. "I hear you. And I'll keep a careful eye on things as they develop."

"Please do that, Al. None of us at the Institute can forget what may be at stake here. For both Benny, and the world."

***

The Osmos Exploration building stood a regal bearing over the other constructions on Waverly Street. It represented power and prestige to those who controlled it and hopes and dreams of upward mobility for those who managed to secure even entry-level jobs within its laboratories.

Little did the many pedestrians who walked or drove past its outward façade realize that it was about to spawn power of a far more visceral form when the exterior mortar of its walls suddenly exploded outward. The cinderblock debris flung from the shattered edifice acted as hardened shrapnel that smashed vehicles and people alike.

The front section of the building continued to explode outward as intense beams of multi-colored radiance shattered the remaining portions of the structure's front entrance as if they were composed of sugar cubes.

The severed head of one of the company's security guards, still wearing its distinctive helmet, lay on the front lawn emitting steam from its emaciated stump. A human-shaped glow soon penetrated through the sooty dust that surrounded the area and stepped into the morning sunlight. Rutger Kaiser, a.k.a., Light-Lord, looked upon his bloody handiwork and couldn't help but smile as he prepared to shift his assault to the surrounding neighborhoods.

"The power I wield in this suit is extraordinary!" he shouted to the sky with shimmering upraised arms that made him resemble an azure statue of some dark deity. "I am now controller of the divine light and lord of all I survey! I am… Light-Lord!"

Having now officially christened himself, the wannabe deity of devastation projected searing orange-yellow beams of pure destructive force at the two nearest parked automobiles, reducing them to shards of shattered aluminum and plastic

169

steel while igniting the gasoline in their tanks. The resulting explosions immediately immolated the traumatized family of three which attempted to hide within one of the vehicles' back seats. Not enough of them remained to be identified.

"I cannot wait until the police arrive so I can crush them!" the raving scientist bellowed. "Let them come, so I can show them who is now king of the proverbial mountain!"

It was when he looked around the devastated streets before him with rage-riddled pride that the scientist turned cosmic realized what was located but a few blocks away on Masten Avenue.

A school! It's called Buffalo Historical School, I believe. Filled with the same type of students who first made my life a living hell; who first made me into what I am now. Holy Christ School many now be long gone, but Buffalo Historical resembles it well enough.

That shall be my first target. I'll show the young fools and their arrogant overseers within exactly what the cruelty of their kind has wrought. They will now receive exactly what they are always so eager to deliver to anyone they deem unworthy of their respect.

With that course of action decided upon, the being called Light-Lord began casually strutting the short distance towards the school. His haughty gait and the multi-hued energy cascading around his clenched fists made him appear to be daring anyone to try and obstruct his unholy goal.

Christofer Nigro

Chapter 19: More Consequences Are a Bigger Bitch

"We'll talk about this more in the TV room tomorrow," Craig Minkel said to Benny as they stood in front of Buffalo Historical School's front exists following fourth class. "I think by tomorrow I'll have… taken all of this in better. Geez, how am I going to be able to keep my mind on things at the Skills Center?"

"Well, you told me that you're always distracted by Beth Hemsford anyway," Benny replied with a grin. "Just try thinking of your future hot date with her instead of the fact that your best friend is a metahuman demi-god. Should be no difficulty if Beth's butt is half as awesome as you say!"

"Yeah, right. On all counts! Well, I'm off now. I decided to walk to the Center today rather than take the shuttle bus. It's only a few blocks away and I think a stroll is just what I need to clear my head. And speaking of which, good luck with Carolyn at lunch today."

"You mean, good luck with me and Carolyn and *all of her friends* at lunch today." Benny released an exasperated sigh. "Well, have fun ogling Beth at the Skills Center, and we'll talk tomorrow."

As Craig exited the glass doorways, Benny gave a forlorn look towards the corridor leading to the lunch room. He gritted his teeth and resolved to try and convince Carolyn to speak to him in a more private setting.

Maybe she isn't trying to avoid talking to me alone; maybe she just didn't "get" what I was getting at by asking her to eat with me in private. It's possible, right? Or am I just rationalizing now? Damn, I have to give it another shot, because she's totally worth it.

His mind made up, Benny strolled towards the lunch room with purpose. What he didn't notice trailing several feet behind him and watching his every move was Al Garrison, faux security guard and soldier extraordinaire. *Please prove us wrong, Benny. I have faith in you, man. Or at least, I really want to.*

171

***

Donovan Jakes sat sipping his orange zinger tea in the break room while enjoying the solitude typically present here at this time of the morning. His somber relaxation period was not to last, however, as a very anxiety-ridden Claire Boone suddenly burst through the doors a mere three minutes into his R & R session. Had the soldier's nerves not been hardened to metaphorical steel after so many combat experiences, he would have been startled enough to involuntarily fling his tea cup across the room at the intruder.

"Donovan!" Claire screamed.

"Jesus shit, woman!" the war veteran shouted back after losing the tea in his mouth. "You're lucky I don't have an itchy trigger finger…"

"Emergency! There's been an enormous expenditure of cosmic energy in the Masten Avenue area, followed by a news report of horrible destruction! The terror I experienced with the people caught in the crossfire is overwhelming, it's horrible *horrible*…"

Upon hearing the words "cosmic" along with the location, Donovan dropped his tea cup to shatter on the table. He leapt to his feet less than an instant later.

"Did I hear you say 'Masten Avenue area?'"

Claire nervously nodded her head.

Donovan gritted his teeth. "Benny, you son of a bitch! Tatti and Garrison were supposed to be keeping eyes on that kid!"

"No, it's not from Benny! Donovan, it's *not him*! It's some other mind, one far more scarred and bitter than Benny's; but the power he's using is similar! He emerged from the Osmos Exploration building on Waverly, which is near Masten. And… he's been blowing everything to pieces, killing wantonly, and… and…"

Donovan pushed Claire aside, as he couldn't concern himself with helping her calm down this time. The situation appeared far too dire, and he had to mobilize his team on the spot. He hit the emergency beacon on his multi-purpose wrist communicator and headed for the nearest planning area.

Within a minute, the trio of Gail Parker, Brett Silver, and Sasheen Kahn were at his side, armed and in full body armor. It was his metahuman-pacifying unit that he began referring to as his "Mega-Force." The planning room they convened had numerous HD television screens linked to local news stations, all of which were recording the one-man wreaker of havoc as he was in the process of plowing through the feeble attempts of the local police to hamper his progress towards Buffalo Historical School.

"We have no idea who the hell this guy is, or how he got that power," Donovan informed his team. "However, it's clearly connected in some way to that Osmos Exploration company. Our investigation of that place will have to wait until we deal with the problem it created. Agent Bauer is out on a mission elsewhere, so the four of us are all there is on the Mega-Force team.

"This unidentified metahuman hostile is clearly as dangerous as they come, and he obviously plays for keeps. He need to call in all available forces, which includes our metahuman agents. And since Agent Lonero, a.k.a., Centurion, is a student at the school that maniac is heading towards, I'm calling on him to guard the building."

"Donovan, are you serious?" Gail angrily interjected. "You're going to unleash Lonero on that guy, when he's every bit as dangerous and crazy?"

"At ease, Agent Parker," Donovan responded. "I've been training him myself. He did well on his first few outings, and frankly, we're going to need his power. We may not be able to stop this hostile without him. The weaponry we have on hand right now is just not sufficient, and this may be more than our other three metahuman agents can handle without Lonero."

"Then we stifle the hostile's progress until the school is evacuated and the National Guard and State Police can be called in!" Gail retorted. "We're more than capable of doing that if we give it our all. Agents Garrison and Tatti can help hasten the evacuation, and then join us for whatever help they can provide. Lonero is a lunatic; he can't be trusted! I *won't* trust him! And you shouldn't either, after what he did to Eddie and those fellow students of his!"

"Gail, I think you're letting your anger over Eddie's injury cloud your judgment just a bit," Sasheen said.

"Quiet, Sasheen. I'll handle this!" Donovan insisted before Gail could respond. "Listen to me, Gail. You need to get past this! Benny has made much progress. He's not evil, he was just hurting really badly…"

"But not nearly as badly as Eddie or those two boys he put in the hospital are hurting, right?" Gail spat. "What about the girl whose face he would have melted off if not for us? And how about the time he disobeyed orders to break out of the Institute, recklessly pursue those gang members, and involuntarily put a civilian in the hospital because of his carelessness?"

"He was properly censured for that, and he gave me his word not to do that again," Donovan said. "As for Eddie and those civilians, that all happened when he was still in a state of mind, prior to being taken into Institute custody for treatment and training."

Gail was now infuriated. "Donovan, he's not a team player, he's a loose cannon! There is just no way someone capable of doing the things he has done can possibly become a hero! You need to accept that! You're letting these foolish paternal feelings for him cloud your judgment, because you have to rescue the wayward little monster that reminds you of yourself! I told you before: He's *nothing* like you, no matter what superficial similarities you may see. You need to stop this now!"

"Stand down, Agent Parker!" Donovan hollered less than an inch from her face. "That's enough! You're out of line! You're letting your emotions paint a troubled young man as a monster with no redeemable qualities. That's not what he is, but that is exactly what we're facing out there! Like it or not, we need his help! And the more we argue about this, the more we delay our response time. So, fall in line, so we can…"

"No!" Gail hissed while stepping into her commander's personal space to make a stand. "I'm not going to participate in this insanity. I'm not going to work alongside Lonero, when he's no better than that other maniac out there! I resign from the Institute, effective immediately!"

"Gail, you can't do that!" Sasheen said. "We need all the people we can get right now…"

"I can't do this, Sasheen?" Gail replied in a snarky tone. "Watch me!" The strong female soldier unbuckled the utility belt which carried her weaponry and let it fall to the floor; that was followed by the removal of her wrist communicator, which she tossed down beside it. "You're as deluded and foolish as Donovan, Sasheen! You're as responsible for this as he is!"

"Gail, I think you're wrong about Benny," the young Indian soldier opined. "You haven't spent the time with him that we have. You haven't seen the person lying beneath all that pain."

"You'll all be sorry for this," the brown-haired young woman decreed. "And so will the world. All because of you. As for me, I can't in good conscience take part in this."

The irate young woman then stormed out of the planning room, and away from the Valis Institute altogether.

"Well, that kinda sucks," Brett said. "Her timing is more perfect than an atomic clock."

"Never mind that, Agent Marks!" Donovan commanded. "We've wasted enough time because of Gail's tantrum. We have to make do without her, and she'd be a liability to us in her present state of mind anyway. Put me in contact with Tatti Lawson at the school right now!"

***

A few minutes earlier, Benny entered the lunch room with more than a little trepidation. He looked across the spacious room to see the table where Carolyn was sitting beside her same-aged niece Jane and their usual crew. He tried to hold back his anger over the newest girl of his dreams lacking the inclination to respond positively, or in any way at all, to his interest in her. *Let's just do this, okay? You can't puss out now!*

174

As the young man finally worked up the nerve to approach her, he suddenly almost buckled to his knees when his cosmic awareness picked up an enormous sensation of energy being deployed in the vicinity of the school. *What the hell? I've never felt anything like that before! Something* big *is going on.*

It was then that an announcement came over the school intercom system, with Vice Principal Hal Carroll's deep voice sounding quite urgent.

"Attention everyone! The school is to be evacuated immediately. Please calmly approach the exits as practiced in our fire drills. Please note this is not a drill! Proceed to the shuttle buses in the parking lot that will take you away from the area. The older students who have their own cars should proceed to their vehicles and leave the school vicinity immediately, and all staff members should do the same. Our security guards will help direct you out of the building in an orderly fashion, and the staff should assist them until everyone is safely out of the building. I repeat, please do proceed *calmly.*"

The students leapt out of their seats and began rushing towards each available exit in a state of alarm. Benny realized this danger must be connected to the surge of incredible energy he just perceived. Without a second thought, his concern for the safety of his fellow students overcame any disappointment in missing his chance to talk with Carolyn.

Craig left for the Skills Center just long enough ago that he should be safely away from the area by now. But Carolyn is still here. I have to make sure that she and the rest of the students get out of here okay, no matter how I may feel about the majority of them personally.

A split second later, Al Garrison acquired Benny's attention when he put a strong hand on the young metahuman's shoulder.

"Benny, we have a serious problem!" Al said.

"Yeah, I know. Mr. Carroll's announcement, the stampeding students, and my cosmic awareness suddenly spazzing out sorta hinted towards that," Benny replied. "What exactly is going on?"

"The Institute just contacted me, and it seems we have an unidentified metahuman hostile approaching the school. He's throwing around blasts of energy that match anything you've ever thrown, if not surpassing it. The police have already been thrashed, so Donovan's Mega-Force team and your fellow metahuman agents from the Institute are headed this way. But honestly, man, we need you in the game if we have any chance of stopping that bastard."

"Consider me officially in the game then, Al. This looks like a job for… Centurion!"

Al couldn't help glaring at Benny as if his zipper had just come undone.

"Okay, so I need to come up with my own original battle cry. But can't I take the inspiration this one provides for now?"

Al's only response was the continuation of his bemused glare.

175

Benny frowned. "Maybe not. Alright, I'll suit up and head for the hostile. Consider the threat as good as nullified!"

***

Just half a block away from Buffalo Historical School, the scientist who just gave himself the *nom de guerre* of Light-Lord kicked aside what remained of the final police car that dared to attempt barring his way.

A lone remaining police officer forced himself to ignore his three broken ribs and dislocated jaw to make one last attempt to halt the progress of the deadly being before him. The debilitated lawman managed to steady his right arm just long enough to fire two more shots. They hit their mark on the back of Light-Lord's skull… or at least they would have, had they not partially melted and fallen to the street when they struck the thin glowing nimbus of energy surrounding his entire form.

"That was quite foolish, officer," the shimmering villain said upon turning around. "Are you determined to sacrifice your life in your futile attempts to stop me instead of doing the wise thing by staying down and pretending to be dead?"

The officer forced himself to utter a partly unintelligible expletive filled rejoinder as he managed to fire another fruitless shot. Rutger Kaiser smiled under his incandescent hood and pointed his arm at the lawman, intending to reduce him to a pile of charred bones and blistered internal organs.

That intention was ruined when the green-clad form of Spring-Heel suddenly delivered a flying double kick to Light-Lord from behind. The powerful blow spoiled the villain's aim just enough so that his projected bolt of energy missed the police officer by a few inches, merely sizzling the air close to the lawman's left ear instead.

But despite its power, the blow from behind didn't succeed in knocking the powerful being off his feet. Instead, Spring Heel bounced off the energies encapsulating his target's body and hit the ground a few feet away. His back impacted in a less than glamorous fashion upon a pile of trash.

"What the hell, dude! You were supposed to get knocked down!" the young leaping hero complained.

"I will never get 'knocked down' again, you insipid little snot!" Light-Lord shouted as he pointed his arm at his portly young adversary. "Now you can immolate in place of that police officer!"

Once again, however, Light-Lord's aim was thwarted when the stone-hard form of the metahuman called Brick suddenly shoulder-slammed into him at full charge. This time, the powerful being was indeed knocked off his feet as the force of the blow caused him to slam into and severely dent the door of an empty Sedan parked several yards away.

"Stay out of this, beef cake, 'cause you're out of your league!" Brick said to Spring Heel as he prepared to attack his enemy again.

"Oh, stick it up your lower orifice, Brick!" the portly young metahuman replied bitterly. "Was I not the one who just saved the cop?"

Not wanting to admit that he had soiled his costume when Light-Lord pointed his arm at him, Spring Heel slowly crawled out of range. The would-be hero hadn't yet decided if he would return to the battle, but he certainly wasn't going to do so unless he first cleaned himself off and got a change of costume from one of the Institute vans parked around the area. Otherwise, at the very least an irritating rash would soon develop on his lower extremities, which would hamper his leaping ability.

"This is so freakin' embarrassing, man," Spring Heel grumbled to himself. "And on top of messing my pants, I now owe one to Brick! What a shitty day this is." *And what a poor choice of words on my part, considering the circumstances. Oh, man…*

Unfortunately for Brick, Light-Lord didn't stay down for more than a second. In a surprising display of fast reflexes, the glowing villain hurled a spherical bolt of yellow energy at the gray-attired, heavily muscled metahuman who charged at him like a frenzied rhino. The bolt struck Brick's left shoulder, and the searing pain drove him right to his knees.

The youthful powerhouse failed to stifle an agonized scream as he went down. "Geez, that felt like fire or somethin'!"

"I can assure you that blast will be a pleasant memory compared to this!" Light-Lord decreed as he pointed his two glowing hands in his fallen opponent's direction.

However, the enraged man's arms were knocked downwards before he could project those twin bolts of destructive energy when they were unexpectedly struck by a sizzling bo staff which appeared to be composed of bright neon magenta energy. Despite its apparently energy-based nature, the luminescent object clearly simulated material solidity.

With impressive swiftness, the neon staff then struck Light-Lord just above his eyes. This knocked the villain back two inches to once again be halted by the metal frame of the Sedan.

Just as Light-Lord regained his full vision a moment later, he saw the lithe form of Shard run towards him, pole vault over his body with her energy staff, land directly behind him, and garrote the front of his throat with the flaring magenta weapon. The quasi-solid staff seemed as hard as steel, and the crackling energy of which it was composed sent a stream of mini-shocks into the powerful villain's throat every second it maintained contact.

177

But the Odic forces pouring into Light-Lord's body by way of his absorption suit gave him more than enough strength to withstand this assault. As a result, he remained on his feet while he grasped the staff and pitted his own energies against those generated by Shard.

"Brick, hit him while I still got him!" the masked heroine shouted. "I can't hold him long, 'cause he's overloading my energy staff!"

"No probs, I'm on 'im!" Brick screeched as he leapt back to his feet and resumed his charge.

The mammoth young man struck Light-Lord directly in the chest, hoping to cave in his rib cage. The impact of the superhumanly strong blow certainly had an effect, even if much less than hoped for, as the powerful villain was sent hurtling back against the Sedan a third time.

However, since Shard was directly behind the energy-throwing villain while attempting to hold him in place with her energy staff, she was caught between his flying form and the door of the vehicle. The force of impact knocked her out cold. Her energy weapon fizzled out of existence as she lost consciousness.

"Aw, shit," Brick lamented. "I didn't mean to do that. You shoulda' gotten out of the way, Shard! I told you I was about to hit him!"

"Thank you for rendering your little compatriot insensate for me, imbecile," a beaming Light-Lord stated as he got back on his feet. "You deserve no less than this."

The scientist gone bad projected one of his stronger beams of energy from his gauntlet. It struck Brick directly in the sternum. The burly metahuman howled in agony as his superhumanly dense form proved no match for the energy projections of Light-Lord.

The tall young hero was hurled back at least a hundred feet by the impact of the blast. His movement through the air was halted only when he smashed into the bolted door of a small deli, knocking the wooden frame right off its hinges. Brick lay halfway inside the store with a steaming burn the width of a basketball seared onto his chest. The mighty young hero was still breathing, but he did not get back to his feet.

"Pitiful," Light-Lord said to himself as he resumed his trek towards the school.

***

A good twenty-five minutes before the above described conflagration began, Craig Minkel had ventured two blocks towards the Skills Center. At this point he became aware of a familiar looking car pull up near the curb alongside him. A sense of foreboding caused his spine to tingle. He then recognized the car as the rust-colored Nissan Versa driven by Rick Kelley. The long-haired, elongated face of Rick then peered outwards to confirm Craig's fears.

The neighborhood where the young man found himself had a long back alley which stretched between two abandoned buildings that operated as cereal mills decades earlier. Craig knew it was no coincidence that Rick parked in front of him at the precise moment he stepped in front of the path leading left into the alley.

Rick quickly disembarked from the driver's side of the car. Zeff Walsh and Jimmy Bonsey simultaneously emerged from the passenger side and back seat, respectively. Craig knew those latter two only in passing, but he clearly recognized them as part of the "in" crowd that included Mick Judge, Jeff Wolfe, and Leah Stanton.

The tall social outcast knew what was about to take place; no words needed to be exchanged from either side. He also realized that though he didn't care for entering the alley, it led to the only way providing him a potential route of escape.

Craig then ran as fast as his lanky but rotund body could carry him into the inner portion of the alley. He knew it exited into an open field where he could make his way to a more populated street.

As he approached the opposite side of the pathway which would provide him ingress to the field, two other teenage boys with an impressive athletic build and flaxen-colored hair suddenly stepped in front of him. They were obviously "covering" the other side, and Craig realized he had been led into a trap. He quickly recognized one of the boys as a popular hockey player from his school named Marcus Eggloft; the other was Ken McRafferty, a friend of Mick Judge from his own neighborhood located on Buffalo's South Side.

Marcus walked up to Craig and shoved him against the brick wall of the derelict factory. "You're dead, Minkel," were the only words he uttered.

"What the hell is this all about?" Craig asked.

"We know what you and that fag friend of yours did to Mick and Jeff," Marcus answered in a completely emotionless tone. "Now we're gonna do the same to you. Haven't you ever heard of 'an eye for an eye,' dickhead?"

Marcus then plunged his fist into Craig's lower abdomen. This immediately caused the larger boy to keel over while gasping for breath.

"No, I get him first!" Rick shouted in a fit of rage.

The medium-sized but well-built soccer player then rushed at Craig and began pummeling him mercilessly. The athlete appeared almost giddy with pleasure at finally being able to unload on the young man he always hated for no reason other than the fact that almost everyone else seemed to.

Though battered by the shorter but stronger young man's initial volley, Craig screamed in defiance while pushing his attacker off him with a single adrenalin-fueled heave. He then leapt to his full height of '6'7" and delivered a rage-fueled haymaker to the bridge of Rick's nose. Much to the young athlete's surprise, two streams of blood began rushing from his nostrils.

While he and his cohorts were still stunned by Craig's uncharacteristic move, the taller boy lunged forward and slammed his full weight into Rick. This took them both to the ground like a pair of MMA fighters. The two young men pounded on each other furiously, with both taking a beating but Craig receiving the worst of it due to the greater strength and fighting experience of his opponent.

The other boys began chanting for Rick to annihilate the unpopular Criag in an almost ritualistic manner. They obviously hoped to give their friend whatever encouragement he needed to get his fill so they could move in and take theirs.

Within seconds, both boys were back on their feet exchanging blows. Craig managed to deliver another good sock to Rick's face, and his lower lip split in half. It didn't take him down, though; Rick simply countered with two blows that succeeded in sending Craig careening to the pavement. The athlete then kicked the towering outcast in the gut, causing him to vomit onto the filthy ground.

"All right, all right, you got him good, Rick," Marcus said while grabbing the arm of his friend and accomplice. "Now let us have our turn."

Rick backed away and wiped the blood from his nose and lip. "Get that fat asshole."

Marcus moved in and began delivering a brutal series of punches and kicks to the badly injured boy, smashing and crushing without let-up. Mick Judge's friend Zeff Walsh then bellowed with rage and took over where Marcus left off, delivering another tremendous beating to the already severely battered teenager. The remaining three were each given their turn as promised, and within several minutes Craig's swollen and broken body lay still in an expanding pool of blood.

Rick ended the whole thing by lifting the broken portion of a discarded brick and slamming it down upon the side of Craig's skull. A very visible crack opened in the skin of his temple area and a quick spray of blood was expelled from it. The boy's body then twitched involuntarily for a second before he was still again.

"Okay, okay, we got 'im!" Marcus said. "Now let's get the hell out of here!"

"But are we gonna, you know, just leave him there?" Ken asked with a despondent expression.

"Wtf!" Marcus exclaimed. "Of course, we're gonna just leave him here, man! What would you like to do, drag him home and nurse him back to health in your bed? Now let's get out of here before someone comes!"

The group of boys swiftly vacated the alley to the two vehicles they used for both arrival and escape. Of the group, only Ken displayed a bit of ambivalence over what they just did, and he gave a quick dejected backwards glance at the battered young man laying unmoving in the alley before following his cohorts in retreat.

For about four minutes Craig lay inert as the pool of blood flowing from his many open wounds and upper body orifices began growing to resemble a huge crimson Rorschach blot.

It was then that an older gentleman who lived in a small house from across the field happened to wander over to investigate the ruckus he had heard. Calvin "Ziggie" Pearson nearly fainted at the horrid human-shaped mess he saw laying near the edge of the alley. And this was a man who grew up in a rough neighborhood and had seen more than his share of disturbing things over a long lifetime.

"Dear lord," were the only words that escaped his mouth at the sight sprawled out before him.

Ziggie forced himself to push past the shock and light-headedness he felt so he could pull his cell phone out of his coat pocket. He then began dialing 9-1-1 as fast as he could.

***

Donovan Jakes quietly extricated himself from the Institute's incognito battle van the second he realized his first three metahuman agents had been knocked into oblivion by Light-Lord. The soldier was immediately followed by Sasheen Kahn and Brett Silver. They each brandished their wireless hyper-tasers and began approaching their target from behind with practiced stealth.

"This is not gonna be fun, boss," Brett said quietly. "Look at what he did to our three metahumans in like, what, seven minutes?"

"If you think this job is supposed to be fun, then you seriously need to quit and secure work at the post office, Agent Marks," Donovan replied. "But this time we're just going to act as back-up for our next big deterrent and hope he's up to this."

"Our next big deterrent?" Brett queried. "Do you mean…?"

"Yup," Donovan said. "That's exactly who I mean."

Light-Lord finally reached the courtyard leading to the small school he had selected to vent his wrath upon. Since most of the students decided not to heed the vice principal's order to depart in an orderly fashion, they were still pouring out of each exit in confused and panic-stricken groups, frequently getting in each other's' way in the process. The remaining staff and security guards were unable to control or calm them sufficiently enough to secure a more systematic mass departure.

"Hah!" the scientist-turned-mad-demi-god said aloud with a sadistic smirk. He raised his arms and concentrated on building up the seething pools of energy that he planned to unleash on the crowd and building before him. "How delightfully easy this will be! It will be like shooting fish in a barrel."

"No, it won't," said a youngish male voice from somewhere out of view.

Light-Lord turned to see a monochrome garbed figure step from the side of the fenced area in front of the school and directly into his path.

"If you want to lay one iota of energy on those students, then you need to get through me first."

"Then I shall gladly do that," Light-Lord confidently rejoined as he raised his arms and summoned coronas of crackling yellow energy around them.

"We'll see," the newcomer replied.

The black-and-white suited figure raised his own hands and bluish-hued energy began coruscating around them. This they did in a manner similar to the more colorful but no less potent energies now cascading about the scientist's gauntlets.

"Hmmm," Light-Lord said. "This may prove quite interesting. Before we begin, though, would you care to tell me who you happen to be?"

The young newcomer's exposed lower face took on an expression that combined a grin with a hint of anger before responding.

"I'm Centurion. And I'm the dude that's going to take you down."

Chapter 20: When Gods Wage War in Da 'Hood...

... it sucks being a mortal who lives there!

"I dispensed with those other costumed metahumans who attempted to stand in my way quite readily," Light-Lord boasted as his gauntlets crackled with arcs of yellow-orange energy.

Centurion stood his ground in a steadfast manner as bluish energy of his own coruscated about his raised fists. The fledgling hero then replied, "That was them. This is me. Know the difference, pollywog."

"You dare call me something like that!"

"Yup. I most definitely dare."

Without another word, Light-Lord howled in rage as he let loose with a double-handed beam of pure destructive force directed at his much younger opponent. Centurion responded in kind, and his own double beams intercepted those of his adversary. The atmosphere itself seemed to be burning at the nexus where the opposing beams collided. The intense buzzing sound these conflicting torrents of energy made as they clashed together was horrendously unpleasant for the human ear to behold.

Light-Lord gritted his teeth under his incandescent hood as he mentally commanded the suit to release exponentially greater amounts of Odic energy on multiple wavelengths. Centurion pushed equally hard with his own outage of power; after about thirty seconds, however, he suddenly found himself beginning to buckle under the seeming impasse.

Light-Lord couldn't help but notice this disparity, which prompted him to make a remark. "So, it would appear the proverbial immovable object to my irresistible force is proving not to be quite so immovable after all."

The evidence for that boast was not lost on the gradually buckling Centurion. "We'll see."

"Hah! It would appear we are beginning to see right now."

Centurion continued to focus his barrage of energy while refusing to yield. Still, it was rapidly becoming clear that his perseverance may not pay off in the end.

This guy is… powerful. I don't know if I can overcome him this way, but I can't give up. The lives of everyone in that school are depending on me. Don't let this peckerhead lay you out, Lonero!

The younger combatant was determined to keep up his end of the stalemate for as long as it took the stampeding students behind him to vacate the vicinity. But the heroic effort on his part was not destined to be successful. Centurion soon had to accept that his arms were beginning to become afflicted with a deep burning sensation as Light-Lord's energy fusillade started seriously overtaking his own energy beams. No amount of denial and stubbornness on his part were going to alter that obvious fact.

Centurion's realization that he had but seconds remaining before being blasted aside forced him to make a quick decision. *Time to change tactics. Like now!*

The young champion kept up his rapidly failing assault for another two seconds as a feint. He then quickly dropped to his knees, thus ducking the destructive energies pouring at him, and immediately projected a single beam of azure Odic energy at Light-Lord's sternum.

The projected beam struck his adversary with sufficient force to knock the former scientist back over fifteen feet. The villain's unexpected flight ended when he slammed up against one of the fence's metal posts.

Centurion then released a war cry of enraged determination just before rushing towards Light-Lord with a speed surpassing that of the greatest Olympic athlete. The scientist-turned-cosmic-menace had promptly scrambled back to his feet, but the bolt of energy he took to his upper body had clearly stunned him.

Before Light-Lord could react, Centurion was upon him. He began the more physical assault with a devastating reverse punch to the side of his adversary's cloaked face. This was followed up with a second punch to the opposite side of his enemy's jaw. The costumed champion then utilized the unarmed combat training he eagerly received over the past few months to deliver a low spinning front kick to Light-Lord's solar plexus region.

The trio of superhuman blows clearly had an effect, as Centurion's adversary buckled back against the fence post and slid to the ground.

"Had enough?" Centurion asked his foe with mock courtesy.

"Hardly, you insipid little brat," Light-Lord retorted.

Despite being down on his buttocks, the demented scientist manifested and hurled a crackling sphere of violet-colored energy around his fist directly at Centurion. As the stood not even a foot away, the explosive force struck him point blank.

The sheer destructive potency of the energy mine sent the young metahuman hurling over twenty feet into the air, and thirty feet distant. Ultimately, he was thrown all the way over the surrounding fence to land on top of one of the vehicles in the lot. The roof of the car caved in while the window on each side of the doors shattered outwards with the impact.

Centurion himself lay barely moving, while misty smoke wafted from his fallen form as he experienced more pain than he thought possible since his transformation to post-humanity.

"Hah! That is what you get for being foolish enough to underestimate me!" Light-Lord swaggered as he got back to his feet. "Your blows were admittedly painful to endure, but they were nowhere near sufficient to take me down. Not with the way my energies provide a thin but powerful protective field of energy around me."

The incandescent villain then began stepping closer to his seemingly fallen young foe.

"You need to cease playing at being a demigod when you are nothing more than an idiotic child trying to exceed your actual capabilities. Should you ever stand again, you had best consider following me rather than opposing me. These snotty louts you're protecting are cruel and inhumane, and they deserve no better than what I am now going to unleash upon them."

Since he believed his opposition to be fully crushed, Light-Lord looked upon the groups of students who continued rushing out of the school in a stampede. A small number of them proved foolish enough to actually remain in the schoolyard to watch the battle while attempting to record footage of it on their cell phone camcorders. The being once known as Rutger Kaiser grinned maliciously under his neon hood as he realized how easy it would be to inflict massive carnage upon this lot.

Like shooting fish in a barrel. Heh…

***

With an expression of fiendish glee in the hazel eyes hidden beneath his hood's goggles, the cosmic power-wielding former scientist raised his arms to summon forth the torrents of crackling energy which immediately began encapsulating them.

These sparks of tremendously powerful energies flashed and blinked numerous colors, both familiar and strange to the human eye, as it swirled about his form while alternately drawing upon numerous frequencies of the electromagnetic and ethereal spectrum. He appeared to become an *aurora borealis* in a distinctly humanoid shape; the indescribable beauty of these constantly shifting energies that whirled and fizzled about his form belied the nightmarish forms of destruction they were capable of wreaking upon human and metahuman alike.

The power of these magnificent and terrible energies now at Rutger Kaiser's command were fully capable of undoing all that humanity had built over 10,000 years of civilization; of showing the ignorant species he once considered himself a part of as nothing more than what Kerry Livgren of Kansas once described as "dust in the wind."

The self-christened Light-Lord could not help but revel in what he had become; at what he could now do to an arrogant race that previously had the gall to treat him as if *they* were the gods and *he* were the ant to thrash underfoot as they pleased. He would not only meet and surpass their pitiable displays of power, but he would show them how readily he could exceed their knack for cruelty as well.

With these encouraging thoughts in mind, the Lord of the Light concentrated his psychotic will into projecting this power at the throngs of panicking students who scrambled for safety in front of him. The former scientist couldn't help but notice how much the lot of them reminded him of the haphazard scattering performed by a group of ants whenever he used to sadistically crush a group of them under his shoe as a child. He beamed eagerly under his glowing hood at the death and pure devastation that he was now about to unleash now that his fellow humans were reduced to the status of ant in his presence.

Or which he *would* have unleashed, if not for the fact that the cosmic-powered villain was suddenly struck in the side of the head by a detached car door that was hurled at him from his left side with great force.

The surprise impact was enough to stagger Light-Lord for a moment. That proved just long enough to allow the once again conscious Centurion to leap in front of the group of students tripping over each other in their hysterical attempts to flee for their very lives; not to mention the smaller group attempting to boldly film the events on their cell phone cams.

"All of you, grow some common sense and get clear!" the young metahuman shouted at them. "I can't keep you safe if you choose to stand here doing the paparazzi thing!"

Thankfully, the authoritative figure's warning was heeded, and the would-be digital journalists fled for their lives. The disguised Benny Lonero couldn't help but notice that the bulk of them were comprised of students who had belittled and even physically abused him in the past. The struggling hero thus fought back a momentary pang of anger and disgust over risking his own person for the sake of theirs. This brief lapse in ethics was successfully sublimated after he quickly reminded himself that taking such indiscriminate risks is precisely what heroes are supposed to do.

Centurion then turned back to his now recovered, and clearly very irate, antagonist. "So, Mr. Christmas Tree Man, where were we?"

"I recognized the look you emoted when you told those fools to flee the area," Light-Lord said in an almost gentle tone of voice. "It was the same expression I had whenever I looked at the peers who hurt me all of my life. You are like me. Or rather, you *were* like me, before one of the Warp Events obviously blessed you with something akin to godhood.

"Yet you protect these imbeciles who treated you like less than the dirty particles they walk over with each step. In the process, you raise hands against one who should be a kindred spirit in many ways, making an enemy of me instead. And all to spare those pieces of walking refuse their just comeuppance. Why?"

The young champion-in-the-making sought a feasible answer from within his heart and was relieved when he promptly found one to respond with.

"Because using these advantages granted to us by Fate to become worse than the worst of them is the easy way. The pain we suffered at their hands does not give us the right to wantonly inflict harm on others, or to take revenge on the world. Change the world for the better, maybe? Yes. But seeking revenge will not accomplish that; it will only make the world worse, and us worse along with it. And to put it more simply: it's just flat-out *wrong*."

The sizzling cascade of energy waves that sizzled about Light-Lord began increasing in their intensity, the air molecules themselves bursting under the force they represented. Clearly the former scientist's state of mind influenced how much power the suit emitted every bit as much as his conscious will. Centurion immediately realized that things were about to get uglier than a human face covered brow to mouth with third degree burns.

"You dare pontificate such naïve platitudes to me! They hated us enough to ensure that we would eventually come to hate them back! They used their own advantages against us to satisfy their own lust for popularity and social power! And now you want to defend the likes of them?

"Listen to me, so we do not misdirect our anger at each other: The vipers in human clothes you're now risking all to defend have always fancied themselves better than us. Well, now we have surpassed them in every conceivable way!"

"Every way… except morality and wisdom. The two factors that count the most."

"I said listen to me, damn you! Fate upended the status quo in our favor, and it was clearly done for a reason. Can't you see what that reason is? It was so we could enact just retribution upon them. Not only for us, but for the numerous similar people out there who suffer in the same manner!"

Centurion cringed upon hearing those words.

"I... used to think like you, dude. But the only way we can really be better than them is to avoid acting like them. I agree we were guided by higher forces to gain these powers for a reason. I agree this reason was likely to help dispense justice in the world. But what you're doing isn't justice, it's simple cold-blooded revenge. I've been there, and it cost me a part of my soul. You have to stop this before it does the same to you."

Light-Lord put his head down for just a second. "It's... too late for that now, my young friend. I've already killed this day. And after all I've been through for 46 years, I couldn't help feeling good about it. It wasn't soul-destroying to me; rather, it was invigorating."

Centurion clenched one of his fists and gritted his teeth. *Oh, man... this could have been me. This was almost me! No, that was me two months ago for a minute. All the hatred, all the insanity, flowing from him like lava spewing from an erupting volcano... and that could have been me. It could still be me in the future if I fail to gain control over all of my remaining baggage.*

The young metahuman held out his right hand in a non-hostile, conciliatory manner.

"Look, this has to stop. I know first-hand how much you're hurting, and what such anger can do to someone. But you don't have to give in. I came back from this, and that means you can too. Let me help you, man. Like it or not, we have an enormous responsibility to the world now. And..."

"I read that comic book story too, you idiot! But unlike you, I always saw it for the naïve sentimental nonsense that it was! How many people with power, from the hallways of a school all the way up to the corporate board rooms and to the Oval Office itself, have ever done anything less than whatever they wanted to do? And to whomever they wanted to do it to? Do not play the fool!"

"Maybe *they* are the fools! Maybe it's important for us to show them that power has to be used *for* the world, not to subjugate it for one's personal benefit."

Light-Lord angrily released a beam of violet-hued energy at the fence a few feet to the side of him; an act which melted the criss-crossing strings of metal like wax. That time, thankfully, it was solely to vent, and nothing more. But that was obviously not going to last.

It was then that the scientist-turned-demi-god made an impassioned request of Centurion.

"I am asking you—pleading with you, even—not to raise arms against one who could be like family to you. Join me, and we can inspire others like us who emerge in the wake of the Warp Events to link up with us. We can now be the true alphas of this world, the apex of power; not the pathetic omegas we used to be, those who are crushed under the feet of the conventional alphas. The mundane alphas will now bow before us, the new breed of alpha in their midst. The meek have become the mighty, and the old guard has been dethroned."

Centurion clenched his fist again, and bluish arcs of energy began sparking around it. *Geez, listen to this guy! His mind is unwrapping faster than a roll of toilet paper on a bad shit day. I need to do something, and fast. As crazy as he sounds, his babbling is making too much sense to me. I can't help empathizing with him. I... can't listen to him anymore. I need to shut him up.*

Centurion closed his eyes tightly for a moment, as if fighting conflicting feelings and loyalties in his still battered psyche. The adolescent metahuman had to concede that he *did* identify with the tormented being of power who was fast descending into a psychotic breakdown before him. He could not deny this.

The pain and memories of the events that nearly drove him into the same dark chasm; the collage of hateful faces and the words they spewed at him like spurts of corrosive acid... all began cascading through his mind's eye like flood waters from a burst dam. The young hero found himself *wanting* to show sympathy and even loyalty to the incandescent man-god before him.

Centurion suddenly realized that he once again found himself at the threshold of two pivotal choices: one that his heart and mind wanted to make in an almost instinctual fashion; and the *right one*. The youth now realized why doing the right thing was so often the hardest choice of all. He had already learned in no uncertain terms how welcoming the road to Hell can be.

Hence, the young man's voice was heavy with emotion when he answered a few seconds later. "I... can't join with you, Light-Lord. It would make me one of the ultimate bullies in the world. What they did to me... to *us*... I just can't do to others with no fear of consequence. It would be *wrong*. We have to fight these temptations, alright? Now, please back down. Or, with all due respect, I'm going to stomp your face into the ground until you do."

The inner pain, disappointment, and feelings of betrayal flared from Light-Lord with an intensity that rivaled the energies he expelled from his suit like a thousand exploding neon lights. In fact, the rage and the phosphorescent candela seemed to symbiotically feed off each other as readily as a couple of mutually enabling drug addicts.

Not only was Centurion himself actually forced to avert his eyes from the severity of that glare, but the surge was excruciatingly painful to any psychic who was present throughout Western New York.

Back at the Queen City branch of the Valis Institute, Agent Claire Boone jumped up from a deep sleep and screamed in horror. The intensity of the nightmare she had just experienced was matched only by the brutality of the waking migraine that made every blood vessel in her cranium feel as if they were about to burst.

***

"You treasonous little piss pot!" Light-Lord screamed. "You'll pay with all the rest for this treachery!"

"The quality of your insults make me suffer enough as it is, dude," Centurion uttered sardonically.

Now beyond the point of frenzy, Light-Lord focused his will into his Odic energy-channeling suit that he wore like a prized suit of armor. This time he used that energy to form a basketball-sized sphere of sizzling plasma that flickered in his right palm like a hundred roman candles. Centurion raised his own energy-flaring hands and braced for what he knew would be a powerful assault.

As it turned out, however, the presumed intentions of Light-Lord were merely a ploy on his part. The plasma ball wasn't intended for Centurion.

Instead, Light-Lord hurled the bright white plasmic sphere far over his opponent's head, towards a portion of the brick roof which extended over another group of fleeing students. And the younger combatant could plainly see that one of them was Carolyn Marsden, the young lady whom he cared about more than he dared admit to himself.

"No!" the rookie champion shouted as he rushed towards the group of imperiled students as fast as his superhumanly enhanced leg muscles could muster.

Nevertheless, the hurled plasma ball had too much of a head start, and it sizzled through the air like a rogue comet towards its intended target. The brick enclosure was struck as intended, which caused the entire structure to be blown clear off the roof. The several ton mass of dislodged masonry began falling downwards towards the hapless Carolyn, who had been driven to her knees by the ear-splitting explosion of the energy sphere's impact.

Carolyn screamed in terror as she saw certain death falling upon her from above. She spent her final seconds praying to God for divine intervention.

He may possibly have answered her devout plea, for a sleek monochrome-attired figure leapt over her a mere second before the enclosure reached the point on the ground where gravity was pulling it. Centurion was barely able to brace his arched back over the girl of his dreams in time to blunt the impact of the huge brick structure.

The limits of his superhuman strength were sorely tested as he felt what must have been one of his vertebrae dislocated from his spine. Despite the agony, he focused all his will and determination into one mighty heave of his enhanced arms to hurl the structure off of him. It tumbled to the ground a few feet away with a loud smash.

Centurion then fell to his knees as the pain of his injured back overtook him. He hit the ground beside the girl whose fragile mortal life he had just prolonged. Carolyn was clearly in a mild state of shock, but she could see the masked visage of her savior through slightly blurred vision.

"Are… are you an angel?" she asked in her sweet voice.

"No. But in my view, I just saved the life of one," was his response.

Damn it, that was sappier than a crushed mustard seed, dude. I hope she was in too much shock to actually hear it. But thank the gods I was in time to save her. Now I pray to Odin or whichever deity is behind the Odic force empowering me that my cosmic energies will heal whatever happened to my back. And I mean within seconds, otherwise I just bought Carolyn a very short reprieve.

The still injured Centurion painfully turned his head to see that Light-Lord had aimed his flaring gauntlets in the direction where there stood both the fallen metahuman and the girl under his protection. The cosmic-powered villain was in the process of building a truly enormous surge of energy which he obviously intended to release directly at them.

The monochrome-attired adolescent didn't know if his superhumanly resilient body was sufficient to shield Carolyn from the coming onslaught. And even if it did, he knew his injured state would be exacerbated to the point that he would be truly taken out of the fight.

Would Donovan's small Mega-Force unit of soldiers be sufficient to save these students if he fell? *I need to concentrate my energies into consciously healing my back. And I need to do it* yesterday!

Centurion focused all of his potent energies inwards, rather than outwards as beams of visible energy. He did so on a creative hunch that both his life and that of Carolyn depended on being successfully carried out.

Within a matter of seconds, the young hero felt the familiar tingle of the energies he summoned being concentrated in the area of his spine, like an etheric Kundalini serpent slithering directly off a Caduceus wand. He literally felt whatever had been knocked out of alignment from his spinal cord being directed back into its proper place by these arcane energies that traveled through his internal organs like water forced out of a spigot. All pain in the area appeared nullified as his potentially debilitating injuries were consciously healed far quicker than they normally would have.

The feeling of triumph and elation that accompanied the success of this act was nothing less than palpable. *Yes! I did it! Thank you, freakin' Odin or whoever!*

The monochrome-costumed youth had not even a split second to self-boast over this amazing new use of his power, however. Because no sooner did

191

Centurion render himself able to stand and walk again than Light-Lord had fully unleashed a mauve-colored beam of destructive force in his and Carolyn's direction. The teen metahuman leaped to his feet in a blur of motion and extended his arms while focusing all his will into blocking the oncoming shaft of glowing devastation.

Much to Centurion's utter astonishment, this instinctual response did not result in countering beams of sapphire-colored energy, as before. While his hands did indeed light up in a thin corona of azure luminescence, this time no shafts of energy were fired from them.

Instead, nothing but a dim bluish glow surrounded the air in a wide rectangular space before him. When Light-Lord's beam struck this glowing wall of atmosphere, however, the energy barraged was abruptly halted. The stream of energy rippled about a few feet short of its intended targets as if it struck an invisible solid object.

This lightly glowing field projected by Centurion effectively blocked his enemy's beam, but the sheer force of impact seemed to be partially transferred directly to the young defender nevertheless. As a result, his body was thrown back several feet up against one of the school's brick walls.

"What in the hell?" Light-Lord pondered aloud. "You can use your Odic force to fuse the surrounding air molecules together to create an effective 'force field?' Not even I have been able to utilize my suit's energies to accomplish a comparable feat."

Less than a moment later, the ex-scientist suddenly found himself pummeled from a distance of four meters, the impact of which caught him off guard knocked him off his feet. This blow was courtesy of a ruby-colored beam of pure concussive force projected from Centurion's eyes, which he managed to do while still on the ground.

"Ha! That's what you get for allowing yourself to get distracted by my impressiveness, guy!"

But how did I manage to fuse those air molecules into a force shield? That seems like yet another of the interesting ways I suddenly "figured out" how to use these energies when I happened to be under some serious duress. Not to mention how manifesting the energy as pure force is still something I need to get used to. And why is it that the force beams project out of my eyes instead of my hands, like the blue disintegrator-type of energy does? It really sort of freaks me out when it projects out of my eyes like that.

Still, I can't let that stop me from practicing how to do it, since it really comes in handy at times. And I'm rambling to myself again, probably because I'm so nervous. I need to calm down and focus.

Once Carolyn saw Light-Lord knocked off his feet and apparently stunned, she quickly pooled her will into forcing herself out of her state of shock and getting back onto her feet. Despite the girl's strong inclination to take advantage of the seeming divine intervention that had saved her life, she found herself unable to do so without first seeing to the welfare of her strange savior. The young woman thus ran up to Centurion just as he painfully stood once again.

"You're Centurion, right? I saw reports of you on the news."

"Yeah, that would be me. I'm flattered that you didn't mistake me for one of the janitors."

The girl almost smiled, despite the situation. "Thank you for saving me. That was amazing. Scary as all hell, but… amazing."

"It was worth every risk."

With that stated, the young metahuman suddenly exhibited a surprising burst of confidence by wrapping his arms around the girl and planting a deep kiss upon Carolyn's lips.

The expression on her face was one of complete astonishment.

"Omg," she whispered aloud.

The incognito Benny Lonero knew this wasn't the time to continue along those lines, no matter how much he wanted to… almost more than saving the world, in fact.

"Yeah, I know," he replied. "Awesome, huh? But you have to go now! I need to deal with this. So, later, okay?"

The surprised girl simply nodded her head and ran towards the western exit to the schoolyard. She did so just as Light-Lord was back on his feet once again. The protective field around his suit again enabled him to withstand massive amounts of force without sustaining serious injury.

Centurion was determined to put the heat on Light-Lord to cover Carolyn's escape, along with that of the few students and staff who were still in the process of evacuating the grounds.

To that end, he immediately pointed his arms and projected beams of force at his opponent. They struck their intended target dead center and sent the cosmic-powered villain skidding backwards several feet. But this time he remained standing.

"Is that your best, you treasonous little fool? If it is, then your worst must be truly pathetic!"

"Maybe I just don't think you're worthy of my best, huh?"

Light-Lord shrieked in fury at the insult and unleashed another pair of energy beams at Centurion, these ones flaring with an incandescent green. The young hero's reaction time proved on the mark as he leapt and somersaulted several meters through the air to evade the beams rather than attempting to counter them via another force field. Especially since he still had no idea how to consciously manipulate air molecules in that manner.

The young hero was well aware that he needed to practice accomplishing that feat at will, rather than only by seeming instinct when under extreme pressure. But alas, now was not the time for that.

Centurion realized for the moment that he needed to use strategy in addition to pure force against his powerful and unyielding foe. To that end he projected a spherical bolt of crackling plasmic force directly at the ground before his adversary's feet; after all, if the energy-wielding opposition could use plasma "mines," then so could he.

As hoped for, the spherical bluish-white mass of energy exploded like a cluster of TNT the moment it landed on the concrete a mere few inches from the target's feet. Though Light-Lord's suit possessed an auric shield that took the brunt of even this blast, he was still stunned enough to be knocked off-balance.

In addition to that, he was simultaneously pelted by the many rocky shards of concrete shrapnel that bombarded his inch-thick energy force field in every direction. That was sufficient to stun him even further, albeit still not quite enough to send him to the ground.

Centurion took full advantage of his foe's momentary disorientation to charge at his opponent. He slammed into the master of light as hard as he could with an ersatz football-style tackle (he duplicated the move as best he could based on the limited number of times he actually watched the sport performed on television or online). Light-Lord was sent flying backwards several yards by the superhuman force of this full body blow, stopping only when he slammed against the intact portion of the yard's steel fence.

Centurion followed up by quickly stunning his adversary yet again with another bolt of electromagnetic force projected from the fingertips of his right hand. This one struck Light-Lord directly in the face. Before the ex-scientist could recover, the young metahuman was upon him unleashing a series of punches to his hooded face, hoping to inflict maximum damage upon the god-like villain.

Light-Lord was clearly under painful siege from the ruthless salvo of superhuman blows. However, just as it seemed he would go down at last, a fit of sheer desperation enabled the cosmically empowered man to cybernetically command the suit to release a tremendous omnidirectional expulsion of energy.

This incredibly powerful discharge had the concurrent effects of melting the remainder of the fence into a chrome-colored puddle on the ground, smashing a seven-foot-long oval-shaped blast pit in the concrete below his feet... and sending Centurion flying away from him for more than fifty yards.

A few seconds later, Centurion's battered form gave off billows of smoke from the painful energy discharge he had just received, as he laid near the center of the schoolyard stunned and unable to get back on his feet. He was barely cognizant enough to cohere a single brief thought:

Man, this day really blows…

***

As the final group of students were rushed off the school grounds, Al Garrison finally caught up with Tatti Lawson. As they reconnoitered, Al sent the other two remaining security guards to follow the last of the students away from the school to safety.

"I'm pretty sure that's all of them," Al said to Tatti. "It seems our boy didn't do too badly, either. We've had some injuries, but most of those were connected to the panic. No casualties to speak of."

"I'm not too sure about that, Agent Garrison," Tatti replied with a depressed tone.

"Say what?"

"Rick Kelley, Zeff Walsh, and a few of their cronies-in-crime weren't anywhere to be seen when that lunatic with the light powers attacked. The only other students who had left the school prior to that were those who attend the Skills Center in the afternoon."

"And Mr. Kelley, Mr. Walsh, and the others don't?"

"No. They don't."

"And they didn't have a pass for some reason?"

"No. They didn't."

"I'm sorry, but considering the ruckus going on around here for the past twenty minutes, I didn't notice they weren't among the groups of evacuees."

"I did."

"Well, of course. You being The Noticer, and all that. But what's the problem if they broke the rules and left early? That was just less who were in danger here today. I'm certainly willing to overlook this indiscretion of theirs."

"You don't understand, Agent Garrison. Craig Minkel, Benny's best friend and often fellow favored target for bullying, does attend the Skills Center. So, he was one of the students who left the school earlier."

"I… see. But that's nothing to worry about, because he went with the rest of the students in the shuttle that takes them there, right?"

"No. I called the Skills Center to verify if everyone who was supposed to be there today was in fact there. Craig never made it."

"But maybe he wasn't feeling well and just went home."

"There was no record in the nurse's office of his asking for a pass; trust me, I took the time to check despite everything that was going on here. Also, I have noticed him taking a walk to the Skills Center twice prior to today, likely as a way of letting off steam. I don't think the near-simultaneous departure of both Craig and Mr. Kelley's crew was a coincidence, Agent Garrison."

"Oh, Jesus. You don't suppose…"

"Yes, I most certainly do suppose. We need to leave the school grounds now."

"You mean we aren't going to give Centurion there some back-up?"

"Donovan and his Mega-Force team can do that, if need be. We, however, need to go looking for Craig, as well as Mr. Kelley and his crew, immediately. You get out your cell phone and call all the local hospitals to check for the admittance of someone fitting Craig's description. And be sure to turn on the police radio in my van so we can scan and replay all recent reports."

Tatti felt her gastro-intestinal fluids begin to boil at the thought of her suspicions proving correct. *Benny, you're going to have to be strong…*

Chapter 21: There Goes the Neighborhood... Literally

"Alright, let him have it!" Donovan Jakes commanded at the top of his lung power.

Immediately following that order, Agents Sasheen Kahn and Brett Silver unleashed the full force of their taser rifles on the seemingly triumphant Light-Lord. Now that Centurion was down, it was all up to them to keep the cosmic villain at bay until Valis Institute reinforcements, state troopers, and the National Guard arrived.

Unless, of course, Centurion turns out not to be dead and gets his silly little ass back into this fight, Donovan mused.

The deranged man-god's azure suit of destruction frequently shifted the radiance of its protective aura as he was repeatedly struck by taser bullets. Though Light-Lord's personal half-inch-thick energy field was weakened from the battle with Centurion, it remained sufficiently intact to prevent the continuing staccato of spherical energy projectiles from penetrating his suit and inflicting major bodily damage. He still felt their impact, however, and the fact that he was brought to his knees by the assault attested to that.

"Keep it up!" Donovan commanded. "Keep hitting him until your rifle's battery runs dry!"

Light-Lord screamed in rage and defiance as the fusillade of taser projectiles buffeted his form from a trio of directions.

"Do you idiots seriously believe this will stop me if that kid could not?" he shouted interrogatively.

"I seriously believe we're going to *try*, asshole!" was Donovan's quick response.

The besieged former scientist proved his determination to make good on his boast by focusing all his will into unleashing a multi-directional series of mauve-colored energy bolts from his central bodily aura. Donovan realized exactly what was about to occur due to the pulsating bubble of energy that suddenly manifested around Light-Lord's person.

"Go for cover!" the battle veteran hollered a mere two seconds before the omni-directional blast of energy burst forth like numerous multi-colored shafts of pure chaos.

The beams projected behind their source smashed what remained of Buffalo Historical's front entrance section as if it were composed of plastic Lego blocks. Donovan and his two fellow Mega-Force soldiers leapt aside with barely a fraction of a second to spare; the beams that missed them struck the row of houses across the street from the school, blasting to pieces the wood, cement, and glass of which they were comprised.

Donovan quickly rolled from his knees to a standing position and could scarcely believe the carnage he saw inflicted upon this section of Masten Avenue. The muted screams of whichever people remained huddled in these houses for what they hoped and prayed to be safety could be heard reverberating throughout the streets.

Jesus H. Christ. I hope to Whomever May Live Upstairs that none of those people were seriously injured, or worse. We have to take this freaking psycho down, and fast!

Sasheen swiftly side-flipped to a kneeling position and fired at Light-Lord again. The expertly aimed energy bullet struck his incandescent adversary directly between the eyes, which snapped back the villain's head and knocked his specialized goggles clear off his head. Light-Lord was taken aback by the unexpected impact but was quick to regain his bearings.

Despite the temporary occlusion of his vision which resulted from the blast, the cosmic-powered menace retaliated with a gauntlet-projected beam of sizzling white energy. The imperfectly aimed beam ripped through the body armor covering Sasheen's right leg as if it were wax paper.

The brave Indian soldier screamed in agony while the air filled with the stench of his calf's burning flesh. Brett immediately ran to tend to his injured comrade as best he could.

"Sasheen!" Donovan yelled in horror. He then turned back to Light-Lord. "You're dead, you son of a bitch!"

"No, ingrate!" the iridescent man countered. "*You are.*"

Light-Lord demonstrated how well his experience wielding the suit had grown by manifesting a sizzling, basketball-sized sphere of golden energy over his gloved palm. He then hurled the searing mass of concentrated light at Donovan, who now leaned against the remaining portion of the fence for support.

The artificially created ball lightening resembled a miniature comet as it sputtered through the air towards its target. The soldier immediately deduced that he would never be able to jump aside in time to avoid the deadly energy orb. He also knew his thin body armor wouldn't be sufficient to shield him from the entirety of its burning effect, especially not at a range of just a few meters.

As a veteran of numerous combat situations, Donovan stoically prepared to meet the fate he always knew would someday be awaiting him. *Just my luck to be killed by a dickwad like this light-throwing nerd…*

Except the spheroid never struck its target; instead, it dispersed against what appeared to be an invisible barrier roughly two feet before it would have struck and immolated the Mega-Force leader. The startled but relieved soldier turned to see a once again conscious Centurion crouching against a partially intact vehicle a few yards to his left, his outstretched hand emitting a shimmering bluish glow.

"I had no idea you could fuse air molecules into one of those force shields of yours from several meters away," Donovan said with a grin.

"Neither did I," Centurion replied, "until I realized that I absolutely *had to*. I wasn't about to let Disco Ball Dude over there kill 'The Man' as long as I'm still alive."

"Welcome back to the world of the conscious, kid," Donovan uttered with a warm smile before his tone turned serious again. "Now go get that dick nozzle."

"This is for what you did to my friend Sasheen!" Centurion shouted as he projected a beam of azure-white energy from his fingertips at his adversary.

The energy beams struck Light-Lord dead center, clearly staggering their target.

"And this is for what you almost did to Donovan!"

That declaration directly preceded another stream of projected electro-force. Centurion's second beam assault hit his opponent directly in the gut and knocked him back several steps, after which he briefly went down on one knee before quickly pushing himself back to his feet.

Light-Lord's protective energy aura seemed to be starting to buckle under fire, but it continued to hold for the time being.

"You're still here?" the scientist-turned-demi-god asked in a contemptuous tone. "You can barely stand, let alone summon sufficient power to actually knock me down."

"I just need to get a second wind," Centurion replied. "Then I'll knock you down plenty."

Determined to make good on that boast and filled with anger over the injury inflicted upon Sasheen, the adolescent hero-in-the-making charged towards his opponent.

This time Centurion focused his will into projecting the golden-hued beams of pure searing heat that he learned he could emit directly from his eyes. The intense energized tingling sensation he felt surging through his retinal nerve cluster was extremely invigorating as his ocular organs delivered twin streams of 1,500 Fahrenheit heat directly into Light-Lord's throat.

The villain's protective aura prevented the beams from burning clear through his larynx, but the sudden surge of pain was incredible. The scientist-made-cosmic clutched his throat with both hands and screamed.

Determined to press his advantage, Centurion leaped over twenty feet through the air to land on his incandescent adversary. There he delivered a reverse punch of great superhuman force to Light-Lord's nasal region, and this blow sent the powerful menace directly onto his back.

The youthful champion now felt himself fueled as much by pure rage and determination as the Odic energies which charged his cells. He mercilessly began pummeling Light-Lord in the face, thus putting severe pressure on the latter's protective energy aura. In the midst of the several blows delivered, Centurion was certain that he felt something on his opponent's face break under the impact of his steel-strong knuckles.

Light-Lord reacted to the relentless assault with an equal degree of rage. He seized his foe by the throat in a crushing grip that forced the young hero to cease his flurry of punches. Centurion suddenly realized he should have anticipated that all the energy channeling through his foe's suit would give him superhuman strength that was at least on par with his own.

Light-Lord immediately followed up his choking clutch by willing several wavelengths of Odic energies into the sophisticated micro-circuitry of his gauntlets. The result of this was a wave of crackling pink arcs of energy which permeated the nerves in Centurion's neck and lower jaw. The adolescent hero bellowed in pure agony, while simultaneously struggling to wrest his enemy's hands off his throat.

Centurion's best efforts along these lines proved insufficient, however. He quickly found himself shocked back to the brink of unconsciousness by the pain exacted upon him by his foe's energy assault. The bio-memetic material of the youth's monochrome suit began melting around his neck region, thus making it clear that his semi-impervious skin underneath was likewise being damaged.

With a quick swell of anger, Light-Lord lifted the badly stunned Centurion over his head like a sack of laundry. He then slammed his young opponent's body down upon the pavement as hard as his cosmically enhanced strength could muster. The resulting blow left the youthful metahuman imbedded within an indentation of roughly human-shaped contours that extended almost two inches into the cement.

Centurion was thoroughly stunned, and he could feel a trickle of blood oozing out of his mouth. Light-Lord then raised his foot and stomped it down with superhuman force on the youth's chest. This caused his opponent to hack up a further expulsion of blood as one of his ribs snapped like a twig and penetrated the lung behind it.

"I'll see you dead, you treasonous little bastard!" the cosmically powered scientist roared. To make good on this intention, he raised a right fist that quickly began manifesting another energy mine around it. "I'll burn your putrid little head right off your shoulders!"

***

Al Garrison quietly ended a call on his cell phone and turned to Tatti Lawson, who was sitting beside him in an unmarked silvery Valis Institute van.

"I just… received a confirmation from Sweet Mercy Hospital. Craig Minkel was admitted there this morning. He was jumped on the way to the Skills Center. He's… in really bad shape."

Al couldn't help but notice Tatti clench her fist and close both of her eyes tightly for just a split second.

"Tatti, this is seriously messed up. It's bad enough that something like that happened to Craig under our watch. But how is Benny gonna react?"

"I think you just asked a seriously rhetorical question there, Al."

"How are we going to tell him this?"

"We'll figure that out after we find Mr. Kelley and everyone else involved in the assault and get them into protective custody. And I mean fast."

"A part of me thinks they shouldn't be protected from the consequences of what they did. As if their crowd hadn't already done enough already to instigate this whole business in the first place."

"I know, Al, but they aren't being shielded from any consequences. When I said protective custody, I still meant *custody*. They're going down for this. Big time."

"But we can't let them go down by Benny's hand. Sometimes violent solutions are necessary, but it still must be done within certain civilized boundaries. And even the most powerful among us must be made to realize they cannot simply do anything they want to do, or to whomever they want to do it to. God help us all when only the 'little people' have to follow the rules."

"Maybe you should tell the people in Washington that. But anyway, can we actually stop him if it comes down to it?"

The lady known as The Noticer sighed and looked down. "I really don't know. We need to inform Donovan as soon as that mess on Masten Avenue is resolved. Assuming he and Benny even live through it, that is. If not, then we may have far bigger problems than Benny's feelings at the end of the day."

***

Rick Kelley cursed loudly when the latest episode of the *Degrassi* series was suddenly interrupted by an emergency news bulletin reporting the disaster now going on in front of his school. The disruption of his viewing pleasure was then extended with a secondary report about a fiasco surrounding a young, allegedly electricity-tossing metahuman from Kentucky whom the press referred to as "Kid Kilovolt." These reports were combined into an impromptu mini-documentary of sorts titled *Metahumans in Our Midst: What Does Their Mean for Human Civilization and the Rule of Law?*

But something worse than the sudden disturbance of his favorite TV show was about to be revealed to him. It began a moment later when his cell phone emitted the downloaded theme of *The Godfather* to indicate he was receiving a call.

Seeing that it was Jimmy Bonsey on his caller I.D., Rick answered it. "What the hell do you want, man? It's bad enough *Degrassi* got interrupted, even if it was to report the good news that some metahuman freaks just thrashed our school..."

"Dude, shut up for a minute!" Jimmy said in an uncharacteristic tone to his alpha friend. "We're in some deep shit. I just heard that Ken decided to turn himself into the cops."

"You gotta be shittin' me!"

"No, I'm not, man. Seriously! But I don't think he's stupid enough to turn us all in."

"Are you really that level of retarded? Do you honestly believe that prick is going to take the rap entirely on his own? And do you think the cops would believe him if he tried? They're gonna find out that he only knew Minkel through us, and then they'll figure out the rest of it!"

"Aw, man! What the hell are we gonna do?"

"We need to get the hell out of Buffalo, that's what! I gotta call Zeff, and we need to split town, into Canada or something! You do have an enhanced license, right?"

"No, man, I don't. I couldn't afford one..."

"It's only 65 bucks, you cheap ass bastard! Look, I know Zeff has an enhanced license, so we're gonna take off for Canada. I know some people in Toronto we can sack with. Maybe I'll get to meet some of the cast members of *Degrassi*, or some shit while I'm there. With Buffalo Historical having just been annihilated, no one will be doing roll call at the school for a while anyway."

"But what about me? I don't have an enhanced license, or a passport, or..."

"Then you're obviously not going to Canada with us, man! You need to find someplace else to go, and you better do it now!"

"Jesus shit, Rick. I have no idea where I can possibly run to..."

"Look, I gotta go! I gotta call Zeff, and we gotta blow this town! Good luck, dude!"

"Rick, wait…!"

But those were the last words a now hysterical Jimmy Bonsey heard before his friend and partner-in-crime terminated the call. And it was also the last time he would ever be able to contact him, since Rick would make a point to immediately toss his cell phone's sim card, just before using a disposable phone to call Zeff and take flight.

Chapter 22: The Final Throwdown

Light-Lord stood prepared to hurl the energy sphere carrying an explosive force equivalent to 200 lbs. of TNT down upon the insensate form of Centurion.

However, a mere second before doing so, the cosmic-powered villain found himself struck from behind by a furious burst of taser fire. The berserk scientist's aim and balance were consequently spoiled, and the manifested sphere of sizzling energy ascended from the palm of its creator like a helium-filled balloon.

Donovan Jakes was once again thankful that his aim proved true. *I hope this bought you a little reprieve, kid. Please don't be dead this time either, because I can't stop this freak without you.*

Light-Lord screeched in rage as he reflexively attempted to "catch" the mass of artificial ball lightening that now hovered several feet away… only to see it fizzle out of existence due to its failure to hit a physical target during the few seconds its charge was "live."

"You again!" he yelled at Donovan. "I'll make certain I kill you this time!"

The grizzled soldier knew this would be no idle vaunt from the scientist-made-cosmic. He thus prepared to do his best to dodge the imminent beams of incandescent destruction that would momentarily be directed towards his frail human form.

***

Several seconds earlier, the felled and barely conscious Centurion had one thought instinctively passing through his mind in a psychic loop: *I have to concentrate… heal these injuries… gotta help Donovan…*

To that end, the young metahuman concentrated every iota of Odic energy coursing through his cellular matrix into the areas where he could sense the worst injuries. He did his best to focus past the nearly overwhelming pain to project a single thought and purpose into these cascading streams of internal energy: *heal me... heal me, dammit.*

Centurion could clearly detect a sensation of intensely charged but soothing energy flowing into the cells of his broken rib cage. He literally felt the jagged edge of a broken rib extract itself from the lung it had pierced, with the ruptured flesh of the vital organ knitting itself back together seconds afterwards. The fractured bone moved back into its proper place with an apparent mind of its own; though in actuality the only will involved was the focused intention of its youthful owner projected into it. In obeisance to his conscious thoughts, the energy began recombining the fractured bones of the rib cage.

Following that, the panacean energies would soon have their course re-directed to the cracked thoracic and lumbar vertebrae comprising the young champion's spinal column.

***

Donovan leapt behind the parked vehicle nearest to him, hoping its frame was solid enough to take Light-Lord's oncoming energy projection without exploding to pieces. Fortunately, the car in question turned out to be a '57 Ford, whose steel construction merely caved in several feet under the force of the beam rather than being blown to bits. *You're one lucky old bastard, soldier...*

The leader of Valis's Mega-Force unit then bounded atop what remained of the vehicle's hood and fired off several shots of his taser at the enraged wielder of Odic fury. Light-Lord was struck by two of the electric projectiles, which were duly felt through his suit's weakened protective aura.

Donovan was fully aware that his returning fire would give away his position, however. Thus, he knew that he had to run behind the next available vehicle to have a chance of surviving the far superior retaliatory power of his opponent. *Man, please don't let this Sedan be made of lots of that newer cheap ass plastic instead of good quality steel...*

That time, however, Light-Lord chose to manifest and hurl an energy mine -- an artificial sphere of destructive ball lightening -- instead of projecting a long stream of energy directly from his gauntlets. The "mine" would lack the precise aim of the beam but would surpass it in pure explosive force. That was a trade-off its wielder was gambling to do a better job of exterminating the troublesome pest in his midst.

Donovan peeked from behind the Sedan and saw the glowing sphere flying towards the vehicle like a flickering will- 'o-the-wisp of impending death.

"I think this is the big one coming, Elizabeth!" the combat veteran punned as he made a desperate bid to vacate the car's vicinity before its front end was demolished in a flurry of immolation.

The soldier spotted a large pine tree located directly across the street, which he made a swift beeline towards. It was his hope that the tree's bulk would be sufficient to block the numerous flying pieces of lethal plastic, glass, and burning rubber shrapnel that was sure to erupt from the vehicle's explosive destruction.

Before the protective quality of the huge pine tree could be put to the test, however, a familiar looking beam of bluish energy struck the flaring yellow energy mine while it was still airborne. This caused the luminous sphere to disperse with a sound resembling a much louder version of a candle flame being blown out. Donovan couldn't help smiling with the realization of where that saving beam had originated.

The veteran soldier then heard Light-Lord release a grating scream of agony. Donovan smiled once more when he saw the reason for the malcontent's sudden pain: The recovered but still-off-his-feet Centurion had grasped his adversary's genital area in his steel-strong fingers while squeezing with all available might.

The youth's gripping hand was surrounded by a miniature corona of crackling and burning energy, even as his eyes flared with an azure incandescence.

"Stop blasting at the soldier or I'll burn off your 'nads!" the young hero demanded in a tone even more firm than his grip.

***

Al Garrison realized that no good news would be reported from Tatti Lawson as she stepped into his office in the security control center of the Valis Institute. The dejected expression on her face made this all too clear. But he knew it was his job and personal responsibility to listen anyway.

"It would seem that Mr. Kelley and the remaining two culprits were tipped off about Ken McRafferty going to the cops," The Noticer said glumly. "They took flight, and their respective parents and siblings claim to have no idea where they could have gone. I also had a 'friendly' little interrogation session with Marissa Robbins and Leah Stanton, who also pleaded ignorance of their whereabouts. I'm convinced all were telling the truth."

Al sighed with great exasperation. "So, we have three scared, desperate, and potentially violent kids on the lam. We don't even know if the three of them ran off together, or in two or more different directions. And we also gotta deal with what will happen when we break the news of all this to Benny; who, by the way, I'm totally optimistic will survive the fiasco going on at the school right now."

"We need to find out where they went," Tatti replied. "I have my suspicions that Rick Kelley, at least, may have fled over the Peace Bridge and is now en route to Toronto."

"What evidence do you have for that?"

"You never noticed that Mr. Kelley sometimes wore a tee shirt to school with a quotation taken from one of the central characters on Canada's popular *Degrassi* TV show?"

"Um, no."

"Well, I did."

"Of course, you would. You're The Noticer."

"Mmm-hmm. I have a niece who is a huge fan of the current incarnation of that show, which is filmed and situationally based in Toronto. I also noticed an image of actress Jessica Tyler, one of the stars of that series, serving as the display pic on Mr. Kelley's iPod tablet. This strongly suggests he's one of the many North American high school students who are fascinated with the show.

"Also keep in mind Toronto is located in a foreign country that can be easily traveled to from here by car in a relatively short period of time. It's also just far enough away to provide a good distance from the border to prevent easy communication between the Buffalo and Toronto authorities. With these factors taken into account, I think it's only logical Toronto is Kelley's destination point."

"Now I totally know why the Valis Institute put you on the job! So that means we can check with customs to see if anyone fitting his description went over the border, and with the same model of car and license plate that he's known for driving."

"Yes, but here's the thing. We have no idea if he took his regular car, as I also noticed he had a promotional keychain from a small car rental business located in South Buffalo. Some checking on my part revealed that car lot to be owned by his older cousin, Merl. This cousin may have been persuaded to lend him a vehicle credit free; or Mr. Kelley may even have stolen one under his cousin's nose, since he had after school employment at the business, and was trusted with full access to the lot.

"We can interrogate his cousin, but I'm not sure what info that will end up yielding. Also keep in mind that since we're not accredited law enforcement agents, we would need to do this carefully and under the radar of both the Buffalo PD and the FBI, not to mention the Toronto PD. We also cannot coordinate our efforts with law enforcement in an overt manner, since not only do we not want the local police to know about the Valis Institute having a branch in Buffalo, but we need to find Mr. Kelley and his partners *before* the police do.

"If the cops incarcerate them in a juvie facility pending a full investigation, it will be exceedingly difficult for us to keep Benny from getting to them there. And this despite the Institute having a mole in the Buffalo PD; and even if we install a secret security detail at the facility to bolster that which is already employed there. If it should come to that, of course."

"Yeah. Of course. This really sucks."

"That would be the word for it, Al."

"So, I take it that a trip to Toronto is in order?"

"You 'take it' quite correctly, Agent Garrison. Especially since Valis so happens to have an institute secretly located in Toronto too."

***

"Release me, you little pissant!" Light-Lord demanded as his younger opponent tightened his electro-enhanced clasp on the older man's genital region. "Release me or I'll kill you all!"

"Yeah, right, like you haven't already been threatening to do that all along!" Centurion rejoined. "Now either lose your threats or lose your junk! Those are your options, Disco Man!"

While this stand-off of sorts was ensuing, Brett Silver finally re-appeared on the scene after having delivered the injured Agent Sasheen Kahn to the Valis Institute infirmary. Within moments of parking the van, he was beside Donovan Jakes once more.

"Whoa!" Brett exclaimed at the sight before him. "Am I seeing what I think I'm seeing, Commander?"

"Yup," Donovan replied matter-of-factly. "The kid has him by the balls in the most literal of ways."

"Sir, should we move in and blast that bastard from behind while the kid has him, you know, distracted?"

"Sounds like a plan, Agent Silver. So, let's – oh shit…"

Donovan's self-interjection came as he noticed that Light-Lord's pain, terror, and desperation were once again combining to cause him to channel a full-body build-up of Odic energy in his suit. This meant that within a moment the cosmic-powered malcontent would expel that vast energy surge as an omni-directional burst of force rivaling the destructive power of a small nuclear warhead.

That this was about to occur was obvious to anyone who had previously witnessed the screeching sizzle of the air accompanied by the formation of a pulsating mauve-colored sphere around the villain's body that always directly preceded such an expulsion wave.

Donovan grasped Brett and pulled him to the ground, even though he knew the act was probably futile. His last thought was one of regret that his loyal soldier had returned to his side only to be blasted out of existence mere seconds later.

Again, however, such a predicted scenario of devastation would not come to pass. The very moment that Centurion sensed the build-up of energy in Light-Lord's suit, he delivered a powerful reverse punch to his opponent's gut. The superhumanly strong blow completely disrupted Light-Lord's panic-driven thoughts, thus sabotaging the impending energy build-up before it reached critical mass.

After Centurion caused his adversary to keel over over, the young metahuman leaped back to his feet and projected as powerful an electro-beam as he could manage at his opponent's chest. Light-Lord was knocked off his feet by the force of the beam and sent backwards until his flight was halted when he crashed into the remaining portion of the schoolyard fence.

Donovan could once again scarcely describe the sense of relief that filled his psyche.

Geez, I swear my whole life passed before me for at least the third time tonight. That kid sure comes through when he has to. But he needs to strike a decisive blow, and soon, because even he isn't gonna last much longer. And if it comes down to reinforcements having to handle this, half the city is likely to be taken down along with this maniac.

Despite the continued weakening of the half-inch protective aura generated around his body by his incredible suit, Light-Lord was still quick to retaliate. He did so with a double handed blast of destructive multi-colored energy at his youthful opponent. Centurion, in turn, was quick to respond in kind, double-projecting a whitish-azure beam of punishing electro-energy.

Though neither of the two Odic-energy wielding titans were up to full strength, what they both still managed to unleash was nevertheless impressive. The very air surrounding the point where the dueling blasts met steamed and crackled with a sound not unlike two powered chainsaws grating against each other.

The dueling demi-gods were simultaneously giving it their all, and though both were visibly buckling under each other's assault, they were equally determined not to give ground. The sparkling fury given off from where those opposing beams clashed seemed to fly in every direction. This provided a sight that was both amazingly breathtaking and nightmarishly terrifying for normal human bystanders to behold.

The energies which Centurion and Light-Lord pitted against each other were nothing less than the fundamental forces of the universe; the power source of the gods themselves, only now wielded by individuals who walked within the world of mortal men. Though humbled by what they saw, Donovan and Brett were no less adamant about bringing down the one who was most obviously not on the side of their fellow mortals.

"Taze the bastard!" the Mega-Force commander ordered, speaking loudly to ensure that the soldier under his command heard him over the cacophony of the clashing energy beams.

Both Mega-Force soldiers brandished their taser rifles and fired several shots of electrical bolts directly at Light-Lord. The energy bullets hit their target from behind at several points, but his weakening defense field was still sufficient to resist them.

"Damn it all," Donovan said to himself, as he initially believed this attack yielded negligible results.

Soon, however, it was to become clear this may not have been the case. The apparent stalemate between Centurion and Light-Lord abruptly ended when both combatants could no longer continue the attack in this manner. As their respective beams appeared to sizzle out at roughly the same moment, the two cosmic combatants fell to their knees from the tremendous strain both had endured to maintain that impasse for so long.

Despite the ostensibly artificial means of summoning and channeling the Odic force, it was clear that Rutger Kaiser's power suit was intimately connected to his own life energies along with his very consciousness.

Light-Lord was no less intent upon obliterating his foe, however. As such, he was the first of the two to manage getting back to his feet. After doing so he immediately began forming another energy mine over the palm of his hand, which he quickly aimed to toss directly at the still fallen Centurion.

"No, you don't, pencil dick!" the young man shouted.

Immediately after that declaration, a spontaneous need once again enabled Centurion to tap a different frequency of energy along the Odic spectrum for a very specific effect. This time it manifested as twin projected scarlet-orange colored ocular beams of pure concussive force.

The twin energy streams struck Light-Lord on his wrist, cracking his ulna beneath what remained of his suit's deflective aura. This not only caused him to scream from the excruciating pain of the sudden injury, but it also caused him to drop the surging sphere of ball lightening he created. The energy mass then floated to the ground to harmlessly bounce twice before fizzling out of existence.

Centurion then leapt to his feet and rushed towards Light-Lord, who was then still holding his fractured wrist. Before the deranged ex-scientist could sufficiently react, the younger man struck him in the side of the face with a superhumanly strong haymaker. The villain's protective aura continued to flicker as he was sent reeling by the blow.

Light-Lord reflexively swung back at Centurion, but the latter's recent intense training at the Institute served him well as he instinctively blocked the mighty counter-punch. With his fortitude and anger on overdrive, Centurion responded with a side kick to Light-Lord's solar plexus, causing his foe to buckle further.

"C'mon, kid, knock that asshole's block off!" Donovan shouted.

"Don't let up, man!" Brett hollered in agreement.

These attempts to add verbal encouragement to Centurion's fuel reserves appeared to work as the young hero continued to rain blow after superhuman blow upon his enemy, absolutely refusing to give ground or to give Light-Lord the opportunity to deliver any form of retaliation.

Centurion could sense the exponential weakening of his enemy's protective energy field under the intense pummeling he delivered. He could likewise actually feel Light-Lord's facial bones fracturing underneath the headpiece of his suit with each connected blow.

Finally, with his rage at its zenith, Centurion launched one final reverse punch directly to Light-Lord's face. The young warrior felt the cartilage of his adversary's nose fragment under its smashing force.

The severely battered scientist flew back against the still standing portion of the schoolyard fence, where he hit the hard metal with a loud clanging sound. He then slid down until he came to rest in a sitting position on the concrete ground.

"You're done," Centurion said as he forced himself to remain on his feet. "Give it up. I understand what drove you to this, but I won't let you hurt any more innocent people."

"You understood... nothing," Light-Lord coughed in reply, as he mentally commanded the Odic energies still coursing through his suit to keep him conscious. "We should have been... friends. You betrayed... one of your own. I will... kill you... for that."

Despite the beating he dealt to the man, Centurion could sense the further building of energies in his adversary's suit.

Light-Lord's entire sky blue raiment began glowing in alternating colors as power continued to course through it, apparently sifting for just the right frequency to bring to bear against the young metahuman standing before him. The lengthy swaths of tubular circuitry which adorned the exterior of the suit began flashing as if colored neon liquid was flowing through them, this making them resemble cosmic-powered fluorescent ceiling lights.

Light-Lord then began raising his left arm in preparation for projecting more deadly energy from the pulsing gauntlets.

"No, enough is enough!" Centurion decreed.

The cosmic-powered youth reached down and literally pushed his hands through the weak remnants of the suit's energy field and grasped its external energy-processing circuitry. Centurion shouted with the effort akin to a human weightlifter pressing a 300-pound barbell over his head as he pulled with all his superhuman might to rip the circuitry clear off the surface of his opponent's azure-hued garb.

Light-Lord yelled with an incredible degree of agony as he lost control of the Odic energy flowing through the contours of the suit. The erratic energies scattered about his body in a flurry of multi-colored incandescent sparks. Centurion was buffeted by the sudden energy surge and received a shocking sensation that momentarily knocked him off his feet.

"Whoa!" Brett again exclaimed as he and Donovan ran closer to the scene of combat.

They arrived seconds later to find Centurion once more pushing himself back to his feet. Right below him, still laying in an upright position against the remains of the schoolyard fence, was the now immobile form of Light-Lord. His power suit was continuously glowing with a frequently changing pattern of colors, but no hazardous levels of energy flowed or crackled about him any longer.

Centurion's clasped right hand held the detached, dangling rings of circuitry that formerly absorbed and manipulated the inestimably powerful Odic energy from the universal fabric. Light-Lord was effectively de-fanged.

"I… I think he's finally down for the count, Donovan," the young man said while struggling to remain standing.

"I think you're right," the commander of the Institute's Mega-Force unit said with a noticeable smile. "Nice going, kid. Now let's get both you and him out of here before the National Guard and state troopers arrive. We can't afford his suit, however damaged, to end up in the hands of any government agency. If this get-up and its circuitry ever got reproduced, the whole world would be knee-deep in shit."

A moment later, Donovan's order was interrupted when Spring Heel Jack leapt clear over the remainder of the fence and landed in their midst with a loud thud. His soiled costume was now replaced with a clean but slightly ill-fitting replacement.

"Hey, guys, what did I miss?"

The pudgy, green-suited adolescent then noticed the unconscious form of Light-Lord. He punctually ran up to the insensate villain and kicked him in the chest.

"Hah, the *coup de grace*!" Spring Heel decreed. "Now he's totally down for the count! I guess I was the *deus ex machina* for you guys, huh?"

"Yeah, dude, I don't know what we would have done if you hadn't arrived just in the nick of time," a thoroughly drained Centurion retorted sardonically as he fell back against one of the schoolyard fence's remaining metal posts.

Epilogue: Loose Ends and Foreboding Futures

After just over three months in the confines of their shared hospital room, Mick Judge and Jeff Wolfe had made satisfactory progress via surgery, physical therapy, and (as their parents had hoped) mutual reassurance. They were due to be sent home soon, and the doctors were expected to provide their parents with a prognosis for when they would be able to return to school afterwards.

Of course, the question of when, or if, they could return to playing sports was separate to the more immediate query as to when they could resume their in-school academic studies and basic life activities.

The two young men had nothing but time over the past three months, and they passed much of it discussing these matters, as well as the implication of the visit they received from apparent law enforcement officers soon after they had both regained full cognizance. They weren't always in accord over how to conduct their post-hospitalization activities in regard to all of the above concerns, but they knew that Benny Lonero would likely continue to be a presence at the school once they finally returned to it.

What would they do about that? What would school be like for them now that venting via bullying Benny and his best and practically only friend was no longer an option? And, perhaps most importantly, was that perhaps something they shouldn't have been doing all along, despite being able to conduct that activity with a heavy degree of impunity?

During the course of those discussions, the two on-the-mend students and (possibly former) athletes never considered an entirely different sort of option than those already spoken about. However, such an option suddenly presented itself to them when an attractive younger woman dressed in smart attire walked into the room one afternoon soon after they had each completed their daily physical therapy sessions and were in the middle of their lunch repast.

"Mick Judge? Jeff Wolfe?" the woman inquired for confirmation.

"Yeah, that's us," Mick replied. "And you sure don't look like someone about to stick us with another needle or take our temperatures."

"No, I'm not," she stated with a firm attitude. "My name is Gail Parker. I'm glad to see you boys on the verge of being released, and able to talk again. I came to tell you that I think what was done to you two was reprehensible. I think the… person… who did this to you should be punished far more than he was."

"Person?" Jeff said with a very nervous tone. "Um, we already gave our statements to the police. We told them how it was a whole gang of…"

"Okay, enough of that," Gail interpolated with a raised hand. "Listen to me, gentlemen. I know exactly who did this to you, and that it was a single individual of… unusual capabilities. He is someone that has hurt more than just you guys. And while I do not condone what you two participated in to set him off, I certainly do not think what he did should have been dealt with as lightly as it was."

Jeff gulped audibly. "Look, lady, we really don't know what you're talking about…"

"Yes, you do!" Gail insisted quite adamantly. "So, let's cut the bull, because I'm here to give you an opportunity to be directly involved in getting justice for what he did to you; as well as other people that he hurt, including someone I care about very much."

The two adolescents were quiet for several seconds, before Mick turned to his friend. "Let's hear what she has to say, Jeff." He then turned back to the strange women who had unexpectedly entered their lives. "Please go on, Ms. Parker. Or can we maybe call you Gail?"

***

Jane Marsden sat beside her same-aged aunt and BFF Carolyn on the latter's bedroom couch where they had had more than their share of "girl talk" in the past. But no secret the two young women had ever shared before came close to measuring up to what Carolyn had just revealed to Jane on this occasion.

"Seriously, girl?" the tall and thin Jane said with more than a hint of surprise. "Centurion seriously kissed you? As in, on the lips?"

"Do you think I'm one to make something like that up, Jane?" Carolyn snipped.

"No, of course not. But this is just… well, crazy."

"No kidding."

"This is amazing, Carolyn! Just totally 'effin' amazing!"

"Yea, I suppose it is. I guess."

Jane looked closer at her young aunt after noticing the chubby-cheeked girl's less than enthused response.

"Wait, were you not excited about it?"

"Well, yea, I guess."

"You 'guess?' What am I missing here?"

"Okay, I meant, it was rather exciting in a way, but... I don't really know how I feel about it overall, Jane. It was sort of creepy the way it went down. I know he saved my life, and I'm very grateful for what he went through to do that, but... I just don't know. I really hope I never see that guy again."

***

Mac Campton, a.k.a., Brick, laid upon an extra padded medical bed in the Valis Institute infirmary as he recovered from the fairly serious injuries he incurred earlier that day. The flat wall-mounted TV was activated, but he paid little attention to the on-screen antics. Instead, he found his mind wandering onto other things. These thoughts were less than enthusiastic, considering his relatively poor showing against Light-Lord.

"Hey, sexy," came a soft, familiar young female voice, along with a casual knock on the wall, to get his attention.

That utterance belonged to Angela Bentley, a.k.a., Shard, who entered the room in her civilian clothing, which consisted of a crop top tee shirt and a pair of tight blue jeans. Her usual peppy exuberance was belying the pain from the injured ribs she received in that same battle.

"Hey, babe," Mac replied in a low voice. "Thanks for coming, but I hate you seeing me like this, ya know?"

"Awww, don't give it any concern, my walking Brick wall." She scampered over to the bulky young metahuman and gave him a quick but deep kiss on the lips. "You still look good, even trussed up like this."

"Yeah, right."

"Seriously, boo." She sat on the extra-sized bed beside him and took his hand. "So, how are you doing?"

"That glowing asshole blew a hole almost half an inch deep into my gut with that energy beam he shoots. Since I got these powers I had no idea I could be hurt like that. Hell, bullets bounce off my hide while barely stinging."

"Just because you're bullet proof, doesn't mean other, more powerful forces can't penetrate that ultra-strong skin of yours. I'm thinking it's pretty fortuitous that you find out what your limits are, so you don't run into future battles half-cocked."

"Nah, don't worry, that part of me wasn't cut in half."

215

"Huh? Geez, that's not what I meant, hun. I meant in the future you need to think and have a plan before you launch yourself into a combat situation with such a powerful foe; especially now that you know you're not totally indestructible."

"Oh, okay. And 'fruit-tu-ey-tous?' You and those big words of yours. Maybe you should be going out with Centurion instead, since he talks like that too and he has way more in common with you than me."

"Eeeeww, I don't think so. I like my big jockie guy just the way he is, okay? You don't have to read a lot to be attractive to me. I think you were pretty brave to engage such a powerful opponent, and you took these injuries while defending innocent people. You're a real hero in my estimation. Even if you did rush into the whole thing half -- ... without thinking."

"Yeah, yeah. I also could have hurt you really bad with the mistake I made. Speaking of which, babe…"

"I'm all right. Just a few cracked ribs. I've had much worse, trust me."

"That's cool. Thank Thor for that. But as brave as you say I was, Lonero was the one who took that dickwad down."

"Not without help from Cmdr. Jakes and his Mega-Force unit. And it's not like Centurion routed Light-Lord without taking a hell of a beating himself first. You're just starting out in this business, remember? You'll do fine in the future."

"But Lonero did fine *now* and didn't wait for the future before doing good. He's gonna end up second-in-command to Jakes of the Institute's Western New York metahuman division. Just watch, I can see it coming."

"I was here before you and believe me when I tell you that Lonero has made his share of screw-ups already. Don't worry about him. He's a loose cannon waiting to blow, and when he does, I'll be there beside you to help take him down."

"So, you think I need your help to really take him?"

"Stop that, Captain Macho. You know that's not what I meant. You just won't have to face him alone when the time comes. Not because you're incapable of taking him mono-a-mono, but because I *want* to help you. And I'm there for you whether you want me to be or not."

"Yeah, but, babe…"

"Shut up, sweetie."

Angela ended the conversation by locking her lips tightly with Mac's own, and the two immediately abandoned all thoughts as they became lost in each other.

***

Benny Lonero sat on an unfolded futon in his quarters-cum-confinement-cell located within the brig section of the Valis Institute facility literally sequestered underneath a mock public gym on 751 Niagara Street, Buffalo, New York. He had spent the past few hours recovering from the grueling battle with Light-Lord.

That battle nevertheless ended in a great victory for him, one which convinced him that perhaps he did have what it took to one day become an actual hero; just like those he often read about in the four-color books, and just like his mentor Donovan.

Benny thought it odd that his calls sent to Craig's cell phone went unanswered, and his voice messages unreturned. However, he figured that his friend simply failed to pay the monthly bill, even though that wasn't like him. In the meantime, he was talking -- or perhaps, *arguing* would be a more apt term – over the phone with his grandmother.

"You still haven't told me when you plan to come home, Benny," Grace Lonero hollered through the phone's speaker.

"It's because I don't plan to any time soon," Benny replied curtly. "You know how I don't get along with you and my grandfather."

"Look, you aren't under the custody of Craig's mother; you're under our custody. We're responsible for you, and your mother is having a fit that you're not home with us. And I think it's terrible how you won't talk to her at all!"

"Oh, well, life tends to be a bitch to those who are bitches."

"Stop being such a little smart ass, Benny!"

"Well, that's better than being a *dumb* ass, right?"

"What? You're not funny, young man!"

"Look, I'm perfectly fine where I am, and I can't come home now. I don't get along with you and my grandfather, and I'm sick of all the fighting, okay? If he can't stand me, then I think I shouldn't be there."

Grace's tone lowered just a bit. "Your grandfather and I love you, Benny."

"But you and him sure as hell don't *like* me. And it's not… safe that we share the same house right now."

"You're being ridiculous, Benjamin! Your grandfather just has no patience for you. And not for nothing, but you're really disrespectful to us, and you can't expect us to put up with that."

"The two of you do not *understand* me, and like too many people, you resent what you don't understand. Respect has to go two ways, and he has no respect for my privacy, or for me as a person. And you usually always take my grandfather's side, even when he starts the fights. That grows old pretty quick. Older than you, in fact."

"Shut up, Benny! You need to understand something: I *need* your grandfather, but I *don't* need you. You have to be the one to learn respect, not us."

"See, that attitude is exactly the reason that you're certifiably insane to expect me to come home. I don't agree that respect is something that only works in one direction. Sorry, but you know I'm a card-carrying youth liberationist. We need to work something out before I can come home."

"What's to stop us and your mother from asking the police to bring you back here?"

Benny's voice suddenly took on a darker tenor. "I wouldn't do that if I were you." He then cleared his throat. "What I mean is, you don't own me, and there's a lot more to being a parent or grandparent than putting a roof over a kid's head or providing food for them. The state does that for prisoners! We need to come to some arrangement before I even consider coming home, but that won't be for a while, okay?"

The typically tedious argument between Benny and one of his immediate family members was interrupted by Donovan Jakes and Tatti Lawson hitting the request bell on the solid steel door that separated his "quarters" from the rest of the brig facilities.

"Benny, we need to talk to you, okay?" Tatti's voice came through the intercom, both loud and concerned.

"Look, I have to go now, Mrs. Minkel is asking me something," Benny told his grandmother. "We'll have to continue this later. Hopefully much later."

He then ended the connection with his grandmother and admitted Donovan and Tatti to his room.

"Do you have news on Sasheen?" Benny immediately queried. "How is he doing?"

"He's stable, just like before," Tatti said. "We'll let you visit him soon. But listen, there's something else. And we need you to stay calm."

"When you tell me something like that, it causes me to become anything *but* calm," was Benny's retort. "What's going on?"

"We mean it, kid," Donovan responded in a low but firm tone. "We need you to hold it together. You've already been through a lot, and you just did so much good today. You need to hold onto the strength you showed earlier."

Benny stood up from his futon. "What is it, Donovan? Stop keeping me in such negative suspense, okay?"

The soldier sighed and put his hands on the young man's shoulders in an atypically gentle fashion. "It's... Craig. He was jumped earlier today and beaten down really badly."

"What do you mean?" Benny demanded, his eyes starting to well with tears. "I mean, I know what you meant, but how bad is he? Can I see him?"

"Benny, he's... not in good condition," Tatti said as softly as she could. "He's suffering from numerous broken bones and a lot of internal bleeding. And, well... he might have some brain damage, possibly severe, and..."

"No!" Benny screamed while covering his face with his hands and falling back on the mattress of his futon. "Who did this to him? Do you know who did this?"

"Yes, we do, Benny," Tatti replied. "It was a group of boys from your school and a friend of theirs who retaliated for... well, bottom line, they think you and Craig hired some local gang members to do what you did to Mick Judge and Jeff Wolfe. One turned himself in, and we're looking for the others."

"Those freaking bastards!" Benny hollered through a wall of tears. "Craig had nothing to do with that! It was me! It was *only* me! And now he got hurt for what I did! Damn it, why didn't they try to come after me first? Now they've really gone too far! I'm going to kill them!"

As grief and anger began to overtake the young metahuman's already unstable psyche, his eyes began flaring with a blue incandescence while arcs of powerful azure energies encapsulated his clenched fists.

"I should have killed Judge and Wolfe! I should have ripped them apart! Why didn't I finish what I started?"

"Because you're not like that, Benny, that's why!" Tatti reassured him forcefully. "Never regret being above a wanton killer, no matter what those people did to you, or to anyone else. Do you hear me?"

Benny's entire body now became illuminated with a powerful cerulean glow. "No! I should have done it!"

"Kid, you need to calm down," Donovan insisted. "I know how much this hurts, and how pissed off it's making you, and you have every right to feel that way. But I trusted you enough to give you this news. Don't throw away all the progress you made, and don't prove all my faith in you wrong. We'll get those guys who hurt Craig, I promise you that, but we're going to do it the right way."

Tatti then put her own hand on the rage-stricken boy's shoulder. "Please, Benny. Please listen to Donovan."

"Nooooo!" was all Benny could say as he turned and punched a hole two inches clear into the thick cement wall on the left side of the room.

It would take every iota of his will to avoid slipping into the abyss of no return, and Donovan and Tatti were *anything but* certain that he was up to it. Nor was Benny himself.

The only thing any of them could be certain about at this point was that the next few months would be the most trying of Benny Lonero's life to date, which was truly saying something. And once this crisis was finally weathered--presuming that it would be--then there would only be the rest of Centurion's potentially very long life to be concerned about.

END

Centurion's saga will continue in *CENTURION: A CERTAIN FURY*. Stay tuned and keep an eye or two out for it! After that, prepare for... *MOONSTALKER VS. CENTURION!*

For those who enjoyed Centurion's debut exploit, please do consider leaving a review on Amazon, BookBub, your own blog, the works! Reviews really do help and will enable me to continue bringing more of Centurion and many other heroes from the Warp Event Universe to you on a regular basis! For those readers who may not have considered this initial outing up to par, my apologies; but rest assured I will strive to make each subsequent adventure of Centurion an improvement over the last! Your purchase and reading of this book was much appreciated, as I would be nowhere without all of you!

Bonus Short Story: Any chance you're wondering how the Warp Events that gave Centurion's Earth its official designation came about and changed everything in this reality? If so, then read on, compliments of the house!

THE WARP EVENT

Christofer Nigro

Colonel Donovan Jakes sat in the briefing room of the Valis Institute's hidden San Francisco headquarters during the early morning hours of June 14, 2006, a mug of coffee in hand. He sipped it periodically, while viewing the awe-inspiring digital satellite video of outer space – specifically, the Milky Way's galactic rim -- where Earth drifted as an all-important mote of cosmic dust.

"It's really beautiful and all that, Ashlee, but what exactly am I looking for?" Jakes queried.

"Just keep watching for another few seconds, as I'm certain that I put the video clip at the correct time stamp," Sub-Director Ashlee Concord replied.

As Jakes viewed the tranquil star-encrusted tableau it was suddenly enveloped by a flash of blue incandescence so intense, it blotted out all the visible stars and nebulae in the video. The veteran military man cringed and felt as if a harsh winter wind stroked his spinal column. Within a second, at most, the azure flash vanished.

"My god, what the hell was that?" Jakes sputtered in astonishment. "I swear that I felt like someone just walked over my grave."

"That's pretty much how we felt the first time my team saw it," Ashlee said. "And our psychics reported both their daydreams and nightly excursions into REM sleep filled with strange images."

"Will I be sorry if f I ask what kind of images?"

221

"Bizarre realms of existence, nothing like our own. That's a direct quote, by the way. Along with what they described as otherworldly beings of great power. Several mentioned a 'menacing but wise older man with a long gray beard and a missing eye.' Also reported were strange 'roaring' vibrations permeating their body and mind simultaneously. Psychics in other parts of the world described visions of the legendary Wild Hunt filling the night skies; whereas others dreamed of close encounters with UFOs, and even abductions by occupants described as tall, luminous blonde humanoids delivering messages like, 'The times are changing' and 'It now begins.'

"I should mention that dozens of these espers needed to be restrained upon awakening. Two committed suicide. Four were diagnosed as catatonic. Lots of others suffered migraines, sudden onset of epileptic seizures, chronic insomnia, and a couple of cases of sudden color-blindness. The less said about the teenage girl who tore out her own eyes during a fit, the better."

Jakes groaned. Yes, he was sorry for asking. He knew that his next question might make him sorrier still, but it remained his job to ask such things. "So, what does all of this mean?"

"We don't know yet, not for sure. But based on preliminary analysis, we believe that this flash of light was the overt physical manifestation of what we're calling a *Warp Event*, for lack of a better term. Experts in our highly esoteric line of work refer to as a *paradigm shift*."

Paradigm shifts had been required reading when Jakes was first recruited. In essence, these consisted of events that literally changed the laws of physics in subtle but dramatic ways. He hadn't wanted to believe in them. Truth to tell, he still wasn't sure that he did.

"Aren't those supposed to result in the rapid appearance of certain anomalous phenomena? Including the manifestation of paranormal abilities in humans, a surge in spiritual & religious experiences, and a slew of technological & scientific breakthroughs that may previously have been highly unlikely, or even near-impossible?"

"Exactly. There have been small-scale events like this across time, much like other recurring 'themes' in nature with huge implications on the world, such as: mass extinctions, ice ages, and collisions with Apollo asteroids or large comets. Paradigm shifts, of which the Warp Events appear to be an unusually dramatic example.

"They may have also occurred periodically, but with potentially even more implications--for humanity and our natural place in the cosmos, to be exact. Some hypothesize that localized paradigm shifts during past eras may have had something to do with the evolution of organisms into more advanced forms, an influence upon the sheer diversity life can take, and with life's ability to evolve to the level of sentience the human species now demonstrates. Note how many technological advances occurred following a paradigm shift believed to have occurred in local space towards the end of the 18th century.

"Another significant factor of that era to note was the increased drive to understand and contemplate various changes in human potential, from the philosophical to the biological. This doubtless led not only to the unprecedented technical advances that took place during the 19th century, but also the emergence of various new religious and occult movements like Theosophy and the brief but noteworthy rise of the Hermetic Order of the Golden Dawn. Along with this came the rise of Spiritualism, the beginning of official scientific studies into psychical phenomena, and the serious interest in lost continents and their attendant advanced civilizations like Atlantis and Lemuria.

"Perhaps most significantly, we then have the appearance of unusually skilled personages whom we may term 'exceptional humans.' This august roster includes Charles Darwin, Aleister Crowley, Harry Houdini, and Madame Helena Blavatsky. Along with them a few bona fide metahuman beings began appearing here and there across the globe. The former slave Albert Miller and archeologist/explorer Emily Atkinson are perhaps the most poignant examples of their number, but there were others of note."

"Wait," Jakes interrupted. "Is there any proof of this phenomenon, Ashlee? By this I mean complete documented scientific evidence."

Ashlee twirled her finger through her long, braided black hair as she answered. "The phenomenon of paradigm shifting is a new course of study, much like quantum entanglement, string theory, the existence of dark matter and dark energy, and the effects of consciousness on the quantum level of reality. But we do believe the evidence is there, even if it's more or less completely unacknowledged by mainstream science. This flash of light and subsequent events of the past four days almost immediately following the latest Warp Event appears to indicate…"

Jakes's eyes went wider, and he again interjected. "*What* subsequent events?"

Sub-Director Concord pulled a series of thick files from her briefcase and began reading the notes aloud to Jakes.

"Sunday, in Moscow, a young female psychic listed in our database reported that during a rather nasty argument with her alcoholic father, all the windows in her home, as well as the great majority of glass and crystal knickknacks in their house, simultaneously shattered when her temper reached what she called its 'boiling point.' Prior to this incident, she never experienced a capacity to even remotely affect physical matter.

"On Monday, in Sydney, a 13-year-old boy arrested on arson charges and placed under psychological evaluation reported that he didn't deliberately set his home on fire; rather, the furniture and draperies burst into flame the moment he experienced his first kiss. He had no previous record of psychological instability or any type of aberrant or criminal behavior, including pyromania.

"On Tuesday, in Big Sur, a technician who had invented a pistol with a carbon battery power source designed to fire quick bursts of plasma -- a gadget that obviously didn't work at all when he constructed it three years ago -- reported to *Astounding* magazine that the device actually fired a few plasmic discharges before the batteries overheated. He claimed to have discovered this following a 'compulsion' to re-test the device immediately following an encounter with a huge triangular craft that was enveloped in a bright pink incandescence.

"Also on Tuesday, in a suburb outside of London, a man who had illegally purchased a relict example of one of those radioactive gold watches that made headlines in the 1970s and wore for over a year, reported that the cancer he developed in his forearm had suddenly gone into total remission. Soon afterwards a 'sky blue' glow surrounded the same forearm and hand. While this odd form of bio-luminescence manifested, he reputedly melted any physical object he touched with the glowing hand without actually producing any discernible heat. The effect lasted for approximately 24 minutes.

"On Wednesday, a graduate student in physics who designed a small anti-gravity device a few years ago that didn't work at all suddenly discovered the apparatus performing much as she hoped it would by suspending several small objects in a projected energy field. She said she was inspired to test the device again following a conversation with an individual at the university whom she described as a rather eccentric gentleman with long blonde hair, a shiny plaid shirt, and dark shades who described himself as 'a visiting professor from Norway.' A copy of her YouTube video displaying the device's 'new' capabilities has been downloaded to our database.

"Also on Wednesday, we have a report from a research institute in Venezuela where a quantum physicist claims to have viewed and briefly 'captured' a tachyon, thus proving the particle to be more than hypothetical. This allegation has yet to be fully verified, but if it turns out to be true, the implications for future technological development -- including time travel -- stagger the imagination. The report went 'live' on *Omniverse's* online journal just a few days later.

"Two of the editors of that issue predicted that if advances like this continue at the present rate, we may actually see a manned mission to Mars by the year 2015, a permanent lunar base shortly afterwards, a space station with sustained artificial gravity, *blah blah blah*... you get the idea.

"As of this morning, we have reports of strange meteorite crashes across the globe, with initial investigators describing the rocks emitting 'strange radiations.' What the ultimate results of this phenomenon will be cannot be determined at present.

Christofer Nigro

"And if that wasn't enough, psychics and astrologers on our staff have reported bizarre synchronistic events across the globe. Particular concentrations, however, have begun appearing in known 'window areas' like a rural hamlet outside Oshkosh, Wisconsin and Arkham, Massachusetts…"

"Okay, Ashlee, I get the gist. I'll read the rest in the files. Right now, my mind is boggling; I'm having trouble just getting used to the idea that something like a paradigm shift is actually possible. And I'm saying this despite all I witnessed during my glorious days performing secret ops for the government."

"Well, Donovan, many phenomena that were nigh-impossible prior to the Warp Event have now officially become *quite possible*."

"Wonderful. So, what does this mean for us?"

The sub-director removed her glasses and rubbed her eyes before answering. "What it means, my good friend, is that all bets are off. Today may be the end of the human race, with the jackrabbits taking over. Or our species might become gods. Maybe the Age of Aquarius is here, with swords beaten into ploughshares and drugs eclipsed by the Golden Apples of Iduna."

"That'd be great."

"That's nice to hear from a soldier type."

"*Ex*-soldier type, lady."

She nodded, acknowledging his point before continuing.

"But this also means that the donors and contributors to the Valis Institute need to pull together the entirety of our resources to investigate all these phenomena. We need to understand what the modified rules of reality are, so it's imperative we get our hands on any of the new exotic technology, as well as establish contact with as many of the emerging metahumans as possible. As soon as most of the world governments discover what is going on, they will scramble to take full advantage of the new additions to the world outside our window. And this includes the emerging metahuman and exotic technological resources that were previously scarce to non-existent.

"Thanks to the Warp Event, our planet and its close spatial environs just became a much more interesting -- not to mention more *dangerous* -- place. So, we need to get as much of a handle on all of this as we possibly can before the world governments begin doing it themselves. Granted we cannot fully stop them, but we need to acquire and maintain a permanent edge. The continued freedom and advancement opportunities now available for humanity must be directed by us, not the world governments and their corporate financiers."

Jakes rubbed his close-cropped beard in contemplation. "Ashlee, you do know who the donors and contributors of this organization are, correct? What you're saying we have to do, I wouldn't exactly call likely, or even possible. But one word I would use is 'very dangerous.'"

"That's two words, Donovan."

"Touché. But you know what the hell I mean, Ashlee."

The sub-director almost smiled, a rare occurrence for her. "But as of now, my dear Donovan, the impossible just got *a lot* more possible. That means the stakes for the world and humanity's future just got *a lot* higher. Either we go for the gold, or the military-industrial superstructure now ruling the world does. Take your pick and choose your side, *ex*-soldier."

Donovan frowned.

END

About the Author

Christofer Nigro is a writer, freelance editor, and publisher who makes his home in the United States. He is a lifelong fan of the comic book medium in general and the super-hero genre in particular. His short stories have been published by Black Coat Press, Sirens Call Publications, Pro Se Press, Grinning Skull Press, Horrified Press, and Local Hero Press. He has previously had novels published by Severed Press. Wild Hunt Press is his first foray into publishing on his own.

www.ingramcontent.com/pod-product-compliance
Lightning Source LLC
Chambersburg PA
CBHW050928120626
46552CB00001B/92